For Al

Enjoy!

Chris

Calder

With thanks — Chris

Payback

Chris Calder

Copyright © 3P Publishing
First published in 2014
This edition published in 2018
3P Publishing
C E C, London Road
Corby, NN17 5EU

A catalogue number for this book is available from the
British Library

ISBN 978-1-911559-77-1

Cover: Marie-Louise O'Neill

www.chriscalder.com

This book is dedicated to the brilliant surgeon who saved my life some years ago. Payback was conceived during my recovery in the hospital in France. It was my first published book and it started me on the road to my career as a novelist. A happy and truly unforseen outcome!

MAIN CHARACTERS

Geoff Summers	Designer of control systems for security company Melford Electronics
Penny Summers	Geoff's wife
Tony Mellon	Managing Director, co-founder of company, who retires
Peter Whittam	New Managing Director who leaves the company
Adam Ford	Production Director who takes over as MD from Whittam
Ray Ford	Adam's father, co-founder of company, now a director
Samantha Bowen	Secretary to Managing Director
Jim Warwick	Chairman, Warwick Motors
Sandra Warwick	Jim's wife
Rosie Warwick	Jim and Sandra's daughter
Mike Stubbs	Manager of Warwick Motors' body repair shops
Shaun Conroy	Works with Stubbs but is also Warwick's 'muscle'
Dave Merchant	Warwick's uncle, now retired to France
Kevin Flynn	Accountant working for Warwick
Robbie Naylor	Boss of 'unauthorised removals' gang, professional burglars
Norman	Naylor's assistant
Paul Hawker	Private investigator
Andy Powell	Chief Superintendent. Essex CID

Frank Rollo	Detective Sergeant
Eddie Smith	Detective Constable
Harry Mortimer	Journalist, crime reporter
Martin Blake	Commander, Scotland Yard Drugs Squad
Ron Standish	Superintendent, Drugs Squad

PREFACE

Geoff Summers turned to look at his wife, reaching mutely for her hand as the doctor leaned forward and placed a document on the desk between them.

"This is the schedule of treatment we propose," he said softly. "But we need to do a few more tests." His manner was sympathetic, his brow lined with furrows of experience. He smiled thinly. "One step at a time."

Geoff turned to Penny again and she was there, yet not there. Her image was ethereal, it had begun to fade. That was the moment when Geoff realised that he was once again in the dream, *that* recurrent dream, unreality seemingly real.

He looked back at the doctor whose appearance was morphing before his eyes. Gone were the kindly expression, the sympathy and the dark hair. The man he saw now was round-faced, with bulging eyes behind tinted spectacles, an image that was menacing and intimidating. It was Ford, *Adam Ford the bastard*. He looked to his right but Penny was not there anymore.

At that point the dream ended abruptly, instantly tipping him back into reality, so that he became immediately aware that he was Geoff Summers masquerading as John Jeffries and living a lie. He was drenched in sweat and he had a thousand-hammer headache. The anger returned, the emptiness and frustration returned, with the bitter recollection of what had happened since that interview with the specialist only four months ago. He glanced at the bedside clock which told him it was six-twenty, so he knew that more sleep would be impossible, and he rose to face another day.

But he knew also that it would be a day like no other, because today he was to take the first irrevocable steps towards his new life.

CHAPTER ONE

"Did you remember the beer?" Geoff Summers asked his wife Penny. "I think Samantha said he likes the strong Belgian stuff." They were in their kitchen, preparing to welcome guests for a Sunday lunch in the garden. She was sorting cutlery onto a tray upon which she had already placed table napkins and glasses.

"A couple of six-packs in the fridge. If he needs any more, he really does like it."

Geoff opened the fridge door and took out one of the beer packs.

"Anything else to go outside?"

"You can take this, just needs the cruets."

Geoff took the salt and pepper pots off a shelf. "What about the desserts?"

"Leave them in the fridge until we need them."

The doorbell chimed just as Geoff picked up the tray. Penny looked up at the kitchen clock on the wall.

"Bang on time," she said.

"Sam's never late, you know that. Can you see them in, I'll take this out and come back to make the drinks."

After their leisurely al fresco Sunday lunch in the garden, Penny shielded her eyes from the sun and watched anxiously as Geoff and Robbie picked their way along the pathway into the house, each overloaded with rattling crockery. The men had volunteered to fill the washer and make coffees,

1

CHAPTER ONE

leaving Penny and her friend Samantha in the garden.

"Hmmm… a rare beast, a man willing to help with the dishes. And he's really quite good looking," Penny observed with a wry grin. "You've been dating for a couple of months, is it getting serious?"

"Yes and no. Yes, Robbie's handsome and no, it isn't serious."

"Bit of a revolving door, with you," Penny teased, twirling a finger in the air. "It rotates to let them in and then whips around again when you fancy a change."

"Rubbish! I'm just happy making new friends."

Penny squinted and reached for her sunglasses on the table. She unfolded them carefully and put them on.

Samantha frowned. "Another headache?"

"It's not too bad today. I'll take a paracetamol when the boys bring out the coffee."

"You seem to be having a lot of them lately. Have you seen your doctor?"

"I've got an appointment tomorrow."

Samantha reached over to dip into a bowl of potato crisps on the table. "My boss Tony gets bad headaches a couple of times a month. He says they are migraines, he goes home as soon as he feels one coming on." Penny knew that Samantha was referring to Tony Mellon, managing director of Melford Electronics, the security firm where Geoff also worked. He was chief designer of their anti-burglar systems.

"Really?" she said, "I didn't know that."

"Mm," Samantha crunched. "He says it's not a big

2

problem. When he gets one he deals with it and is back at work the next day. Don't worry; I'm sure you'll be fine."

"He's over seventy, isn't he? When is he going to retire?" Penny asked casually. She noticed immediately that Samantha reacted to the question. Penny leaned forward, her eyebrows arched.

"He's not, is he?"

"It's not official yet, but yes, he's decided to leave."

The men emerged from the kitchen, carrying mugs. With a glance at them Samantha whispered, "Not a word about that, please, Pen."

Penny responded with the faintest of nods.

"Coffee up, girls," said Geoff. "And the dishwasher is loaded. What would you do without us?"

Penny smiled. "I'll be happy to tell you. How long have you got?"

Geoff was at work when Penny saw the doctor and she did not call him as he expected. So maybe, he thought, the headaches were not a symptom of something more serious.

"How did it go?" he asked that evening when he got home. She was setting out the table for their supper.

"He asked me some questions and looked inside my eyes with a sort of torch thing."

"And?"

"He doesn't think there's a problem, but he is arranging for me to have a scan. Just to be sure, he said."

Geoff frowned. "When will you have that?"

"We'll get the date by post."

"Is he giving you anything for the pain?"

"I've got a prescription for some pills. I have to take them when I feel a headache coming on."

"What did he ask you?"

"Oh, mainly about diet. Every time it happens I've got to keep a note of what I've eaten. He said that migraines can be caused by something you eat."

Geoff pulled back a chair. "Can't say I know too much about migraines, but at least it's something we can deal with."

On the golf course Adam Ford squared up to his ball and struck it cleanly; a near perfect drive.

"Nice shot," said his father Ray as he shaded his eyes to follow the trajectory of Adam's ball. "There's hope for you yet."

"I don't know about that," Adam replied. "I could never take the game as seriously as you do."

Ray stooped to place his ball on a tee and stood back. Settling into his stance for the drive, he said, "A few more like that and you'll be hooked, wait and see." He slammed his ball into the distance, watching it all the way. "Keep straight, keep straight," he muttered, then turned to drop his club into the bag in his trolley. "But you'll have to play more often, give it more time."

Adam fell into step with him as they made their way down the fairway. "To tell you the truth, Dad, I really don't have the time, or the inclination right now. Too much going on."

"Have you given in your notice at Daneplan?"

"A fortnight ago. I'll be leaving them in a couple of weeks. But they weren't surprised; I told the chairman last month that it could happen."

"You know," Ray said, "I had some doubts that after being a managing director you could settle into a lesser job at Melford. You'll be taking orders instead of giving them. Is that going to be a problem for you?" They paused when they reached Adam's ball, Ray's was forty yards further down the fairway.

"Nah, I'll be fine. I like Peter Whittam, he'll be a good MD and I'm sure we'll get on. It would have been the same with Tony, if he was staying on. I'm comfortable about coming into the firm at a lower level; I'll be better prepared for the top job when I take it on, sooner or later." Adam selected a club from his bag. "And I'm a fast learner. Anyway, I've had enough of fitted kitchens, high time I joined the family firm."

Adam squared up to his ball. "I've got plans for Melford and when I get a couple of my own people in, the sky's the limit." He took a mighty swing, then swore softly as his ball soared aloft before drifting into the rough.

Ray shook his head. "Bad luck. You really do need to play more often."

They made their way forward and Ray asked casually, "So you don't see yourself going back into property development at some time in the future?"

"Are you asking as my dad or as a Melford shareholder?"

"Just wondering if you had got it out of your system."

CHAPTER ONE

"Property development's a great way to make a lot of money when times are good, as I did." He paused to stoop and replace a divot. Patting it down with his foot he said, "But it wouldn't be in Cyprus again, that's for sure. Too much corruption, too many arseholes who think I'm to blame for their losses." He straightened. "Anyway, it's a taboo subject as you well know, Dad. I made my pile and got out, but I will *never* set foot in that place again."

Ray stopped by his ball and looked at his son. "Good," he said simply. "It was a bad business and your mother and I were quite worried."

"Nothing to worry about, it's history." Adam moved off towards his own ball.

Ray looked ahead to the green. Selecting a club he said, "Now, I should be able to get there with a seven."

Geoff was working late one evening at his computer at Melford Electronics, engrossed in the design of a complex layout drawing. In the silence of the deserted building, echoing footsteps heralded the approach down the corridor of Tommy the security man, long before he reached the door to Geoff's office.

Tommy pushed the door open. "Blimey, you still here?"

"Nah, this is a mirage, the real me is out there swimming the Channel."

"Oh yes, very funny," said Tommy. "Haven't you got a home to go to?"

Geoff liked Tommy. He was always cheerful and

he enjoyed their verbal fencing. He looked up from his desk. "Some security man you are. How do you expect to nab an intruder when your size twelves can be heard a mile off?"

Tommy leaned forward and looked at his feet. "I'll put in for bedroom slippers if you sign the ticket."

"OK, it's a deal."

Tommy gestured. "Tell you what, if you can just cruise around a bit, you know, have a little look in the offices and such, I can nip down to the pub for a quick pint. No sense in us both being on duty this time of night."

Geoff glanced at his watch. "OK, I can take a hint. I'll just finish this and be down. About another ten minutes, I'm nearly done."

"Take your time, take your time," said Tommy. "I've got all night. I'm not going anywhere until Paul relieves me at ten." He shut the door and clumped away down the corridor.

The next morning Geoff was summoned to see Tony Mellon. The door into the managing director's office was ajar, so Geoff knocked and pushed it open. Tony was on the telephone but he waved Geoff forward as he spoke, and indicated that he should sit down. It became apparent that he was talking to one of the company's component suppliers.

"That's all very well," he said, "but it's not our problem. Either you match Sandersons or we will have to go with them." He paused to listen, then spoke again. "Well, Peter rates them and that's good enough for me." He was talking about Peter Whittam the production director who was Geoff's immediate boss.

Tony was still engaged in this conversation when the communicating door to his secretary's office opened. She put her head around the door, smiled at Geoff and silently mouthed the question "Coffee?"

He nodded and whispered, "Yes please, Sam."

Tony wound up his call. "That's it then. Speak to Peter again and we'll see what he makes of it. He'll tell me what he thinks. OK, goodbye."

Peter Whittam was a man so completely on top of his job that Tony had total confidence in him. It was expected that when Tony retired Peter would become MD, and Geoff believed that when that happened he would take Peter's place as head of production, one step from the board.

Tony put the phone down and leaned back in his chair.

"Well, Geoff, the reason I asked you in is that I have some news." He smiled. "And it's good news, at least for you."

Geoff sat up, not knowing quite what to expect.

"I'm stepping down," said Tony quietly, "and not before time, if I am to believe the rumours in this place."

This news was not altogether unexpected but it caught Geoff on the hop. Was it going to be what he hoped it would be? He paused before answering hesitantly.

"I don't know what to say, but…"

"My choice, it had to happen sooner or later. I can't go on forever."

Geoff knew that his managing director was now well over seventy but more than fit enough in mind and body to stay on longer if he wished.

"In that case and if it really is what you want, congratulations."

"Thank you. I will miss being here day to day, but don't write me off, I still own the company and I am still Chairman, so I won't be disappearing altogether."

"What are your plans?" Geoff resisted the urge to ask how this news would affect him.

"First, a long holiday. God knows, Paula deserves it. After that, I'm going to have to learn how to retire."

Geoff smiled. "It's hard to imagine you doing nothing."

"Anyway," said Tony briskly, placing his palms on the desk, "back to business. I told the directors at the board meeting on Friday. We'll break the news to the staff today, but I wanted to tell you about this myself. Peter will take over formally at the end of the month but to all intents and purposes he is running the company as of now."

Geoff was bursting to ask what this would mean for him, as Tony went on.

"It's a good thing that you're ahead of schedule for the jobs in hand," he said evenly, "because you're going to need time to work closely with Peter for a while. After that, if he's happy and you're happy and *I'm* happy," he paused and inclined his head, "you'll be the new production manager."

Geoff felt a surge of elation, he wanted to jump up and punch the air. Instead he grinned. "Thank you,

Tony, you know I won't let you down."

"Make sure you don't. You've earned it and you're pretty bright, but you'll have to work harder if you want to go further because it won't be me looking over your shoulder."

The door to Samantha's office swung open and she came in carrying a tray with two cups on it. When she glanced at Geoff before putting the tray on the desk, he knew at once that she was aware of this development and approved. He thought he would have felt at twenty paces the genuine warmth generated in that look. She was one of the few people from Melford whom Geoff and Penny counted as friends and she and Penny were particularly close.

Tony thanked her and she left smiling gently at Geoff. Not for the first time, he wondered why she was still on her own four years after being widowed.

Cradling his cup in his hands Tony said, "We think you should be able to take over production in about a month's time, but there's no set timescale." He took a sip from the cup and put it down. "One other thing; Adam Ford will be joining us soon. I think you've met him?"

"Yes, once or twice."

"He's been MD of a kitchen manufacturer's, but as Ray's son he was bound to join the firm sooner or later. He'll be on the board of course, replacing Peter and heading up production. You'll be answering to him."

Geoff nodded. "Will Danny be taking over from me?" He was referring to his assistant.

"Yes, but he'll need a deputy on the design work."

"Do you have anyone in mind?"

"Make your own choice," he said, "perhaps Jack or Stephen. Talk to Danny, I think he should be involved in the decision. But we need you to remain hands-on with development projects. Danny's good but he doesn't have your flair for invention."

"Thanks, it's nice to know I'm appreciated."

"Don't get too carried away, you'll have to prove you can handle all the problems that come with running a big department. There's a lot more to what Peter does than just making sure assembly runs smoothly and keeping an eye on stocks of components. You're going to have to work overtime to keep on top of it all."

"No problem, I'm up for it."

"Anyway, Debbie does much of the routine stuff, which should help."

Debbie was Peter's secretary, a woman whose calm manner and motherly appearance belied the sharpness of her brain. She it was who updated daily all the information relating to components, including suppliers, costs and stock levels.

Tony sipped his coffee and put the cup down. "What are you working on in development?" he asked.

Before Geoff could tell him about his ideas for enabling and disabling alarm systems remotely, Tony's intercom buzzed. He pressed the response button.

"Yes, Samantha?" Geoff heard Samantha telling him about a caller whom she had put on hold. "Put him through in a moment," said Tony. Turning to

CHAPTER ONE

Geoff he said, "Liaise with Peter, we'll talk later about
your new salary package."

Geoff thanked him, rose and walked out,
unintentionally leaving behind an untouched coffee
cup. With so much on his mind he had completely
forgotten it was there.

On the way home Geoff stopped off at a
supermarket and bought a chateau-bottled claret, one
that he knew Penny liked.

"Celebration," he said as he put it down on the
table.

"Oh, a Margaux," she squealed. "What are we
celebrating?"

Geoff told her about the promotion and how Tony
had hinted at the prospect of more to come.

"What did he say?"

Geoff smirked. "Oh, something about me being
very bright."

"Tosh! What did he *really* say?"

"He said that if I worked harder I would go
further."

Her eyes twinkled. "Damn, I knew there had to be
a catch." She tilted her head. "Did Sam know?"

"What do you think?"

"I expect she did. Cunning little minx. I spoke to
her yesterday and a couple of times last week but she
didn't let on."

"You know Sam, soul of discretion."

"I'll get my own back. I'll give her a call right now
and pretend to be annoyed with her."

He smiled. "Good luck!"

12

The following Saturday Geoff and Penny were at breakfast when the letterbox flap banged shut. Its spring was so strong that Penny had once likened it to an alligator's jaws.

"I'll go," she said. She returned a minute later holding a white envelope with a logo on the front. "There's just this. It's from the hospital, probably my scan appointment." She sat down, opened it and withdrew a letter which she began reading.

Geoff looked up. "What does it say?"

"The appointment's for the thirtieth of next month. It's a Friday." She handed the letter to him.

Geoff scanned it quickly. "Over a month from now. Doesn't say much for the system, does it?"

"I expect they're busy."

"I can understand the scanner being busy, but it's been over a fortnight since you saw the doctor. Why does it take two weeks just to put you in the queue?" He tossed the document onto the table. "It's disgraceful."

"Well, it's not as if it's urgent. For me, I mean. I expect they do the urgent ones first."

Geoff picked up the letter again and looked at it. "Fridays are not good for me."

"You don't have to come. I'm sure I can manage on my own, a scan is only a check."

"Hmm, OK. I'd like to be there, but there's no point in asking for another date, not if it's going to add another two or three weeks."

"I'll be fine," Penny said, "don't worry."

Later that week Geoff was in his new office checking

stocks of electrical items when he noticed a possible problem. He looked over at Debbie.

"Have we had an answer from DCS about the connectors, Deb?"

"They say they'll be with us in the middle of next week. Don't worry. They can be slow sometimes, but they're pretty reliable."

"I hope you're right, we can't afford to run out."

The intercom on his desk rang and Geoff picked up the handset.

"Summers."

"Geoff? Rod Thompson." Thompson was the sales director. Geoff liked him and they got on well.

"Hi, Rod, what's up?"

Thompson snorted. "Adam's blood pressure, that's what! Seems you pulled his chain, big time, today."

"Well, yes, we did have words. Who's been talking?"

"The man himself. I had a couple of things to see him about, went to his office. He was ranting, spitting nails, said you were incompetent. I thought you should know, could be trouble for you."

"Oh, I'll be OK. I was promoted recently, remember? Not something that happens if you're incompetent. My contract was approved by Tony Mellon and signed by Peter and the ink is still wet. Still, I wish I knew what Adam's problem is. I can't make it out."

"If I get wind of anything, I'll tell you. Specially as Peter's dropped his bombshell about leaving. Adam seems to be front runner for taking over."

"Hmm. There's an uncomfortable thought."

"Anyway, I was really calling to tell you that Stork Hill has postponed. We won't be going there next Thursday; they want us to do the survey two weeks later, on the Tuesday. Is that OK for you?"

"Should be fine. Hang on a minute, I'll just check." Geoff opened his desk diary on the page for that day. "Tuesday the sixth. Yes, that's fine, Rod. I'll mark it."

"Thanks. Oh, there's something else. There's a new enquiry. Warwick Motors, do you know them?"

"Warwick Motors? The car dealership near the M25?"

"Yes, that's the one. But the survey is for the owner's private house. Warwick Hall, near Braintree."

"Uh, huh. When do you want it done?"

"No hurry, it'll be in about three weeks, after Stork Hill. I'm away next week, we'll fix a date for it when I get back."

"Going anywhere special?"

"Sorry, mate, I'm not telling. I'm taking a complete break; I don't need any calls about work."

"Fair enough. Have a good time, and to hell with any emergencies, eh?"

"Thanks, I will. But you know, the big difference between your job and mine is that there are no emergencies in sales."

"You're right. Bye." He put the receiver down slowly. Maybe Rod was right to be concerned that Adam could make trouble for him.

Debbie had been listening. "Did you say Warwick Motors?"

"Er – yes, we've had an enquiry from the owner."

"I've heard about him, Jim Warwick." She

15

shuddered. "A nasty piece of work by all accounts."

"I just do my job, Deb, and socialising with the customer isn't in my brief."

"Just so you know," she said, "I'm sure you can look after yourself."

The next time Debbie was out of their office, Geoff called Samantha on the intercom.

"Sam? Geoff."

"Yes, Geoff."

"Deb's just nipped out. I have to ask you, is it true?"

There was a short pause. "About Peter leaving?"

"Yes, and will it be Adam who takes over?"

"Um. You know I never talk, but the first bit is now common knowledge, Peter will be leaving."

"And?"

"At the moment nobody knows who will be the new MD. I suppose it could be Adam."

"OK. Thanks, Sam." Geoff put the phone down. Not good news.

Geoff had the answer two weeks later when Peter Whittam left the company and Adam Ford was promoted to the post of managing director. Almost immediately, Geoff became aware that his concerns appeared to be justified. Adam seemed to have something against him. He decided one day that he had to find out if that was the case and he went to ask Samantha for her opinion. He made his way to her office, which was adjacent to Ford's, but paused before entering. A man he had been following down the corridor had just gone into Ford's office.

Geoff recognized the man but momentarily could not place him. Quite suddenly he remembered. Kevin Flynn! Flynn the bent accountant, who lied in the Crown Court when Penny's cousin Brian Hammond was convicted of fraud and jailed. What on earth, he wondered, was he doing visiting Ford? Samantha was typing at her keyboard when Geoff entered.

"Hi, Sam," he said, "got a minute?"

She looked up and took off her stylish reading spectacles. "Of course, what can I do for you?"

"Something I wanted to ask you. But first," he said nodding towards Ford's office, "what is Kevin Flynn seeing Adam for?"

She looked at him blankly. "Who?"

"Kevin Flynn. An accountant, or maybe by now, an ex-accountant."

"I've absolutely no idea," she said. "Wait, I'll check." She called up the diary page on her computer. "As I thought, nothing in the book for him this afternoon."

Geoff shook his head. "Strange."

"Who is he, anyway?"

Geoff paused. All he really knew for certain was that the man had run an accountancy business and that he had been directly involved in the false conviction of Brian Hammond. Too complicated to explain.

"A man who did some dodgy business a couple of years ago." He frowned. "No matter, there's something else I'd like to ask you."

CHAPTER ONE

Not sure how he could find out what he wanted to know without compromising her loyalty to her boss, he thought it best just to ask. Pulling a chair forward, he turned it back to front and sat down with his arms folded over the top of the backrest.

"How are you getting on with Adam?"

If she was surprised by his directness she did not show it. She picked up the spectacles, folded them slowly and put them down again.

"Why do you ask?"

"Because I think I may have a problem. I get the feeling that he has something against me and I have no idea why."

"Have you fallen out in some way?"

He shrugged. "Not exactly, but he seems to be going out of his way to make things difficult for me."

"Well, he's different, that's for sure. But if you are asking whether I like working for him I would have to say not as much as I liked working for Peter or Tony."

She had skilfully avoided answering the question, so he did not push it and tried a different tack.

"OK, off the record, is there something going on that we don't know about?"

She arched her eyebrows and smiled. "Well, *if* there was and *if* I knew, I wouldn't really be in a position to say, now would I?"

Geoff grinned. "I forgot. You don't do gossip. Bugger."

She laughed and he changed the subject. Penny had asked her and her current boyfriend over for dinner on the following Saturday. Samantha had accepted but said she would be coming on her own.

Geoff stood up and turned the chair around. "See you Saturday. If you come early you just might get one of my martini specials."

He started to leave but before he reached the door Samantha spoke again. "Off the record, the answer to your question is 'maybe', but ask me again on Saturday, *before* you serve the martinis."

On the day, he waited until they were relaxed and enjoying the meal. Samantha told them that in the short time that Adam had been in the job he'd had several visits from people who she thought had worked for him before. She said she really did not know much more because on the few occasions when she had entered the room while they were talking, they had fallen silent. That, she said, was something she did not like at all.

Adam Ford had been a private client of Kevin Flynn for four years, but this was Flynn's first visit to the Melford factory. Adam watched as he opened his briefcase, withdrew a folder and handed it over.

"Your annual report. In person, as always."

Adam took the folder, opened it and scanned the first page quickly. "I'll go over it at home tonight and come back to you if I need to. Anything from Cyprus?"

"Nothing new. The usual moaners bitching about losing their money. Kemal is dealing with them, for the moment anyway."

Adam snorted. "All investments are speculative in the property business, they knew that." He flicked through the folder to another page. "Things are looking OK in Anguilla," he said, referring to his bank account in the tax haven.

"Solid. Best left alone for now."

Ford closed the folder. "OK, I'll call you later if I need to."

CHAPTER TWO

Easing his Bentley through the gates of Warwick Motors to the parking area reserved for staff, Jim Warwick swore. His spot, the one plainly marked with a sign, "Reserved for Chairman", was occupied by a saloon car he did not recognize. He glanced around and seeing no free spaces, swore again before positioning the Bentley across the back of the other car, blocking it in.

Receptionist Elaine whose desk was near the entrance to the showroom, greeted him with a respectful, "Good morning, Mr Warwick." Jim merely nodded in response.

"There's a blue Toyota in my parking space," he snapped. "Whose is it?"

"I don't know," she replied nervously, "but I'll find out now."

Jim's office was the last of four glass-walled enclosures down one side of the showroom. Striding towards it he said over his shoulder, "Don't bother, he'll turn up. Let me know when he does."

On the opposite side of the room Sales Manager Eddie Sharp and his two salesmen at their desks suddenly became totally engrossed in paperwork. They did not look up, as to do so might risk making eye contact with the Chairman, an intimidating experience. The cold blue eyes and close-shaven head could strike fear into his employees, most of whom were motivated to stay in their jobs only by the fact that they were extremely well paid.

CHAPTER TWO

Managing Director Mark Allen looked through the glass wall of his office and saw Jim arriving. He grimaced and picked up a folder.

"Into the fray," he muttered, rising. To Brenda, the secretary he shared with Jim he said, "You know the drill, no interruptions."

"He's early. Good job I've already sorted the post." Her first task every day was to sort the post, placing on Jim's desk anything addressed directly to him.

Jim Warwick had direct access to all the computers at Warwick Motors from his home, so he always knew exactly what was happening in the business. He invariably called in on Monday mornings, when the meeting with Mark was always the first business of the day.

"Good morning, Jim," Mark said as he came into his boss's office. Mark was the only staff member who addressed the Chairman by his first name.

Jim had removed his jacket and draped it over the back of his chair. He sat down and reached for the small pile of unopened letters on the desk.

"Is it?" he said, sifting through the envelopes. None of them drew his immediate attention, so he put them aside. "Sales down two units on last week," he growled, "not such a good morning."

Mark took the chair on the opposite side of the desk. "But last week we were four up on the week before."

"Your fat salary and perks are for moving metal, not finding excuses. What's in the pipeline for this week?"

Before Mark could answer, the intercom on Jim's

desk buzzed. He glanced at the display and saw that it was Mike Stubbs, manager of the company's three body repair shops.

Jim pressed a button. "Yes, Stubby?"

"Guv? Elaine's just called me. The arsehole who parked in your space is an insurance assessor, came to see me. He's in reception."

"OK, let him wait," said Jim. "Can you come over?"

"Be round in a tick."

Jim clicked off the intercom and looked up. "We'll go through the lot," he said dismissively, checking his wristwatch, "in twenty minutes." As Mark rose he added, "In the meantime I want you to take a hard look at the part-ex figures for last month. Eddie should be wearing a sodding Santa Claus outfit," he snarled, "some of the deals lately look like Christmas presents."

"Will do," Mark replied, nodding.

A few minutes later Mike Stubbs' bespectacled round face, brush moustache and toothy grin appeared at the door. Jim was on his mobile phone, so Stubbs paused, then entered as Jim waved him in. Stubbs, one of the few whom Jim trusted completely, had been with him since the early days. Jim finished his call and looked up.

"Nice friends you've got, is he still in reception?"

"He's asked to see you. Wants to apologise, says he's got another urgent appointment."

"I'm busy. Let him sit on his brains for a while."

Stubbs shrugged. "Whatever you say, guv, but his company is important to us. And to be fair, it was his first time here."

"Should we be dealing with people who can't read a big sign? In plain English?"

"He won't do it again, that's for sure."

"Here's my keys." Jim shoved his bunch of keys across the desk. "You can let him out. He was lucky I didn't have time to let his tyres down."

Stubbs grinned. "I'll tell him that if he does it again, I'll use the transporter to park his car for him, somewhere nice."

Jim lowered his voice. "We've got the nod on the next Dutch consignment. No change from the last time, the new routine's working well. Week after next and Shaun will be going with Kevin again. I'll let you know the exact date. You'll get your usual wedge, of course."

"Fine with me," Stubbs replied, "I could do with a nice bonus."

Sunday was the only day in the week when Jim Warwick allowed himself the luxury of a delicious, fat-dripping "full English" breakfast, which his wife Sandra cooked to perfection.

"Lovely," he grunted, shoving a piece of bread around his plate to mop up the reddish-yellow ketchup and egg fluid which was all that was left. "Bloody lovely".

"I wish you wouldn't do that," she said, leaning over to refill his coffee cup.

Jim slapped her bottom playfully. "Only showing my appreciation, love."

"Lots of other ways you could do that."

"I have my moments, as you know." He grinned.

"Behave!" She tapped his head, which he had kept close-shaven since his hairline had begun to recede some years before. The first time she saw it he had asked what she thought about his new look. She had paused, tilting her head to scan his solid six-foot frame.

"You look like a thug," she said.

"Do I? Good!"

Jim liked the way he looked. It was important to be fitter, stronger and smarter than other people, he believed, especially those whom he employed. His car dealership and three motor body repair shops were the businesses on which he paid his taxes, high profile and above board establishments. But some other ventures were neither, and they were the ones that had contributed most to making him a millionaire many times over well before his fiftieth year.

Jim's success had brought him from modest beginnings in Dagenham to the mansion he now owned in the Essex countryside. He had extended it and fitted it out to suit his lifestyle, with home and office under one roof. Known formerly as "The Larches" it was now "Warwick Hall". The building had CCTV cameras but lacked anti-burglar protection, something Jim had been looking into lately. He had held back because the best of those systems had alarms linked automatically and silently to the nearest police station and that was something with which he was not at all comfortable.

Not that he was afraid of burglars; he had a shotgun and would not hesitate to use it on an

CHAPTER TWO

intruder. Jim knew that he had made too many
enemies who wanted to hurt him, people who knew
he was wealthy and that he had a teenage daughter. It
was a recipe for a kidnap, something he never forgot
and the one thing he really feared.

It suited him in his business dealings to be tough
and to be perceived as such, an image he cultivated
for business. At home he was different, a man who
had a solid if tempestuous marriage and who doted
on their only child, Rosemary.

Lifting his cup he asked, "Rosie down yet?"

Sandra hesitated before answering quietly, "She's
out."

"Out?" Jim glanced at the wall clock. "She must
have been very quiet. I didn't hear her go out.
Where's she gone?"

Sandra refilled her own cup and sat down opposite
him. Jim noticed immediately that the question
seemed to unsettle her. She paused and reached for
the milk jug before answering.

"She's at a party."

"A party? What, on a Sunday? In the *morning*?"

Sandra stared mutely into the cup, stirring her
coffee.

Jim sat up; there was more to this. "Has she been
out *all night*?"

Sandra put the spoon down and placed her hands
in her lap under the table. "She..."

Jim interrupted, his voice rising. "Where is she?
Did she tell you she was going to be out all night?"

Sandra shook her head. "No – I mean yes," she
said. "She said not to stay up, she could be back late."

26

Jim stood up and moved to the sideboard to pick up his mobile phone.

"Where did she go? Where was the party?"

"Fiona's, I think."

He had already jabbed at the button and was waiting for an answer.

"Come on, come on," he muttered impatiently.

"Hi, Dad."

"Rosie? Where are you?" Although relieved to hear her cheerful greeting, Jim could not hide the anxiety he felt.

"In the car, with Tony. He's dropping me home." In the background Jim heard Rosie's muffled voice whispering, "Stop it," followed by a giggle.

Jim stiffened. The Italian! And God knows what was prompting the goings-on in the car.

There was an edge to his reply. "Where exactly are you right now?"

"We're just turning into Heather Lane, Dad. Should be home in a few minutes."

Jim was thinking fast. If the Italian was bringing her home, had he picked her up yesterday? If not, where was her own car? And where had she spent the night?

"Dad?"

"Yes, I'm here, love." His questions would have to wait. As calmly as he could he said, "See you in a few minutes then."

Sandra looked up enquiringly.

Jim said, "She's on her way home, in the Italian fellow's car. Be here in a few minutes."

"His name is Tony," Sandra said quietly. "Tony

27

Bellini."

"Never mind his bloody name," he barked. "Where the hell has she been all night? With him?"

"Calm down, love, I'm sure there's nothing wrong."

"Calm down?" he shouted. "What, when our child, our little girl, has been out all night with some gigolo?"

Sandra stayed calm. "She's hardly a child any more and this *is* the twenty-first century, love. Lighten up, she's a big girl, she's sensible and she knows how to look after herself."

Jim was staring at the CCTV monitor in the corner of the room, breathing heavily, scarcely able to contain his anger. He watched the main gates, waiting for the car to pull up alongside the intercom located directly under the camera, but the gates opened automatically. Rosie must have her keys with her, he realised. A black Audi coupe drove through onto the drive.

"Right, they're here." Jim's jaw was clenched and he stood up. "I want a word with that young man."

"Jim," Sandra exclaimed. "Wait, there's something you should know."

"What?"

"She's in love with him. She told me she wants to marry him."

Jim's head snapped around. "What? *Marry* him? She hardly knows the man."

"No, *you* hardly know him. They've been together for months."

On the monitor they watched the couple emerge from the car and embrace.

Sandra shrugged. "He seems nice enough to me and from the look of the car, he can't be doing badly. Rosie said he owns an estate agency in Leyton."

"I want to know where she spent the night," Jim snapped, "and I intend to find out right now."

As they watched, Tony climbed back into the car and Rosie waved to him as he started it up and headed back down the drive.

Jim frowned. "Damn, the bugger's not coming in."

"Why don't you ask her yourself? Maybe later when you've calmed down a bit. You'll only upset her, and yourself."

"All right, it can wait." He turned abruptly and strode through the communicating door to the extension.

Jim went straight to his desk and looked up a telephone number in his diary. He dialled it using one of the four mobiles that were on the desk. It was answered immediately.

"DS Rollo."

"Frank? Jim Warwick."

"Hello, Jim, what can I do you for?"

"Cut the crap, I need a favour."

"OK, what is it?"

"Have you got anything on a guy called Tony Bellini? I think that's B-E-L-L-I-N-I. Dark hair, medium build, mid-twenties. Drives a black Audi sports coupe."

"Does he now? Nice. Got an address?"

"No, but he owns an estate agents in Leyton."

"The company name?" He paused, but when Jim

29

did not answer he said, "OK, estate agent in Leyton, no name. No problem, I'll check it out and call you back."

"Do that, and don't hang around."

Ten minutes later Rollo rang back to the same mobile, saying that Bellini worked for estate agents Mercer and Treadgold; he definitely did not own the business. He added that there was nothing on record for him.

Jim checked his diary for another number and dialled it, using his landline phone. The number rang six times before switching to answer mode.

"Paul," said Jim tersely, "it's Jim Warwick. I have a job for you, call me."

A few minutes later Hawker Investigations returned his call.

Rosie stared into her coffee mug. "He's upset, isn't he, that I stayed out all night?"

Sandra shrugged. "Are you surprised?"

"I'm not a kid any more, Mum. Why doesn't he understand?"

"You know your father."

"And anyway, nothing bad happened. You must know that." Rosie rotated the mug thoughtfully between the palms of her hands. "Has he gone to his den to sulk?"

"Your father doesn't sulk. If something upsets him he gets angry and steamed up, but he never sulks."

"Is he very angry?"

"Mmm, just a bit, but he'll get over it. He goes into a strop and then he gets over it, he always does. You know that."

"I wish he'd just..." Rosie shook her head, "*trust* me. I'm not a kid."

"Course he trusts you, love. But he worries about you, he really does."

Sitting around the kitchen table to chat had been a family habit for years. The house had a comfortable living room and a formal dining room, both tastefully furnished, but it was the kitchen to which they gravitated naturally.

Sandra said, "He went off to calm down, which he will. But maybe it's just as well that Tony didn't come in this time."

"He had to meet a client for a viewing; it wasn't that he didn't want to come in."

The lobby door swung open and Jim entered, his face expressionless.

"I smell coffee," he said. "Pour us a cup, love."

Rosie closed her eyes and breathed in deeply. If he had been angry, at least he did not seem so now.

Sandra rose and moved to the sideboard. "Feeling better now?" she asked lightly.

Jim ignored the comment, sat down in the chair next to Rosie and said, "OK, what's it all about then?"

"Nothing happened, Dad."

"Fine." He gestured. "If nothing happened, then nothing happened. Where did this nothing happen?"

"I didn't go to his flat, if that's what's worrying you. We went to a party at Fiona's and it went on a bit late. Then some of us sort of stayed on and we talked and drank coffee all night. Actually it was great, we just relaxed."

CHAPTER TWO

"Why didn't you come home then, or phone?"

"I thought about phoning but I didn't want to disturb you, there was no need."

Sandra put the mug of coffee down in front of Jim. "And before you ask," she said, "she didn't drive home because she thought she'd had too much to drink. Her car is at Fiona's."

Jim looked at Rosie. "OK, so nothing happened. Tell me about this guy, your mum says it's serious."

Rosie perked up instantly. "Oh, Dad, he's *wonderful!* I love him and I want to marry him."

Jim's eyebrows arched. "Do you now? Has he asked you?"

Rosie inclined her head. "Well, not exactly, not yet. But he will because we love each other and we talked about getting engaged soon."

Sandra cut in. "That's a start. And you have to admit, he's a bit of a charmer and quite handsome, really."

Jim shot her a glance, folded his arms and leaned on the table.

"What does he do for a living?"

"He's very successful. I know that's important to you, Dad. He's an estate agent. Actually he owns the business, they have five branches. He works in Leyton."

"Would I know them?" Jim asked evenly.

"Mercer and Treadgolds, their branches are all around London."

"Can't say I've heard of them."

Sandra chipped in. "I have, they're quite well known."

"Not to me," said Jim. "Where's their head office?"

Sandra answered, "In the East End somewhere, Stratford, I think."

"Stratford? Really? Not Leyton, then." He leaned back. "What about his family? Have you met them?"

Rosie answered. "I've met his mum and dad, and his brother and they are really nice. They live in Ilford."

"OK, sweetheart," Jim said, "no harm done, then. Just make sure he doesn't take any liberties. Know what I mean?"

Jim had decided not to push it further. He would soon find out all he wanted to know about Mr Tony Bellini. In the meantime, best to lighten up. No point in upsetting her, he did not want her doing anything foolish.

CHAPTER THREE

Penny got home from her Tuesday afternoon shift at the school to find that the message indicator light on the phone was blinking. She pressed the playback button.

"Mrs Summers, sorry I missed you. It's Kerry Black, practice nurse at Doctor Mead's surgery. The doctor would like you to come in to see him at five tomorrow afternoon. If that is not convenient please call us back. Otherwise we'll see you tomorrow."

"I'll come home early," Geoff said when Penny told him that evening.

"You sure? I don't think you need to come with me.

"Just the same, I want to hear what he has to say."

Penny shrugged. "If you like."

Alarm bells were ringing in Geoff's head. Why did the doctor want to see her so soon? No way was he going to let her go on her own.

The next afternoon Geoff was home in good time to go with Penny to the surgery. They arrived ten minutes early, just as the last scheduled patient, an elderly man hobbling with a walking stick, was called into the doctor's room. At ten past the hour they were still waiting.

Geoff shifted in his seat and crossed his arms. "Twenty minutes," he fumed. "What's he *doing*?"

"Stop fidgeting," Penny said evenly. "We've got all day."

Geoff stood up and strode over to the low table in the centre of the room upon which was a stack of magazines. He picked one up and flicked through the pages indifferently before tossing it back onto the pile.

"Old rubbish, and probably full of germs, like they say."

The door from the doctor's surgery opened and the old man came through, leaning heavily on his stick. He nodded to them briefly and made for the exit.

The loudspeaker on the wall blared, short and crisp. "Mrs Summers, come in, please."

Penny stood up and Geoff took her elbow. "At last," he muttered.

They walked through a short corridor leading to Mead's office. The door with his name on it was ajar and they heard the doctor's voice, raised slightly, from within.

"Come in, please, Mrs Summers."

Penny pushed open the door. Mead, a small wiry man whom Geoff had not met before, was seated in a high-backed leather swivel chair at his desk. There was a telephone on the desk and beside it a monitor screen, a brown cardboard folder and a note pad.

"My husband is with me," Penny said, turning to look at Geoff.

Mead nodded briefly. "Mr Summers." He waved a hand. "Sit down, please."

Penny took one of the chairs indicated and Geoff sat on the other. Doctor Mead spoke to Geoff in clipped tones, saying, "I believe you are on our books, but this is your first time here, I think?"

"We registered when we moved into the area a few months ago, doctor. First thing we did."

"Yes, yes, good." He turned to look at Penny. "And how are you feeling Mrs Summers? The headaches?"

"The same, doctor, about twice a week." She opened her handbag and removed a folded sheet of paper which she held out to him.

"I kept a record of my meals, like you told me to."

Mead took the paper, unfolded it and glanced briefly at Penny's neat script.

"Yes, thank you." He put the document to one side, brought his hands together and leaned forward. "We have the results of your scan. Your headaches are not migraines." He opened the folder and looked briefly at Geoff, then turned to Penny.

"I'm afraid that you have a small growth, a tumour, behind your right temple, but let me assure you that we believe we can deal with it."

Geoff saw the shock in Penny's face and he responded immediately.

"What? A *tumour*? Are you sure?"

"Yes, unfortunately. But we have no reason to believe is it not benign. And as I said, we can deal with it."

Geoff felt his chest tightening. "Deal with it? How?"

"I'd like to make an appointment for you, Mrs Summers," Mead said, turning to address Penny, "to see a specialist, Mr Ganesh Mehta."

Geoff glanced at Penny whose face was ashen. He asked sharply, "A surgeon?"

Mead nodded. "Mr Mehta is a neurological surgeon, one of the best." The doctor leaned back and his expression softened. "He has seen the scans and I have spoken to him. We think that you will need surgery, but it's not as bad as it sounds, believe me."

Penny asked quietly, "What will that involve?"

The doctor seemed to be choosing his words carefully. He inclined his head.

"I understand that there are a few alternatives. First we have to find out exactly what it is, so a biopsy may be indicated. After that the specialist will be able to suggest the best course of action." He looked from one to the other. "You need to discuss the options with him. So if it's all right with you, I'll make the appointment for you. You should hear from his office in a few days' time. He's based at King Edward's Hospital in London."

On the way home they said little to each other. Geoff was too upset to speak and Penny stayed silent. Geoff drove slowly and was deep in thought, looking straight ahead.

Penny turned towards him. "He said we would hear in a few days."

"Uh-huh."

"The sooner the better. I'm fed up with the headaches."

Geoff realized that she was looking beyond the meeting with the consultant. Even beyond the surgery, already anticipating a successful outcome, a future without headaches. She was amazing, he thought.

"Well, he said it could be dealt with. That's good news."

"Yes, so stop worrying, it'll be fine."

Geoff frowned. He was not so sure and certainly could not stop worrying.

Private Investigator Paul Hawker arrived at Warwick Hall on a stormy grey morning, with a howling wind whipping rain horizontally across the windscreen. He turned into the cul-de-sac that led to Warwick's home and drew up outside steel gates set within a high brick wall. On a concrete post by the wall was a metal intercom box and he parked the car as close to it as he could. Paul removed his spectacles and placed them carefully on the passenger seat to keep them dry. Lowering his window just enough to allow him to squeeze his arm out, he reached forward and pressed the call button.

A metallic voice answered, "Yes?"

"Paul Hawker to see Mr Warwick."

"Just a minute."

Paul drew his arm back into the car and hurriedly raised the window, leaving only a small gap at the top. It did not prevent cold rain spattering his face, or keep his sleeve from getting soaked.

"Mr Warwick is expecting you, Mr Hawker, come through please."

"Thank you," Paul shouted before raising the window fully.

As the double gates yawned open he put his spectacles on again and drove forward. He had been there before, so he headed straight for the office at the end of the gravelled drive. It was a large house, even by Essex millionaire standards, with a long single-storey extension to one side. Paul followed the curving drive past the front porch and double garage of the main house to the extension, pulling up beside the heavy glass door that was its separate entrance. Hugging his briefcase he stooped as he bolted for the doorway at a trot. The door was being held open for him by a slim youngish man whom he had not met before.

"Come in, please, Mr Hawker. I'm Clive, Mr Warwick's PA." As Hawker entered he closed the door, instantly silencing the wind.

Hawker set his briefcase down. "Phew," he said, removing his coat. "It's wet out there."

Clive held out his hand. "Let me take that."

"Thanks."

"You're a little early but we can go in, Mr Warwick is expecting you."

Paul took a handkerchief from his pocket and wiped his spectacles. He picked up his case and followed Clive down a short corridor into Jim Warwick's office. It was a spacious, expensively carpeted room, fitted with a comfortable suite of furniture in red leather, an antique sideboard and an imposing leather-topped double pedestal oak desk, where Jim was sitting working on a laptop, a notepad at his elbow. Against one end of the big desk and at right angles to it was a smaller one on which were a CCTV monitor, a desktop computer and a filing tray with papers in it. Warwick sat with his arms on the big desk, studying the screen of the laptop. He looked up briefly as they entered.

"Paul, come in and take a seat," he said. "I'll be with you in a minute."

"Good morning, Mr Warwick," Paul replied. He found Jim's habit of trying always to dominate others childish and tiresome, but he was a good client who paid his bills, on time. Paul moved to one of the armchairs, sank into it and put his briefcase on the coffee table.

Clive had paused at the door. "Coffee?"

"Yes, please, white no sugar."

"I'll bring a tray, then you can help yourself." Clive left through a door that led to Jim's personal gym and leisure suite.

Jim Warwick stared at the screen, making a few notes before putting the pad aside and shutting down the laptop. He swivelled his chair to face Paul, when one of the mobile phones on his desk trilled. Paul noticed that in addition to the normal landline there were no fewer than four mobiles lined up side by side on the desk, each a different make or model to the others. Jim picked up the one on the end of the line.

"Yes?"

After listening for a few moments he spoke again. "Eighty? *Eighty*? That's five more than the last lot."

There was another brief pause while he listened. "Well, I don't believe that; it's just an excuse, they're bloody thieves," he snarled. "OK, eighty, but tell them it has to be the best, otherwise it will be the last we take. Sort out the details and let me know when you are ready."

Hawker had opened his briefcase and removed a notebook and a slim file of documents bound together within a plastic presentation folder. Under the transparent cover the first page on Hawker letterhead was entitled "GEORGIO ANTONIO BELLINI". The exchanges he had just heard meant nothing to him; it was none of his business.

Jim leaned forward and picked up another of the mobile phones. Paul noticed that it was the one on the opposite end of the line. Jim pressed a button on the pad, waited for a response and spoke.

"Everything OK?" He paused to listen, and then said, "It's ready. Eighty this time, sort it, will you? I have enough here to cover that, pick it up tomorrow. We collect on Tuesday and Shaun will be going with you. Your meeting is at eleven, same place. That's eleven their time." He paused, then said tersely, "Keep me posted."

Jim put the mobile down, swivelled his chair again to face Paul, and stood up.

"Now, young man, what have you got for me?"

Paul Hawker was good at his job. He did not mind being slim and below average height, or that his thin face and heavy spectacles combined to make his appearance unremarkable and unmemorable. In his business these were assets, as were his sharp intellect and his attention to detail. At their previous meeting Jim Warwick had demanded to know everything about Tony Bellini.

"Everything?" Paul had asked.

"Everything." Jim had counted off the questions on his fingers. "Where he works, where he lives, how much money he's got, where it comes from, where it goes, what family he has and who his friends are."

Paul had nodded. "I understand."

Jim had not finished. "I want to know what makes him tick. What's his past and does he have a future? I especially want to know if he is shacked up with a woman and who she is. If not, when was the last time, and how many before that? Get the picture?"

Paul had answered in the affirmative. And now he was here to present his findings to his client, sitting across the table from him. He held out the presentation folder and handed it to Jim.

"It's all in here, everything. All you asked for and a bit more."

Jim opened the folder and was scanning through it.

"Anything interesting?"

"Giorgio Antonio Bellini," said Paul, looking at his notes. "He prefers to be called Tony. Twenty-six years old, born in Bedford. His parents emigrated from Italy to Bedford in the sixties, then moved to Ilford about twenty years ago."

Before he could go further, the landline phone on the desk rang. Paul paused.

"Bugger," said Jim, slamming the folder onto his knee. He rose, went over to the desk, glanced at the caller identification and picked up the handset.

"Give me a minute, I'll call you back," he snapped. Turning to Paul, he said, "Can you leave the file? I'll go over it and get back to you. Something's come up and I have a few calls to make."

It was plainly a dismissal, clumsy and insensitive, but Paul was not going to make anything of that.

"Yes, no problem," he said quietly, collecting his papers.

At that moment Clive entered, carrying a tray on which were two mugs, sugar and milk.

Paul looked uncertainly at Jim who said, "We're going to have to pass on the coffee, Clive, Mr Hawker is just leaving."

Paul knew that Jim was not a polite man, but this was insensitive to the point of rudeness. He got up to leave.

"I'll wait to hear from you then," he said. Jim Warwick did not answer.

As Clive escorted him out of the office, Paul said half in jest, "Is he going to use a mobile to call me? I wonder which one he'll use. I've never seen anyone use so many at the same time."

"Dunno, mate," was Clive's deadpan answer, as he held the door open. "There's a push switch on the post inside the main gate that opens them. End of the drive, right-hand side."

Paul remembered the arrangement from his last visit. He nodded and thanked him. Outside, the wind had abated and the rain was now just a fine drizzle.

Geoff and Penny were having their supper, tucking into the vegetable lasagne that Penny had cooked.

Geoff thought it delicious. "Mmm, this is good, makes a change from the usual."

"Fresh veg, straight from the stall in the market. By the way, I met Brian there."

"Brian? A bit off his beat, isn't he? Haven't seen

43

him lately, how is he?"

"He's fine, got a new girlfriend, she lives somewhere local. We had a coffee in the cafe." Brian Hammond was Penny's cousin and they had been close friends since childhood. He had spent thirteen months in jail for fraud and false accounting, and had not long been released.

Geoff put his fork down. "How is he coping?"

"He seems to be doing fine, actually. He said he had been a bit 'down' when Marie left him, but he's got over it."

"A lady with expensive tastes, that one. Too fond of the good things in life. Is his new relationship serious?"

"I think so. Her name is Jackie, she teaches art. He seems keen."

"Why don't we invite them over for dinner sometime? Then we'll find out for ourselves."

"Good idea." Penny was silent for a moment. She shook her head. "I still can't believe it really happened. I *know* he couldn't have done the things they said he did."

"He was stitched up," said Geoff flatly. "By his boss, that man Flynn. It was obvious that he was lying in the witness box and his statement to the police was a pack of lies too."

"Brian is too trusting, always was."

"There was too much that just didn't add up. Not for me, anyway. Dodgy businessmen and a bent copper, it stinks."

"Anyway, he seems settled now. He's got a job in a public library. In the Hackney area, I think he said."

"He's probably had enough of accountancy."

"I'll give him a call; it'll be nice to meet his Jackie. It's about time he had a decent break."

The following morning Penny called Brian and at his request they agreed that the couples should meet for dinner at a restaurant. He said that Jackie was a bit shy and he thought she might be more comfortable with that.

"Controlled chaos," Geoff observed when he and Penny stood in one of the two queues waiting at the main reception area of the hospital.

"Controlled? Doesn't look like it." Penny replied.

A mélange of the sounds generated by a score of waiting people, passers-by in wheelchairs and on foot, four receptionists and several telephones all clamouring for attention at the same time, contributed to the impression of chaos.

A woman of ample proportions behind the counter managed a harassed smile when Geoff and Penny finally got to the front. She had just put down a phone which immediately started ringing again. She picked it up but held it unanswered while she spoke to Geoff.

"Can I help you?" she said.

"We have an appointment with Mr Mehta in Neurology," Geoff replied.

"Neurology? Second floor," the woman pointed. "Lift's in the corner. Turn right when you leave it, Doctor Mehta's office is at the end of the corridor." She turned away and put the phone to her ear.

"Thank you," said Geoff. Under his breath he

muttered, "I hate hospitals."

Penny smiled. "Are you going to be Mister Grumpy today?"

Geoff took her hand in his as they moved towards the lift. "No, I'm never grumpy."

"Not much, you aren't." She squeezed his hand.

In the lift he reflected. Married nineteen years and they still held hands sometimes. There was something truly comforting about that, not feeling the slightest embarrassment at this very public display of their affection for each other. He looked at her tenderly. Shit, he could lose her. No, that wasn't going to happen, it couldn't.

The lift doors sighed open to reveal a sign on the wall opposite, pointing to the department of neurology. They were still holding hands as their footsteps echoed down the corridor, his muted and hers measuring her strides in loud clacks from her high heels.

The white plastic sign on the door said in black letters, "G. Mehta, FRCS". Geoff pushed the door open and Penny followed. Geoff looked around. If this was typical of a senior consultant's room, he thought, the National Health Service isn't paying them enough. Senior? Mehta might be a surgeon, but he looked scarcely old enough to be out of college. But the shock of dark hair and smooth light brown skin probably served to make him look younger than his years, Geoff mused.

The consultant was wearing a perfectly cut, expensive dark blue suit. He was sitting in a padded swivel chair at his desk, a laptop open and switched on. The man spoke in a firm but quiet manner.

"Did your doctor show you the scans?" he asked Penny.

"Yes," she answered.

Geoff leaned forward slightly. "He said you would tell us about the options."

Mehta turned towards his desk and picked up a compact disc in its sleeve.

"Let's look at them again." He fed the disc into his laptop and turned it so that they could all view the screen. He tapped the keyboard and an image appeared. Geoff pulled his chair forward for a closer view. Mehta pointed with his little finger.

"Here," he said. "The tumour is in the temporal lobe behind your right temple. As you can see, it is well defined."

"Does that matter?" Penny asked. "It's strange to be looking at something inside my own head."

"Broadly, it's good. It means that it is likely to be of a slow growing type, sometimes called benign." Mehta tapped the keyboard and a different view appeared. "Your headaches are the result of pressure of the growing mass upon the brain. For this type of tumour, surgery is usually the best option."

Benign? Geoff shot out the burning questions. "If it's benign, does that mean that it won't spread? And if you take it out, will that get rid of it completely?"

Mehta brought his hands up and locked the fingers together. "I can understand your concern," he said softly, "but I must tell you that nothing is certain until we get confirmation of the type of growth it is. We

47

do that with a biopsy. For the moment I am prepared to say that I believe that a biopsy is likely to confirm our initial diagnosis. If so, the tumour will not spread and it can be removed by surgery."

Geoff asked, "What does the biopsy involve?"

"A minor operation, a few days in the hospital. Using an endoscope we remove a small piece of the tumour and analyse it. The lab is downstairs, so we get the results very quickly."

Penny asked, "If it…if it's what you think it is, what happens next?"

"The good news is that you will almost certainly not need chemotherapy or radiotherapy. We would schedule an operation to remove the tumour altogether. In the meantime, you need to take medication to inhibit further growth." He closed the lid of the laptop. "No cause for alarm. Your condition is serious, but not immediately life-threatening."

"What sort of timescale would it all involve, Doctor?" Geoff asked.

"First the biopsy, in a couple of months' time. All being well, the main operation will be scheduled about eight weeks later. I'll give you a prescription now for the medication; steroids for the tumour and something to help you manage the headaches."

Geoff breathed out audibly. "Wonderful. Thank you, Doctor."

They were on their way home. "I suppose it could have been worse," Geoff said.

"It could have been *a lot* worse," Penny replied.

"I'm lucky really, when you think about it."

"I wouldn't exactly call it good luck."

"I promised to call Sue after seeing the consultant. I'll ring her tonight." Sue was Penny's elder sister who lived in Australia, but the geographical separation made little difference to the closeness of their relationship.

"Uh-huh."

"She made me promise. As soon as we had the results."

God, Geoff thought, that won't be easy. "When did you last speak to her?"

"Saturday. She'll probably want to come over before the op."

They both knew that it would be difficult for Sue to make the trip. Her husband Bob was a hospital porter and they had three teenage children.

"I don't think they can afford it," Geoff said.

"That won't stop her."

"No, you're right. She'll borrow the fare if she has to."

They were silent as he slowed to negotiate another roundabout. Penny turned in her seat to face him, about to speak, but he interjected.

"I know what you're thinking but it's out of the question," he said flatly. "You're simply not well enough to make the trip. Anyway there won't be enough time."

After another short silence Penny said quietly, "It's something I really want to do." She placed a hand on his arm. "Whatever happens. The doctor said that the biopsy wouldn't be for another couple of months, so there should be enough time. Before that, I mean."

Geoff frowned and turned to glance at her. "I get the impression that you may be more worried about all this than you are letting on."

"Maybe, just a bit. I want to see her again, just in case. And I'm well enough to travel but if you want, we could break the journey in a stopover. It would be part of the holiday, not just a break."

"All right, I suppose that's possible."

God forbid that the worst should happen, Geoff thought, but if it did, the time she has left is *her* time, so if going to Australia to see her sister was what she wanted, she should go. It was up to him to make it happen.

"OK, but it will have to include two stops at least and for three or four days each time."

"Thank you, darling."

He slowed the car before taking the last bend into their road. He was thinking about how the trip should be planned, with long stopovers both ways. He would need a lot of time off work but did not think that would be a problem.

Then there was the cost. They had moved house and taken out a heavy mortgage only a few months previously and their bank balance was not healthy. No matter, he thought, one way or another he would find the money. Of that he was grimly certain.

CHAPTER FOUR

Jim Warwick picked up his calculator and tapped in a figure. Eighty thousand Euros, around seventy grand for Kevin to collect. No problem, he had a lot more than that in cash in his safe. In a couple of weeks it would become a sum close to a quarter of a million, less some piddling expenses on the way. Lovely.

His mood changed as he picked up one of the mobiles on his desk. He jabbed at the dialling button, he needed to answer the last call to his landline. Dave; he might have known. Why doesn't the old sod *listen*? He had been told time and again not to call him on the landline. The phone at the other end was answered immediately.

"Hello, is that Sunny Jim?"

"I'll give you 'Sunny Jim', you stupid old bugger."

"Now is that any way to speak to your uncle? And me a pensioner and all."

"Bollocks. You know you're only supposed to call the mobile. And then I call you back. It ain't rocket science."

"Sorry, mate. I lost the number."

"What, again? I can't be sodding about buying new mobiles every five minutes. Go get a pen and paper."

A minute later Dave returned. "OK, I'm ready."

Jim gave him the number of the mobile he was using and told him to keep the note handy by his phone. "I don't want you losing it again. Now listen. The next lot's ready. Kevin and Shaun will be at the usual place in Dunkirk at eleven o'clock your time on Tuesday. Got that?"

"Eleven, Tuesday, OK."

"You can get to the factory, pick up the stuff and be back home in Lille in time for dinner Tuesday night."

"Yeah, no problem. Kevin going back by train?"

"Yes."

"I'll drop him off at the Eurostar, then, same as before."

"Fine. I'll tell Pete Mount to call you to confirm his pick-up; it'll probably be the next day, Wednesday. He's got a house removal on hold at the moment, a domestic heading for Leeds. It'll go with that. The Mounts will overnight at their Canterbury depot."

"Wednesday pick-up, OK. Shaun going back on the wagon with Pete?"

"Yes. We'll pick him up from Canterbury."

"OK, we'll put him in the spare bedroom again. I'll call you Tuesday night."

"The mobile, remember."

"OK."

"Make sure you do. Drive carefully and don't mess up."

Jim clicked the phone off and sighed. It was impossible to be angry with the man. For one thing, Dave Merchant was his uncle, a man he had known all his life and, for another, he was always so bloody cheerful. When Jim was growing up Dave was a petrol tanker driver whose job it was to deliver to filling stations but he always had plenty of money and was fond of splashing it around. He was generous to the boy and Jim loved and idolised him. One day when he was about ten years old he asked Dave how it was that he always had so much money. "Never you mind," Dave had responded. Touching the side of his nose he winked and added, "We work very hard, you see." It was to be some time before Jim discovered that Dave's wealth was more to do with dodgy fuel level measurements than with hard work.

Paul Hawker parked in his marked bay behind the parade of shops. Will it ever stop bloody raining, he wondered? A light drizzle clouded his spectacles as he clutched his briefcase and headed briskly towards the alleyway connecting the parking area to the main road. He hurried along the pavement past the brightly lit window of Bobbie's hairdressing salon and stepped into the alcove that provided access to that establishment and to the staircase that led to his office above.

There were two doors on the landing at the top of the narrow wooden stairs. The brass plate fixed to the first read, "HAWKER INVESTIGATIONS". On the second was a printed plastic strip declaring it to be "PRIVATE". Paul pushed open the first door. It was not a large room, being furnished only with two desks, four inexpensive office chairs, some steel filing cabinets and a small fridge in the corner, adjacent to a table upon which were the essentials for making and consuming tea and coffee. At one of the desks was a swivelling armchair occupied by Paul's sister, a smartly dressed woman of generous proportions who was working at her keyboard. She lowered her head to peer over her spectacles.

"You're back early. How did it go?"

Paul put his briefcase down, took his raincoat off and shook it. "Wish I could tell you, but the meeting was cut short."

"Oh?"

"He took a phone call and that was it, end of meeting. I was a bit miffed at the time, but it's OK, I left the file."

"Did you remember to leave the invoice?"

Paul smiled. "Relax, sis. I put it in the file, right at the top where he can't miss it." Her name was Christina, usually shortened to Tina but he had always called her "sis".

She reached for a ledger on her desk, opened it and ticked a column against the Warwick job number. "Invoice dispatched," she muttered.

Paul picked up his case. "Any messages?" he asked over his shoulder as he went through into his office.

"Mrs Hodder called in."

"Mavis Hodder? What did she want?"

"She just popped in to say hello. She has her hair done at Bobbie's sometimes, said she never stops recommending us to people."

"That's nice," said Paul absently. Eighteen months earlier Paul had traced Mavis Hodder's missing teenage son and brought him back from Liverpool where he had been living rough. The Jamie Hodder case had resulted in a good bit of publicity for the business. Tracing missing people was time-consuming and expensive, but that one had been worth the effort.

A few minutes later Tina came into the room bearing a brown folder and a mug of tea, both of which she placed on his desk.

"Richard Ellesworth, Southend-on-Sea. In case you've forgotten, you're serving papers on him this evening for Parveys."

Parveys were solicitors acting for a major bank and Richard Ellesworth, so far as Paul could determine, was a man whose small taxi business had failed and all he had left was his house.

Paul sighed. "OK," he said heavily, picking up the folder. The unfortunate Ellesworth probably had plenty of other problems, but a job was a job. Papers were best served after hours, when the recipient was most likely to be at home and off guard. God, there were times when he hated having to do this sort of thing.

Geoff and Penny had decided to keep the news to themselves. Geoff was sitting at the kitchen table staring morosely into his coffee cup and Penny stood leaning with her back to the worktop. She turned to put her coffee mug on the draining board.

"I'll have to tell Mrs Taylor. She'll need time to find someone else to cover for me." Geoff was still staring into his cup. Penny said, "Geoff?"

He looked up. "Sorry, I was miles away. Mrs Taylor? Yes of course, the school." He nodded. "Shouldn't be difficult, I'm sure there are plenty of part-time primary teachers around."

"And I want to tell Sam."

"Yes, of course."

Penny glanced up at the clock on the wall. "She'll be in the office, I'll do it now." She moved to pick up her handbag, which was on the end of the worktop, fished out her mobile and scrolled down to call Sam's number. Moments later Samantha answered.

Geoff listened as Penny said, "Oh, not too bad. There's a problem, and I'm going to have an op in a few months' time to sort it. In the meantime I'm on a course of medications, which will help."

Geoff was paying close attention. After a brief pause, Penny said, "It should be fine, after the op. For now they said I should take it easy for a bit. No, no need to come around right now, but this evening would be fine, if you're free." After a brief pause she laughed and said, "OK, see you later."

Still smiling, Penny put the mobile back into her bag. "She's coming around tonight."

Geoff asked, "What's the joke?"

"Eh? Oh, when I asked if she was free, she said something. And no, you don't want to know."

Geoff smiled. "I'm glad she's coming over. Do you want to call Sue?"

"Yes, I'd better do that. I told her I'd call after the consultation." She looked up at the clock again. "It'll be just after nine in the evening in Australia, should be OK."

"Just tell her that it's good news and what you need is a holiday, so we'd like to visit. You can tell her the rest when we get there."

"She'll want to know when."

"I'll get on to the travel agents tomorrow." For the first time that day, he smiled broadly, lifting his head. "Tell you what, Pen, let's do it in style." He gestured. "First class all the way and five-star hotels."

"First class? Huh," she snorted. "That's crazy,

how much quicker will we get there in first class?
Economy will do. And there's nothing wrong with
good clean three-star hotels."

He stared at her. She had a *brain tumour* for God's
sake. He wanted to hold her close and remind her
that saving money would only make him feel worse
than he did already. They talked it through and in the
end she agreed to compromise, accepting business
class flights provided that they booked only one two-
night stopover each way.

"What's the point of staying any longer on the
breaks?" she had asked.

"You are going to need to rest."

"But two nights means three days of rest and that
will be enough. I don't want to lose an extra day each
way for nothing."

He gave in. "I'll make the arrangements
tomorrow."

The following day Geoff telephoned the agents and
gave them an outline of the intended itinerary, asking
for costs to be worked out. He made an appointment
to see them on the Friday afternoon. That way, he
thought, he could call in on the way home from work
without Penny being there. He was determined to
book the best hotels for the stopovers. By the time
she found out it would be too late for her to do
anything about it.

On the Friday Geoff left the office early and went
into the travel agent's shop in the high street. There
were four attendants, all young women dressed

identically in light blue jackets, each at a desk equipped with a keyboard and monitor. Three of them were occupied with customers. Geoff moved forward and spoke to the fourth.

"I have an appointment with Brenda Fuller. My name is Summers."

"I'm Brenda," she replied, flashing a wide-mouthed smile. "Please take a seat, Mr Summers, I have the file here."

Geoff sat down as Brenda opened the file and took out three pieces of paper.

"I've got three draft schedules for you to look at, two with Hong Kong stopovers and one in Singapore." She passed the papers across to him.

Geoff read through them while she waited.

"The Singapore stopover looks good."

"It's the best, but it's the dearest. Would you like me to see if I can tweak it a bit?"

"If you can get it down a bit, that would be good. But I'll take it anyway. Pencil it in and I'll be in touch with you after the weekend."

"How did it go?" Penny asked when he got home.

"All sorted," he said.

"How much will it cost?"

"A lot less than I thought it would."

"Is it going to be a problem?"

"A problem? No, why should it?"

"There's not too much in the bank at the moment."

"Oh, we'll manage. Don't worry about it. We can get a loan if we need to, but that's not likely."

She seemed satisfied with that.

In his office on the Monday morning Geoff checked the number for his local bank. Nine or ten grand, no problem raising that, he thought. He was put through to the investment and loans manager who had helped arrange a bridging loan some months previously when they moved house. Geoff made an appointment to see him the next day at one-thirty in the afternoon.

He had just put the phone down when his secretary Debbie said, "Rod just came through. He said please could you call him."

Geoff thanked Debbie and called Thompson on the intercom.

"Rod? Geoff."

"Thanks for getting back to me, Geoff. A couple of things: First, Warwick Motors called. He wants the survey visit put back by a week, to Thursday the twenty-sixth. Can you make it?"

Geoff thumbed through his diary. "Looks fine, morning or afternoon?"

"Eleven o'clock. It's not far, a place called Warwick Hall, near Braintree."

"Warwick Hall," said Geoff, making a note in the diary. "Yes, you told me. No problem. What was the other thing?"

"Sorry about the short notice but something has come up. Can you come to Birmingham with me tomorrow?"

"Tomorrow? Tomorrow's a bit difficult for me, Rod. What's so urgent?"

"Stork Hill Galleries, I finally got the nod from them."

"Great. Well done." The order was worth over

sixty thousand pounds and they had worked hard for it.

"Yeah, thanks. But they want to meet us for a final look at the proposal."

"But that's been fixed since our amended quote went in. What is it, two, three weeks?"

"Look, Geoff, you know how it is. Sometimes they muddy the waters just looking for a reason to shave a bit off the bottom line."

Geoff grimaced. This was a matter of negotiation, very much Rod's department. Why should it involve him? His priority was to get the trip to Australia organized, booked and paid for.

"Well, if they've given you the nod it means they want to go ahead. Why do you need me?"

"They want to see if we can reduce the cost by making a few small changes to the design."

This was getting ridiculous, thought Geoff. He did not want to make a trip to Birmingham anyway, and certainly not just to mess around with the integrity of the design at the eleventh hour for the sake of a few pennies.

"Sorry, Rod. I'm not comfortable with that, it could compromise total security."

"All I want you to do is to take another look at it, listen to their suggestions and then if you have to tell them it can't be done, so be it."

Geoff waited for a few seconds before giving what he thought was a measured answer. He liked Rod and got on well with him, but he was not ready to tell anyone at Melford about Penny's illness and the matters he needed to address urgently.

"To be honest, Rod, I have a problem. It's a big problem and it's personal. I have to deal with it and that means I have to be somewhere else tomorrow. If it has to be tomorrow, can you take Danny?" He was referring to Danny Hall, who had been promoted to chief designer following Geoff's own promotion.

After a brief pause Rod said, "OK, Geoff, I understand."

Geoff got the impression that Rod was not happy but he felt sure that Danny was perfectly capable of standing in for him. After all, what could possibly go wrong?

At the ferry terminal in Dunkirk Dave Merchant pulled his Transit van into the car park. Plenty of time, he thought, to treat himself to a snack at the café where he could pick up a copy of the *Sun* fresh in from an earlier boat. With a bit of help from his nephew Jim Warwick, Dave and his wife Glenda had retired to a quiet hamlet south of Lille two years earlier.

He collected coffee and croissants from the counter and settled at a table towards the rear of the room. Now, he thought, turning to the back page of the paper, how is Manchester United doing?

Shortly after, Dave watched as the ship docked and vehicles disgorged from the yawning doors, bumping their way down the exit ramp and up onto the dock road. The men he was waiting for were Kevin Flynn, Jim Warwick's personal bookkeeper, and Shaun Conroy who worked in Jim's business. They would be arriving as foot passengers. Dave disliked Flynn and was surprised that his hard-nosed nephew employed him as a bag man. But he knew also that Shaun was there to guarantee Flynn's loyalty. They wouldn't exactly be travelling together, but Flynn and the bag would never be out of Shaun's sight, never more than a few feet away.

They came in separately. Flynn first, a thin man of average height whose stooped gait and narrow face below thinning hair made him seem smaller. He had a briefcase in one hand and a bulky holdall in the other. He made his way to where Dave was sitting and put the briefcase on the table and the holdall on a chair.

"Everything OK?" he asked.

"Fine. You?"

Flynn removed his coat. "No probs. I'm getting a coffee. Want one?"

Dave shook his head. "Just had one." He noticed that Shaun, carrying an overnight bag, had entered and moved to the counter, making no sign of recognition.

Dave knew that Shaun was one of the few people whom Jim trusted totally. Fifteen years earlier Shaun had been a professional light-heavyweight boxer; good but not quite good enough to reach the top. He'd won more fights than he'd lost, but was best remembered as the man who had never ever been knocked down. A journalist once said that you could hit him with a truck if you really wanted a new truck. After a spell as a doorman at a nightclub, Shaun had been hired by Jim. He was paid to valet cars, but he doubled as Jim's bodyguard whenever required, an activity for which he received generous bonuses in cash.

Since his pugilistic days Shaun's six-foot-one frame had bulked out, but it was all muscle. Dave watched him collect a cup of coffee and ease his way between tables to sit at one near the door. Flynn then picked up his coffee, paid for it and returned to Dave's table. Ten minutes later Shaun caught Dave's eye, nodded and left the cafe with his bag. Dave casually folded his newspaper and looked at his watch. "Time to make a move," he said quietly.

They had been on the road for over an hour and were not quite half way to their destination. Dave had been driving steadily, well within the speed limits. Flynn was in the middle seat and Shaun had taken the outer one, with the holdall on the floor by his feet.

"Can't this thing go any faster?" Flynn complained.

"Not today," said Dave. "Strict instructions: take it steady, no risks."

"It's boring."

"It wouldn't be boring if we got pulled up," Dave replied.

Flynn sighed. "God, I hate France."

Shaun turned to look at him. "We're in Belgium," he said drily.

"France, Belgium, all the same to me. Anyway, going a bit faster isn't going to damage that thing in the back," he said, jerking his thumb towards the load area behind them.

"Relax," said Dave. "No speeding. This is a French van, French registered, with a French two hundred litre domestic water heater in the back. All legal and above board, even if we are stopped. He pointed at the holdall. "And if we're pulled up and you're worried about *that*, as long as you keep it and your mouth shut, everything will be fine." He eased the van out to overtake a slow lorry. "Anyway, we'll be there soon, so just relax."

Flynn rolled his eyes without commenting.

A little over two hours later they arrived at their destination, a small factory unit on an industrial estate between the towns of Breda and Tilburg in Holland. Dave stopped the van outside its tall roller-shutter door. He stepped out carrying his anorak.

"Stay in the van," he ordered. He glanced around casually while he put his anorak on.

The unit was in a cul-de-sac of about thirty similar ones. It was lunchtime and there did not seem to be much going on, apart from some activity at the bottom end of the close where a burger van was serving a queue of hungry workers engaged in noisy banter. Perfect, he thought, making his way towards a half-glazed door adjacent to the roller door. A sign above proclaimed the premises to be "NEDERLAND LINDEN ELEKTROTECH-NISCH B.V." He pressed the doorbell and was let in.

Shortly after, the shutter door rolled up half way. Dave climbed into the van and drove under it to pull up inside the unit. At once the door was lowered, squealing in its track all the way to the floor. Shaun and Dave unloaded the water heater and carried it to a storeroom at the rear, with Flynn following with the holdall, which he put down on a counter.

"I'll get the cover off," said Shaun, armed with a small screwdriver.

The factory owner, a plump man called Henk, rubbed his hands briskly and tipped the bundles of money onto the counter. He began counting the notes slowly and diligently.

"It's all there, no need to worry," Dave said.

Henk smiled crookedly and inclined his head. "Of course I believe you," he replied in perfect English with a Dutch accent. "But I check anyway." When he was finished he pulled forward a cardboard box that was on the counter.

"Your goods, gentlemen."

Dave nodded. "I'll start checking these," he said to Shaun. "You get the bags and the aerosol from the van."

Dave counted out twenty-four small fabric bags and carefully checked the contents of each. Meanwhile Shaun pulled on a pair of latex gloves and used the aerosol, a strong deodorant, to spray the insides of six heavy duty polythene bags.

"OK, all done," said Dave.

The fabric bags containing the drugs were put into the polythene ones, which were then folded over, sealed with tape and placed inside the heater. Shaun replaced the cover and he and Dave loaded it back into the van.

Henk smiled broadly. "Thank you, gentlemen, it is good to do business with you."

As they left, he said, "Goodbye, give my regards to the boss; see you again."

CHAPTER FOUR

Inside the burger van at the end of the cul-de-sac a man flicked a switch and spoke softly into his headset microphone. "*Ze hebben net weg,*" he said. In the Rotterdam office of the anti-drugs section of the KLPD, the National Police Services Agency, Chief Inspector Annika van Houten's assistant Marta logged the time of the van's departure, just as she had recorded the time of its arrival.

She turned to her boss. "They are just leaving."

The chief inspector nodded. As far as she knew, this particular vehicle had not been observed at their target site before. The van's visit had been recorded on the surveillance team's CCTV, so she knew that a trace on its French registration would quickly yield details of its owner and location.

Ten minutes later Jim Warwick picked up the fourth of the mobiles on his desk and pressed a button. In Holland Henk's landline telephone rang.

"Ja?"

"It's me, everything OK?"

"They just left. Everything is good, no problems."

"When the stuff gets here I'll see for myself if everything is good."

"Of course it is good. Would I cross you?"

"You'd only do it once!"

"You make good jokes. You want to make a date for the next batch?"

"No, not now. I'll call you when I want to order again."

"Fine, then I hear from you when you are ready."

"OK." Jim put the mobile down on the desk.

Jim Warwick was careful to limit this side of his business activity. This would be the third time they used this particular method for shipment of the goods to England and as long as it worked, he felt that four or five shipments a year were quite enough.

He reflected that it had been nearly two years since the last time they had used couriers. That had ended in disaster when the two men were intercepted at Dover. But the new system had been working for nearly a year. It was slick and professional, and working well. Lovely.

CHAPTER FIVE

Geoff made sure that he would be in good time to keep his appointment at the bank, but he had been kept waiting in the lobby.

"Come on, come on," he muttered, "I haven't got all day."

Finally after fifteen minutes he was ushered in to see John Knowles, the loans manager. Knowles stood to greet him, adjusting his navy blue tie with the bank logo on it. On his desk were a keypad and monitor and a brown folder with a notepad beside it.

"Nice to see you again, Mr Summers. Sorry to keep you waiting. Are you well? Enjoying your new home, I hope?"

"We're fine, thank you, and settled in."

Knowles sat down and leaned back. "What can we do for you?"

Geoff came straight to the point. "I would like a loan or a higher limit on my overdraft."

"A loan? Fine." Knowles sat up and pulled the notepad forward. "How much do you need?"

"Ten thousand pounds. No, better make that eleven."

Knowles arched his eyebrows and inclined his head. "Eleven thousand?" He made a note on his pad. "May I ask what it's for?"

"I'm taking my wife to Australia for a long holiday and I want it to be first class all the way. Travel, hotels, everything."

Knowles put the pen down and looked up. "Er… have you made any improvements to the house?"

The question surprised Geoff. "Not really. There are a couple of things we want to do but to be honest we can't afford it at the moment. The holiday is the priority right now. Why do you ask?"

Knowles opened the folder. "The reason I ask," he said, "is that you seem to be a bit, ah, extended just now." He looked at his monitor screen. "You are near the limit on the agreed overdraft and you don't appear to have much leeway on your cards. Any changes to your mortgage?"

"No."

Knowles scanned a page of printed information in the folder. "Hmm… I was hoping that you may have reduced it a bit. What with the dip in house values, it's unlikely you have sufficient equity in your property to provide the necessary collateral."

"*What?* Not enough equity? That house is worth a hell of a lot more than the amount of the mortgage."

Knowles' tone was apologetic. "What it comes down to is that the bank's first consideration is to establish your ability to repay the debt and frankly on your current income it may be difficult to make a case for a loan of this size."

Geoff shifted in his chair and shook his head. "It's hardly a fortune. Ten or eleven grand? Almost credit card stuff."

"Yes, for some people. But these are difficult times and we have to keep to the bank's strict lending criteria."

This was not sounding good but Geoff had with him the letter of appointment to his new post, just in case it was needed. He reached into his jacket and took out the envelope, withdrew the letter and placed it on the desk.

"You might like to take a look at this."

Knowles picked up the letter and scanned it quickly. "Ah, this looks good." He nodded. "A recent promotion, I see."

"And a substantial rise."

"So I see. This will make a difference; I think we should be able to do something. Do you mind if I take a copy?"

"Go ahead."

"Thank you."

Knowles swivelled his chair, placed the letter on his printer copier and pressed a button. When the copy emerged he glanced at it and handed the original back to Geoff.

Knowles put the copy into the folder. "I'll set the wheels in motion; we should be able to get back to you in a few days' time."

"How long will it take to get the cash into my account?"

"We'll send you a letter when the loan is approved. You come in to sign the documents, then it's an immediate transfer into your account."

"Good, but could you phone me instead of sending a letter? The holiday is a present for my wife and I don't want to spoil the surprise."

"It's not the usual procedure. Normally it would be sent to you from our head office, but I'm sure they'll send it here if we ask. What's your mobile number?"

Geoff told him and he wrote it down.

"Just one thing. I think it would be better if we put

the loan request in for improvements to your house, if you see what I mean."

"Whatever it takes," Geoff replied dismissively.

They shook hands and he left. Once outside the building he took in a deep breath. It felt good to have sorted out the biggest potential problem.

At ten past two that afternoon Geoff got back to the office. Debbie was at her desk, looking worried.

"Adam's been after you. He's called twice in the last fifteen minutes, asking where you were."

"What did you say?"

"I said I didn't know."

Geoff picked up the intercom handset and pressed the button for Adam's line. "I'll call him now."

He answered immediately. "Ford."

"It's Geoff, you wanted me?"

"Where the hell have you been? I want to see you *now*."

What's this? Geoff wondered. Rude bastard. "I'll come straight round."

There was a click as Ford put the phone down without answering.

Debbie's expression mirrored her concern. "Trouble?"

"Don't know. He seems annoyed about something."

On the way to Ford's office Geoff tried to control his rising anger. In all the years he had been with the company, nobody had ever spoken to him like that. He knocked at Adam Ford's door and went straight in.

CHAPTER FIVE

At his desk the managing director was poring over an open folder. He did not even look up as Geoff approached and then waited; deliberately it seemed to Geoff, before slowly closing the folder. Geoff noticed the title of the file on the cover: STORK HILL GALLERIES. So that's what this is about. What could possibly have gone wrong, he wondered? Ford picked up the folder and tossed it across the desk.

"Have you any idea," he said coldly, "how much work has gone into this project?"

Geoff was thinking fast. If something had gone wrong it was unlikely to be his fault. The layout was one of the best he had ever done and the last time he talked to the customer's head of security, they were well pleased. He was still standing, feeling awkward because he had not been asked to sit, but he was determined to stay calm.

"Is something wrong?"

"Wrong?" said Ford. Raising his voice he said again, "*Wrong?* Yes, Summers, something is *very* wrong. We are on the brink of losing a sixty-grand order because the customer is pissed off. Why didn't you go to the site with Rod Thompson today?"

Mustn't let this little sod get to me, Geoff thought. He answered slowly, in a deliberately measured tone.

"It was a sales matter, not technical. In any case Danny went and he has all the knowledge and information that I have, so what exactly is the problem?"

The eyes behind the tinted spectacles bulged. "The *problem* is that the customer was expecting *you* at the meeting, not your bloody assistant. They've postponed *again* and I hold *you* responsible."

"*What?* Just because Danny went in my place? If they haven't signed there must have been a better reason." Geoff was immediately aware that he had raised his voice. Not good, he thought, must be careful.

Ford glared at him. "We'll find out when Rod gets back. In the meantime, you haven't answered my question. Why didn't you go to the meeting? Where did you go that was more important than helping the sales director to get a large order signed?"

Geoff stared at him steadily for a few moments, inwardly seething, but he was determined not to show it. In clipped tones he answered as calmly as he could.

"I had some personal business to attend to, and it was very important to me."

Ford leaned forward, his eyes narrowed and his nostrils flared. There was venom in his reply. "More important than keeping your job?"

It was the first direct threat. That's it, thought Geoff. There's no future for me here any more. The bastard is deliberately winding me up, he wants me to tell him to stuff his job.

Geoff dearly wanted to grab Ford by the scruff and smash his fist into his stupid face but he knew that this was no time to let his emotions rule his head. He simply could not risk dismissal at this time. Though seething, he controlled his emotions sufficiently to answer evenly, determined to say nothing about his meeting at the bank.

CHAPTER FIVE

He could feel his face reddening when he said, "I'm sorry, but I don't see it like that. I had an important private appointment to do with the fact that my wife is unwell, and it was in my own time, my lunch break. My presence at the meeting was not essential and Danny was well qualified to handle it."

Ford did not let up. "We'll see about that when I have all the facts from Rod about what happened. In the meantime, I remind you that you were late back to work, *and* you swanned off early on Friday. Not the sort of behaviour this company expects from its senior managers."

Geoff was now certain that he was being goaded deliberately, because Ford knew perfectly well that he was not a clock watcher and that he worked after hours on most days. Ford was waiting for him to react but he was not going to take the bait. This was not about a petty issue like timekeeping.

He gritted his teeth. "I understand."

There was a brief silence. Geoff had nothing more to say, believing that Ford knew that he had failed to force him into quitting on the spot or doing something that could justify his immediate dismissal.

Finally the man narrowed his eyes, waved a hand and said coldly, "You can go now, I will want to see you again later."

Geoff turned and left without another word. His heart was hammering and he felt his face flush with anger. He knew he had come close to venting his feelings but that would not have done at all. He walked back to his office slowly, taking time to think about the implications of this extraordinary interview. If Ford wanted him out, why didn't he just fire him? Why try to force him to resign? The more he thought about it, the clearer it became that from Ford's perspective his voluntary resignation would be the neatest option, because if they sacked him, he would have a strong case for suing the company. In that event his twenty-two-year record of employment, substantial pension rights and recent promotion could prove expensive for them.

Making him redundant unfairly would carry the same risk, so Ford was obviously trying to get him to quit. No chance, he thought bitterly, let the bastard do his worst, he will find that I am more than a match for him.

Later that day he discovered from Danny that the meeting at Stork Hill Galleries had actually gone well. Danny had amended the proposed design and Rod had agreed a small reduction in the price for the job. The order would be placed formally as soon as the customer received confirmation of the changes. Rod was delighted with the outcome and Danny was with him in his car when he phoned in the news to Adam Ford. The meeting had been successful and Geoff now knew that Adam Ford must have known that all along.

So, his career with the company was finally over, and through no fault of his own. The realisation hardened his resolve to get out because he now knew exactly where he stood. He decided that he would leave Melfords, but he was determined that *he* would decide the manner and timing of his departure. If he had to leave, he would make certain that all the years of his life spent with the company would not have been wasted.

Shortly after, Adam Ford had a guest in his office. He made an expansive gesture. "Piece of cake. No problem for a man of your experience. Worth making the move for an extra fifteen grand a year, wouldn't you say?"

Across the desk from him Ken Lever looked pleased.

"My only concern is that my knowledge of electronics is, frankly, nil."

"You'll get into it soon enough, so stop worrying, Ken, it'll be a doddle. Running a factory is your forte and as for knowing what goes where, you don't need to, at least not to start with. You'll soon pick it up and the design guy we have is pretty good."

"Would that be Danny?"

"Yeah, Danny Hall. Short, heavy glasses, you met him."

"What about… what's his name? Summers? You said there could be a problem."

"All in hand. He won't be here much longer." Adam leaned forward to press his intercom button.

"Could you pop in, Sam?"

Moments later Samantha came through the communicating door.

Adam looked up. "Could we trouble you for a couple of coffees?" To his guest he said, "White, no sugar, isn't it, Ken?"

"Yes, please."

Adam smiled at Samantha and said, "You

remember Mr Lever? He visited us a couple of times last month."

Samantha nodded. "Yes, I do. How are you?"

"Fine, thank you. It's good to see you again," he said.

Adam said, "Mr Lever is going to be our new production director."

Samantha left the room.

Back at her desk, Samantha wondered what was going on. As far as she knew, Geoff was managing the production department and everyone expected that, sooner or later, he would be promoted to the board as production director. She was troubled, and as she made the coffees she wondered, could Adam have been planning this all along?

That evening Geoff was at the computer desk he kept beside the bed in the spare bedroom, when Penny came in.

"Sometimes I think you spend too much time on that thing," she said, setting down a mug of coffee.

"Hmm, thanks," he replied absently.

Penny leaned forward to look at the screen. She saw a spreadsheet with names and numbers on it.

"What is it, Melford stuff?"

"Just something I need to keep tabs on." He picked up the mug. "How are things with Sue?"

Penny had been talking on the telephone to her sister, as she did regularly at that time of night.

"She's fine. She keeps asking when we are going over."

"I haven't finished sorting the arrangements, but you can tell her it won't be long. We'll let her know as soon as we have a firm date."

Penny bent over and kissed him lightly on the cheek. "I'm off to bed, don't stay up too late."

"I won't. Have you taken your medicines?"

"Yes, stop worrying."

She left, closing the door softly behind her. How could he stop worrying? She had good days and bad days and the medication seemed to give her some relief, but nothing could take away his concern. He turned his attention to the screen again. There were six names on the spreadsheet until he added one more, Stork Hill Galleries. He smiled to himself. Another nail in the coffin? Perhaps, if the germ of the idea that he had could be brought to fruition.

Peter and Charlie Mount had a good business doing domestic removals between France and the UK. They took turns to drive their removals van. After delivering a load to Toulouse they were returning to their French base in Orleans and Charlie was driving.

It had been a long day and beside him on the passenger seat of the cab, his brother Peter dozed away the motorway miles. They had a ground rule: if either was tired, the radio stayed off. It was off, so it was not the radio that disturbed Peter's rest, but the tinny mangling of Beethoven's "Fur Elise", his mobile's call tone.

"Shit," he muttered, reaching for the instrument in his jacket pocket. He pressed the answer button and drawled, "Mount Continental Removals."

"Pete? Jim."

Pete recognised the caller immediately. "Yes, Jim."

"You on the road?"

"Where else? But I can talk, Charlie's driving."

"It'll be ready for pick-up at Dave's on Wednesday morning."

"OK. We'll be loading the Leeds job Tuesday and it'll go with that."

"Shaun will be coming back with you, same as last time. I'll send a vehicle to Canterbury to pick him up, and the goods."

"No problem."

"Dave's got your envelope."

"That's what I want to hear, thanks."

Pete pressed the off button and slid the mobile back into his pocket. "A man of few words is our Jim." He yawned. "Dave's got our dosh and we'll have Shaun for company again on the way back."

Charlie nodded. "Naturally."

After a brief silence Charlie spoke again. "Is it worth it?"

"What?"

"The risk. All this cloak and dagger stuff." He took a hand off the steering wheel and made a gesture. "I mean, we don't even know what's inside it, could be anything."

Pete shrugged. "I have a pretty good idea, but it's nothing to do with us. We load it on the back of the wagon with the stuff for Leeds, take it to our depot in Canterbury and they pick it up. Money for jam."

"We should at least know what the hell it is. I mean, what if we're stopped?"

"Stopped?" Pete shook his head. "Nah, nothing to worry about. It's routine, just one thing in a wagon-load of stuff being moved back to England for the Rogers family." He stretched and yawned. "Anyway, who's going to look inside a water heater, for God's sake?"

Charlie thought for a moment. "Still, you never know," he said darkly.

Pete settled back into his seat and put his feet up on the dashboard.

"We never look inside customers' stuff. So *if* someone does, and *if* they find anything that shouldn't be there, it's not down to us, is it? Like I said, it's none of our business, we just haul the goods." He put his head back and within minutes was snoring gently.

Jim put down the mobile and smiled. All was going to plan, just as he thought it would. He'd had his doubts about the Mount brothers at first, but now that they had already done two collections for him they were well and truly in the loop, for them there could be no going back. The business had been dormant for a while before he had re-started it. No more couriers, he thought, they're risky and bad news and the last couple are still doing time. No, this was a much better system and like it or not, the Mounts were in it up to their necks.

Dave and Shaun dropped Flynn off at the Eurostar station in Lille just over two hours after leaving Holland. They continued on to Dave's house, where

Dave parked the Transit in his garage. The following morning the Mounts' moving van arrived, already loaded with the household effects they had picked up for delivery to Leeds, and parked in the drive.

"This thing's heavy," Charlie moaned when he and Pete were loading the water heater, a white steel cylinder eighteen inches in diameter and four feet tall, onto the removals van.

"Rubbish," said Dave who was watching. He took a sip from his coffee mug. "I put it on the Transit all on my own. And I'm a pensioner."

Charlie grunted. "Bollocks, I don't believe that."

"OK, I might have had a bit of help. But only for a minute." He turned, went into the porch and leaned into the hallway. Behind him on the drive the lorry's engine throbbed impatiently.

"Shaun, where are you? The boys are ready to go."

Conroy came out of the house carrying his overnight bag.

"No need to shout, I'm here." He went over to the lorry and climbed onto the step of the cab. Hauling himself into the cabin with his bag he shut the door and waved to Dave.

"See you next time," he called as the van pulled away.

At Dover the queue of lorries filtering through the Customs and border checks was moving slowly. Pete was driving, with Charlie alongside him in the middle and Shaun on the offside seat by the passenger door. They had passed through the Customs checkpoint without being stopped and were approaching the police border post.

"Passports," said Pete, keeping the vehicle in the inside lane and holding his hand out.

They passed them over and Shaun asked, "Ever been pulled over?"

Pete shrugged. "A few times, mostly when we first started, but not so much now."

"They know us," said Charlie. "Bloody good job, too."

Shaun grinned. "They waved us though, but you were shitting yourself, mate. You had your eyes shut."

Charlie straightened. "Bollocks."

Pete smiled. "We're left-hand drive, French registered, with English signing in big letters on the sides, and we are in and out all the time. Not too many others like us."

He drew up alongside the kiosk and handed the three passports to a bored-looking officer who reached out and took them whilst briefly perusing the occupants of the cab.

The officer flicked through the passports, barely glancing at the details. He closed them, put them together and was about to pass them back into Pete's outstretched hand when quite suddenly he stopped, drawing his arm back.

"Wait a minute," he said, re-opening one of the passports to examine it.

Pete sensed his brother's sudden tension. Charlie had stiffened.

Raising his voice to be heard over the noise of the lorry's engine, the officer called out, "Shaun Conroy? I thought I recognized you last time you came through."

Shaun leaned forward so that the man could see him.

The policeman was smiling. "I remember you. I was there the night you clobbered Lou Sammes. Round one. Shoreditch, wasn't it?"

"Yeah," Shaun replied, loudly, "geezer thumbed me in the eye, twice. So I done him, quick."

Pete glanced at Charlie briefly. He had shut his eyes and breathed out slowly.

The policeman nodded. "Good for you, that was some right hook. You in the moving business now?"

Pete cut in hurriedly. "We're just giving him a lift."

Handing over the passports the officer said to Shaun, "Well, good luck to you, you were a hard bloke."

"Thanks, mate," said Shaun.

Shaun was relieved to see a battered Escort van when they pulled onto the forecourt of Mount Continental Removals' depot in Canterbury an hour later. It was Stubby's van. Stubby could have had his pick of any car in their business but refused to give up the old van. They transferred the heater from the lorry to the little van and after Shaun had handed Pete his brown envelope, he and Stubby were on their way.

"This van stinks like a bleedin' ashtray," Shaun complained as they headed off.

"You can always walk. If I want to use my van as an ashtray, I will. Tough cheddar."

Shaun grimaced. "Don't you know what that shit is doing to your lungs?"

Stubby made a deliberate show of inhaling deeply on his cigarette. "When did you become my doctor?"

"Disgusting, should be illegal."

"It is in some places but not in my house, or my van."

Traffic on the motorway had slowed to a crawl and Shaun was suffering. He wound the window down and discovered that it did not go further than half way.

Stubby glanced across. "It doesn't go any further, it's stuck."

"Why don't you bleedin' fix it, then?"

Stubbs grinned. "I leave it like that to wind up guys like you." He lowered his own window. "But I'll open this one, just for you."

The traffic had now stopped altogether. Ahead was a solid mass of stationary vehicles.

"At this rate it'll be dark before we get there," Shaun observed.

"That'll suit the boss."

Shaun nodded. "That's true, and he don't like hanging about. In and out, the stuff will be gone tomorrow."

"I'd better give him a call." Stubbs flicked his cigarette stub out of the window. "Tell him we're running late. Don't want him worrying himself sick, do we?" He flashed a toothy grin.

"That'll be the day. Anyway, it don't matter. It's not as if we'd be disturbing anyone. He's sent Rosie and Sandra up west overnight, again."

"Harrods, dinner, a show, and a fancy hotel. It's a hard life, for some."

An hour and a half later it was already dusk when Stubbs used his remote to open the gates to the Warwick mansion. The main house was in darkness, but there were lights on in the extension. He steered the van past the main entrance and around to the side of the extension where he pulled up and reversed to stop outside the second garage.

It was a large room with two sets of shutter doors, one of which was open with the interior light streaming through. Jim was standing in the doorway like a Colossus, silhouetted by the light behind. The moment the van was inside and clear of the door he pressed a button on the wall to bring the shutter down.

CHAPTER SIX

Adam Ford pointed to the spreadsheet displayed on his screen. "There's really not enough here to justify any bonuses for this year," he said, shaking his head.

Seated across the desk, sales director Rod Thompson shrugged.

"Our order book is full for the next four months. Sales are doing OK, and I'm not the one who sets the margins."

Ford grimaced. "We've got to do better than this. Let's see what Sandy thinks." He picked up the handset on his intercom and pressed the button to call the company's finance director, Sandy Macgregor.

"Morning, Adam. What can I do for you?"

"I've got Rod with me. Looking at the figures, there's not enough to justify much in the way of bonuses this year."

"Then he's got to get more sales, or bigger orders."

"He says the order book's full, and I agree with him."

"Uh-huh."

"Can we take a look at the margins? Are we charging enough? Do we need to squeeze our suppliers harder?" The questions had been delivered in a rapid staccato.

"Well, Rod won't want to raise prices, it's a competitive business. You'd have to talk to Ken Lever or Geoff Summers about supplier contracts and as for the margins, we can go over a couple of the recent jobs together if you want to assess the situation."

"Ken's not been here long enough; sounds to me like Summers is not up to the job."

"I wouldn't say that, but it can't hurt to push a couple of our bigger suppliers harder."

"OK." Adam paused to look at his diary. "I want to get this sorted. Can you come to my office this afternoon, say, around three o'clock?"

There was a brief pause before Macgregor answered. "OK, three's fine for me."

"Can you bring the pricing breakdowns for the last three jobs?"

"OK, no problem."

"Good." Adam put the phone down.

The door to his secretary's office opened and Samantha put her head around it.

"Can I bring in today's post for you, Mr Ford?"

Adam waved her in, and looked at Rod. "I'll go through the figures with Sandy this afternoon. We'll see what we can do."

Rod got up to leave. "I'm in the office all day today, if you need me."

As Rod Thompson left, Samantha put a small pile of letters on the desk in front of Adam.

"There's a confidential one from a bank," she said. "It's on top."

It was Samantha's job to sort the post every morning. She opened the envelopes and scanned the documents inside before putting them into the 'in' tray of the department for which they were destined. Anything for the managing director she took directly to him and anything confidential remained unopened.

Adam picked up the envelope. It was addressed to

"Mr P Whittam, Managing Director."

"Huh," he snorted, looking at the logo. "It's not our bank. And it's addressed to Peter Whittam, probably some sort of promotional mail shot. You'd think that if they mark it confidential to get it noticed they would at least do their homework."

Samantha left as Adam tossed the envelope to one side and started to go through his letters. He decided that none required his immediate attention, so he opened the envelope from the bank. He read their letter, paused, then smiled. This, he decided, was one he would answer himself, using his own computer and printer rather than dictating his reply to Samantha. The bank requested answers to enquiries about Mr G J Summers. It would be his pleasure, he thought, to provide them.

The next day Geoff was called to Adam Ford's office but he had been given no reason for the summons. He knocked on the managing director's door and went straight in. Ford was seated at his desk with an unmarked brown folder in front of him.

Ford looked up and nodded towards a chair. "Come in and sit down," he said.

Geoff wondered what was coming next. Ford's manner was calm and businesslike, very different to the last time Geoff had been in this room. He sat down.

Ford put his hands on the brown file and leant forward.

"I take it you realise that I am not happy with your performance?"

Geoff answered slowly, choosing his words carefully. "You have made it clear that you don't want me around, but I have to say that I have no idea why. My recent promotion and salary increase are testament to my competence. There is nothing wrong with the way in which I perform my duties."

"That may be what you believe. Nevertheless, I want your resignation, and I want it now."

The man was talking calmly and dispassionately. Well, Geoff thought, I can play that game too. "I do not wish to resign, Mr Ford, and I have no intention of doing so."

Ford looked directly at Geoff. "I want you out, but there is no reason why we cannot come to an amicable arrangement. I am prepared to offer you, without prejudice, a severance bonus of five thousand pounds in addition to payment in lieu of notice. Your company pension fund is worth a bit and my advice to you would be to keep it going."

Geoff met Ford's gaze and waited a few seconds before answering.

"I am afraid that I must decline your offer. I am not prepared to resign my position."

"What a pity." Adam Ford leaned back, opened the folder and withdrew a piece of paper. "This is a letter from your bank," he said. "They are asking the company to confirm your salary level and have requested our opinion as to your integrity and your ability to repay a loan."

Geoff sat up. Ford was actually *smiling*. Geoff could think of nothing to say.

Ford went on. "I will give you an excellent

reference, Summers," he paused and pushed his spectacles back with a finger, "and all you have to do in exchange is to give me your letter of resignation."

Geoff considered this for a few moments, then looked directly at Ford.

"I cannot resign just now. The fact is, my wife is ill and she is due to have surgery in a few weeks' time. She wants to go to Australia to see her sister before the operation and that's why I have to keep my job and why I need the bank loan."

Ford appeared unmoved. "I see."

"I still do not know why you want me to leave, but I realise that I no longer have a future with the company." Geoff shrugged. "There's no point in staying on where I'm not wanted, so I'll go. But not just yet; I shall leave in a few weeks' time, when my immediate problems are resolved."

From behind the tinted spectacles Adam Ford stared unblinking. Geoff was unable to read the man's mood.

Ford sat back again and said, "You'll get your reference."

"Thank you. I shall keep my word and leave the company but in the meantime I must ask that the matter of my wife's illness remains confidential. It's of no concern to anyone else."

Adam Ford nodded. "Very well."

That afternoon Samantha was checking the time yet again. Four o'clock, he's going to be late if he's not careful, she thought. Adam Ford and Sandy Macgregor were locked in a meeting with a man from the firm's auditors. The meeting had over-run. She decided that she would have to interrupt them and pressed the intercom button.

"Yes, Samantha?"

"Sorry to interrupt, Mr Ford, but you may be cutting it a bit fine for your dental appointment."

"Yes, yes, I know; we are just winding up." He sounded stressed and impatient.

Another ten minutes elapsed before Macgregor and the accountant left. Adam yanked opened the communicating door and leaned into Samantha's room.

"I'm off now. Can you ring them and say I've been delayed in traffic? Oh, and there's a letter in my out tray that needs sending, first class."

She nodded. "Will you be back later?"

He glanced at his watch. "Er… no, probably not." He closed the door, rushed out of his office and down the corridor.

Samantha sighed. Never a "please" or "thank you". Was he born rude, she wondered? She checked the local directory and telephoned the dental surgery to make his apology, saying only that Mr Ford was sorry he would be delayed. If he wanted to tell a lie and blame the traffic, he could do that himself.

She put the phone directory back on its shelf and went through to Adam's office where she saw the envelope on his desk. It was addressed to Midwest Bank and marked "confidential." She picked it up and was about to leave when she noticed that Adam's computer had been left on. This was unusual, probably due to the fact that he had departed in a hurry, she thought.

The monitor was displaying a screen-saver. Samantha leaned across the desk to start the shutdown sequence, but the moment she touched the mouse, the display on the screen changed to show a document. The file had been left open.

She would have to close the file before shutting down, but what she saw on the screen stopped her short. It was the letter to Midwest Bank, but it was the heading in bold script that caught her attention. It read: "Re: Mr G J Summers, your enquiry regarding credit risk."

Samantha's immediate reaction was to turn away from the screen. She sat down in Adam's chair, realising at once that she had a problem. If she closed the document without saving it, there would be no record of the letter unless Adam had already printed off a copy, something she did not know. She made a quick search on and around the desk, but did not find one.

Samantha concluded that if Adam had made a copy, it was likely to be in his locked filing drawer. She reasoned that her best option, therefore, would be to print off a copy and *not* leave it on his desk. If the question of a copy arose later, she would give it to him, saying that she had made it because in the circumstances there was no other option. But if he did not raise the issue she would say nothing.

She printed a copy, folded it in half and placed it in the drawer of her own desk. She was pleased that despite all that she had done, she had not actually read the letter. She reflected that Adam Ford of course, would never believe that.

Geoff had become used to setting the breakfast table on his own. Penny's headaches kept her awake some nights and when that happened Geoff let her oversleep. He was in the kitchen one morning when he heard the letterbox snap.

There was only one envelope on the mat. It bore the logo of King Edward's Hospital and was addressed to Penny, but Geoff tore it open and removed the letter inside. It was signed by Mr Mehta and stated that Penny's biopsy would be carried out on the twenty-ninth of the following month. That's seven weeks from now, he thought. Later than expected, but it would have to do. At least things were now on the move.

That afternoon Geoff was in the factory. The plan drawing for Sadlington Manor lay on the assembly bench and Geoff was going over a few details with the senior installer, when they were interrupted by the ringtone of Geoff's mobile.

"Sorry," he said, reaching into his pocket.

"Summers."

"Mr Summers?" It was a vaguely familiar voice.

"Yes, Geoff Summers here."

"It's John Knowles, Midwest Bank."

"Oh, hello. Can you hold for a second please?" To his colleague he said, "Won't be a moment," as he walked out of earshot.

"Hello, Mr Knowles, what news?"

"I have your letter but you asked me not to send it

to your house."

"I'll call in to pick it up."

"When can we expect you?"

Geoff checked his watch. Ten past four, he could get there before they shut for the day.

"I'll be with you in twenty minutes."

He returned to his office and told Debbie that he had to go out and might not be back that day. If Adam Ford didn't like it, he thought, bugger him.

Geoff fidgeted in his chair, waiting to see John Knowles, who was talking to a young couple. When they left he ushered them out of his office and then came over to Geoff.

"Come in please, Mr Summers," he said, showing Geoff into his interview room.

"Thank you." Geoff sat down. "Well, is it a yes or a no?"

Knowles looked uncomfortable. "I have the letter here."

He opened a folder, removed an envelope and handed it to Geoff. "Please understand," he said, holding up a hand, "that I am not in a position to discuss the matter here."

Geoff ripped open the envelope and read the document. It was brief, saying only that the bank regretted that it was unable to proceed with the requested loan, but thanked him for making the application.

"What the hell is this? *Unable to proceed?* Why not?"

Knowles was clearly embarrassed. "I am really sorry but I am simply not able to give you an answer."

"In that case I would like to see the manager."

"Mr Summers, these decisions are made only at our head office. It is entirely out of our hands at branch level. If you wish to pursue the matter, I suggest you write directly back to the department that sent you the letter." Knowles looked genuinely sorry. "Why not try someone else? I have the names of a couple of good finance houses. The bank... well, let's say that they rarely change a decision on loan applications."

Geoff took the information offered and left.

On the way home he tried to make sense of what had happened. He had never had a problem with his credit rating. Like most people the level of his borrowings fluctuated, and he thought that his record was probably no better or worse than most. As far as the bank was concerned, he had a secure well-paid job and the amount he wanted to borrow was hardly a fortune. He decided that he would go to a finance company and saw no reason why he should have a problem. But the bank's unexplained rejection niggled and he wondered anxiously what could possibly have been behind their decision. Something was not right.

The bank's rejection of Geoff's loan request had an unwelcome knock-on effect; the finance companies turned him down. In both cases he had to declare that he had recently been declined a loan and he was told that this had a negative effect on his credit rating. Worse, it had been more than three weeks since he had made his first loan application and he was angry that nothing had been achieved. Eventually he took a loan from a company that specialised in providing cash to borrowers who were considered risky by others, but lost another week in the process. The fact that the interest rate demanded was iniquitous did not concern him, but he bitterly resented the loss of another month of precious time, something, he felt, that could have been avoided.

The intercom on Samantha's desk buzzed and she picked up the handset.

"Sam, it's Sheila. Do you happen to know where Mr Lever is? He's not at his desk and I have his wife on the line. She says he's not answering his mobile."

"He's with Mr Ford."

"Really? Fancy that. OK, thanks, I'll put her through to his office but don't go away, I'll call you back in a minute, something interesting."

Sheila could be a bit scatty sometimes, thought Samantha, but she was intrigued, Sheila liked to pass on gossip. Moments later she called again.

"Sam? Guess what?"

"What?"

Sheila whispered. "Ken Lever. He's Adam's brother-in-law."

"Is that so? How do you know?"

"She told me. His wife. Well, she didn't actually say that, but when I put her on hold trying to find him, she asked me to try her brother's office. When I asked who that might be, she said Adam Ford. Talk about keeping it in the family!"

"Well, well...thanks, Sheila."

Samantha replaced the handset slowly. So, it

seemed that Adam had almost certainly planned all along to replace Geoff. This triggered her memory to recall that the copy of Adam's letter to the bank was still in her desk drawer. It had been there for nearly a month and in that time she had not given it a thought. Should she now read it, she wondered? It would go against her sense of duty but she had a powerful urge to find out what it said. She decided that she would read the letter and then destroy it. Whatever the contents, nobody need ever know that she had seen them.

She took the letter out of the drawer, unfolded it and put it down on the desk. She read it quickly, then sat upright and blinked. Was this real? She read it again, carefully. The bastard. *The bastard!* The palm of her hand had been open and face down on the document. Without realising it, she had begun to draw her fingers into a fist to crush it into a ball. Then she stopped, smoothed it out and read it yet again.

Dear Sirs,

Re: Mr G. J. Summers—Your enquiry regarding credit risk.

I refer to your letter of the 20th and the information requested therein.

Your letter was addressed to my predecessor Mr P. Whittam. For your information Mr Whittam is no longer here and I am now the Managing Director of this company.

I can confirm that Mr Summers is currently in charge of our production department and that the salary figure quoted is correct at present.

With regard to your enquiries concerning our views as to his

*ability to repay a loan and as to his personal integrity, I regret
that it would be inappropriate for me to comment. I regret also
that I am unable to offer any other comments or observations.*

Yours faithfully,

A. D. Ford

Managing Director

Samantha slowly took off her reading glasses and put
them down. With her elbows on the desk she put her
face in her hands and thought about the situation in
which she found herself. Confidentiality was the very
core of her job as personal assistant to the managing
director, so she felt instinctively that she should
destroy the document and forget that it ever existed.
And yet this was different. It was about Geoff. In
the end she decided that she would keep the letter but
not reveal its contents to anyone unless it became
necessary to do so. She folded it and tucked it away in
a pocket inside her handbag.

Geoff Summers was in the passenger seat of Rod
Thompson's car and they were on their way back
from Warwick Hall to Melfords.

"Strange bloke," said Geoff, flicking through the
notes on his clipboard.

"Takes all kinds."

"He seemed much more interested in showing off
his stuff than talking about the nitty-gritty of security.
The flash cars, and that coin collection. That is
something else."

They had paused at a T-junction and Rod swivelled
his head to look both ways before proceeding.

"Sovereigns, Krugerrands, all solid gold. What did he say his collection is worth?"

Geoff snorted. "Well over a quarter of a million. Do you believe that?"

Rod shrugged. "Who knows? Not our business. Anyway all he wants from us is a good security system, and a discount, of course."

"What will you do about that? We don't do discounts, do we?"

"Once in a while you have to go along with it. His demanding a discount is not about getting the job at a cheaper price, it's to show us how tough he is." Rod grinned. "What we do is add a bit extra up front for contingencies, then wring our hands when he negotiates us down mercilessly."

Geoff smiled. Rod was a smart guy, he thought. "Odd that he wants to leave out the automatic link to the police."

"Well, maybe not that unusual. Not everyone wants the grief it causes when there's a glitch. And they do happen, sometimes. Imagine the place swarming with coppers."

"Who are not pleased when they discover it's a false alarm," said Geoff. "I'll get on with the design, but I'll need to know if he's having the stuff for beefing up the garage protection."

"Put it in as optional. He can tell us later if he wants it."

"Like I said, strange bloke," Geoff mused. "Why the extra bits for the garage? I mean, his expensive motors would all have the best built-in protection anyway."

CHAPTER SIX

"The vintage ones won't," Rod pointed out.

Geoff grinned. "Maybe he's got a secret hobby he doesn't want anyone to find out about, especially the cops."

Rod smiled. "Like a lot of seriously rich people. Personally I prefer selling to companies. Corporate clients are easier to deal with, rich individuals can be a pain in the arse."

Geoff's mobile phone trilled and he took it out of his jacket pocket.

"Summers."

"Mr Summers?" It was an unfamiliar female voice. "Mr Geoffrey Summers?"

"Yes, I'm Geoff Summers, who is this?"

"Sir, this is WPC Matthews, Essex Constabulary. I got your number from your office. Could you please confirm that you are the owner of a blue Ford Focus, registration number KN5AZG?"

Geoff's heart missed a beat. "That's my wife's car, is everything all right?"

There was a slight pause. "I'm afraid she's unwell, sir, she's been taken to hospital. She's at West Essex General."

Geoff's stomach knotted instantly. "Has she had an accident?" he asked sharply, panic rising inside him. "Is she hurt?"

"No, she wasn't hurt, sir, but it looks like she felt unwell when driving because she pulled into a lay-by, that's where I'm calling...."

"Was there an accident? What happened?"

"No, there's been no accident, sir, but a motorist parked in the lay-by noticed she wasn't well and called an ambulance. I think you should make your way to the hospital as soon as you can."

Geoff was still holding his mobile. He struggled to respond.

"Problem?" Rod enquired anxiously.

Geoff cupped the phone in his hand and answered quietly. "It's the police. Penny's been taken to hospital and I have to get there at once." He raised the instrument and spoke into it.

"When did this happen?"

"About fifteen minutes ago."

"I'm on my way."

Rod responded immediately. "Where are we going?"

"The hospital, West Essex General."

"I'll take you straight there; I know where it is." He gunned the car into the overtaking lane and accelerated.

Twenty minutes later they arrived at the hospital and learned that Penny had been admitted to the intensive care unit. She had suffered a suspected stroke and was in a coma.

At Melfords Adam Ford fumed. "They're all so bloody *complacent*. Here I am trying to find ways to cut costs and improve profits, and what do I get?"

The rhetorical question went unanswered by Ken Lever, sitting across the desk from Adam who had not finished.

"Nothing." He made a dismissive gesture. "All they want to do is chug along in their old sweet way." He slammed his hand down on the desk. "Well, bugger that. I want results."

Ken Lever crossed his legs. "You said you wanted to talk about component costs. What do you have in mind?"

"Let's start with the controllers. We're paying too much for parts. We have a good relationship with Stalmanns; they served us well at Daneplan. Let's see what they can do. The people here seem to be married to Sandersons."

"I can get Geoff Summers to talk to them."

"Summers? What for? He's a systems man, what does he know about business? Anyway like I told you, he won't be around much longer."

Lever seemed uncomfortable. He uncrossed his legs. "You know his wife's in hospital? Intensive care, I heard."

Ford shrugged. "Yes, unfortunate. But nothing to do with us." He put his hand to his mouth and cleared his throat. "What I'd like you to do is to take a finished controller off the production line and get Stalmanns to look at it. Let them take it apart and see what they come up with."

Lever nodded. "OK, when do you want it done?"

"Soon as you can. I'd like to get us all a decent bonus this year."

The following evening Jim Warwick was at home, waiting for the confrontation that he had planned. This was a serious matter that needs sorting, he thought. No way was he going to allow his Rosie to get engaged to the Italian, let alone marry the guy. Unthinkable. But he had a plan to flush out this gold-digger. Jim had asked Tony to call around for a chat, saying that it would be just the two of them man to man, and now he was at his desk, keeping an eye on the CCTV image of the main gates of Warwick Hall. Shaun Conroy was sitting on the big leather settee.

They watched as Tony Bellini's car pulled up outside the main gates. Jim pressed the switch to open the gates before the young man had time to push the intercom button. He wanted him to know that he was expected. The gates swung open and Tony drove through, guiding the Audi past the front door of Warwick Hall. He stopped outside the entrance to the office extension and Jim switched the CCTV to the camera that covered that area.

Tony took off his polarized designer shades, folded them and inserted them into a spectacle pouch which he slid into a storage slot. He tilted the internal mirror to inspect his image and turned his head from side to side to check that all was well. Apparently satisfied, he opened his door and stepped out of the car. He reached inside and lifted his jacket off the passenger seat, stood up and shrugged himself into it, tugging at the bottoms of his shirt cuffs. Then he took a small aerosol from his jacket pocket, opened his mouth and sprayed. Jim and Shaun had been watching.

"Arrogant sod, we'll soon find out what you are made of," Jim muttered. He had prepared well for the meeting, arranging it for the Saturday evening and ensuring that Sandra and Rosie would be out. Jim would not be alone, as Bellini would expect, because he had called in Shaun for a couple of hours' overtime.

Shaun leaned forward for a closer look. "You expecting bother, boss?"

Jim nodded at the screen. "From him? Nah, but I want you around. The guy thinks he's struck gold but he's in for a nasty reality check."

At the sound of the doorbell Shaun sat up. "Want me to show him in?"

"No, I'll do it." Jim pointed to the door to the adjacent leisure suite. "Turn the TV on and help yourself to a beer. I'll give you a shout if I need you."

"Thanks, boss." Shaun left the room.

Bellini had been waiting at the door for a full minute but as there was no response to the bell, he pressed the button again. Unknown to him he was still being watched by Jim, who smirked as he waited to find out what Tony would do next. Would he be patient, or impatient, he wondered? After another half minute, Tony pressed the bell push again, this time keeping his finger on it for about ten seconds.

"Right," Jim muttered. "Arrogant *and* impatient, I've rattled him." He walked down the corridor to the glass door and opened it. Tony Bellini was standing outside looking flustered.

"Come in, come in, lad. Sorry to keep you waiting," Jim lied affably.

Tony stepped forward. "Uh, thank you."

Jim led the way to his office and opened the door. "Take a seat. My PA who makes the coffee isn't here, would you like a beer?"

"I'm fine, thanks. Uh, driving, you know."

Jim saw that Bellini, though still uneasy, was

starting to relax. Time to get down to business. Bellini had chosen to sit in one of the armchairs and Jim sat down opposite him, on the settee.

Crossing one leg over the other, Jim appeared completely relaxed. "So, young man, I believe you want to marry my daughter."

"We want to get engaged."

"Is that so?" Jim stroked his chin and stared directly into Bellini's eyes. Before the man could answer he stood up abruptly and headed for the door to the leisure suite. He stopped and turned.

"I'm going to get a beer. Sure you don't want one?"

"Er, no, I'm fine, thanks."

"As you wish."

Jim opened the door and put his head around it. "Get me a beer from the fridge, will you, Shaun?" He kept his eyes fixed on Tony as Shaun fetched a beer can from the fridge. "Thanks," he said, taking it. "Come in and meet Mr Bellini, he wants to marry my daughter." Indicating with the can in his hand he said, "Take a seat."

"Hello," said Shaun nodding to Tony.

Jim noted the look of surprise on Bellini's face; he would not have expected anyone else to be present. Keeping the young man guessing was exactly what Jim wanted to do.

Jim used the ring pull and the can hissed. "Now, where were we?" He sat down. "Oh yes, you want to get engaged." Keeping his gaze locked on Bellini's eyes he took a swig from the can. "I'm sure you realise, young man, that all her life my daughter has had the best of everything."

"Yes, sir."

"The best. I am a wealthy man, a *very* wealthy man." Turning to Shaun he asked, "Isn't that so, Shaun?"

"That's a fact, boss."

Jim narrowed his eyes. "You see, Tony–it is Tony, isn't it?" Bellini nodded as Jim continued, "I have a bit of a problem. When Rosie leaves the nest, so to speak, she needs to be with someone who can keep her in the style she is used to." Holding the can, he inclined his head and pointed with his index finger. "Know what I mean?"

Tony Bellini shifted uncomfortably. "Yes, sir," he said with a wan smile.

Jim pointed at Tony again. "My problem, Tony, is that I don't actually see *you* being able to do that." He took a swig of beer as he stared at Bellini. "Because if you could, you would own that fancy car. But you don't, it's leased and," he waved his index finger from side to side in admonishment, "you are way, way behind with your payments. Tut, tut."

Tony swallowed; he was sweating. "I...we love each other, and..."

"Rosie says that you are in estate agency, and that you own the business." He took another swig from the can and wiped his mouth with the back of his hand. "Five branches, isn't it?" Tilting his head, Jim looked for the reply.

"We...there are five branches," Tony stuttered, again shifting in his chair, "but..."

Jim cut in sharply, leaning forward. "But what?"

Tony mumbled quietly. "I don't own the business, I

just work there. Rosie must have misunderstood."

For a few long moments Jim stared at Bellini, saying nothing. Finally he leaned back. "Now let me tell you something." Speaking slowly he said, "Rosie has no inheritance. Nothing. Zilch. Zero." He formed an "O" with his left thumb and forefinger. "What do you think of that, eh?"

Tony Bellini's face betrayed his astonishment. He did not answer.

Jim Warwick was enjoying this. He pointed his index finger at Bellini.

"I decided years ago that she could either marry well, or make her own fortune, like I did." Jim was staring at Bellini again. Without taking his eyes off him, he leaned forward and put the beer can down on the table. This was the point at which he had confidently expected the man to crumble. Gold-diggers give up when there is no gold. But to his surprise, there was no sign of that. Instead, Tony straightened and stood up.

Quietly but firmly he said, "Mr Warwick, you seem to have gone to a lot of trouble to find out things that I would have been happy to tell you, if you had asked. I don't want your money, I intend to marry Rosie if she will have me, and I'll do my best to..."

Jim jumped up, his face contorted. "Then why did you lie to her?" he snarled.

Tony took a deep breath. "I do not lie." He held up a hand, palm outwards. "When we first met, I did give her the impression that I was well off, but it was just talk."

Jim raised his voice, almost shouting. "*Talk?* Is

there another way to lie?"

Tony was stung into responding, his own voice rising. "I'd only just been introduced to her. How was I to know she would be the one for me? I was just chatting her up. Just talk, like I said. Now, if you don't mind, I think I'd better leave."

Jim's jaw tightened, his nostrils flared and he leaned forward menacingly. Shaun interrupted immediately.

"Boss," he said quickly, "you want him to stay?"

Jim's head snapped around to face Shaun. He realized at once why Shaun had interrupted. He blinked, then turned back to Bellini.

"Sit down," he snapped.

Tony stood still and did not move. After a few tense moments Jim spoke again. "Sit down. I know what this is *really* about." Tony sat down.

Jim strode across to his desk, wrenched open the top drawer and withdrew a cheque book. He picked up a ballpoint pen and slammed the book angrily onto the desk.

"I'm writing you a cheque. Twenty grand, enough to clear your debts." As he wrote he said over his shoulder, "I want you to take it, and *get out*."

Jim ripped the cheque out of the book and moved over to Tony, who had stood up. Thrusting the piece of paper at him, Jim snarled, "And don't come back. I swear that if you come anywhere near my daughter again, I'll break both your fucking legs."

Tony's face and neck had reddened, betraying his mounting fury. He snatched the cheque from Warwick's extended hand and gritted his teeth.

"You know what? You are the rudest, stupidest

man I have ever met. You think you can buy anybody?" He held the cheque up in front of Jim's face and slowly tore it in half. "*This* is what I think of you and your money, you can take your money and stick..."

Jim Warwick, eyes bulging in a face contorted with fury, suddenly leapt forward swinging his clenched fist towards Bellini's head. Tony was slow to react, having time only to move his head slightly before Warwick's fist struck his left cheek with considerable force. There was a loud crack and Bellini fell over. Shaun leapt forward, too late to intervene, as Tony Bellini sank to the floor where he lay motionless.

CHAPTER SEVEN

Penny's bed was the one nearest the window. There were four in the room but only two that were occupied: Penny's and one near the door, where an elderly woman with wispy grey hair and translucent, parchment-dry skin lay motionless. The stocky old man who had just entered nodded to Geoff and put down the shopping bag he had been carrying.

He inclined his head towards Penny. "Any change?"

Geoff's chair was between Penny's bed and the window. He had an open book on his lap. He closed it and shook his head.

"No, she's the same."

The man peeled off his shabby anorak and placed it carefully across the bottom of the old woman's bed.

"They brought your lady in yesterday, didn't they?"

"Yes, early afternoon."

"She's so young. Rotten shame, that's what it is." He shook his head. "My Daisy's had a good life, seventy-seven this year, bless her." He sat down and looked at her.

"Now, my chick, how are we today?" He turned to Geoff. "Chick, that's what I call her." There was no response from the prone figure in the bed.

"How long has she been here?" Geoff asked.

"Let's see– ten days, I think. Yes," he said, "this is her tenth day." The man turned to look at his wife. "Ten days, innit, Chick?"

The man looked up again. "But she's a fighter. They're weaning her off the ventilator, slow like." His mouth moved into a twisted smile. "Funny word, that, 'weaning', but as long as she's getting better I don't care what they call it."

Geoff had been told that Penny's condition was stable and if it remained so, they would arrange an operation as soon as possible. He looked at the tubes and wires connecting her to the life support equipment. She looks so helpless and frail, he thought, not at all like her. She was always fit and slim; she jogged most mornings when she wasn't at school and had never had any illness worse than a cold. And now this. In just twenty-four hours his world had been turned upside down. He wiped his hands across his face, looked out of the window and sighed. How long would it be before he got her back?

The ward door burst open and a nurse bustled in.

"Good morning, gentlemen," she said, moving swiftly to the foot of the other bed. "Doctor's on his rounds, he'll be here shortly." She picked up the clipboard that was hanging on the bed rail and scanned it. "She's a bit better today, Mr Robbins."

Turning to Geoff she said, "Your wife had a quiet night, Mr Summers. The doctor asked if you were in, I think he wants a word." Geoff nodded and thanked her.

A few minutes later the door opened again and a young man in white overalls with a stethoscope around his neck entered, carrying a clipboard. He spun around to hold the door open as a smartly-dressed grey-haired man sailed through imperiously, as if he was accustomed to having doors held open for him everywhere. He was followed by a short, thin, middle-aged nurse taking rapid steps to keep up with the men.

Geoff stood up as the grey-haired man strode over to Penny's bed. He looked at Geoff and held his left hand out behind him to receive the clipboard which the younger man handed to him.

"Mister Summers?" He glanced briefly at the clipboard.

"I'm Geoff Summers."

The man looked up. "Good morning. I'm Doctor Pallister. This is Dr Farrow. I believe you saw Dr Stevens yesterday when your wife was admitted.

"Yes, in the afternoon."

"We have your wife's medical history from your GP," Pallister said, checking the clipboard. "Dr Mead, I believe you told us?"

Geoff nodded. "She has also seen the neurologist, Mr..."

Pallister interrupted, "Mehta. Ganesh Mehta. I've spoken with them both this morning." He looked over at Penny. "She had a good night; no new problems," he said, sitting down on the end of the bed. He passed the clipboard back to his colleague and put his hands in his lap. "The consensus is that she should have an operation as soon as possible to remove the tumour. No point in waiting. If you agree, Mr Mehta can schedule the procedure for Thursday this week, Friday at the latest. He has a full diary but he will clear a space."

Geoff had not been expecting this. "So soon?"

"Yes, but I don't want you to get the wrong impression, or to worry too much. It needs to be brought forward only because we cannot be certain as to what caused her to pass out." He inclined his head. "It's for the best; for you, too. You'll have her back as good as new, I promise you."

That evening in Mike Stubbs' house the phone rang and rang again. Stubby was ensconced in his favourite chair with his stockinged feet up on a stool and a beer glass in his hand, watching football on television. He was not about to get up and was relieved when the ringing stopped. A minute later when it started again he groaned.

From the landing at the top of the stairs his wife called down. "Are you going to answer that? I'm just out of the shower."

"Shit," he muttered, muting the TV sound as he got up to take the call. He picked up the receiver. "Mike Stubbs."

"Can you get over here quickly?" It was Jim Warwick.

"Evening, guv. What's the problem?"

"I need you here at my place, right now."

"I was just going out for a takeaway, OK if I make it say, in an hour's time?"

"Stubby, listen to me. This is a fucking emergency!"

"I'm on my way."

"Don't stop for anything, and don't tell anyone where you are going."

"Right," he said. Don't tell anyone? Why? Better not to ask.

"Stubby, another thing. Make sure you bring your

113

spare keys for Stirrup Lane."

"Stirrup? OK, but what..." Jim had already put the phone down, so Stubbs did not have a chance to ask why he needed the keys for the car body repair shop at Stirrup Lane on a Saturday.

Forty minutes later Mike Stubbs drew up outside the office at the Warwick mansion. The door opened and Shaun came out, motioning Stubbs to take his van around to the side of the building.

"Take it around to the garage, the boss is waiting."

And so he was, with one of the shutter doors open behind him. Jim Warwick waved his arm in an arc, motioning Stubbs to drive his van into the building.

Jim pressed the button to lower the door as Stubbs stepped out of the van, slamming the driver's door behind him. Stubbs looked at the Audi.

"Whose is that?"

Jim ignored the question. "You took your time," he said sharply.

"Weekend drivers. What's up, guv?"

Jim pulled open the door into the office suite. "We have a problem."

Stubbs followed him into the room, where Shaun was standing by the desk. Stubbs' eyes widened when he saw Bellini's body on the floor.

"Who's this?"

"His name's Bellini," said Shaun flatly. "He's dead."

Mike Stubbs stopped in his tracks. "*CHRIST!*" He walked forward slowly to stand by the body. "You sure?"

"As a door nail."

114

Jim sat down heavily on the settee. Stubbs was stooping over Bellini.

"What happened?"

"I hit him and he died," said Jim simply.

Shaun commiserated. "You only broke his jaw, boss, the rest he done himself."

"Anyone can have a heart attack," said Jim defensively, "even young guys."

Stubbs straightened, shaking his head. "Bloody hell, what you going to do?"

"I've had a bit of time to think," said Jim.

"Why didn't you call an ambulance?"

"Are you mad?" Jim exclaimed. "He's dead; it wouldn't have helped him and definitely wouldn't have helped me."

"Shit, what a mess," said Stubbs. "Who is he, anyway?"

"One of Rosie's friends." The question had reminded Jim that his wife and daughter were due home at any time. He had to get Bellini and the Audi out at once.

"Did you bring the keys?"

Stubbs reached into his pocket, withdrew the ring of keys and held them out. "What do you want them for?"

Jim nodded towards the prone body. "We have to get rid of him fast, and the car. Torching it won't work, they have to disappear. I'll drive the car to Stirrup. It's a weekend, we have time to dismantle it and lose the parts."

Stubbs pointed at the body. "What about him?"

"You and Shaun can drop him into the quarry lake.

115

Plenty of heavy stuff in the yard at Stirrup," he said, referring to the place where they stored wrecked cars and metal scrap.

Jim pointed at a small pile of effects on his desk: a wallet, a mobile phone, some loose change and a gold-coloured wristwatch. "I've been through his pockets and taken out any stuff that could identify him."

Mike Stubbs turned to face Conroy.

"Let's get on with it, then. We'll put him in the van. You take the heavy end, I'll grab his legs." They took the body out to the garage and put it into the back of Stubbs' van.

Jim opened a drawer in his desk and placed Bellini's effects into it, carefully checking that the mobile phone was switched off. He removed from his pocket the two halves of the torn cheque that he had picked up off the floor, screwed them up and threw them in with the rest. He then closed and locked the drawer, picked up the handset of the landline phone and pressed a pre-dial button. He waited a few moments and Sandra replied.

"Yes, love," she chirruped.

Although breathing hard, Jim controlled his emotions and made a conscious effort to speak calmly. "Where are you?"

"On the A127, near Horndon and the traffic is diabolical, as usual."

Jim knew that it would be at least half an hour before they got home. That's good, he thought. "No hurry, take your time. I've got to go out, but I'll be back later."

"What, tonight?"

"Yeah, something cropped up."

"What about your tea? I've got lamb chops."

"You carry on, I'll get a burger or something." He knew that Sandra would know better than to ask when he would be home.

"OK, love, see you later."

On the dual carriageway Rosie was overtaking a slow lorry. A large four-wheeled-drive vehicle bore down rapidly on the Mini from behind, its headlamps flashing. Rosie glanced in her rear-view mirror and calmly began to pull into the slower lane. The road hog rocketed past.

"Dad working late, then?"

"You know your father."

"Did he say anything about Tony?"

"No. Why?"

"Mum! You *know* Tony came to talk about us getting engaged."

"Oh, sorry. No, he didn't mention it."

Rosie frowned. "Can you give him a call?"

Sandra had been gazing out of the window. "Who?"

Rosie shook her head. "Sometimes you're impossible. Tony, of course. I want to know how he got on." Rosie's mobile was in a cup holder by the gear lever. She picked it up and handed it to her mother.

"Here, use this. He's on the speed dial."

Sandra found the list, scrolled to Tony's name and

tapped the phone and listened.

"No answer," she said. She tried again, waited, and then turned the phone off.

"Must be switched off or something," she said, putting the instrument back into the holder. "We'll be home soon, you can try again from there."

From Warwick Hall the unlikely convoy made its way to the car body repair premises at Stirrup Lane, with Jim leading in the Audi, Stubbs in his van and Shaun in the rear in his old Range Rover. Once inside the premises they locked the gate behind them, leaving Shaun's car outside the building and taking the van and the Audi into the large repair shed.

Jim parked the Audi in a vacant repair bay inside the shed and was sitting in the passenger seat with the door open.

"Nip around the back to the scrap pile, Shaun," he said, "you know what we need."

"Right, boss."

To Stubbs he said, "Take a look in the boot and under the bonnet, I'll clear this out."

Jim opened the glove box, where he found a plastic envelope with the letters BCL printed on the front. Inside were documents on headed paper which proclaimed them to be from Bellingham Car Leasing. He put it on the driver's seat and turned his attention to other storage pockets, from which he removed a pair of designer sunglasses, a map of the Greater London area and a London road atlas. He flicked the pages of the atlas, briefly wondering why it was there since the car had a built-in satnav system. His thoughts were interrupted when Stubbs called out from under the bonnet. "Guv, come and look at this."

Jim climbed out of the seat. "What?"

"It's only got a fucking tracker!"

Jim moved around to join him. Stubbs was pointing at the device mounted on the bulkhead.

"Oh *shit!* I should have guessed."

Stubbs held up a hand. "Don't touch it, I'll check it out first."

Warwick followed Stubbs into the foreman's office in the corner of the shed. Stubbs turned on the light and switched on the computer on the desk. It was one that had seen better days. While they waited for it to start up, Jim looked around the desk and picked up a ballpoint pen and a piece of paper.

"I'll get details off the tracker." He walked back to the car just as Shaun returned, carrying two large rusty leaf springs, a length of heavy chain and an old tarpaulin.

"This lot should do it, boss," he said as he dumped the load near Stubby's van.

"It's got a tracker," Jim said. "I'm going to see if there's a label. Take a look inside the boot, Shaun."

Jim put his head under the bonnet to examine the unit more closely. There were two paper labels on the device. He found the model details on the larger one that was stuck to the front.

Shaun looked up from under the raised boot lid. "Everything OK here, boss, you want me to start taking it apart?"

"Hang on a minute, we're checking out the tracker."

Shaun ambled around to the front. "You hungry, boss? I'm starving."

Jim checked his watch. He was hungry too. "OK, we have time. Get the gate keys from Stubby and pop down the road to the chippy."

Jim made a careful note of the details on the label and returned to the office. He handed the piece of paper to Stubbs, saying, "Here. Find it."

Pecking at the keyboard with his two index fingers Stubbs entered the details on the keyboard. It took two minutes to find the information he wanted and when it appeared on the screen he smiled broadly.

"Good news. There's no tamper alert on this model; we can take it out. It's geo-fenced, but there's no fancy extras."

"Probably restricted to the south-east," said Jim. "Good, we'll take it out."

He went back to the car and around to the driver's side, removed the lease documents and the maps and put them in his jacket pocket. "Shredder fodder," he explained. He dropped the sunglasses in their soft case on the floor and stamped on it twice. Then he picked it up and strode over to a steel barrel which served as a dump bin for general waste.

"How often is this thing emptied?"

"Every week," said Stubbs.

"That'll do. Now, where are the overalls?"

Stubbs and Warwick pulled on overalls to start stripping the car immediately and Shaun departed to buy fish and chips.

Stubbs nodded towards the raised bonnet. "What about the tracker? Could be a record of the track in the car lease place."

Jim was kneeling behind the car, unscrewing the number plate. He looked up.

"Yeah, you're right. Hook it up to a battery, drive it somewhere away from here and junk it." Screwdriver in hand, he turned his attention to the number plate again, then stopped.

"No, wait. Take it on a Cook's tour first: shopping mall, seaside, anywhere well away from here." He waved his arm in an arc. "Use your imagination."

Stubbs nodded. "We'll start with a trip to the old quarry lake, got a parcel in the van to get rid of first."

"Leave the tracker in Shaun's motor while you're doing that, park it up somewhere safe *before* you go to the quarry."

"How about the Stars and Stripes?" Stubbs was referring to the nightclub in Rainham where Shaun had once worked. "Nice big car park, cars coming and going all night."

"Perfect. Do it tonight, the sooner the better. Actually, that would be a good place to close the trail, just trash the tracker there. Better than taking it on a tour."

Stubbs nodded. "OK, Guv."

"You don't need to drop me home tonight; I'll use one of the courtesy cars."

"OK."

"Something else: on Monday pick yourself another motor from the used stock, then take your van to the wreckers. Make sure they crush it immediately."

"Will do, boss. You think of everything." He shook his head. "I'm gonna miss the old bus but it needed changing, anyway."

They decided that all three would work on stripping the Audi that night and the following day, so that by the Monday there would be little trace of their activity. By putting unmarked parts on the used spares shelves, smashing up the glass and scrapping the rest, the chassis could be parked at the back of the yard with other wrecks, and covered with scrap. Stubbs would strip out the major mechanical parts later. He declared that if any of the staff asked any questions, he would tell them that it was one of his private jobs.

Jim Warwick rose early the following morning, but he did not want to linger over a leisurely Sunday breakfast. He went downstairs wearing a tracksuit and carrying a sports bag that he placed on the floor by the kitchen door. Sandra had laid out the ingredients for his breakfast, ready for frying.

"No fry-up today, love," Jim said. "I've got to go in to work."

"On a Sunday?"

"It's something I have to do myself. Don't worry about it."

She protested. "You can't go out on an empty stomach. Look," she pointed. "Everything's ready, it'll only take five minutes."

"No time, can't stop." He reached for the coffee pot.

"Have some cereal," she said. "I'll make you toast to go with the coffee."

At that moment Rosie came in, wearing a dressing

gown over her nightie. Jim looked up in surprise. "You're early, princess. Makes a nice change."

"Morning, Dad." Rosie came over to plant a kiss on Jim's cheek. "I have a reason."

Jim was pouring cereal into a bowl.

"Oh yes?" He grinned. "Is it going to cost me money?"

Sandra passed the milk jug to Jim. To Rosie she said, "You'll have to make it quick, he's going in to work today."

Rosie looked from one to the other. "On a Sunday?"

Jim took a spoonful of cereal, swallowed, then gestured with the spoon. "I have to make money to keep up with all your shopping."

Rosie pulled out a chair, turned it and sat down facing Jim. She put her hands in her lap. "How did it go last night, Dad?"

He looked at her blankly. "How did what go?"

"Dad! Don't tease. Your chat with Tony. I've tried to call him but his phone is off."

Jim shrugged. With his mouth full of cereal, he gestured. "We had a talk and he left."

"He *left*? What do you mean?"

Jim was pouring himself a glass of fruit juice. He turned to look directly at Rosie. "Sweetheart," he said, putting the jug down, "I had to find out what sort of man he is. Did you know that he's up to his eyes in debt?"

Rosie's eyes widened. She shook her head. "No, but what..."

"Over twenty grand. I found that out before I

asked him over. So I offered him the money, on condition that he went away and left you alone."

Rosie's face betrayed her horror. She put her hand to her mouth, mutely shaking her head. Sandra looked up. Eyes wide, she asked, "And he took it?"

Jim nodded. "I wrote a cheque on the spot. He took it all right, nearly took my arm off."

Rosie spluttered. "You – I don't..."

Jim reached for Rosie's hand. "You see, princess, he should have refused. Then, we would have known he is the man for you." He shook his head. "But he didn't."

Rosie pulled her hand back. *"No! It can't be,"* she screamed. She covered her face with her hands and sobbed, shaking her head. "No, no, no."

Sandra rushed around the table and put her arms around her daughter.

Jim stood up. "I'll get my cheque book, so you can see for yourself." At the door he paused and turned. "It was the only way, princess."

Seated at his desk in the open plan CID office, Detective Sergeant Frank Rollo was worried. He had just received a text message on his mobile. *"Call me now. Urgent. J"*.

Jim Warwick never sent him a text unless he wanted something; and to Rollo, Warwick's requests were tantamount to commands. What the hell is this, he wondered? He tapped out an answer: "Five mins", sent it, and stood up. Then he took his jacket off the back of his chair and slipped it on.

"Just popping out to get some fags," he announced

casually to the others in the room. In fact he had a full packet in his pocket, but he needed a reason to be outside when he made the call. He also needed a cigarette.

Rollo made his way out of the building, heading on foot towards the newsagent's shop two streets away where he was a regular customer. He paused to light a cigarette before crossing the road and inhaled deeply. Within a few seconds the nicotine fix had done its job. He was ready to make the call. Rollo was too careful to have Jim Warwick's number on the list stored in the phone, so he had memorized it. He dialled the number and continued walking, holding the phone to his ear.

The response was immediate and abrasive. "What kept you?"

"I was in a meeting and had to get outside. What's up?"

"Remember that Italian I asked you to check out a couple of weeks ago? Name of Bellini."

"Yes, I remember."

"I needed the rundown on him because he said he wanted to marry my Rosie."

"Fair enough."

"He came to see me. I sussed him as a chancer straight off, so I paid him to sod off."

"So what's the problem?"

"His car is leased, and now he and the car have disappeared. I had a call from an insurance bloke asking questions."

Rollo stopped walking. "Nothing to do with you, surely?"

"Of course it's bloody nothing to do with me. But the car's got a tracker, so they know he was at my house."

Rollo didn't like the sound of this at all, but there were a number of reasons why he simply could not risk upsetting Jim Warwick.

"What do you want me to do?"

"Simple. The guy was here, he left twenty grand richer and now he's done a runner. Chances are the insurance or whoever could pay you a visit and I do NOT need noddies from your place stomping around here in their size twelves giving me grief."

Rollo walked across to a shop awning and stood under it. "When was this?"

"Saturday."

"Far as I know nothing's been reported, but I'll check and get back to you."

"No need, I'm not interested. Just put the fucking lid on it, know what I mean?"

Bloody hell, thought Rollo, where is this leading? But aloud he said, "No problem, Jim, will do."

"Good man, see to it." Before Rollo could reply Warwick added, "And Frank, give my regards to your lovely missus, Jean, is it?"

"Thanks, Jim," said Rollo. He rang off. Under his breath muttered, "Thanks for nothing, arsehole, and her name is Joan."

CHAPTER EIGHT

Unusually for her, Chief Inspector Annika van Houten arrived at her office that morning a few minutes late, the traffic in Rotterdam had been heavy. She put her smart leather three-quarter overcoat on a plastic hanger, unwound the pale blue silk scarf from around her neck, and hung both on the wooden coat stand just inside the door.

The office was a small room, containing three desks, a few chairs and four steel filing cabinets. Modestly furnished, it gave no hint of the importance of the work carried out there, save for the whiteboard that covered a large part of the surface area of one wall.

"Traffic chaos," said the Chief Inspector to her assistant, Marta. "If it gets any worse, I'll have to put in for a personal helicopter."

From Marta's initial reaction, Annika thought that she might have believed the jest, if only momentarily.

"What you need is a patrol car from Traffic," said Marta, rotating a solitary index finger vertically. "Complete with flashing blue lights, assigned to you for your exclusive use."

"While you are doing that, make sure you get me a handsome young driver." Annika moved briskly to her desk. "What's in?"

"There's an email from Paris. I've printed it out for you." Marta picked up a brown folder on her desk and took it over to Annika. "And a couple of attachments, surveillance photos."

The phone on Marta's desk rang, so she moved

back to it and picked up the handset.

"Special unit," she declared, then continued in conversation with the caller.

Annika was looking through the information she had been given. It was a response to her department's enquiry about the French registered Ford Transit van that had been observed at the electrical spares business near Tilburg a few days previously. She was mildly surprised to learn that the owner, one David Merchant, was a citizen of the United Kingdom, but much more so when she read that he was a pensioner who, with his wife, had apparently retired to live in France. Annika looked at the five pictures that accompanied the email. They showed the front view of a modest house in rural surroundings, with the white van parked on a gravelled area at the front. The photos were taken in sequence, as the man climbed into the vehicle and drove off.

The man was, she guessed, in his sixties. He appeared to be in good health, with a full head of grey hair, and he was wearing a blue anorak, jeans and trainers.

So, she thought, a UK citizen but a French resident. And from here he had travelled through Belgium. Definitely worth watching, but she would have to be careful not to tread on any international toes. The note said that Merchant had no criminal record in France, and that he was not being investigated there. It concluded by offering assistance and cooperation, if required. Precisely as intended, Annika took this to mean, "Keep us in the loop."

The message was sent by Pierre Broussard,

assistant to Jean-Luc Duroux, head of the French equivalent to Annika's department. She had met Duroux and had spoken to him occasionally, always in English, which they both spoke fluently. The email, however, had been sent entirely in French.

To herself Annika muttered, "D'accord, Jean-Luc!"

Geoff held out the polystyrene cup. "Milk, no sugar."

Samantha took it from him. "Thanks. Actually it's not bad, for machine coffee."

Geoff sat down beside her. They were in a waiting area outside the operating theatre in West Essex General hospital, its walls plastered with garish posters warning of the dangers of pursuing anti-social habits involving the injection or inhalation of various nasty substances.

"You're right," he said. "It's not bad at all. In fact it's terrible. Plastic, like the cup and these chairs."

Samantha checked her watch. "What time did they take her down?"

"About eleven." Geoff had been at the hospital since eight, Samantha had arrived just after noon. "What time are you going back to work?"

"Not until they've wheeled her out and we know how she is. Did they say how long it will take?"

"The surgeon reckoned between four and five hours."

"The middle of the afternoon, then." She took a sip of coffee. "I don't think I'll bother going back today."

"Oh dear. You might upset Adam."

She looked at him sideways. "Hmm. I can live

with that."

Geoff said, "There's a café on the ground floor. You hungry?"

She smiled. "You asked me that ten minutes ago, before you went for the coffee."

"Did I? Oh. I forgot." He looked at her. "Well?"

"Well what?"

"Are you? Hungry, I mean."

"Geoffrey Summers, sometimes I wonder how Penny's put up with you all these years."

"Me too." He grinned. "But I'm not complaining."

"Well, she *is* a bit special." She drained her cup. "At school, when we were kids, you know, we used to talk about boys."

"No, really? Why do I not believe that?"

She ignored the remark. "There were three of us, Penny, Joy Miller and me. We were always together. We talked about lots of things, especially boys. Penny used to say that she wanted to marry a fireman. They were big and strong and had lovely uniforms."

"Unfortunately, she got me. What about you?"

"Me? My dream was to marry a footballer. At the time it was George Best. Then I met Phil, the least athletic man on the planet!"

"He was a lovely guy. Do you still miss him?"

She nodded slowly. "Yes, at times. But I'm over him now." Her face clouded over and she stood up suddenly. "Come on," she said, "you can buy me lunch. She's not going to be out before we get back."

Two hours later Ganesh Mehta left the theatre tight-lipped, saying nothing. He removed his gown, mask and cap, rolled them into a ball and binned them.

"Do you want me to tell the husband?" the senior theatre nurse asked.

"I'll do it, if you like," said Daniel Glover, the surgeon who had assisted Mehta.

Mehta ripped off his bloodied gloves and hurled them into the bin. "No. It's my job, I'll do it."

He felt drained of all energy. Medically we did all that we could, he thought. But how am I going to explain to the husband that despite everything, sometimes things do not go as expected? The operation had been timed at three hours and twenty minutes. Three hours and twenty minutes; scores of times he had carried out procedures that had taken more than twice as long. Difficult, complex procedures, unlike the comparatively simple one he had just done. Yet he was exhausted. Always the way, he reflected wryly, when we lose a patient, rare though that was. Ironic, considering that he had actually done a good job. Try telling that to the husband! He cleaned up and left to do exactly that.

"Yes, sis," said Paul Hawker answering his mobile on hands-free in his car.

"Where are you?"

"On my way back, not far. Why, what's up?"

"You have visitors."

"Visitors? Nothing in my diary for this afternoon, far as I know."

"They don't have an appointment, they just dropped in. I told them you were out but they said they didn't mind waiting."

"Fine, I won't be long. Any idea what they want?"

"They're a middle-aged couple." She paused. "Are you ready for this? Name of Bellini."

"Bellini? Any relation to..."

"Yes, the parents."

"You sure?"

"They said their son Tony's gone missing, ten days ago. Mavis Hodder recommended us; apparently Mrs Bellini met her in Bobbie's." Paul was silent, rapidly considering the implications.

"Paul?"

"Yes, I'm here, just thinking. I'm really not sure we can take it on."

"That's why I called, I thought you'd like to know."

"OK, thanks. Make them comfortable, I'll talk to them." He rang off.

The man looked much older than his wife, anxiety drawn in every line of his gaunt, leathery face. He thrust his stubbled chin forward.

"We go to police, but they don't do nothing." He made a dismissive gesture. "Nothing. My boy is gone ten day now, *ten day*, still they don't do nothing."

Beside him his chubby grey-haired wife, clutching the handles of a small black handbag nestling in her ample lap, nodded vigorously and said, "I go to see them three, four time, but always they say is no news. They say maybe he go to Italy or somewhere."

"Look," said the husband reaching inside his shabby garlic-perfumed anorak, "I got his passaport. Here, you look."

He handed the passport to Paul Hawker. Paul took

it from the man and opened it. An unflattering image of Georgio Antonio Bellini stared out at him.

The wife interjected, "They say maybe he go away. How can he going away with no passaport, eh?" Turning to her husband she nodded towards Paul and said, "*Mario, dargli i documenti.*"

From one of the outer pockets of his anorak Mario withdrew a folded sheet of paper and a photograph. He passed them to Paul.

"This all his informations: address, telefono, where he work, car number, everything."

Paul looked at the photograph, a picture of a young Tony Bellini on a beach, wearing only skimpy swimming trunks and a wide grin. He had one arm around the waist of a shapely bikini-clad blonde and a beer bottle in the raised hand of the other. Paul unfolded and read the piece of paper, discovering that he knew all the facts listed, and reflecting that he knew even more.

"Thank you, Mr Bellini, this will help. When did you last see your son?"

His wife answered. "He come for Sunday lunch with us, before the Saturday tenth last month."

Paul was making notes. "Saturday the tenth. Was that the day he went missing?"

"Yes." She nodded vigorously. "He tell us he go to see his girl's papa to ask for getting married." She sniffed, wiping a ball of crumpled handkerchief on her nose. "But we don't see him after."

Paul wanted to help them but was still considering the implications of taking this one on. It was extraordinary that they had come to him, of all people. He put the note pad aside and stood up, extending his hand.

"I'll see what I can do. I have some friends in the police I can check with."

Bellini stood up, his pale blue rheumy eyes locked onto Paul's. Grasping Paul's hand he gripped it firmly with both of his.

"You find him, please. You find my son."

Paul then shook the wife's hand. She asked awkwardly, "Mr Hawker, how much you charge?"

Her husband's face hardened. "*Il costo non e importante!*" he exclaimed sharply. To Paul he said, "Don't worry the money."

Paul showed them into the outer room where Tina gave him a knowing look as the couple left. She arched her eyebrows. "Now *there's* a turn-up for the books. What are you going to do?"

"Not sure, I need to think about it." He frowned. "If we take it on, what's the worst that can happen?"

"All depends on why Jim Warwick wanted Tony Bellini researched in the first place," she replied tartly. "What did he say about that?"

Paul stroked his chin.

"Actually I don't remember. Come to think of it, I don't even remember asking him about his motives. Not something I would do, really, unless I felt I needed to know." He moved towards the door to his room.

"But if Jim Warwick knew Tony Bellini wanted to marry his daughter, that could have been more than enough reason. Let me think about it. At the end of the day we're professionals, so we should take it on regardless of where it ends up. But I'll call Eddie Smith at the nick anyway, to see if they've found out anything."

"Thanks." Paul Hawker scooped up his change from the bar as the barman turned away. He grasped the beer mugs and picked his way carefully through the noisy crowd.

Detective Constable Eddie Smith picked up the pint glass of dark ale that Paul had placed on the table in front of him.

"Cheers." Eddie's round open face and blue eyes under a mop of blond hair combined to make him look considerably younger than his thirty years.

"Personally I prefer lager," Paul said, taking a seat opposite the policeman. He gestured, indicating the busy room. "Why did you suggest coming here?"

"Safer here. I usually get lunch in the canteen at the nick, but when you mentioned Bellini, I felt it would be better to meet away from the office. Easier to talk here."

"You know something?"

"Not exactly, but I'm pretty sure there's something going on, something that Frank Rollo wants to keep hidden."

"Really?"

Smith took a swig of beer. He put the glass down. "Bellini's been missing what, a couple of weeks?"

Hawker nodded. "About that."

"Rollo took the case on, seemed keen. The Chief wasn't interested, just another guy who's done a runner. From debts, he reckoned. Frank then said he

135

would look into it, not worth wasting resources, he said."

"You think Rollo knows something about Bellini's disappearance?"

Smith leaned back in his chair. "Absolutely. And I'll tell you something else." He jabbed the air with his index finger. "Whatever it is, he wants to keep it under wraps. This is a man who never volunteers for *any* job. So why this one?"

"You don't like him much, do you?"

"No, I don't, but I don't have to. I have to work under him, but I'm a career cop, my feelings don't get in the way of me doing my job. Bellini's parents have been in a few times and every time it was Rollo who went to speak to them. A few days ago I was on my way out, when Mrs Bellini collared me in reception. She asked if I was a detective, and when I said yes, she told me enough to convince me that her son's disappearance needs looking into."

"And Rollo has done nothing? Are you sure?"

"Certain. Twice I asked him if I could look at the file. The first time he brushed me aside saying that he was dealing with it. The second time he told me to eff off, he didn't need help from me or any other amateur." Smith coloured slightly.

"Why don't you go to his boss?"

"With what? A hunch?" Smith snorted. "Don't get me wrong, the Chief is a good man. I'm pretty sure something stinks, but with no proof, all I would do is made trouble for myself."

"Do you think Rollo is on the make somehow?"

"Between ourselves, frankly yes. Why else would

he go to the trouble of keeping a lid on this?"

Paul reflected. Why else indeed? What motive could Rollo have unless he was being leaned on by someone with the money, power and influence to do so? Hawker was thinking that Jim Warwick fitted the bill, and also, probably had the motive.

Keeping his suspicions to himself, he asked casually, "Do you have any ideas?"

Smith grimaced. "No, and it's driving me mad. It needs looking into and I can't do a bloody thing about it. Yesterday Mrs Bellini was in again, getting nowhere, and I felt awful." He drained his mug. "Your call is just what I needed. When you said your clients were the Bellinis, I could have punched the air."

"Actually I haven't decided yet whether to take it on. I thought it could be a lot of trouble for not much return, but now, maybe not."

"Great, marvellous! Go for it, and if I can help, even if I have to stick my neck out a bit, call me."

Smith stood up and pointed to Hawker's beer mug. "Another? I'm just going to check out the sandwiches."

A typical bachelor flat, Paul Hawker thought. He stood in the open doorway, looking around the bedroom. Tony Bellini's room. What he saw was a wardrobe, a guitar propped up in a corner, a wicker chair and a double bed, neatly made. There was also a chest of drawers on which were a sheaf of papers and a laptop. On one wall were a full-length mirror and two posters of a heavy metal band and on another, two framed prints of sports cars. It was, thought Hawker, a young man's pad.

Standing behind him, Tony's flatmate Mike Layborne said, "He's not the tidiest bloke in the world, his mum came around and tidied up. She also sorted his dirty washing and made the bed."

Paul moved across to the chest of drawers and picked up the papers.

"You say you've heard nothing from him since the day he went missing?"

"Not a word. I keep trying his mobile but there's no answer."

Paul sifted through the papers. "And before that, did he say or do anything to give the impression that he might be going away? A short break or a holiday maybe?"

"No, nothing. It's like he's just vanished. I can't understand it." Layborne shook his head.

Among the papers was a large brown envelope upon which the words "Car Lease" had been scrawled. Inside were documents relating to the Audi and its leasing terms. Paul took out his notepad and scribbled some notes. Most of the other papers were unpaid bills. He opened the wardrobe door and scanned the interior.

"Do you know if there's anything in here that he would have taken with him if he was planning a trip?"

Layborne shook his head again. "No, I don't, but I'm not sure I'd know that, anyway."

Paul closed the wardrobe door. "How long have you shared this flat?"

"A couple of years. Tony was living with his

parents and wanted a place of his own. I'd been renting a room but didn't like it much, so we got together to share the rent on this place."

"Does he have many visitors?"

"In the beginning, quite a few. Girls, mostly." He smiled crookedly. "Well, he's a good-looking bloke, flash car and everything."

"And now?"

"Now there's only one, Rosie Warwick. He's crazy about her. She's been here a couple of times since he left and she keeps calling me to find out if I have any news. She's convinced something's happened to him, she can't believe that he would have just taken off without a word. The last time she spoke to him he was in his car on the way to see her dad to talk about them getting engaged. That was the day he didn't come back here. Poor girl, I feel really sorry for her."

Paul knew then that if he was to take this further he would have to speak to Jim Warwick. "If you had to guess, what would *you* say happened?"

Layborne did not answer immediately. He was looking out of the window at the street below. He turned and said slowly, "I have absolutely no idea. But I can tell you this, I'm certain he hasn't taken off. It's not like him; plus," he gestured, "all his stuff's here."

Paul made a few more notes. Without looking up he asked, "Has anyone else been here asking about him?"

"Apart from his parents and Rosie, only some bloke from an insurance outfit, but he was looking for the car. He left a card."

CHAPTER EIGHT

"Can I see it please?"

"Yeah, sure, I'll just get it." Layborne headed for the door, then stopped and turned. "Oh yes, there was a copper here too, before that. Bloody useless, he was."

Paul followed him out of the room. "Really? Why?"

"He told me that Tony had been reported missing. That was a surprise. Anyway, he was in and out in five minutes. Didn't ask me anything, just went through Tony's things and left." He shook his head. "Strange, that. I asked him what they were doing to find him and he just said that they didn't have time to chase after someone who's done a runner. He said people disappear on purpose, that it happens all the time."

"Did he leave you his contact details, name, phone number?"

"No. But he took Tony's work briefcase away. I asked him why and he said something about needing time to check every possibility. He said he would return the case later, but he hasn't. You know, I got the impression he wasn't really bothered." Layborne frowned. "You'd have thought he would have asked me to call him if Tony turned up or phoned or something, but he didn't."

"Can you remember exactly when the policeman came? I mean, was it on the day Tony didn't come home?"

Mike shook his head. "No, it was a couple of days later, in the evening on the Monday. I remember that because I was about to go out. To be honest I had no idea that Tony was missing, he sometimes stays overnight with friends, often at weekends." He paused and frowned. "Come to think of it, he hasn't done that for some time. I guess that's because Rosie's parents are probably not the sort of people who would encourage it, if you know what I mean."

"Why do you say that? Have you met them?"

"No, but from what Tony says, they don't seem the sort." Mike went over to the fireplace and picked up a business card from the mantelpiece.

"This is the card the insurance guy left," he said, holding it out.

Paul took the card and read it. "Loss adjusters," he murmured. He made a note of the name of the company and its agent and the telephone numbers.

He handed the card back. "Thanks."

As Paul was leaving, Layborne said anxiously, "You will let me know if you find out anything, won't you? Tony's a good bloke and I'm really worried."

"Of course, and if he turns up here, you call me. Here's my card," he said.

When he got back to his car Paul opened his notebook, took out his phone and dialled the number of the loss adjuster. His call was answered immediately.

"Vincent Gregory."

"Mr Gregory? My name is Paul Hawker and I am an investigator working for the parents of Tony Bellini. Can you spare a minute?"

"Hold on. I'm driving, I'll just pull up."

A few moments later Gregory spoke again. "Now,

who did you say you are?"

"Paul Hawker of Hawker Investigations. I've been retained by the Bellinis to find their son Tony."

"How did you get my number?"

"From his flatmate; you left your card."

"Oh yes. OK, what can I do for you?"

"Just wondering if you have anything on his whereabouts."

"Sorry, no. I wish you luck, but actually I'm more interested in finding the car."

"Any information on that?"

"Not yet. We know where he went...or the car, anyway, but nothing for the last couple of weeks."

"So the car has a tracker?"

"Yes, but...Look, I'd like to help you, but I can't really say any more. I suggest you contact our clients yourself. Client confidentiality and all that. You know who they are?"

Paul checked his notes. "Bellingham Leasing?"

"Yes. Sorry about that, but I'm sure you'll find them helpful. Also I have a lot of other stuff on my plate just now."

"That's fine, I'll do that."

"Speak to Kulwant Singh, he's your man. That's K-U-L-W-A-N-T."

Paul wrote it down carefully. "Thanks, you've been a great help."

"No problem, good luck." Gregory rang off.

CHAPTER NINE

Geoff Summers slouched in his armchair, clutching a tumbler of whisky. Nine days, he reflected bitterly. Nine days since Penny had left him and three since the service at the crematorium. In that time he had slept little and fitfully, and had not eaten much. Only now was he becoming truly aware of the magnitude of what had happened. She was gone and nothing would bring her back. The pain was always there, the bitterness, frustration and anger that were eating into him because he believed that he had failed her.

He thought it his fault that he had not immediately taken her to Australia as soon as her illness had been diagnosed. His fault too, that he had hung on at Melfords, instead of leaving so that he could devote all his time to her. His fingers tightened around the glass. Thanks to me, he thought bitterly, the last three months of her life have been wasted. He drained the glass, reached for the bottle and picked it up. It was nearly empty. Bugger, he thought, I need some more.

The persistent trill of the telephone finally cut through the fog in his head. He rose unsteadily to cross the room, went into the hall and picked up the handset.

"Hullo," he growled.

"Geoff? Is that you?"

"Uh, oh, hi, Sam," he drawled.

"Are you all right?"

Frowning in concentration he answered, "Uh, fine, I'm fine."

"You don't sound fine."

His head was clearing, slowly. "No, really, I'm OK."

"Anything you need? I've got to go to the supermarket anyway."

"Er, can't think of anything."

"I don't want to butt in and I know you can look after yourself, but how are you managing?"

Geoff ran his fingers through his hair. "Uh, this is going to sound really daft, but since you ask, there is one thing. I don't know how to work the bloody washing machine. It's driving me mad. I tried pushing all the buttons..."

She sniggered. "You silly devil. Why didn't you say?"

"OK, I suppose it does sound funny. But I'm nearly out of clean underwear."

This time she laughed. "I'll be round in twenty minutes. And I'll bring a pizza or something, just in case all your meals lately have been liquid."

"Thanks, Sam, you're a brick."

He put the phone down and looked around. His coat was draped over the newel post, a pair of dirty trainers nestled untidily at the foot of the stairs and there was a pile of envelopes on the door mat. God, what a mess. He wiped his hands across his face and looked at himself in the hall mirror. His eyes were veined and lifeless, his face drawn and pale, his cheeks and chin covered with a six-day stubble. "I'm a mess, too," he muttered. Twenty minutes, he thought, better get a move on.

It took him no more than fifteen minutes to get upstairs, strip off, shower, shave and get dressed again. He felt tired but refreshed as he busied himself making the living room presentable, before starting to do the same in the kitchen. He was slotting plates into the dishwasher when the doorbell rang.

Geoff opened the door wide to let her in. "Hi, Sam."

Samantha stood in the doorway, holding a carrier bag in one hand and her handbag in the other.

"Well, you're looking a lot better than you sounded on the phone," she said.

"Come in." He leaned forward to kiss her proffered cheek. "I had a quick shower and change. But you're right, I was a mess."

Samantha held the bag up. "Dinner." She headed for the kitchen. "Come on, I'm hungry. Are you?"

"A bit."

Samantha placed the carrier bag and her handbag on the worktop. She opened the carrier and took out a frozen pizza, a stick loaf, a bottle of red wine and a carton of fresh milk.

"Now," she said briskly. "Let's put your microwave to use. We can tackle the washing machine later." She handed him the wine bottle. "Make yourself useful and open this. You like reds, don't you?"

He nodded. "Yes, I do."

"Pizza isn't the ideal Saturday night fare, but it'll do," she said cheerfully.

When they had eaten Geoff complimented Samantha on her choice of the wine. She shrugged. "A fluke. It had a fancy label with gold print, so it had to be good."

She had taken only one glass of the wine and had nursed it through the meal, saying that she was not a great wine drinker and anyway she had to drive home. Later they went into the living room and she took the glass with her.

Samantha sat on the settee with her shoes off and her legs drawn up beside her. Geoff had carried the bottle out and relaxed in his armchair. Samantha stared into her glass. They had been talking about his return to work at Melfords.

"I suppose it could help to take my mind off things," he said gloomily.

"The longer you leave it, the harder it will be."

"Maybe, but right now Melfords is hardly a priority. I should have got out of there ages ago."

"Even before you fell out with Adam?"

"Yes, before then. Mind you," he said lifting the glass and raising his index finger, "that doesn't exactly help. Twenty-two years, *twenty-two* bloody years I've grafted for them. And all for nothing. I'm too loyal, it doesn't work these days."

Samantha's face was expressionless. Geoff went on.   "If I'd quit three months ago, I could have taken Penny to see Sue in Australia, but I didn't. It was the one thing she really wanted. Her last wish and I let her down. I don't know if I can live with that."

They sat in silence for a few moments. Finally she spoke, softly.

"No, I don't think you let her down, and Penny wouldn't think so either."

He shook his head emphatically. "No, no, it was my fault. I wasted *weeks* messing around." He waved his hand to emphasize the point. "With the bank, finance people, travel agents – and now it's too late, she's gone." Again there was a long silent pause.

Samantha looked at Geoff; a broken spirit, a shadow of the strong, positive man who had been, for so long, the spouse of her best friend. A man for whom she had nurtured a secret love for many years. Now, with Penny gone, she could not help but hope that he might perhaps, one day come to realise how she felt. That unspoken thought immediately brought on a pang of guilt. But it was illogical to feel disloyal to Penny. It was different now, and she wondered if Geoff would ever discover how she felt about him. It hurt to see him beating himself up, unfairly.

Quietly she asked, "Was the problem the delay in getting a loan?"

Geoff frowned. "How did you know about that? Did Penny say something?"

She hesitated, then swung her legs off the settee and stood up.

"No, it wasn't Penny. But you must stop beating yourself up. I have something interesting to show you; it's in my bag in the kitchen."

He sat up. "What?"

Samantha went into the kitchen and returned holding a folded piece of paper. She held it out to him.

"Take a look at this. But before you read it I should tell you that I will be handing in my notice at

Melfords next Friday."

"*What?*"

"Read it, and you will understand."

She sat down again and watched him closely as he read the letter.

They had talked for hours, with Geoff doing most of the talking. Samantha had been a sympathetic sounding board for his violent swings of emotion, from fury to self-pitying depression. In the end he settled to a steely calm, manifested by his determination, expressed in strong language, for vengeance at any price. He still felt partly responsible for his failure to fulfil Penny's last wish, but he came to believe that it was that man Adam Ford who was really to blame. Despair, disappointment and frustration combined to propel what had been formerly mere dislike of the man, into an all-consuming, burning hatred that cried out for revenge. Now he was ready to do whatever was necessary, however long it took, to bring down Adam Ford, regardless of the consequences.

After several cups of strong coffee, Geoff was able to articulate his feelings clearly.

"I'm going to get the bastard for this," he said, "whatever it takes."

Samantha replied quietly. "It's easy to see why you're so angry. Understandable. But I'm worried, hate can be poisonous. Don't let this eat into you."

Geoff shook his head. "I don't care, Sam. He *knew* about Penny's illness and he knew what the loan was for. The *bastard!* I'm going to get him, I promise you."

Samantha looked at him for a few moments, then stood up. "Another coffee?"

Geoff checked his watch. "No, I don't think so. It's nearly midnight and I have things to do."

She raised her eyebrows. "Things to do? What you need right now is sleep." She smiled. "Me too, I'd better be going."

Geoff sighed. "You're right. The way I feel right now I could sleep for a week."

He saw her to the door and kissed her lightly on the cheek. "Thank you," he said simply. "Be careful on the roads, I'll speak to you tomorrow."

Geoff went to bed around midnight, but despite being emotionally and mentally spent, sleep eluded him. In the twilight of semi-consciousness, his mind shuffled the options constantly, at first achieving little except to deny him the peace of slumber until slowly an idea began to take shape. The more he thought about it, the better it seemed. Suddenly he was alert, and excited. He had a notepad on the bedside table and three times he rose to scribble notes upon it, until about four in the morning when he abandoned altogether any attempt at sleep. There was just too much on his mind.

He picked up the notepad and went downstairs to the kitchen to make a mug of strong coffee. Then he sat down to marshal his thoughts and develop the idea which, if he got it right, would satisfy his craving for vengeance. Two hours later, after he had made several pages of notes and drunk four mugs of strong coffee, he was done. On the last page of notes he had written in large letters, ASK SAM TO STAY ON. He pushed the pad aside and went upstairs to fall into bed, where he slept soundly until late the following morning.

Making that call was Geoff's first thought on waking. At the other end the phone rang six times before it triggered the recorded message.

"Hello, this is Samantha Bowen. Sorry I'm not here to take your call. Please leave a message after the beep and I will get back to you."

"Sam, it's Geoff. I don't have your mobile number. Please call me, there's something I need to ask you. It's important."

He had woken refreshed and alert. He showered, dressed and was making himself a late breakfast of coffee and toast when his phone rang.

"Geoff Summers."

"Morning, Geoff, it's me. How are you feeling?

"Hi, Sam, thanks for getting back. I'm OK, much better than I felt last night."

"That's good. Now, what's so important?"

He got straight to the point. "You said you would be putting in your notice on Friday. Did you mean it?"

"The letter is already in an envelope addressed to Adam. When I put his post on his desk on Friday, it will be at the top of the pile."

"Before you do that, we need to talk. I have a big favour to ask."

"A favour? What is it?"

He took a deep breath. "Last night I did some heavy thinking. I now know what I want to do, what I *have* to do."

"Uh-huh."

"I've worked out a plan and I need to stay in my job for another few weeks. If you could do the same it would be a big help. Would that be a problem for you? I mean, maybe you have something else lined up?"

There was a slight pause. "No, I want out, but I could stay on for a bit if I have to. What's this about?"

"Before I leave Melfords there's something I need to finish. If I resign I probably won't be allowed to stay. Ford is more likely to pay me off to get rid of me immediately."

"But surely if he wanted to, he could just fire you. Anyway, why do you need me to be there?"

"He'd prefer to fire me right now, but he won't, because there would have to be a good reason. He doesn't have one. It would be messy for him and expensive for the company. That's why he has been trying to force me to resign."

"I see," she said slowly, "but why do you want me to stay on?"

"I need to do some after-hours overtime, Sam. Quite a bit in fact, and I need to keep a low profile."

"But they already know you do a lot of work after hours."

"I don't want anyone to know exactly what I am doing. I don't think they'd check, but just in case they do, I would need to know. And I think you would be likely to hear about it if they do."

"Ah, I get it now. You want me to spy for you."

Geoff started to interrupt, "Not exactly..."

"Tell me straight. What you are doing, is it legal?"

"Sam, I promise you, I'm doing nothing illegal. It's a project I've already done some work on, and I don't want anyone knowing what it is, especially not Adam Ford."

"Aha. It sounds like you're the one who has something in the job market lined up, a competitor maybe? And you want to finish your project first."

"Something like that. Everyone knows that there isn't much that happens in Melfords that you don't know about."

"That may be true, but they also know that it doesn't go any further."

"Also true. Will you do it, then? Delay putting in your notice, I mean?"

"All right, I'll leave it for now, but sooner or later I would like to know a bit more about what you are up to."

"Thanks, Sam. Just give me a little time, you'll know soon enough."

"Isn't there something else?"

"Something else?"

"What's the underwear situation? We didn't do the washing machine last night."

"Oh, that. Don't worry, I'll find a laundry. There must be one around somewhere. I just haven't been thinking straight lately. I needn't have troubled you at all, but I'm glad I did."

"So am I," she said simply.

"I've decided to go back to work tomorrow. I am ready for it now."

"Good. See you tomorrow, then."

"Thanks again, Sam. Bye."

"Bye."

It was a quieter, more subdued Geoff Summers who went back to his job at Melford Electronics on the Monday morning. There were none of the usual cheerful exchanges of banter that were his forte. Geoff noticed that nobody seemed surprised at the change in his demeanour, he was after all, recently bereaved of the love of his life. He was greeted generally with sympathy and deference and he knew that his well-meaning colleagues were giving him space to grieve. Geoff was grateful for that and thought wryly that a degree of detachment would suit his objectives perfectly.

Debbie smiled when he walked into his office. "Welcome back, Geoff, we've missed you."

"Thanks, Debbie."

She nodded towards his desk. "As you see, there's a pile of work waiting for you."

He sat down in his chair and switched on his computer. Pushing the chair back slightly he looked at the paperwork. "I wouldn't have been surprised if you had done it all yourself."

She looked up. "Well, I've dealt with most of it, but not the stuff only you can do. You'll be a bit behind with that."

"Fine," he said, drawing his chair up to the desk.

CHAPTER NINE

He reached for his "in" tray, picked up the pile of papers and files and placed them on the desk.

At that moment the door opened and Ken Lever came in. Geoff had not talked to his new boss since the morning of the day that Penny died. Later Ken had attended the cremation service but not the reception after, although he and his wife had sent a card of sympathy.

"Geoff, glad you're back," Ken said. "My deepest sympathies, we're so sorry about your loss." Turning to Debbie he said, "Good morning, Debbie." She nodded in response.

"Thank you," Geoff replied. "And thank you for your card."

"There's a lot on at the moment, so it's good to see you back."

Geoff did not comment and Lever went on. "If there is anything we can do to, er, help, all you have to do is ask."

This is just what I want, Geoff thought. He smiled.

"Well, actually, there is something. Would you mind if I worked flexible hours for a while? There are a few personal things I need to attend to."

Ken shrugged. "Well, er..."

Geoff gazed up at his boss without blinking. "Just for the next two or three weeks, but as I'm on my own now, any time I take off working hours I will of course make up in overtime."

Ken nodded. "I understand. I'm sure that will be fine."

"Thank you."

Ken turned to leave. "I'll let Adam know."

As he closed the door behind him, Debbie snorted. "Hmmph, he should be thankful you even bothered to ask."

"Just keeping my nose clean."

"After all you have done, the least they should do is to give you as much time off as you want. That's what I think," said Debbie. "And just about everybody who works here would say the same."

Geoff looked across and smiled. He decided he would take mornings off, and make up the time working overtime after hours. He had got what he wanted and it had been much easier than he had expected.

There were six names on the list. Just such bare details as would be found chiselled into the granite of most headstones: name, date of birth, date of demise. They had in common three things: all were male, all were born about the same time as himself, and all had died very young.

Geoff put the list into his pocket and checked his watch. He had to be back home by eleven-thirty to meet an estate agent whom he had asked to call, then get to Melfords by two o'clock. That should be no problem, he thought, as he left the leafy peace of Manor Park cemetery in East London.

Later, researching the names on the internet revealed that the ideal choice was one John Elliot Jeffries who had died in infancy. He appeared to have no living relatives in the United Kingdom, so Geoff did more research. He discovered that the parents had emigrated to Australia a few months after the baby died. He whispered the name to himself, "John Elliot Jeffries." He liked it. It had a good ring to it and it could be shortened to "Jeff," which could be useful. Perfect.

Geoff opened his front door to the negotiator from the estate agency. She was a willowy, smartly dressed young woman armed with a briefcase folder. He showed her in.

"Please take your measurements or whatever, anything you need. I just want to sell the place as quickly as possible."

The woman launched into a sales patter, cheerfully assuring him that despite the depressed market, she was confident her company could secure a good price for the property and do it in a reasonable timescale.

Geoff was impatient to the point of rudeness. "Look, all I want you to do is to sell the house, quickly. Do whatever you have to, but sell it immediately. That's why I haven't called in any other company. You have an exclusive; please just get on with it."

The sales patter dried up. "Yes, Mr Summers. We are happy to take your instruction on that. We have a few good prospects looking for properties in this area and I'm certain at least one of them will be happy to get a bargain."

"Good. A quick sale, as fast as possible. I've made arrangements for clearing my stuff out next week."

She opened the folder and withdrew a cardboard wallet, which she handed to him.

"Copies of our literature and terms," she explained, as she also took out a printed document. "If I can ask you to complete this instruction form with me, we can get on with it. But can I suggest you leave clearing out until after we have a firm sale? An empty house is less appealing to viewers."

"OK, that makes sense."

"Thank you. And it would speed things up if you allow us to carry out accompanied viewings on your behalf."

"Fine, I'll give you a set of keys."

He had to hang around while she took room measurements and photographs. Finally she handed him her business card.

"Thank you for your instruction, Mr Summers. We'll put it on immediately."

"Thanks," said Geoff glancing at the card, "Tracey."

She smiled. "Right. I'll get back to you within the next few days, hopefully with good news. Give me a call if there's anything else we can do."

The following morning Geoff was in Leigh-on-Sea, standing outside a double-fronted Edwardian villa in Elm Drive, a quiet street off the London road. With cars parked on both sides, negotiating the narrow space between made for an interesting slalom. Geoff knew what to expect because he had driven past on a reconnaissance three days previously.

The signboard in the front garden stated in large script, that this was Gamages Guest House. Smaller lettering below indicated with an arrow the guest parking area to the rear, down a gap at the side of the house. Geoff had not parked there, choosing instead to leave his car further down the road.

He stepped into the half-covered porch. On the wall above a steel plaque bearing the number 67 was a brass doorbell push, which he pressed. Moments later the door was opened by a small grey-haired woman who welcomed him with a wide smile.

"Mr Jeffries?"

"Yes. And you must be Mrs Hallam."

"That's me, but call me Gloria. Come in, please."

Geoff entered the wide hallway. "When I phoned I half expected to be speaking to a Mr or Mrs Gamage."

She directed him into a large room off the hallway. "There hasn't been a Gamage here for over thirty years. The previous owners and the ones before kept the name because the hotel had a good reputation. Still has, I like to think. My hubby and I bought the place fifteen years ago. This is the guest lounge," she said sweeping an arm around. "Plenty of comfortable seating and a nice big telly." She drew back a curtain. "And it looks onto the road. The dining room is through there." She indicated a double door on the opposite side of the room.

"It all looks very comfortable."

"You were enquiring about a room for a few weeks?"

"I'm not sure exactly how long I'll need it, but it will be a month at least, maybe two."

"Would that be bed and breakfast only, or full board? We do excellent evening meals."

"Just B&B to start with, I'll be working most evenings."

Gloria then showed him to a single room upstairs, which was clean and comfortably furnished. A window looked out onto the car park at the rear.

"You have a pedestal hand basin, shaving point and a mirror," she said, indicating. "The bathroom is on the landing, right opposite."

"This will be fine," Geoff replied. "I'll take it, starting immediately."

They went downstairs to a reception desk at the end of the hall where Geoff registered as John Jeffries, writing in a fictitious address in Liverpool.

She turned the book around and looked at the entry. "Liverpool?"

"I work for a company in the security business. I'm here on a project for a client," he said casually.

She tilted her head. "I expect you'll be going home at weekends then?"

"I might, but probably not, it depends on the job."

Her eyebrows arched. "It must be quite an important job," she said expectantly as she placed on the desk a key fob with two keys on it.

Geoff realised that the sociable Mrs Hallam was also an inquisitive person. He would need to be careful, nosy people were usually gossips.

"Not really," he said. "It's fairly routine work for us but of course, confidential. We don't talk about it much, that's how it is in our line of business, I'm afraid."

"Oh." The disappointment was evident on her face. She picked up the key fob. "The larger one is your room key; the other is for the front door, which is never bolted on the inside."

"Ah, that reminds me, there's something I need to ask, Mrs Hallam..."

"Gloria."

"Gloria. I'm going to be late getting in sometimes, will that be all right?"

"I'm sure that will be fine, Mr Jeffries, but we do ask guests coming in late to try not to disturb anyone."

"I assure you, I'll be as quiet as a mouse."

Her face brightened when Geoff paid her in cash for a month's accommodation before leaving, saying that he would be back soon.

Geoff parked in his space at Melfords, his mind on work. Not the work on his desk, but the tasks he had to perform to complete his special project. He walked into the reception area and saw Samantha chatting to receptionist Sheila. Samantha turned.

"Oh, Geoff, can you spare a minute?" To Sheila she said, "See you later."

She fell into step with Geoff as they headed for the stairs.

"Are you OK?" she asked.

"Yes, fine, nothing I can't handle. Even the underwear situation is sorted."

She smiled. "You found a laundrette then?"

"Better than that, I found the instructions for the washer. You know what they say, when all else fails?"

On the landing at the top of the stairs they paused because their offices were in different directions.

Geoff said quietly, "Thank you for being so patient. The good news is that I've nearly finished my project."

Samantha shrugged. "No hurry, you said you'll tell me what you are up to when you're ready. I can wait."

Geoff had started to turn away, but stopped. He was now nearly certain that he was going to achieve his first objective; all that remained was a physical test. Why wait to tell her? He said, "You know what I'd like?"

"What?"

"When I'm finished, why don't we have dinner somewhere quiet and I'll tell you everything over a good, relaxing meal?"

Samantha smiled. "It's a date."

Geoff had found the name he was looking for in Penny's address book, but the details were scored through. Of course, he thought, Brian had moved in with Jackie, and Penny would not have had the new address. Still, it shouldn't be too hard to find a Brian Hammond who worked in a public library in the Hackney area. Ten minutes' research on the internet yielded five possible establishments.

After drawing blanks on the first two phone numbers on his list, he got what he wanted.

"Yes," said the woman who answered. "We do have a Brian Hammond. Would you like to speak to him?" Geoff answered in the affirmative and she put him through.

"Hammond here."

"Brian? It's Geoff, Geoff Summers."

"Oh, hi, Geoff, this is a nice surprise. What can I do for you?"

"Sorry to trouble you at work but I couldn't find your number. I need to ask your advice."

"Advice? From me? That's a first. What's it about?"

"It's a bit complicated. I'll need to explain; can we meet?"

"Fine, where do you suggest? We work Saturdays here, but Thursday is my day off."

"At the moment I am free most mornings. How about next Thursday?"

"Thursday morning's fine, why don't you come around to our place? Come for lunch. Jackie will be at work, but I can knock something up for us."

"Thanks, Brian. It's kind of you, but I'm going to have to pass on lunch this time, I have a couple of things to sort out in town before getting back to my office. Would around ten o'clock be OK?"

"Ten is fine; I'll have the coffee pot on."

"I'd better have the address, then, and your home contact numbers."

Brian gave him the information and Geoff thanked him before ringing off. Another box ticked. He knew that what he intended to ask of Brian was outrageous, and he wasn't sure if Brian would help, but it was something he had to try.

CHAPTER TEN

Paul Hawker sat in his car looking at the plain red brick building for a few minutes before pulling into the parking area at Bellingham Car Leasing's premises. It was a small factory unit on an industrial estate in Edmonton in north London, just off the North Circular Road. Not the sort of place he had expected to find as the headquarters of a company that specialised in hiring out prestige motor cars. The façade at the front was a plain brick wall with a half-glazed entrance door and an adjacent window, both heavily fortified by steel bars. Surveillance cameras and lights at high level complemented the other security measures.

Briefcase in hand, Paul entered the building to find himself in a room where an L-shaped counter separated the reception area from the office behind. To one side was a door upon which was a sign: "Workshop Staff Only".

The woman occupying the desk behind the counter looked up.

"Can I help you?" she asked. She was in her fifties, Paul guessed, with an attractive face that once would have been quite pretty.

He handed her his business card. "Paul Hawker. I have an appointment with Mr Singh."

She took the card and glanced at it. "I'll just get him for you." She stood up, went past the end of the counter and through the workshop door. A few moments later she returned.

"He'll be with you in a minute, Mr Hawker."

CHAPTER TEN

Shortly after, the door swung open and a tall, bearded Sikh came through. He was wearing a smart leather jacket, designer jeans and a yellow turban, which added to his already considerable stature. Paul found himself under the concentrated gaze of a pair of unblinking brown eyes beneath bushy eyebrows.

He extended his hand. "Paul Hawker. We spoke on the phone, Mr Singh."

Kulwant Singh's grip was firm. "Yes, about Mr Bellini and our missing car. Like I told you, our insurers haven't come up with anything yet." He gestured towards the end of the counter. "Come in please."

Singh led the way to the back of the office where he sat down in a padded swivel chair in front of a double pedestal desk. On the desk was a computer with its monitor displaying the swirling pattern of a screen saver.

Singh nodded towards an adjacent chair. "Sit down, please." He tapped at the keyboard. The screen saver disappeared, replaced by a desktop background picture of a red Ferrari sports car. Singh clicked on an icon.

"Now, let's see... Bellini," he muttered. He stabbed out the name on the keyboard, using only his two index fingers. A document appeared on the screen. Singh looked up.

"Here it is. Bellini, file number DL 045." Then he clicked on a tab and scrolled down.

"This is the track of the car for the last week before it disappeared."

Paul leaned forward. "Can we look at the evening

of Saturday the tenth?"

"Normally, we only keep records of daily movements for two weeks, but when there's a problem, as in this case, we do not delete until the problem is sorted."

Kulwant Singh clicked on the date. The display on the monitor changed to a map on which a track was shown in red. He pointed with his index finger.

"These white stars are the coordinates where the vehicle stopped. Not in traffic, only places where it was stationary for more than five minutes."

Paul leaned forward for a closer look. As he had half expected, Warwick Hall was marked with a star. The track led from there to an address on the Rayleigh industrial estate and then on to an address in Rainham, where it terminated.

"When did the transmissions stop?"

"Early hours on the Sunday morning, but there was an interruption on the Saturday night." Singh pointed the cursor at one of the stars. "Here, at eight sixteen. Apparently it's a car repair place," he said, rolling his eyes upwards.

"Really?" Paul looked closely at the map. The location indicated was at Stirrup Lane on the industrial estate.

"For how long was the transmission interrupted?"

Kulwant Singh's bearded face broke into a wry grin.

"It arrived there at seven fifty-three and the interruption occurred twenty-three minutes later. The break was around four minutes, just about long enough for the tracker to be transferred to another vehicle, or more likely, to be connected to a battery. It did not have a tamper alert."

"Pity."

"Unfortunately we can't afford to fit the most expensive trackers to every vehicle, sometimes we have to compromise. Depends on the circumstances, value of the car, client's job, that sort of thing. In the end it's a judgement call."

"Do you fit them here?"

Singh nodded. "Yes, it's not difficult, our electrician does it." He reached down, opened the bottom drawer of the desk and withdrew a cardboard box.

"This is the standard unit we use, like the one fitted to the Audi." He opened the box, removed the tracker and handed it to Paul who examined it. The device was a small, plain black rectangular plastic box fitted with an electrical mains lead. The maker's details were on a printed label attached to one of the broad, flat sides. On one of the narrow sides was an adhesive plastic sticker, upon which were printed the words Bellingham Car Leasing.

Paul handed it back. "Do you always put your sticker on the side?"

"Yes. We have them printed on a roll, self-adhesive."

Paul pointed to the star on the map identifying the previous stop, Warwick Hall. "What time did it leave here?"

"Seven minutes past seven."

Forty-six minutes, thought Paul. About right for the journey from Warwick Hall to the industrial estate, allowing for Saturday evening traffic. He stood up.

"You've been very kind, Mr Singh. Any chance that you could perhaps let me have a printout of these details?"

Kulwant Singh frowned and inclined his head. "Our insurers have had all this and they have got nowhere, and the police are not interested. The people at these addresses deny all knowledge of the car and our customer, but if you can do better, good luck. You can have the details, but there are a couple of conditions. First, you must pass on to us anything you discover." Paul nodded his assent as Singh continued. "Secondly, no bills, please, this has already cost us a bomb."

"No problem, my costs are covered." Paul reflected that he had come a long way for a short interview, but it was worth it.

Kulwant Singh stood up. "Good. Can you email me with your request, and that you agree to the conditions? I'll give you one of my cards, it has the email address on. I'll reply with a printout of the tracking information. "

Paul confirmed that he would send the message, and left shortly after.

Geoff decided that the time had come to keep his promise to tell Samantha about his experimental project. But since Penny died, so much had happened that he scarcely knew where to begin. He knew it had to be done; he would delay it no longer.

A few paces from her office he paused. What would she think when she learned the truth? He had told her that he was not doing anything illegal.

Perhaps not altogether truthfully, because when she had drawn an incorrect inference, he had not corrected her. He had allowed her to be misled, so in effect, he had lied to her. That, he concluded, was what she would probably think.

He stopped outside the door. He had a disturbing gut feeling that something was not right, but could not quite put his finger on what it was. Why did he now feel that it mattered so much that he had misled Samantha? Was he not emotionally dead, single-mindedly bent on revenge at any cost? He turned around slowly and began to walk back towards his own office. He needed time to think, to sort his head out and identify the reason for his unease.

Slowly it came to him. He realised that it was because he did not want to hurt her, their relationship had changed. She had been Penny's closest friend and by extension a good friend to him. But now he realised that she had become much more. Penny had been the love of his life. Was it possible that so soon after losing her, he could have similar feelings for Samantha?

Geoff stopped in his tracks. Bloody hell. Was he about to do something that would turn her away from him? But he had to go ahead with his plan to bring down Adam Ford; no way would he consider abandoning that. Slowly he came to realise that he had found the dilemma that was the root cause of his unease. In the end he decided that he had no choice but to tell Samantha the whole truth, but not until he had worked out how he could do so without losing her.

"Ken Lever called in," Debbie said when Geoff got back to his office. "I told him you had gone down to the factory."

"Did he say what he wanted?"

"Adam wants you to be around on Friday week. It's the next board meeting and they want to call you in at some point."

"Really? What for?"

"He didn't say. I checked your diary, you have nothing marked."

Geoff picked up the handset of his intercom and pressed a button. "OK. I'll ask Ken."

His call was answered immediately. "Lever."

"Ken? Geoff. No problem; I'll be in all day on Friday week. What's it about?"

"Adam wants you to stand by, he's going to call you in to the meeting."

"Did he say why?"

"Something to do with control panels, I believe. I don't know any more than that, but he did say that it is important that you are there."

Control panels? Had they found out, somehow? Geoff's stomach knotted. No, surely that was not possible, he had been too careful and he was nearly finished, with only the final test to be carried out. He made the effort to answer calmly, "Fine. Thanks, Ken."

A little later when Debbie was not in the room Geoff called Sam on the intercom. She answered immediately, her tone uncharacteristically brisk.

"Samantha Bowen," she snapped.

CHAPTER TEN

"Hi, Sam. Geoff."

Her tone softened. "Oh, Geoff. Sorry, I was a bit short."

"It's not like you. Are you OK?"

"I am now. Boss-related stress. That bloody man!"

"What's he done now?"

She was dismissive. "It's his manner, I'll never get used to it. But nothing to worry you about. What can I do for you?"

"We have a date."

"What?"

"I owe you a dinner. And an explanation. I've finished my overtime project and I promised to tell you all about it when I was ready, remember? I am now."

"Good. You can tell me right now, I can't wait to get out of this place."

"Can't do it here, and not on the phone, Sam. Tomorrow night OK?"

"What, no overtime then? Tomorow's fine."

"After tonight, definitely no more overtime," he said with feeling. "Where would you like to go?"

"Hmm...How about the King's Head? Do you know it?"

"That place on Woodbridge Road?"

"Yes, near the cricket field. About seven o'clock?"

"Seven's fine."

"I'll meet you at the main bar. It's on the right as you go in. You can't miss it."

"OK."

"See you there, then."

"OK, bye." Geoff put the phone down

170

thoughtfully and took a deep breath. This meeting was something he really would have to handle correctly.

Tommy the security man was on a routine round of his night shift. As usual, Geoff heard the measured clump of his approaching boots down the long corridor well in advance of Tommy's arrival. Damn, he thought, just at the critical moment.

He knew that he had about a minute before he could expect to see Tommy at the door. He threw a cloth over the small battery-powered black box on which he had been working, then turned to focus his attention on the control panel beside it on the workbench.

Before Penny's death Geoff did overtime only when absolutely necessary. After her illness was diagnosed he had resented every moment away from her, but pressure of work sometimes made it necessary. Now it was different. He was able to work alone on his project, quietly and without interruption. Without the visceral motivation of cold revenge, he would have had neither desire nor reason to be working overtime again. The experimental work on the special product he needed in order to further his plan was tantalizingly close to being finished, so he was nearly there.

When Tommy entered, Geoff was bent over the test bench, with various small electronic components spread around.

Tommy shut the door behind him and whistled. "By golly, you're a glutton for punishment."

"Oh, you know. Needs must when the devil drives."

The security man strolled over and sat down on a stool. "That's nearly two weeks to my certain knowledge, four hours every night except one."

Geoff smiled. "Ah, that must have been the night I got some sleep."

Tommy looked concerned. "None of my business, lad, but aren't you overdoing it, maybe just a bit?"

Geoff put down the screwdriver he had been holding. He looked up and spoke softly.

"It's good of you to worry, Tom. Yes, I have been pushing it a bit lately, but it helps. These days I'd rather be here than at home."

Tommy's weathered face softened. "Like I said, none of my business, but whatever this lot pay you, it ain't nearly enough!"

"Thanks, mate," said Geoff simply.

Tommy stood up. "I'll leave you to it, then."

Geoff's fingers tingled with excitement as he waited impatiently until the sound of Tommy's boots had faded altogether. He was ready. He re-assembled the small black box carefully, put the cover back on the control panel and switched the unit on. The system controller was then "live" as it would be when installed in a building. His pulse hammered and his hand shook as he took a deep breath, picked up the black box and tapped into it the code he had pre-programmed into the control panel.

A muted 'click' confirmed that it had switched off, and the red "system off" indicator light came on. In a moment of sheer elation Geoff made a fist and punched the air.

"Yes!" he whispered, exhaling a huge breath. Then he cleared a space on the bench and reached under it to pick up one of the four other control panels he had retrieved from the production line. Four more and he was done.

Geoff arrived at the *King's Head* early and took a stool at the bar, from where he had a good view of the main entrance. The room was crowded with people waiting to order drinks, and others milling around searching for vacant tables. This was no place for a quiet talk. Looking around he saw that there were patio doors to one side, leading to an outside terrace with tables and seating. He ordered a scotch with ice and waited.

Just after seven o'clock Samantha came through the door. She was wearing a white silk blouse with a wide collar open at the neck, and a tight black skirt that showed off her slim shapely figure. Geoff thought that she looked stunning. He stood up and waved her over. As she approached he raised his voice over the hubbub of background noise.

"Let me get you a drink." Pointing to the patio doors, he said, "We'll take them outside where it's quieter. What would you like?"

"Small gin and large tonic, please. Lemon, no ice."

"G and T coming up. Find us a quiet corner outside and I'll join you there in a minute. I've booked a table in the restaurant for seven-thirty."

When he took the drinks out, he saw her seated at a table in a corner of the terrace. He went over and put the drinks down.

"Good choice, it's quieter here."

"And away from the smokers," she said, picking up the tonic and mixing her drink. She raised her glass.

"Good health."

Geoff sat down and looked at her for a few long moments. Samantha coloured slightly and smiled, inclining her head downwards.

He shook his head, then said, quietly, "Was I staring? Sorry. Can't help it, you look gorgeous."

She smiled again. "Thank you."

Geoff picked up his glass. "Good health. Here's to a new start."

She arched her eyebrows. "You'll have to explain that."

"A new beginning, for me at least. I've sold the house."

"That was quick. Have you found another place?"

"I've taken a room in a small hotel. It'll do for now. And I've cleared out the house."

"What, everything?"

He nodded. "Yup, all of it. I kept some personal stuff, like photographs. Memories of good times with Penny. Clearing out everything else that we shared together is part of starting again."

She took a sip from her glass and put it down again. "Sounds like you have a new job. Are congratulations in order?"

"I'm leaving Melford, but it won't be to start another job."

Her eyebrows arched. "No job? What will you do?"

"I have a plan that will make me enough to kick-start my new life."

Samantha's arms were on the table. She was holding her glass in her right hand, and her left was resting on the top. Geoff reached forward and placed his hand gently over hers, while looking directly into her eyes.

He sighed. "I have a problem, Sam. I am about to do something that you won't like, and my big fear is that when you hear what I have to say, you may not want to have anything more to do with me. All I ask right now is that you hear me out, and then tell me what you think."

Her eyes widened. "Are you serious?"

Geoff drew his hand back and picked up his drink.

"Totally. You have a decision to make. If you decide that you don't want me around any more, I promise I'll go away. But it has to be *your* decision."

He drained the glass, then stood up and walked around the table. "Now let's go and have dinner, we have a lot to talk about."

Samantha was still wearing a baffled expression when Geoff took her elbow gently and led her through the patio doors. The room was crowded, so he held her hand as they eased their way past the bar to the restaurant beyond. Samantha said nothing but she did squeeze his hand. Geoff's heart missed a beat.

At the door they were greeted by a young man holding a clipboard.

"Table for two, sir?" he asked. "Do you have a reservation?"

175

Geoff drew Samantha closer and answered in a deliberately clear voice, but looking directly at her and not at the young man.

"Yes. I made a reservation for seven-thirty. My name is John Jeffries."

On the evening of the following Saturday Paul Hawker drew up outside the gates at the end of the cul-de-sac that was Stirrup Lane. The paint on the adjacent metal sign was in poor condition. Scarcely a good advertisement, he mused, for the services of the enterprise it represented. "Stirrup Lane Car Body Repair and Paint Services," it said, and below that in smaller print, "A Warwick Group Company." Surprise, surprise.

Paul checked his wristwatch. On this Saturday evening traffic had been light and he had not hurried, completing the run from outside Warwick Hall in just forty-one minutes. The gates were shut and secured by double steel chains and padlocks. Beyond, the premises appeared deserted. Coils of razor wire decorated the top of the boundary wall and the tops of the gates, which had been fabricated from welded box section steel.

He would have liked to take a closer look around inside, but had to settle for what he could see. The main building was a large metal structure, with a double-width roller shutter door. At the front was a lean-to cabin with a door, and a sign that said "Reception". Paul noticed that CCTV cameras with infra-red sensor floodlights were mounted at high level, giving total surveillance coverage of the grounds.

Cars and vans were parked in the area to the front of the building, but Paul could not see what lay to the sides or rear. There was nothing else he could do here, so he climbed back into his car to resume retracing the route that the Audi had taken. Or rather, the tracker and the battery that had powered it. He doubted whether the Audi would ever be seen again. It was time to move on to the final destination.

On the last leg of the route Paul reflected that there was strong circumstantial evidence that Jim Warwick was indeed involved in Tony Bellini's disappearance. And he could not have acted alone. Even if the surveillance cameras at the body repair shop were linked to recorders, there was no chance that Warwick would allow them to be examined. Paul hoped that he might fare better at the next stop.

Thirty minutes later his satnav announced that he had reached his destination. He pulled up briefly in front of the building, to look at the entrance. This was the place where the tracker had stopped transmitting. It was a large Victorian structure set back from the road, with tarmac-surfaced car parks to each side. Stone steps led up to a mock Palladian façade with a pair of heavy wooden doors. One was open and through it the rhythmic thumping beat of booming rock music escaped, doubtless to delight the ears of the customers entering. Paul shook his head; he was definitely too old for this.

A signboard on one side of the steps declared in garish neon lighting that it was the "Stars and Stripes,

CHAPTER TEN

South Essex's own Rock Disco Heaven". Above the
main doors, hewn into the stone, was the legend that
revealed the original purpose of the building:
"Rainham Gospel Hall 1896". Paul smiled at the
irony. They should have called the nightclub "Rock
of Ages".

At just after eight thirty, it was too early in the
evening for the place to be in full swing, but already
there was a steady stream of people making their way
up the stone staircase from each side. Paul parked his
car towards the front near the road to ensure that he
would not be blocked in, and made his way up the
steps. He joined the queue waiting to pass through,
feeling distinctly out of place among the smartly
dressed chattering young people out for their night's
entertainment.

A sweating dinner-jacketed bouncer with slicked-
back hair and built like a road block was busy frisking
each male entrant in turn. Beside him a middle-aged
blonde with crimson lips on a heavily made-up face
was checking the females.

As Paul approached, the man said, "Arms up,
please. You a member, sir?"

Paul raised his arms and the man ran his meaty
hands expertly down his body.

"Not really. I'm here on business. I'd like to see
the manager, if possible."

"Talk to Gail at reception." The man tilted his head
towards a young woman seated behind a counter
nearby, before turning his attention to the next person
in the queue.

Gail was a pretty, ponytailed young woman whose

178

loose halter-necked top showed off her shapely bust to maximum effect. As Paul walked towards her she looked up with an expression betraying some surprise. Probably, he thought, because he did not look the disco nightclub type.

"Membership, sir?"

He smiled and shook his head. "No, thank you, Gail. I think I may be a bit geriatric for this place. I'm looking for the manager. I'd like to have a word with him if possible."

"Certainly, sir," she said deadpan. "But you'll have to raise your voice."

"Oh, does he have a hearing problem?"

She grinned. "Not really. He's on holiday in Spain."

Paul Hawker laughed out loud. "Wonderful, you've made my day."

"Sorry, just a joke. No offence meant."

"None taken. Who's in charge when he's not here?"

"His assistant, Barry. But he's busy with the DJ at the moment. Can I help?"

Paul thought quickly. With the manager away, the assistant might not be too keen to make any non-routine decisions. Paul felt he could do worse than speak to this bright young woman.

He took a business card from his jacket pocket. "Do you have CCTV cameras covering the car parks?"

"Yes, as it happens, so you're out of luck if you're selling them."

"Nothing like that." He handed her the card. "I'm

Paul Hawker of Hawker Investigations and I'm trying to find one of your customers who's gone missing. I'm working for his family."

"I should think lots of our customers go missing, especially after a skinful of beer. How can our CCTV help?"

"We think he was here on the tenth of last month, three weeks ago today. It would be a big help if I could take a look at the coverage for that night, if you still have it."

She raised her eyebrows. "Guess what? You're in luck, Mr Hawker."

"Paul."

"OK, Paul. This is your lucky day." She stooped to reach below the counter. Paul appreciated the view.

She straightened. "A couple of weeks ago we had the exact same request from another guy." She held up a compact disc in its plastic sleeve and put it on the counter. "An insurance man. We made this copy of the recordings for that night and gave it to him. He brought it back the next day. You can have it if you like."

Paul's eyebrows shot up. "Is it all on this one disc? The whole evening?"

"Uh-huh. There are four cameras and two screens, one in the manager's office and the other one here. They show all four pictures at the same time." With her index finger she outlined a square in the air. "You know, one in each quarter of the screen. You can come around this side and take a look, if you like."

"Thanks, I will." He made his way around to the back of the counter and stood behind her.

Gail pointed at the screen. "The two cameras on the left cover the left side of the building, the other two show the other side. It's a bit jerky 'cause the cameras take pictures every two seconds, but they're not bad." She tossed her head and the ponytail swung. "That's the good news."

"And the bad news is...?"

"The guy said he found nothing useful on the disc."

"Just the same, I'd like to give it a go." Paul picked up the disc. "What do I owe you for this?"

"Nothing, it's no use to us. It's just sitting on the shelf here."

"Well, if you're sure you don't need it any more. Thank you, I'm really grateful."

"No problem. When you've finished with it you can use it as a bird scarer. Or a frisbee, for all I care," she said dismissively.

He thanked her again and as he turned to leave she winked.

"Good luck. You can owe me a free investigation, if you like."

"It would be my pleasure," he replied.

Back in his study at home Hawker pored over the CCTV images on the disc, working steadily for nearly three hours and it was now after one o'clock in the morning. He sat back, blinked, took off his spectacles and rubbed his eyes. Then he picked up and drained his glass of scotch and soda.

The images were in monochrome and Paul surmised that would be because the cameras were used mainly at night. Monochrome worked better in poor light conditions. Gregory's people had found nothing, but Paul persevered, determined not to give up until he had checked every single frame, if necessary.

He looked at his notes. The tracker had arrived at the nightclub at 10:55 on the Saturday night, and it stopped transmitting at 01:35 on the Sunday morning. He had examined the footage minutely, frame by frame, backwards and forwards until finally, his efforts were rewarded. He noticed something which could be significant. He decided that he would go back to the nightclub's car park, to do a careful search of a particular parking bay that he had identified as being worth a closer look.

The following morning Hawker went back to the nightclub. As he expected, the car park was deserted, it was a Sunday morning, after all. He parked close to the bay in which he was interested and began to examine the tarmac surface closely. Three weeks had elapsed since the cameras had recorded the scene, but it was just possible that he might find what he was looking for. Worth a try, he thought. A few minutes later he bent down for a closer look at something, then knelt to pick it up. He straightened, examined it in the palm of his hand, and smiled in satisfaction.

Hawker returned to his office and made a quick telephone call to Detective Constable Eddie Smith.

"Sorry to trouble you on a Sunday, Eddie. Are you in your office?"

"Yes, but it's OK, I'm on duty anyway."

"Got a pencil handy?"

"Fire away," the young CID officer replied.

"Range Rover, about ten years old; I need the owner's details, but keep them to yourself, for now."

"OK, colour?"

"Sorry, I don't know."

"Registration number?"

Paul gave him the number. Then he said, "One more interview and I should be ready to fill you in on what I've discovered."

"You've found Tony Bellini?"

"Not exactly, but I think I'm getting close. You'll know soon enough."

Two days earlier Adam Ford had been winding up the board meeting. "Right," he said, "we can move on to the last item: Any Other Business." Seated at the end of the table his father Ray spoke up.

"Oh, good. Is this when I finally find out why you dragged me in? Don't get me wrong, guys," he said, looking around. "I love board meetings, just not every month, that's all."

Adam smiled broadly. "Absolutely. I have a surprise for you. He had several files on the desk in front of him and he moved one to the top. Then he turned to Samantha who was taking the minutes.

"Can you tell Summers to come in now, Sam?"

Samantha went over from the long table to Adam's desk and called Debbie on the intercom.

"Debbie, could you please ask Geoff to come to Mr Ford's office?"

CHAPTER TEN

A few minutes later Geoff entered Adam's office, which on this day as on the final Friday of every month, was being used as the boardroom. He had been given no reason as to why he was needed and he wondered if Adam had prepared some sort of gibbet for the public hanging he was expecting. If this circus had been organized for the previous board meeting, he might have been a tad apprehensive. Not now. They were either going to fire him, he thought, or not. They may even have found out about the secret project, but he was past caring. He felt strong because after what he had been through, nobody and nothing could hurt him. Certainly not this obnoxious, devious little sod.

Adam actually stood up. "Ah, Geoff, come in. Take a seat, please."

Did the man say "please"? And he used my name. Geoff was momentarily caught off guard. He looked at Samantha and saw the slightest hint of a shrug, and raised eyebrows.

"Thank you," was all Geoff said as he sat down. He noticed that Ken Lever was present; perhaps he was to be confirmed as the next production director? Who cares?

Adam swivelled his head and smiled at all present. "Gentlemen, thank you for your attention, I don't want to keep you but this won't take long. This is about our control panels."

Geoff heart skipped a beat but managed to keep a straight face. He had involuntarily tensed, but Ford's next statement relaxed him immediately.

"As you may know, I have been trying to find ways

to increase our margins. Well, Rod tells me that it would not be right to increase prices." He nodded towards Rod Thompson.

"Not unless you want sales to collapse," Thompson declared.

Adam smiled. "Understandable. But there are other ways, and cutting the costs of materials without compromising the quality of our product is what I have achieved." He beamed and looked around.

Sandy Macgregor put his elbows on the table. "News to me," he said.

Adam picked up a document and glanced at it. "Frankly gentlemen, this company appears to have been dragging its heels when it comes to making improvements in design, and especially sourcing cheaper and better components."

"Dragging our heels?" Geoff was the only one who spoke. With an edge in his tone he asked, "What do you mean?"

"I'll tell you *exactly* what I mean, Mr Summers." Ford held up the piece of paper. "On current levels of sales and production, we are going to save over twenty thousand pounds per annum, with no loss of quality or function." He lowered his hand and looked around; to Geoff it was clear that he was milking this moment.

"OK, tell us how," Ray Ford said from his seat at the end of the table. "I've been waiting all day for this."

Adam answered with a question. "Why are we still buying hardware from Sandersons? Eh?"

Geoff sat up. "Because they have worked with us

for years. Their products are the best; I can't recall ever having a problem, and they are totally reliable on delivery promises."

Adam sneered. "Don't you realize, Summers, that they have also been quietly creaming us for tens of thousands, every year." He paused for effect. "I've finally put a stop to *that*." Adam nodded towards Lever. "I authorized Ken to take one of our control panels to Stalmanns who took it apart and they have come up with alternatives, identical in function, that are a damned sight cheaper."

"What?" Geoff exclaimed. "The control panels are *my* design, worked out with a lot of help from Sandersons."

Adam Ford coloured. Raising his voice he said, "If you are suggesting that I have given away a trade secret, let me assure you that anyone, including Stalmanns, could easily acquire a panel from one of our customers, if they want to. You may have helped with the design, but to suggest it was a secret is absurd."

Ray Ford intervened. "Now let's just calm down. Geoff did not say that."

Geoff sat back and folded his arms across his chest. "But it's true, isn't it?"

Adam's eyes bulged. He slapped his hand down on the table. "All right, I'll make it crystal clear. The reason I asked you to attend this meeting is that I want you to use Stalmann components, starting today. Ken has details of their compatible part numbers."

Geoff unfolded his arms and leaned forward. "Has one of our panels been fitted with Stalmann components and if so, has it been tested?"

Adam looked across at Lever. "Ken? Can you confirm what we both already know?"

Ken Lever shuffled his papers. "Er, yes. Fully tested and guaranteed by them."

Adam inclined his head towards Geoff. "Are we satisfied now, Mr Summers?"

"Actually, no. We tested their components a couple of years ago and found that they were not totally reliable."

From the look on his face it was clear that Adam knew nothing about this. He shifted in his chair. "What do you mean?"

"Quite simply, they failed under continuous intensive testing; they were not one hundred percent reliable."

Ford had coloured again. He looked around. "Nothing is *one hundred percent* reliable."

Calmly Geoff said, "In our industry, anything less is unacceptable."

Adam seemed to have recovered his composure. "Given the savings to be made, as far as I am concerned ninety-nine point nine percent is acceptable. It would be irresponsible to turn our backs on the enormous benefit of increased profits."

Geoff did not answer. Adam continued, his tone calm and, Geoff thought, smug.

"Good. Now that's settled, you are to switch to Stalmann components as of now. Is that understood?"

Geoff nodded. "Understood. Just two things, Mr Ford. First, what do we do with existing stocks?"

CHAPTER TEN

Adam snorted. "I should have thought that is obvious. Keep them as spares. What was the other thing?"

Geoff said evenly, "Could I please have your instruction confirmed in writing?"

There was an audible gasp and one or two exchanged glances. Adam's eyes bulged again, and his answer was delivered in verbal icicles. "Since you think it necessary to question my judgment, my answer is yes." He stared at Geoff for a few moments. "Thank you for attending, Mr Summers, you can go now."

Geoff stood up and left without another word. Soon he would let his expertise speak for him, his day was coming. He breathed in deeply, savouring the thought and felt a distinct buzz as the adrenalin flowed through him. In the meantime he had something else on his mind, a bit of research into Stalmann Electronics.

CHAPTER ELEVEN

Geoff had to wait until the following Thursday to take the next step. He had no trouble finding Brian's place, a semi-detached house with a neatly lawned front garden, in a quiet street on a modern housing estate.

Brian came to the door and they went through into the kitchen, which was at the end of the entrance hall.

"Coffee?" Brian asked.

"Sounds good. Milk, one sugar, please."

The kitchen was a small efficiently laid out room adjacent to the dining area. Brian busied himself with making the coffee and Geoff's eye was drawn to a framed watercolour on the wall. It was an ethereal misty landscape, of a narrow boat on a canal. He walked over to take a closer look.

"This is good. Superb, who's the artist?"

"It's one of Jackie's, a canal lock in Leicestershire. At dawn."

"Really? She's very talented."

"Yes, she is. Why don't you take a look at the others in the dining room and I'll bring in the coffee."

When Brian came in Geoff was standing near the dining table admiring another landscape, this one featuring a pair of shire horses. Brian put a mug on the table.

"There you go, milk, one sugar."

"Thanks."

They had not met since the reception following the cremation service for Penny. Brian sat down and asked, "How are you managing?"

Geoff shrugged. "Oh, you know, good days and bad days. You?"

"I'm OK, my bad times are over, thank God. Now, you said something about wanting my advice? Though for the life of me I can't imagine why you should want my advice about anything."

Geoff pulled up a chair. "Well actually, it's your help I need rather than advice."

"How can I help?"

"That evening," Geoff said slowly, "when we had dinner in the restaurant with you and Jackie, it would have been a couple of weeks before..." he paused, "before Penny — before she died, do you remember what you told us about your former cellmate? Billy, wasn't it?"

Brian's eyebrows arched. "Yes, I suppose I do. What about him?"

"You told us that you went through hell because you were innocent and it was the blackest time of your life."

Brian grimaced. "It was."

"And you said that the one good thing that came out of it all was the bond of friendship you formed with Billy."

"He kept me sane. He believed me. After only a couple of days he said that it was obvious that I was innocent, I didn't belong. As he put it, I stuck out like a choirboy in a casino."

Brian picked up his coffee mug. "Look Geoff, what's this about?"

"There's something I need. Just a name, a contact, and I'm hoping that he can help. But I'll come to that in a minute. First, do you remember you told us that at the trial your boss Flynn and that copper had lied to frame you, but you thought that there was someone else involved? Why were you framed?"

Brian's expression hardened and he sat up. "The reason they framed me was because they wanted me out of the way. It didn't take long to figure out why."

"Well, it didn't seem to make any sense. Why did they want you out of the way?"

"Essex police had just made a major drugs arrest. Remember that? It was about two years ago, it was in all the papers."

Geoff nodded. "I remember."

"They got the stuff and the couriers, but nothing else. The newspapers said they were looking for the person or gang who had bankrolled the operation, and they were looking in Essex. I knew of course that Flynn went off to the Continent on short trips every few months, but at the time it never occurred to me that there might be a connection." He shrugged. "It was not unusual for him to move cash around, something he does often, quite legally."

Brian paused to take a sip from his mug. "A few days before, I happened to be in his office on my own and he came in. He went ballistic, accused me of snooping. He rushed to his desk and scooped up some papers. He said he'd fire me if I ever looked at his private papers again. As it happens I never even glanced at them, but I was staggered by his reaction. Over the top, well over the top, it made me think." He took another sip of coffee. "Anyway, a couple of hours later I had a phone call from a policeman. He said he wanted to talk to me about something and asked if he could see me at home that evening."

"Was it Rollo?"

Brian nodded. "You've guessed. He took my address and came to see me. Marie was out at the time. Rollo asked me some questions and to tell you the truth, I had no idea what he was on about. He wanted to know if I had any information about Flynn's business activities. He asked if there were any 'irregularities', and I told him that as far as I knew, it was a normal accountancy business."

"What happened then?"

"He said to get in touch with him if I found out anything suspicious about Flynn, especially about movements of large sums of money. He said there was an ongoing investigation and he advised me to make a statement, so that, as he put it, I would be 'covered' if anything came to light later. He took my statement and left."

"The statement that he said in court was a figment of your imagination."

"Yes. They were clever, no doubt about that. A couple of days after Rollo came to the house, Flynn told me that a set of documents was needed urgently by a client in Anguilla, a Mr Roberts. He said the papers were too sensitive to be trusted to couriers, so I was given the job. There and back in four days." He grimaced. "When I returned, I was arrested and charged with fraud."

"And you knew nothing about it?" Geoff said slowly, "Now I know why you want to find the money man. Didn't they open a bank account in Anguilla and put what – twenty-five grand into it?"

"That was done to coincide with my visit there. There was no client. A man phoned me at my hotel and said he was Roberts. He asked me to meet him at a cafe in the town and bring the documents with me." Brian shook his head. "I still can't believe what a mug I was. The whole thing cost somebody over twenty-five thousand to set up, I reckon, not counting whatever it cost to bribe the bank teller to testify that it was I who opened the account."

"A lot of money just to get you out of the way."

Brian's mouth turned down. "Not really, because they got most of it back. Flynn had transferred the money from a client's account direct to Anguilla using *my* office computer. After I was charged the money was returned to the client with an apology from the firm. That refund must have come from someone else, because Flynn doesn't have that sort of loose change, and I can't believe that Rollo has either. I'm guessing that after the trial the original stake would have been withdrawn from the bank in Anguilla and returned to the money man."

Geoff eyebrows arched. "Bastards!"

Brian shrugged. "So the client got his money back and an apology from the firm. The money man got *his* money back, and what *I* got was a jail sentence."

Neither spoke for a few moments. Then Brian held up his mug. "Another coffee?"

"Thanks." Geoff handed Brian his mug and rose to follow him into the kitchen, where he sat on a stool.

"So Flynn and Rollo must have been involved in the drugs thing?"

"Absolutely, but not on their own, it was too well organized. There *has* to be somebody else, the people who put the money up."

Brian rinsed out the cafetière, filled the electric kettle and switched it on. He opened the canister of ground coffee and began to spoon some into the vessel.

Geoff frowned. "Presumably one of Flynn's private clients. As a matter of fact, I know one who might fit the bill."

Brian looked up sharply, holding the spoon in mid air. "What? *You do?* Who is it?"

"I can't be sure, but it does seem possible."

"Who is it?" asked Brian, his voice raised. "*Who?*"

"I don't think you know him. His name is Adam Ford." The kettle hissed in the background but Brian ignored it.

"Adam Ford? Who the hell is Adam Ford?"

"As it happens, he's the managing director of the company I work for. I saw Kevin Flynn going into his office recently. I know he didn't have an appointment so I did a bit of digging."

"Wait a minute. Are you saying that *your boss* is a drug baron?"

"No, but what I am saying is that it is *possible* he may be involved. I've checked the facts. A few years ago he was in the construction business in Cyprus, made a lot of money in a short time. There was a scandal and he got out fast. Dozens of people lost money they had paid his company for villas which were not built, or not finished. What I *am* saying is that he is not a man of integrity."

194

"You think he's one of Flynn's private clients? I never heard Flynn mention anyone called Ford."

"I think it likely. What I discovered is that in Cyprus it is normal to have bank accounts in sterling and Turkish lire, a perfect situation for moving sterling directly to tax havens from a Cyprus branch of a Turkish bank."

"What? Now that's exactly the sort of thing Flynn could do." He filled the cafetière and turned to face Geoff.

"If you're right, is there any way can we prove it?"

Geoff shook his head. "I don't know. If it is true, it won't be easy to prove. I'm not even sure I know where to start. How many other people worked with you in Flynn's business?"

"It was a small outfit, six altogether including Flynn and myself. I really don't think any of the others would be involved, but I could be wrong."

Brian drew up a stool and sat down. Quite suddenly his face lit up.

"Wait a minute; I think I know someone who might be able to help." His lips parted into a crooked grin. "What's more, I think he might enjoy trying."

"Really?"

Brian nodded. "A journalist; he was in the courtroom at my trial. He came to see me in the nick, said it was obvious that I had been stitched up. He said he would try to help. He told me to write down my side of the story, everything I could remember, and that he would return a week later for a chat and to pick up my notes."

"What happened?"

"In the end, nothing. But he did come back and we went through it all, pretty much the same story I've just told you, but nothing came of it." He shrugged. "About a month later he came to see me again. He said that he hadn't been able to get any further, but that if I remembered anything else or found out anything which I thought might help, I should call him."

"Have you seen him again?"

Brian shook his head. "No, but I'm pretty sure he would like to hear about your Mr Ford. I'll call him and ask him to get in touch with you."

"Fine, what's his name?"

"Harry Mortimer. He used to be a senior crime reporter on the *News of the World,* but after a bust-up with the owners he transferred to a local weekly, the *East London Bugle*."

"That must have been quite a comedown."

"It happened after the phone hacking scandal. Apparently Harry unearthed stuff that his bosses didn't like. There was a huge row and they demoted him."

"Why didn't they just fire him?"

Brian shrugged. "I don't know, but I think he'd be a hard man to silence. It wouldn't surprise me if they just wanted him where they could keep an eye on him. He's his own man, and a bit of a loose cannon." Brian's expression changed to one of concern. "Just a thought, would this cause any problems for you at work?"

Geoff shook his head. "It doesn't matter; I won't be there much longer. And anyway, I won't be Geoff

Summers for much longer."

"What? What the hell are you talking about?"

"Funny you should ask," said Geoff grinning broadly. "It's to do with why I came to see you in the first place."

"You said you wanted my help with something?"

Geoff took a deep breath and looked straight into Brian's eyes.

"It's a long story but the bottom line is that I need a name, a contact," he said quietly. "Someone who could tell me where or how to get in touch with a team of professional burglars."

Brian sat bolt upright. "You need *what?*"

Geoff chose his words carefully. "This is really important to me, Brian. All I am asking is for a contact name or just the name of a place where I could try to get in touch ..."

Brian's eyes narrowed. "You're joking, right?"

Geoff shook his head. "No, I am perfectly serious."

Brian stood up, his temper rising. "You're mad. I want nothing to do with it, and if you think I would do anything to involve Billy..."

"Brian, wait," Geoff held up a hand. "That is exactly what I do *not* want. Not for you and certainly not for Billy, all I want is to know where I would need to go to have the best chance to make contact with them. I've heard that I could try a certain pub in Becton but I've no idea whether that's true."

"*Forget it!*" Brian was shaking his head, his teeth gritted and his face flushed. Placing his hands on the table he leaned forward and hissed, "You know

197

nothing, *nothing* about what it's like on the other side. You start asking questions in a place like that and you'd be lucky to make it back to the car park alive."

Geoff's mood hardened. "Do you really think I give a damn about what happens to me? I have lost my wife, the home we shared, my job and the twenty-two years spent working to make things better for us. The way I feel right now, nobody and nothing can hurt me. Believe me , I will do whatever it takes to get Adam Ford." He was breathing heavily. "And if it means taking a risk or two, so be it."

Brian sat down again, put his elbows on the table and drew his hands down his face.

"All right, all right," he said. "Look, Geoff, I know that you work in security. I think I can figure out what's going on here, and I can tell you that I absolutely do not want to know anything about it. But why don't you wait and see what my journalist friend uncovers, before you go off at half cock? You might get what you want without taking any stupid risks."

Geoff did not answer immediately. He needed time to think, but he felt that Brian was right, it would not hurt to see if the journalist could help. It seemed worth a try.

"Maybe you're right. How can I get in touch with him?"

"Better to leave it to me, I'll ask him." Brian moved to the sideboard and opened a drawer to remove a piece of paper and a pencil. "What's your mobile number?"

Geoff told him. "You'd better make a note that

I'm now John Jeffries, not Geoff Summers."

Brian smiled. "Jeffries, OK. How do you spell that?"

Geoff spelt the name out and Brian wrote it down, then asked if he had also changed his address.

"Yes. I'm selling the house; I can't live there any more, too many memories. I've moved into a small hotel. If you want to make a note, it's called Gamages and the address is 67 Elm Drive, Leigh on Sea, but I'm John Jeffries there, not Geoff Summers."

Geoff had already used the address, omitting the name of the hotel, when applying for a duplicate birth certificate for John Jeffries and it had arrived there only the day before.

"Sorry to keep you waiting," Elaine the receptionist apologized. "Mr Warwick shouldn't be too long now. Would you like another coffee?"

"No, thank you," Paul Hawker replied. Not her fault, he thought, that he had been sitting there for nearly twenty minutes. Typical of Jim Warwick to keep him waiting, even though when Paul had asked to see him it was Jim who had nominated the day and time and insisted that the interview had to be here. The appointment was scheduled for ten-thirty and Paul had arrived early, but he was not surprised. He picked up another motoring magazine from the coffee table and began flicking through the pages.

Elaine's phone rang. She picked up the handset and answered briefly before replacing the instrument.

"Mr Warwick will see you now. It's the last office on the left."

Paul thanked her, picked up his briefcase and made his way to Warwick's glass-walled office.

Jim waved him in and pointed to a chair. "Come in," he said briskly.

Paul sat down. "Good morning, Mr Warwick, thank you for seeing me."

Jim squared his shoulders, crossed his arms and thrust his chin out. He hunched forward on his desk, frowning and staring directly into Paul's eyes.

"I don't have too much time, and I really don't know any more than what I've already told you, the police and the insurance people."

Paul recognised the attempt to intimidate him. He ignored it, crossed his legs calmly and placed his notebook on his knee. "Just a couple of loose ends, it shouldn't take long."

Jim made a show of looking at his wristwatch. "Fire away."

Paul spoke softly. "Tony Bellini is missing and I have been hired by his family to try to find him." Jim Warwick nodded, saying nothing.

Paul checked his notebook. "He came to see you at your home on the evening of Saturday the tenth, and left just after seven."

"So?"

"It seems that neither he nor his car have been seen by anyone since he left your house."

Jim's eyes narrowed. "I know all this, and so do the police. What's your point?"

Paul looked at him steadily. "Did your meeting with Bellini have anything to do with the dossier I made on him for you?"

Warwick straightened, sitting bolt upright. His expression hardened and he waved a hand. "Of course it did. He lied to my daughter, conning her into believing he was rich, when as you know he was twenty grand in debt."

Hawker felt the slightest flicker of surprise. Was? *Warwick had used the past tense.*

He made a note in his book and asked, calmly, "So you confronted him with all this. What happened then?"

"I knew I could show him to be a cheap gold-digger," Jim said. He was breathing heavily. "The cheeky bastard came to ask if he could marry my Rosie. No way was I having *that*."

"Was there an argument?" Paul asked quietly.

"An argument? Bollocks to that. All I had to do was offer him money, which I did. He just took it and buggered off. Good riddance, end of story."

What? This was something Hawker had not expected to hear. He was certain that Jim Warwick was lying.

"Are you saying that you gave him money?"

Warwick's mouth shaped into a twisted grin. "What's the matter? You don't believe me?" Paul did not reply. Warwick swivelled in his chair, reached down and lifted his briefcase off the floor. He put the case on the desk, slid the lock catches and flipped the top open. From one of the document pockets in the lid he withdrew a cheque book, then pushed the case aside.

Warwick held the cheque book up. "This is my personal cheque book." He opened it and flicked through the stubs until he found the one he wanted. Keeping the book open with a thumb, he held it up to show it to Hawker.

"Twenty thousand pounds, to A. Bellini. Look at the date, the tenth of last month." He leaned towards Hawker and thrust the cheque book forward. "Take a good look."

Paul Hawker looked at the cheque stub and nodded slowly. He sat back.

"Has it been cashed?"

"Not yet, as far as I know, but I don't give a shit. Not my problem." In a tone dripping with sarcasm Warwick sneered. "As you see, quite a few cheques written after that date, so if that stub ain't genuine, that's some trick." He closed the cheque book, slammed it down on the desk and snarled, "Explain *that,* mister investigator!"

Paul Hawker drove back to his office unhurriedly, deep in thought. He had more than enough circumstantial evidence to convince him that Jim Warwick had been lying, but the cheque was a surprise. It did not make sense; it did not fit into the picture that was emerging.

Without solid proof to back his suspicions, he could not risk a direct confrontation with the man. In effect his enquiry had hit a wall. He decided that he had no choice; it was time to involve Eddie Smith. He knew that the detective constable did not trust his boss Frank Rollo, therefore involving Eddie could make serious trouble for him. Still, Paul thought grimly, he had no choice now, it would be Smith's problem and he would have to find his own way around it.

Journalist Harry Mortimer stirred under the duvet, his slumber disturbed by noises from the kitchen. His partner Stella was bustling around, preparing breakfast.

"Harry," she called through the open door, "you up yet?"

"Uhhh," he moaned, pulling the duvet down just far enough to expose only his head. Two clumps of tousled hair above his ears decorated each side of the bald pate between. With his wrinkled brow and bags under his half-shut eyelids, Harry Mortimer sometime ace crime reporter, bore more than a passing resemblance to a weary turtle.

He watched as Stella moved to the kitchen door and looked towards the bedroom. She raised her voice.

"*Harry*, time to get up, I'm putting the coffee on."

He was awake now, not quite fully alert but conscious, and watched contentedly as she moved across the open doorway in her floral housecoat. He was awake enough to appreciate the slight shapely figure and pretty oval face, which he knew would be moving between the fridge, the worktop and the two-seater wooden table, getting things ready.

She called out again. "Cereal? Or toast? In case you need reminding, it's Sunday. You feel like some cereal? Or toast? Or if you feel like a fry-up, I can do that instead."

Better, he thought, much better than I deserve.

Not just attractive, but loving and considerate. Definitely better than I deserve. She had asked what he felt like and he was sure that whatever his answer, it would appear on the table within minutes. Trouble was, some mornings he just felt like shit. He smiled to himself. Not a joke he could share with her. Harry pushed the duvet aside, sat up, yawned, and scratched an armpit.

"I'm not hungry, pet, maybe just a couple of eggs." He rubbed his face and yawned again as full consciousness returned. "And some bacon, plus a few bits on the side."

"Full English fry-up, then."

He stood up and padded across to the kitchen door. "Maybe just the one egg, got to watch my weight."

"Full English with one egg." She pointed with a butter knife at the considerable bulge above his striped boxer shorts. "But if you're serious about reducing *that*, you could start by cutting down on the beer."

He was about to protest when they heard the melodic call of his mobile phone.

"Oh shit. Surely not the bloody office, on a Sunday." He turned to return to the bedside table where he had left the phone.

Stella said, "Make it quick, this'll be ready in five minutes."

Harry slouched on the bed and picked up the phone.

"Hullo," he said in a flat tone.

"Is that Mr Harry Mortimer?"

"The one and only, who's asking?"

"Brian Hammond."

Now who the hell is Brian Hammond? Harry wondered.

"Brian Hammond. The one who got stitched up by Flynn and Rollo, the bent copper. You came to see me in the nick."

The wheels clicked into place. "Ah! Brian. Yes, I remember. How are you, dear boy?"

"I'm fine. You said to get in touch if there were any developments. You said that my case was the tip of an iceberg. A big story waiting to be uncovered."

Harry promptly sat up. "What have you got for me?"

"A possible lead on the man who bankrolled the stitch-up."

"Aha. That's good. Just a minute, I'll get my notebook."

The notebook and a pen were within reach on the bedside table beside his two spectacles cases. He picked up the book, pen and his reading glasses and padded back to the kitchen. Stella was standing by the cooker, with a frying pan in one hand and holding an egg up in the other.

Harry cupped the phone in his fist and whispered, "Sorry, love, I've got to take this."

Stella sighed and rolled her eyes. With the frying pan she pointed to a chair.

"Sit. I'll get you a coffee."

"You're an angel," he whispered as he sat down at the table. He took his reading glasses out of their case and put them on. Sweeping the cutlery aside

CHAPTER ELEVEN

with a forearm he put the book down and picked up
the pen.

"OK, I'm ready."

"Right. Actually it's quite a long story, better face
to face. Can we meet? I work in a public library in
Hackney, but I'm off all day on Thursdays. Can I
come to your office at the paper?"

"Er...no, not at the paper, too many ears, old son.
Anyway I don't have a separate office there and even
if I did, we would still have ear trouble."

"Can you come to the library? It's the one on
Church Street. Any day except Thursday, I can take a
tea break when you turn up."

Harry thought for a moment. "How about
Tuesday? Day after tomorrow, say mid-morning?"

"Tuesday morning's fine."

"Good, I'll see you there, then."

CHAPTER TWELVE

Paul Hawker looked at the young CID officer sitting across the desk from him. Eddie Smith was wearing an expectant look on his boyish face.

"You did say to come over to see you in my own time, didn't you?" Smith asked.

"Yes, thanks for coming," Hawker replied. "Fact is, I have a bit of a problem.

"How can I help?"

"I've made some progress on the Bellini case, and..."

"You *have?*" Smith interrupted. "Fantastic!"

Hawker waited a few seconds for Smith's exuberance to abate. "Yes. As I was saying, I've made a bit of progress but don't get too excited, there's a problem. I've uncovered some evidence that points in a certain direction. But it's only circumstantial and that's the problem."

"Circumstantial? Is that why you wanted me to come in unofficially?"

Paul Hawker nodded. "Yes. Right now I can't take it any further, but if I pass what I have on to your people, *you* know where it will finish up."

Smith pulled a face. "Rollo. It'll end up on his desk. Or buried under something else on his desk, more like."

"Exactly."

Smith seemed crestfallen. "What do you want to do?"

Hawker had a DVD in its plastic sheath on the desk and beside it, a brown padded envelope. He pulled them forward.

"Let's take a look at what we've got, then we can decide how to play it. Did you know that Tony Bellini's car was fitted with a tracker?"

"No, I didn't. Not much I do know, I've not been allowed to see the file. Don't tell me you've actually traced the car?"

"Well, yes and no. I haven't found the car, but I've been able to follow the track. All the way, until it stopped transmitting on the night that Bellini disappeared. Looks like the tracker was moved into another vehicle."

Smith perked up. "The Range Rover?"

"Uh-huh."

"Owned by a Mr Shaun Conroy, as I found out. I was tempted to follow it up but I didn't, like you asked. But I did do a quick routine check on him. Nothing on record except an affray, a street punch-up a long time ago. Anyway, I'm guessing that you are going to tell me what this is all about."

"I don't know at this stage what it's *all* about, but I think I know where it's heading." Paul came straight to the point. "Have you heard of Jim Warwick?"

"Of Warwick Motors? Everybody knows him. Hobnobs with the assistant chief constable, they are Masons in the same lodge. Why?"

Paul chose his words carefully. "I think he may be directly involved in the disappearance of Tony Bellini."

"What? *Warwick*? Are you sure?"

"Yes, but proving it is another matter. Anyway, I'd be surprised if the driver of the Range Rover isn't one of his employees. The tracker was in Bellini's Audi, which went to Warwick's house early in the evening that he disappeared. Later the same evening it turned up at a nightclub in Rainham, in the Range Rover. On the way it made a stop at a car body repair place owned by Warwick."

"Bloody hell!"

Hawker then explained how he had obtained details of the track from Bellingham Leasing and how he had followed it through to the car park of the Stars and Stripes, where he had acquired the CCTV disc. He picked it up. "And here it is."

Eddie Smith was clearly impressed. Eyes wide, he asked incredulously, "Are you telling me that's the actual CCTV disc for that night? How did you get hold of it?"

Hawker smiled. "Hard work, charm and a bit of luck." He inserted the disc into the DVD tray of the computer and started it up. He swivelled the screen on the desk so that they could view it together. "What I discovered took a bit of finding. I had to trawl through all the footage from all the cameras but it was worth it. This is not the original disc; it's a copy that shows just the bits we need to look at, the interesting bits."

"You still have the original?"

"Of course, and you can have a copy if you wish. We'll talk about that after you've seen what's on here. That's why I asked you to come around unofficially."

Paul started the programme and an image appeared on the screen. In shades of grey it was a view of a car park at night, illuminated by floodlights at high level.

He explained. "There are two car parks, one on each side of the building. Two cameras cover each of the two. This footage is from the ones that cover the west side." He pointed to the date and time display.

"This was the view at precisely 22:54 on the night of Saturday the tenth."

Eddie Smith peered at the screen. "Quite a big place. And it's nearly full."

"Yes, but there are some spaces at the far end, here." Paul pointed.

The screen flicked to another view. "Now take a look at the entrance just here," he said, pointing again. "A Range Rover appears, followed closely by an Escort van."

Smith moved closer to stare at the screen. "Aha, so this is the one?"

Paul nodded. "Yes. As you see it goes to the very end on the far side, and pulls up right in the corner, nose in to the wall in the last space. Lots of closer places available, so it looks like they chose that one on purpose, well out of the way. Just as well really, considering what I found there later." He paused. "Look, the Escort van stops alongside. Then you see the Rover driver gets out and locks it. See the hazard lights winking?"

Eddie nodded, clearly fascinated, and Paul went on. "He gets into the van on the passenger's side. The van turns around and leaves the car park."

"Leaving the tracker still working?"

"Yes. And it kept going for about another two and a half hours."

Paul moved the image fast forward and stopped it to show the same view later.

"It's now 1:34 a.m. Some cars have left and we see others which were not there earlier."

He pointed. "Look at the entrance again, the same Escort van comes into shot and heads for the Range Rover." They watched the action. "Now it's pulling up alongside. The passenger gets out of the van and goes to the back of the car. Same man who parked it earlier."

Eddie Smith stared intently at the screen. "He's opened the tailgate."

"Now watch. He's reaching into the boot. This is the really interesting bit."

Moments later Smith exclaimed, "Look, look at this! He's thrown something on the ground *and he's stamping on it.*"

Paul Hawker grinned. "One dead tracker."

Eyes rivetted to the screen, Smith watched as the man bent down, hurriedly picked up something and put it into his pocket. "He's picking up the bits."

The man on the screen glanced around briefly, then climbed into the Rover.

"Not quite all the bits," said Hawker quietly, as they watched both vehicles driving off.

"What?"

Hawker picked up the brown envelope and shook it gently. A small, dirty shard of black plastic fell out onto the desk. It was about five centimetres long and two wide, with a stained piece of plastic stuck to it. He picked it up and held it in the palm of his hand.

"He left this behind. It's part of the tracker's

casing."

The detective constable's eyes widened. "Bloody hell," he exclaimed, "*bloody hell*!"

Twenty minutes later Eddie Smith put his notebook away. Hawker had told him about his interview with Warwick, covering every detail.

Smith sighed audibly. "To be honest I don't know what the hell to do. This is dynamite, in more ways than one."

"Yup," Hawker agreed. "Warwick's cheque stub is genuine all right, of that I am sure. And he is definitely involved in Tony Bellini's disappearance."

"You didn't ask him if the cheque has been presented?"

Hawker shrugged. "Yes, I did. He said not yet, but it didn't bother him one way or another. Anyway it's something I can't follow up. Your lot could, you have the clout to look at his bank account and I don't. The cheque book was from the Midwest, Brentwood branch."

Smith looked grim. "OK, I'll ask you straight. Do you want me to take this all on board officially, as a CID officer?"

Paul rubbed his chin. "Well, it's your call. Like I said, it's all circumstantial. Not a shred of hard evidence to implicate Warwick and not a lot to definitely nail Conroy, or the driver of the van. Though I suppose you could lean on them, forensics on the vehicles and all that. My guess is that they went off together to get rid of something in the van."

"A body?"

Hawker shrugged. "Your guess is as good as mine. Anyway, as far as I'm concerned, my investigation has hit a wall and I can't move it further. For me now, it's simply a question of whether or not I pass on what I know to the police."

"Rollo is the officer on the case and I can't see him doing anything about it," Smith replied, glumly.

"If I don't pass it on, it all stops here and we will probably never know the whole truth."

Smith shook his head. "I just can't let that happen. I *can't*. I'm a copper and I have to look at myself in the mirror every morning. Rollo's going to make my life hell, but in conscience I really don't have a choice. I'll take it, officially. I have to."

Paul Hawker smiled. "Good for you."

"You're a hard bloke to get hold of these days," Geoff said to his old friend Horrie the Fixer who was sitting across the table from him in the cafe.

"Nonsense. You can get hold of me whenever you like, just ask anyone. But I'm here now and so are you." Horrie waved a hand over his plate. "Like I said, a good masala dosa washed down by a glass of cold mango lassi is more than enough reason to bring you across town to Wembley." He picked up the glass to gulp down a mouthful of the beverage. "But if it's just info you want, we could have done it over the phone, saved you the journey."

Geoff saw that his friend had not lost his fondness for the Indian curried pancake roll.

"You're right about the dosa. And it's good to see you again."

Horrie da Silva grinned. It was a wide smile, full of perfect white teeth.

"You too, man. You're looking good. Keeping up with the hockey?"

Geoff shook his head. "To be honest, I haven't played for years, far too old now."

"Rubbish. Look at me, forty-five and they still wheel me out sometimes. But I guess, mainly to frighten the shit out of young hotshots."

"You were some full-back. Best road block in the game."

"I seem to remember that you were no slouch yourself. But the game's changed since we played together. These days full-backs are actually expected to run around." He grinned again. "Not something I'm good at any more." He pushed his plate aside and looked up. "Now, young man, what can I do for you?"

Geoff looked evenly at the man whom he had first met nearly twenty-five years earlier. The years had been kind to him, he reflected. Under the neatly parted greying hair, the lightly pock-marked brown face was unlined, the sort of face people were inclined to trust instinctively. Horrie had built a good business importing Indian artefacts and silks into the UK.

In his community Horrie was known as "Horrie the Fixer". He had declined overtures from political parties seeking to gain influence with voters of Asian origin, and remained from choice, an independent councillor in North London. Geoff knew that Horrie da Silva was undoubtedly the man to ask about passports.

"I'm looking for a bit of information, but it's not the sort of thing I could comfortably ask over the phone."

Horrie sat back. He gestured. "You know me. If I can help, I will."

Geoff knew that the law now required any adult applying for a first passport to attend an interview. Posting a copy of a birth certificate would by itself, no longer suffice. He leaned forward, lowering his voice.

"I need a new passport, a good, clean one."

Horrie's eyes widened. "Come again? You need a new passport, but *not* through the usual channels?"

Geoff nodded. "Can you help?"

Horrie's mouth twisted into a crooked grin. "You old rascal." He raised a hand, palm outwards. "Don't say another word; I don't want to know why." Then he shook his head. "Sorry, mate, I can't help you, but I know a man who might be able to. Got pen and paper?"

Geoff reached into his jacket and withdrew his notebook and a ballpoint pen.

Horrie leaned forward. "Prakash Pharmacy, Green Lane, Kilburn. He does the best passport photos."

As Geoff started to write, Horrie said, "The best *photos*. For the other you will need to ask." Horrie spelt it out. "That's P-R-A-K-A-S-H."

"Thanks ..."

Horrie raised a hand again. "Wait, you'll need one of these."

He reached into his hip pocket and took out a fat

leather wallet. From the wallet he removed one of his business cards, turned it over and scrawled his signature on the back.

"Also a few hundred in cash, I don't know exactly how much. Prakash is a careful man, but he knows my signature."

He pushed the card across the table. "And I'm careful too. Very careful. Good luck with whatever it is you're up to."

Prakash's was an ordinary chemist's shop, a typical high street pharmacy. Geoff entered and made his way past display cabinets on each side of a wide aisle to a counter at the rear, where an elderly Asian man was serving a customer. Behind him a younger man, assisted by a girl, was engaged in making up packs of prescription drugs.

"Your medications, Mrs Gibbs," said the old man, handing the customer a paper bag. "See you again next time." She thanked him and turned to leave.

Over half-moon spectacles perched at the end of his long, narrow nose the man looked up at Geoff.

"Yes, sir?"

"I'd like a passport photo, please."

The man inclined his head. "Passport photo. Yes, of course." He lifted a horizontal wooden flap at the end of the counter. "This way, please. The camera is in the next room."

Geoff followed him into the room, where the man flicked on a light switch. Geoff saw that to one side were a desk and chair, behind which shelves were stacked untidily with books and papers. In the centre of the room a camera on a tripod had been set up to face a side wall. The man went over to the wall and drew down a white roller blind, then pulled forward a stool.

"Sit, please," he said.

Geoff perched on the stool. "Are you Mr Prakash?"

The man was checking and adjusting the camera. "Yes, that is me."

Geoff reached into his jacket pocket and took out Horrie Da Silva's card. "I need a passport," he said quietly.

Immediately Prakash stiffened. Without turning around he said, "This is a photo room, sir, I am not able to do that."

Geoff leant forward and held out the card. "Will this help?"

Prakash took the card and lifted his chin to peer through his spectacles. He turned it over and studied the signature on the back, then nodded. "You have birth certificate?"

Geoff took it out and held it forward. "I have it here, but I can't leave it."

The man took the document from Geoff. For the first time, he smiled.

"No need. We do not keep any information about clients, Mister, er..." He looked down to read the name on the document. "Jeffries. I am just needing date and place of birth."

Prakash moved to the desk where he noted on a pad the details he needed.

"It is seven hundred pounds, cash. Five now, the

rest when you collect."

"Can you send it on to me by registered post?"

Prakash shook his head. "No, I am sorry that is not possible." He moved over to the wall and turned on a switch, flooding the stool and its occupant with light, before returning to the camera to view the image.

"You must collect. We do not keep address or any other information. Sit up please and look straight ahead." Geoff did so and the shutter clicked.

"Good," said Prakash. "One more please." The shutter clicked again.

Geoff stood up. "When will it be ready?"

"Ten days. Don't phone, just come, in ten days it is ready."

Geoff understood. Horrie was right, Prakash was indeed a careful man. He counted out the money, handed it over and left.

The Golden Fleece was the sort of public house not much seen since the seventies. The fifteen minutes during which he had been waiting at the bar had been time enough for Geoff to look around and conclude that this was almost an old-fashioned "spit and sawdust" establishment. The sort that offered its patrons alcohol, bagged potato crisps and a limited selection of tired-looking sandwiches only. No other food, neither hot nor cold. Were it not for the outside courtyard to which the smokers repaired with their pint glasses, Geoff mused, it would probably have closed down when the smoking ban was introduced.

PAYBACK

Geoff was perched on a stool with two pint mugs of beer on the bar before him. The man he awaited could be short or tall, thin or fat, Geoff had no idea what he looked like. During their brief telephone conversation Harry Mortimer nominated this place for their meeting and Geoff had asked how they could recognize one another.

"No problem," Harry had said. "I'll know you immediately. You'll be the guy sitting by himself at the bar with two beers in front of him, one for yourself and a Yorkshire bitter for me."

Geoff positioned himself so that he had a good view of the front door, wondering if he would be able to guess which incoming patron would be Harry Mortimer. In the event it was not difficult. A large man wearing a creased brown leather jacket, brown corduroy trousers and heavy spectacles under a grey trilby hat shambled into the room and looked around. It had to be him. The man acknowledged Geoff with a nod and came over. Geoff slipped off his stool, stood up and held out his hand.

"Mr Mortimer?"

"The same," he replied, taking Geoff's hand.

Harry picked up his beer mug immediately. "So kind," he said, gulping down a good third of the contents. "Ah, that's better," he said. "Now let's find a pew."

Geoff led the way to an unoccupied table in a corner of the room where they sat down, putting their mugs on the table. Harry removed his hat and placed it carefully on the table beside his beer. Then he looked up, smiled, and came straight to the point.

CHAPTER TWELVE

"Now, sir, I believe you are looking for a firm in the unauthorised removals business."

Geoff smiled at the journalist's colourful choice of words but was slightly taken aback.

"Don't you want to talk about Adam Ford?"

Harry waved a hand in the air. "Tut, forget him; I am not interested in mister Adam Ford. I've checked him out. An unscrupulous rat, I grant you, but a drug baron he is not, oh no. No contacts for supply or distribution, no evidence at all. Plus a guy like him wouldn't have the balls." Dismissively he added, "In my view he's small fry. No story there."

He stopped to swill down another mouthful of beer, while Geoff found himself staring, fascinated, at the bald dome decorated by the tufts of growth above the ears.

Harry put his mug down again, sat back and steepled his fingers.

"Now tell me your *other* story, much more interesting."

Quite suddenly Geoff felt uncomfortable. He needed this man to get the information he wanted, but he was after all, talking to a newspaper reporter who was looking for a big story.

He hesitated. "I don't know how much Brian has told you."

"Tell me why you want the removal firm. From the beginning in your own words, Geoff. I think I know what you want but I would like to hear it from *you*. I know that you work for a security company, and the managing director is one Adam Ford. Tell me the rest."

"To be honest," Geoff said slowly, "I'm not exactly sure where to begin. You've checked out Adam Ford. What did you call him? An unscrupulous rat?" Mortimer nodded.

Geoff leant forward. "He's ruined my life. I have the chance to get even and I will not rest until I have brought him down."

"I understand. But there's something you should know. The sort of people you want to contact would slit your throat and dump you in the Thames without blinking, if it suits them. But *I* can talk to them, because they know that I am not a threat. Nothing to do with trust, they don't trust anybody, but they know I can be useful to them, and sometimes I am."

He picked up his mug, took another swig and put it down.

"It's like this," he said evenly, wiping his mouth with the back of his hand. "Brian knows you, and he says you are on the level. I believe him. Enough anyway, to make me want to hear more. So now I want *you* to tell me what happened, from the beginning. If I buy it, I may – and I say, *may* – be able to get you a meet with the sort of firm you are seeking. After that," he waved a hand, "you're on your own, at least until you get a result. If you do and are still alive to tell the tale, I'll be around. You can be sure of that."

Geoff nodded. "OK." He needed a few moments to think. He stood up and pointed at Harry's glass, although it was still a third full.

"A refill?"

"How kind." Harry picked up the vessel and

CHAPTER TWELVE

drained it.

Geoff made his way to the bar. Yes, he thought, Harry Mortimer did seem to be in a position to give him the information he wanted, but Harry needed to be convinced that Geoff was serious. On reflection he supposed that it was not really surprising, ordinary law-abiding citizens do not suddenly become criminals. At least not without good reason. Well, there was more than enough reason. He decided that he had nothing to lose; he would tell the man the whole story, making it clear to Mortimer that if he did not help him he would find his own way to the right people, regardless of the consequences.

Later Geoff went to see Roger Mantle, his solicitor. Mantle was the man who had dealt with the legal formalities when Geoff and Penny moved to their new home.

"It's good to see you again Mr Summers," he said. "Is your wife well?"

The direct question unsettled Geoff. "My wife– my wife had a brain operation recently which was not successful. She has passed away."

The solicitor's face changed instantly. "Oh, I am sorry to hear that. I am really very sorry," he said. "Such a lovely young lady. Please accept my sincere condolences. And of course, I am here to help in any way if you should need me."

"Thank you," said Geoff quietly. "I've sold the house; I just can't live there any more. Could you deal with the legal side for me, please? Everything has been cleared out, it was sold with vacant possession."

"No problem, we shall be pleased to act for you. In fact, I've already had a notice of sale from the estate agent. It arrived a few days ago, so I guessed that you had probably told them that you would be instructing us.

Geoff smiled. "Estate agents are usually quick off the mark." He reached into his pocket, took out a piece of paper and handed it to Mantle. "This is my mobile number, and details of my bank account. I'm in temporary accommodation at the moment so if you need me, please give me a call. I'll be staying in the area for the next few weeks at least."

"I shall need you to sign the contract. Have you notified the utilities?"

"All done, in writing. I've also given them your contact details. I think there should be around thirty thousand or so left over after costs." Geoff grimaced. "Not a lot, considering the value of the house. But I just wanted a quick sale."

"Understandable, in the circumstances. May I ask, what are your plans?"

"Nothing firm. I could do with some time off. I'm thinking of taking a trip to see Penny's sister and her family in Australia. After that, who knows?"

They were finished, so Mantle stood up. They shook hands and Geoff left, wondering how long it would be before Roger Mantle would be asked if he knew where Geoffrey Summers had fled to. He smiled to himself. Australia's a pretty big country.

Geoff was in his office later when he had a call from Rod Thompson.

"Geoff? Rod."

"Yes, Rod."

"You OK?"

"Yeah, fine. What can I do for you?"

"Jim Warwick just called, he's accepted our quote."

"That's good. Does he want the extras for the garage?"

"It's one of the things he wants to discuss. He says he's ready to order, but wants to clear up a couple of things first."

"Sounds like you were right, he just wants a bit off the bottom line. I'm guessing you want me along?"

"If that's OK with you."

"When are you seeing him?"

"The appointment's for tomorrow morning, at eleven. Sorry about the short notice but the guy insisted. He said he's out of the country next week and he wants to sort it now. Can you make it? If there's a problem I can ask Danny to go with me, but I'd be happier if it is you. It's one of your designs."

Geoff had planned to go to London the next morning but he knew he could postpone his business there.

"Yes, I can make it, no problem. What time do you want to leave?"

"About half past nine. OK for you?"

"Fine, I'll be ready."

The next morning they made good time, pulling up outside the gates of Warwick Hall ten minutes early. Geoff watched as Rod leaned forward and pressed the intercom button. When it responded, he answered. "Rod Thompson and Geoffrey Summers, Melford Electronics. We have an appointment with Mr Warwick."

"Just a minute." A brief pause. "Come in, please. End of the drive."

The metallic voice clicked off. The gates squealed open and gravel crunched as they drove towards the office extension.

Clive held the glass door open for them and took them to Warwick's office. The man himself was seated at the desk, studying the image on his laptop. Without taking his eyes off the screen, he raised an arm to acknowledge their presence.

"Take a seat. Be with you in a minute," he said.

Geoff chose a corner of the settee and placed his document folder on the low coffee table. On the other side of the table Rod sank into one of the two armchairs and put his briefcase on the floor beside him.

They did not have long to wait. After a minute or so Jim closed his laptop, picked up a folder off his desk and crossed the room to join them. He sat down in the vacant arm chair and opened the folder.

"Right," he said briskly. "Time for a reality check. Let's take another look at your quote."

Geoff glanced at Rod, who smiled crookedly and rolled his eyes.

For the next ten minutes Jim and Rod went through the details of the quotation together, with Geoff contributing little to the discussion. He watched fascinated, as he observed Jim's repeated attempts to intimidate Rod, all of which failed. Rod stayed calm and polite, ignoring Warwick's boorish manners. Jim Warwick appeared increasingly frustrated at his failure to dominate the proceedings; he was not getting his own way.

Finally Warwick closed his document folder, tossed it onto the table and sat back.

"That's it then," he said. "If you really want my business you are going to have to move on the final figure. If you don't I'll have to re-consider."

Rod Thompson smiled. "Of course we want your business. We wouldn't be here if we didn't." He shifted slightly in his chair. "I've met a few tough negotiators in my time," he said, inclining his head. "But you, Mr Warwick, are one of the toughest. I take my hat off to you."

Geoff squirmed inwardly, but the immediate change in Warwick's demeanour showed that the crude flattery had worked. Warwick relaxed and within a few minutes he added the optional items to the order in exchange for a small reduction in the price.

From his folder Warwick took out a cheque book. He filled in and signed one, which he handed to Thompson.

"Here's your deposit. It's a personal cheque. As I told you, I don't want to put the order through Warwick Motors. Your invoice should be made out to me and sent direct to my personal accountant."

"Thank you," said Rod.

"I'll get you his card," said Warwick, making his way back to his desk. He drew open the middle drawer and took out two business cards. Rod and

Geoff were standing by the coffee table, waiting to take their leave and Warwick handed a card to each. Geoff put the card into the file he was holding and thought no more about it.

Detective Constable Eddie Smith paused at the door to collect his thoughts. His boss Sergeant Frank Rollo was at his desk in the open plan CID office, working on a file.

Eddie approached Rollo with some trepidation but he steeled himself. This had to be done.

"Sorry to interrupt, Frank, but can I have a word?"

Rollo looked up and to Smith's surprise, he smiled.

"Yeah, sure," he said. "Just closing this file. The school break-ins. I've found bloody big holes in two of the witness statements. Got the bastards," he declared.

Smith understood why Rollo was in a good mood. There had been a succession of burglaries at a local school and the Chief had been on the receiving end of a verbal assault from a county councillor. She had berated him for what she called the "unbelievable incompetence" of his CID officers, whom she referred to as "Keystones". If Rollo had just uncovered anomalies in witness statements, it was no wonder he was in a good mood.

"That should please the Chief," Smith said.

"Yeah and get him off our backs. Now, mate, what can I do for you?" Rollo asked cheerfully.

"It's about the Bellini case..."

Frank Rollo's mood changed instantly. He threw his arms up.

CHAPTER TWELVE

"Oh shit, not *that* again. How many more times do I have to tell you to *butt out?*" He turned away from his subordinate, waving a hand dismissively. "Bugger off and sort out the fucking traffic, or something."

Smith stood his ground. He tried to control his anger, quietly but firmly saying, "There's new evidence. I think we need to look at it."

Rollo sat up. "*Evidence?* Where would *you* get evidence? You've been told not to get involved. Are you deaf or stupid, or maybe looking for an official reprimand?"

Smith had had enough. He held up the DVD in its sleeve and spoke through clenched teeth.

"See this? *This* is evidence. Have you heard of a man called Shaun Conroy?"

Rollo appeared astonished at this outburst. "No. Who is he?"

"An ex-boxer and nightclub bouncer, muscle for hire. This is a CCTV disc. It shows him trashing the tracker from Bellini's car the night he disappeared."

Rollo was momentarily visibly shaken, but he seemed to compose himself.

Truculently he asked, "So?"

The background hubbub of the office had fallen silent. In his peripheral vision Eddie Smith noticed that several of their colleagues were now following this exchange with interest. Within the next few seconds he would discover for certain whether Rollo had been deliberately blocking an enquiry into Bellini's disappearance, and crucially, whether his actions had anything to do with Jim Warwick. Smith locked his gaze on his superior, then raised his voice slightly, speaking slowly.

"You say you don't know Conroy, but have you heard of his boss?" He paused for effect. "Mr Jim Warwick?"

Rollo's eyes widened and his jaw dropped open. It was as if he had been struck in the face with a brick. "You– he– there must be a mistake," he stammered. "Where did you get that?"

Bingo, thought Eddie. He had his answer and he smiled thinly in satisfaction.

"No mistake, Frank, absolutely no mistake."

With a lightning fast movement bordering on raw panic, Rollo lunged forward and snatched the disc from Smith's hand.

"Give me that," he said hoarsely.

"Certainly," Smith replied. "You'll need it. I brought it in to hand over to you, because it's your case." He reached into his jacket and withdrew an envelope.

Placing it on the desk in front of Rollo he said, "You'll need this too. It's my full report. Oh, and don't worry too much if the disc gets accidentally mislaid, there are copies."

Ashen faced and with sweat beading on his brow, Rollo picked up the envelope and slowly began to open it. Eddie Smith felt it was a good time to leave the office. As he strode out he saw that his colleagues had turned away from Rollo, nobody was looking at him now. Several were smiling and a few nodded to Eddie as he passed.

The next morning Chief Superintendent Andy Powell

was seated behind his desk, looking up at the young detective constable who stood before him. Powell was trying not to show his true feelings. There was a look of apprehension on Eddie Smith's boyish face. He probably believed that he had been summoned to receive a reprimand, Powell thought. But the Chief Superintendent had been impressed by Smith's tenacity and the initiative he had displayed.

Powell put on a grave face. "By all accounts, that was quite a scene you made yesterday, Smith."

"Yes, sir. I'm sorry, sir."

"What have you got to say for yourself? Eh?"

Smith's face displayed his abject misery. He appeared unable to articulate an excuse. Instead, he blurted, "I deserve a bollocking, sir. Sorry, sir."

Powell nearly choked in his effort to keep a straight face. He swivelled his chair to one side and put his hand over his mouth. Taking a few moments to recover his composure he feigned a cough, before turning the chair around again.

"If you had misgivings about your immediate superior, you should have come to me."

"Yes, sir."

"Now I want to know, where did you get the CCTV disc?"

"A private investigator, sir, Paul Hawker, he has an office in Towngate. He gave it to me. He's working for Bellini's parents."

Powell had heard of Hawker, but had never met him.

"I see." He stood up. "Well, Smith, you can go now. But I want you to stay out of this case, I'm taking it on."

"Yes, sir," said Eddie, visibly relieved. He turned to leave but as he reached the door, Powell said, "One other thing."

Smith turned around. "Sir?"

"Well done for keeping at it, and for getting the information."

Eddie Smith beamed. "*Thank you,* sir."

"Off you go. And on your way out ask Laura to come in, will you?"

The chief superintendent sat down and reached for his desk diary. He would ask the WPC to find a contact telephone number for Paul Hawker, whom he wanted to meet. He also wanted to make an appointment to see the assistant chief constable, Charles Haddow. He needed to talk to both those people for different reasons, about a certain Jim Warwick.

Powell decided to send Frank Rollo to get a statement from Warwick, and he had his reasons for ensuring that the detective sergeant should go alone. Powell also knew that Warwick Motors was a generous contributor to police charities, so he would need to tread warily. But he resolved to get to the bottom of this, and soon, without poking a stick into the hornet's nest.

CHAPTER THIRTEEN

Geoff was making final changes to the production schedule for the order placed by Jim Warwick.

"He's having the optional items, Debbie," he said, "so the parts list needs to be altered."

"You've got the file," Debbie answered. "Pass it to me when you've put in the additions."

Geoff opened the 'production requirement' folder, which contained copies of the Warwick job quotation and began to sort through the papers. A business card slipped out from between the sheets of paper. It was the one that Jim Warwick had given him. Geoff picked the card up and held it between his thumb and index finger. It read: FLYNN ASSOCIATES, Accountants.

Flynn? Could this be the same Flynn, he wondered, who, with the bent copper had stitched up Brian? A thought struck him. If that was the case, could *Warwick* be the money man who had funded the plot to silence Brian? He was certainly wealthy enough. Rich enough to be a drug dealer? It was a "Eureka" moment.

Geoff sat back in his chair and pondered the likelihood. It was certainly possible, he reflected, but was it probable? The more he thought about it, the more likely it seemed that he had stumbled upon the truth. He got on with his paperwork, but all morning the issue niggled at the back of his mind. He did not want to contact Harry Mortimer again just yet. Not when all he had were suspicions. He had to find out somehow, whether Flynn and Rollo's relationship went beyond their common involvement in the Brian Hammond case.

Later when Debbie left the office to go to lunch, Geoff looked at the business card again. He had an idea. To himself he said, quietly, "Let's fly a kite, Geoffrey."

He picked up his desk phone and dialled the number on the card. A female voice answered.

"Flynn Associates."

"Oh, good afternoon, I wonder if you can help. I'm calling on behalf of a colleague, Detective Sergeant Rollo. Is Mr Flynn available?" Geoff was hoping that Flynn would be out to lunch, he had no intention of actually speaking to him.

"I'm afraid Mr Flynn has gone to lunch. Can I help, or do you want to call back later?"

Perfect. "Please ask him to contact Mr Rollo when he gets back. Do you need the number?"

"I'll give him the message. No problem, he has the number."

"Thank you." Geoff rang off. Well, how about that? After a few moments he took out his "Jeffries" mobile. Time to make a quick call. He scrolled through the stored numbers, paused, then tapped the display.

"Harry Mortimer."

"Harry? Geoff Summers. Can you spare a minute? I think I've discovered something that you may find interesting."

In fact they talked for several minutes. Before ringing off, Harry told Geoff that he had made some progress in the matter of the removals firm and would be contacting him soon with news.

Next day Geoff received a text message from Harry. It said, *"Jacko's cafe Mile End Rd 2 mins Stepney Grn stn. 10 AM Monday. Go alone, take folded Times paper. No car. U will be picked up by taxi. Confirm if OK. HM.*

Geoff read the message twice, then answered with a simple "OK".

The following Monday Geoff arrived at the cafe fifteen minutes early. Jacko's was set in a Victorian terrace of properties, to the front of which the pavement had been narrowed to accommodate a bus stop lay-by. It nestled between a fried chicken house and a Chinese take-away, neither of which was open for business at that hour. Jacko's, on the other hand, was doing enough business to create a condensation problem on the inside of its plate glass window.

The window and adjacent glazed entrance door spanned the width of the establishment, with the name "Jacko's" painted in a rainbow across the top. Geoff pushed the door open and went in, carrying his laptop in its case and a folded copy of the *Times*.

A centre aisle divided the seating areas, one to each side. At the bottom of the aisle across the width of the room, was a serving counter.

Geoff looked around. The place was short of being full, but there were enough customers to generate a warm noisy ambience, the air heavy with the appetizing odour of frying. There did not seem to be anyone waiting on tables, so he went over to the counter. Behind it stood a middle-aged man wearing a stained white apron and a three-day stubble and behind him, a small woman in a pinafore was busy attending to hissing tea and coffee machinery. The man looked up.

"Yes, mate?"

"A cup of tea please."

The man inclined his head to glance over his shoulder.

"A cuppa for the gent, Maisie."

To Geoff he said, "Coming up. Milk? Sugar's on the tables."

Geoff nodded. "Please."

Maisie slopped a dash of milk into a partially filled tea cup, placed it on a saucer and passed it across the counter. The man rubbed his hands.

"Anything else to go with your cuppa, mate? Bacon sarnie maybe?"

Geoff declined politely.

"That'll be fifty pence, then."

Geoff paid him and made his way to a vacant table, choosing a seat with a good view of the front door. He put the cup and saucer on the table, placing his laptop and the folded *Times* newspaper beside them. Geoff sat down and noticed that an elderly bald man in a donkey jacket, sitting alone facing the interior, half bowed his head and made a quiet call on his mobile.

Geoff spooned sugar into his cup and stirred his tea, glancing at his watch. Any minute now, he reflected, he would be stepping into the unknown. That morning, waking in the still unfamiliar surroundings of his room at Gamages, he knew that this was the day on which he intended to step across the line that divides law-abiding citizens from the rest. At the time he felt no emotion other than impatience, he just wanted to get on with it.

But now with the irrevocable step imminent, the reality of what he was about to undertake finally struck him and a feeling of deep apprehension came over him. His stomach knotted and his mouth went dry. His heart pumped faster, and as he lifted the cup to his lips he was alarmed to find that his hand was shaking. This would not do, he thought, get a grip.

Slowly Geoff put the cup down on its saucer. He had prepared well, he told himself, reassuringly touching his laptop case. In his mind he had a clear picture of the proposal he was about to make and he had brought with him convincing proof of his ability to deliver his part of the deal. But he knew that it would not work unless he calmed down immediately and steadied his nerves.

In the months since Penny died he had tried to blank his mind to his colossal loss. It had been impossible. There had not been a single day when he had not been reminded of her in so many ways. But thinking about Penny and the loss of their life together made him angry, with himself, and with fate for the hand it had dealt him.

He put his elbows on the table, cupped his face in his hands and breathed deeply for a few moments. Now was the time to use that anger to channel his emotions into cold, controlled indifference to everything but the need for revenge. With that thought he slowly began to recover his composure.

He told himself that above all he would need to be calm and dispassionate, keeping in mind the fact that once they had heard his proposal, the people he was about to meet would need him more than he would need them. They would be driven by greed whereas he, Geoff Summers, being already emotionally dead, was not. Nobody and nothing could hurt him now. He was ready.

A few minutes later the door was shoved open and a short man wearing a flat cap entered. He stood still, raised his head and looked around.

"Taxi for Mr Summers?"

Geoff stood up. "I'm Summers."

"Right you are, guv." The man held the door open. "This way, please. I'm Dennis."

The taxi was a standard London black cab. It was parked at the kerb with its diesel engine throbbing and there was a man seated in the passenger compartment. Dennis opened the door for Geoff and he climbed in. The man in the back was slim, impeccably dressed in a charcoal grey suit with a blue silk shirt open at the neck. A matching silk handkerchief was tucked into his breast pocket, and his shirtsleeves protruded just far enough to reveal monogrammed gold cuff links. He had a narrow face with high cheekbones under a well-groomed head of greying hair. Geoff reckoned that he was in his late forties. The man smiled.

"Mr Summers? Good morning. Take a seat, please." The cut-glass accent was that of an educated man. Not at all the sort of person he had expected, given the nature of the business he was in.

The man held out his hand. "My name is Norman."

"Summers." Geoff shook the proffered hand and sat down on the bench seat beside him.

Dennis put the taxi into gear and eased it forward into the traffic. Norman turned, changing his position slightly so that he could look at Geoff.

"This is our private cab," he said. "The best sort of company car for London, wouldn't you say?"

"Yes. Are we going far?"

Norman tilted his head. "Not far. The office is in West Ham."

"West Ham?"

"It should take us between ten and fifteen minutes to get there. If you're wondering why we didn't arrange to pick you up a bit closer, there's a reason."

"A reason?"

"Our company has several divisions. Each has a manager and they all report to me."

At that moment a cyclist just ahead stood up on the pedals of his machine, to power his way forward. He wobbled unsteadily and veered into the path of the taxi. The cab lurched to the right as Dennis swung the wheel to avert a collision.

"Bloody lunatic!" Dennis shouted, shaking his fist.

In the rear Geoff and Norman were thrown against their seat belts. Geoff was slightly shaken but Norman carried on, ignoring the incident as if nothing had happened. A cool customer, Geoff thought.

"And I report directly to the chairman," said

Norman evenly. "He is a busy man, Mr Summers and to be frank, not in the best of health. He wants me to hear your proposal first. In effect he has left it to me to decide whether or not it would be worth his while to meet you. When we get to the office, either we shall go in together to meet the chairman, or I shall disembark, and Dennis will take you back to Stepney Green." He gestured, waving a hand. "Or to a nearer underground station, if you so wish." He looked directly at Geoff. "You have ten minutes, Mr Summers."

Norman's lips parted into a facsimile of a smile. It looked contrived, as if glued on to his face. His steely brown eyes sent out a different message, they were not smiling.

This development caught Geoff unawares. He did not answer immediately, but took a few moments to think before speaking. If this was some sort of test, he would have to show that he was equal to it. He looked at his watch and then spoke slowly, tapping the laptop case on the seat beside him.

"Inside this I have a laptop and a CD which is an important part of the proposal I have come prepared to make. The disc shows a diagram of an actual installation at a retail jeweller's. I could show it to you now but if it's all the same to you, I really would prefer not to have to go through my presentation in the back of a taxi."

If Norman was sympathetic he showed no sign of it. OK, thought Geoff, suit yourself. Norman's indifference served only to stiffen his resolve. Geoff shrugged.

"Fine. I'll get on with it, without the demo disc. If not seeing it prevents you understanding or fully appreciating the opportunity you are being offered, so be it."

Norman frowned. "Just tell me what you are offering, and what you expect in return, Mr Summers. There will be time enough to – ah, fill in the details later." He flashed the artificial smile again. "If, that is, we decide to proceed at all."

The man's arrogance was offensive. Geoff decided that he would give as good as he was getting. He made a show of looking at his watch again.

"Nine minutes left. Should be enough," he said. "No problem."

Norman arched his eyebrows but said nothing.

Geoff continued. "I am Geoffrey Summers, production manager and chief designer at Melford Electronics, a major company in the security industry. I will shortly be leaving them, but for reasons of my own I have ensured that a few of the systems recently installed, or soon to be installed, can be disabled. This can be done remotely, covertly, and without risk of detection. But only by me."

Norman's deadpan expression changed slightly. There was, Geoff thought, evidence of some interest and perhaps a hint of respect, although Norman still did not make any comment.

From a pocket in the side of the case Geoff removed a piece of paper which he held in his hand.

"Disabling these security systems is of no use to me without the means to exploit the opportunity that I've created. As I do not have the resources to do that myself, I am looking for a partner who has." He looked directly at Norman. "Are you with me so far?"

Norman nodded. "Yes."

"Good." Geoff held out the sheet of paper.

"This is a list of all the establishments with security systems that have been compromised."

Norman took the list and read it. He frowned. "There are only five names on this."

"I could only work on what was actually in production at the time. Seven orders were in process of being prepared, and the other two were unsuitable subjects."

"Unsuitable? How?"

"A bank and a gemstone cutting establishment. Both have duplicate security protection and in each case our system is only one of the two."

"I understand."

A red London bus had stopped to disgorge passengers and take on others. The taxi stopped behind it, unable to pass because of a stream of traffic coming from the opposite direction. Its diesel engine chugged impatiently.

Geoff went on. "I can switch off the security alarms at these places at any time, remotely, provided that I am within a couple of hundred yards or so when it needs to be done."

Norman's eyebrows arched. "Really?"

"Yes, really," Geoff replied drily.

"What happens, er, after we are finished?"

"We leave the equipment switched off. That way, anyone looking for a reason as to why the equipment failed will believe that the owners simply forgot to turn it on. It happens all the time."

Geoff took the sheet of paper and put it back into the case.

"That's the proposal. Do you have any questions?"

Norman seemed genuinely impressed. "I have to say, it appears to be very clever. If it works."

"Oh, it works all right," said Geoff dismissively and with conviction.

The taxi slowed to filter into a left turn lane. Geoff was not too familiar with the area but he had been there once, many years before. He thought that they were now heading towards the Bromley gas works.

Norman's attitude had changed. In a more friendly tone he asked, "What do *you* want out of this?"

"Fifteen thousand after each job, in cash. Seventy-five thousand. Not much, considering that the total value of the stuff you would acquire could be in excess of five million."

"Really?" Norman inclined his head, eyebrows raised, his mouth turned down at the edges. "So it *is* about money. I was told that your motivation is revenge; that you just want to get even."

"That's the main reason, yes. But they have wiped out my career, so I need to recover what I have lost. To say nothing of losing twenty-two years' worth of benefits."

They were silent for a minute. Norman was looking straight ahead; Geoff gazed out of the window. Then he looked down, glanced at his watch and turned to face Norman.

"Under six minutes," he said. "What's your decision?"

Norman was staring ahead, he did not answer immediately. His expression betrayed nothing.

"Not sure, yet. Let me think about it for a few minutes."

Geoff felt his nerves on edge but hoped it did not show. He looked out of the window, trying to stay calm and appear casual. The huge gas storage tanks came into view as the taxi made a right turn.

Finally Norman reached into his jacket and took out a mobile phone. He looked at the keyboard, pressed a button and put the phone to his ear.

"We're coming in," he said. "Tell Mr Naylor."

The taxi wound its way through the back streets of east London, and Geoff wondered what sort of place they were heading for. Remembering Harry Mortimer's wry comment about the firm being in the "unauthorised removals" business, he did not know quite what to expect. A room above a pub, perhaps, or above a bingo hall? In the event, it was nothing like that.

They drove into an industrial estate where the taxi slowed and turned through double gates into a large yard in front of a two-storey brick building. It had parking bays on one side and, in front of the building, an external storage area for all manner of builders' materials.

Norman pointed at the sign above the main entrance to the premises.

"Here we are. Builders' Supply and Tool Hire, known in the trade as BST."

Geoff was tempted to ask which trade Norman

had in mind, but thought better of it. Quite a lot here, he thought, that would be useful in the unauthorised removals business.

Dennis parked the taxi around the side of the building and they went in through an unmarked side door. Their footsteps clanged as they ascended a steel staircase to a landing, from which a corridor took them past two rooms with fixed windows, revealing them to be a canteen and an office. At the end of the corridor Norman opened a wood-panelled door.

"Come in," he said. "This is the Chairman's office."

Geoff looked around. The furniture in the room was basic and lacked style. The walls were covered with floral patterned paper, with road maps pinned up on them. One was of the United Kingdom and the other of London and its environs. Near the centre of the room was a long table with a veneered chipboard top, and six plain office chairs. In one corner was a large television, beside which were an old lumpy armchair and a door with a sign: "Private". On the opposite side of the room were a matching chair and a sofa, upon which a tall casually dressed black man was seated, reading a tabloid paper.

Norman gestured towards the man. "Meet Mac," he said, "the chairman's right-hand man."

Mac folded his paper and put it aside. "Left hand, more like," he said in a strong Cockney accent. "You're his right hand." Mac stood up.

Geoff was standing by the door. He nodded to Mac. "Geoff Summers," he said.

Norman flashed the plastic smile. "We have a small

ritual for new guests," he said, motioning Mac forward. "Security. Nothing personal, I hope you don't mind." Then he put his hand out. "Your case, please."

Geoff shrugged and handed it to Norman. "Fine, take a look."

Mac moved in front of Geoff and motioned with his hands.

"Raise your arms."

Geoff stood still and raised his arms. Mac ran his hands expertly over Geoff, then stood back. "Clean," he said.

Norman handed the case to Mac who took it to the table and zipped it open.

"What are you looking for?" Geoff asked.

The men ignored him. Mac removed the laptop, the disc and Geoff's notes, and laid them on the table. He lifted the lid of the laptop.

"Is there a recorder in this thing, or a camera?"

Geoff smiled thinly, resisting the temptation to make a sarcastic comment. "No."

Mac closed the laptop and stepped back. "All yours," he said.

Norman went over to the door in the back wall of the office.

"Take a seat," he said. "I'll just let Mr Naylor know we've arrived."

Mac returned to the settee, his face expressionless. He stared at Geoff in silence for all of the three or four minutes during which they waited. Geoff was going through his notes at the table when the door opened. Norman came in and held the door for

Naylor, who was dressed casually, in a loose grey pullover and blue jeans. He was older than Geoff had expected, and he stooped slightly, leaning on a stout walking stick.

Norman said, "This is our Chairman, Mr Robert Naylor."

Naylor looked up at Geoff, nodded, limped to the table and sat down heavily. He hooked his cane over the end of the table top and drew his chair forward. Norman took a seat next to Geoff, and Mac sat down opposite him.

Norman had said that Naylor was ill, and to Geoff he certainly appeared so. His face was sallow, with a prominent nose between sunken cheeks. Wispy, thinning hair failed to cover the liver spots on his balding head. But his eyes immediately drew attention, steely grey under bushy, close-knit brows. Naylor rested his arms and elbows on the table and Geoff noticed that some of his fingers were swollen with arthritis. He pointed a crooked finger at Geoff, speaking slowly.

"I hear you got something to tell us."

Geoff leant forward. "Thank you for seeing me." Naylor's lips twitched, but he said nothing.

Geoff continued. "I've explained to Norman how I can disable high security alarms remotely, in five places that have items of value in them. I designed..."

Naylor interrupted brusquely. "What makes you think we are interested?"

The question threw Geoff. He sat up. "This meeting was arranged by Harry Mortimer who knows exactly what I am asking for. It was he who told me to go to the cafe where I was picked up, so he must have..."

"All right. Forget that. Norman says you got a list." He crooked his index finger. "Show me."

Geoff handed the list to Norman, who passed it over. Meanwhile Naylor, without looking at Mac, had extended his right hand palm up, towards him. Mac reached into his jacket, withdrew a spectacles case and placed it in Naylor's outstretched palm.

Naylor opened the case and took out a pair of glasses. As he fumbled to put them on his mouth fell open slightly. He peered at the list in his hand.

Geoff thought he looked well past retirement age. Quietly he said, "Three millionaires' homes, a retail jewellers, and a fine art gallery."

Naylor dipped his head to look at Geoff over his spectacles.

"What's Sadlington Manor?"

"The country mansion of Sir Stanley Blake-Wellings, QC."

"Matthew Pratt?"

"The real name of the pop star called Granite."

"I've heard of him. What's Warwick Hall?"

"The home of Jim Warwick, who owns a motor car franchise and other things including a large collection of gold coins."

"What about this gallery place?"

"Stork Hill, dealers in antique and modern fine arts. They say that their showroom has the best collection of small oriental pieces in the country. Mainly jade and ivory."

Naylor put the list down and said to Mac, "Tell

Steph to bring us in some coffees." Mac stood up. "And some chocolate digestives," Naylor added.

He turned back to Geoff. "Right. I'm still listening. Let's start with what's on that disc. And before you leave, I want to make a copy of that and a copy of your list."

Geoff had no problem with that. The information would be useless without his remote device. He switched on his laptop, moved it slightly so that they could all see the screen, inserted the disc and chose a file. A picture of a double-bay corner shop appeared, showing also an adjacent alleyway.

"Babcombe and Horsfield," Geoff said. "Jewellers in the high street in Longford, Buckinghamshire." He pointed. "Window displays on each side of the front door into the shop. Inside there's a display counter on the left and glass cabinets on the right. Behind the shop there's a store room which has been extended at the back. The extension has a flat roof, easy to get onto from the alleyway. Above the shop there's an empty apartment."

Norman interjected. "Is it still unoccupied? When was this picture taken?"

"Sorry, I don't know if it's still empty. You'll have to check. I took the photo from across the road about three weeks ago." Geoff clicked on another file and a plan drawing appeared, showing ground floor and first floor levels.

He pointed again. "These are the points of entry, all connected to the alarm system. See this window?" He indicated. "It's on the staircase landing and it looks over the flat roof. The window has a metal grille on the inside, but it's rubbish. A pair of good bolt cutters is all you need to deal with that. With the alarms off you could be in and out in a matter of minutes." He looked up. "Any questions, gentlemen?"

Naylor asked, "How come you know so much about the inside?"

"I do the site surveys. Then I design the alarm systems. This," he pointed and paused for effect, "is *my* drawing."

Norman asked, "Do you have drawings of the others?"

"Of course." Geoff shrugged. "But not with me. I didn't bring them. No point, until we have an agreement."

Norman shot a glance at Naylor.

The meeting lasted over an hour. Geoff went on to give them broad details of the layouts of each of the other four premises on the list. He told them where the points of entry were and he answered all the questions they asked.

"We're done, then," said Naylor, looking at his gold Rolex. "For now, anyway. We want you back here Thursday morning, come about eleven. Just go into the store and ask for Norman. We'll give you our answer then. If we decide to go with it, we'll start straight away."

Geoff closed his laptop. "Thursday's fine for me."

Norman said, "It will give us time to check out some of these places."

Geoff nodded. "Once we start, the sooner we get

them all done, the better."

Naylor looked at him sharply. "In and out quick, is that it? What you afraid of?"

Geoff returned his gaze. "Sooner or later, some insurance investigator is going to figure out the common link. When that happens, all recent Melford installations will be suspect. At best, that will be the end of the operation." He closed the file in front of him on the table. "At worst we could be met by an unfriendly reception committee somewhere. We need to get them all done, in the shortest possible time."

Robbie "The Nail" Naylor seemed impressed. He tilted his head towards Norman, saying, "The man's right. That man is *right*."

Naylor looked at Geoff again, and lifted a crooked index finger. "Just one more thing. Bring one of those control whatsits with you. Then you can show us how smart you are, when you switch it off without touching it."

Geoff knew it would not be easy to comply without risking his position at Melford. Naylor must have sensed this, Geoff realised, because he actually smiled, something he had not done before.

Geoff answered. "I'll do my best, but it might not be..."

Naylor interrupted. "You're one of the bosses there, ain't ya?" His brow furrowed, he leaned forward towards Geoff and hissed, "No proof, no deal. Savvy?"

He was about a metre away, yet close enough for Geoff to be as offended by the man's breath as he was by his manner. "I'll find a way," he replied.

Norman stood up. "I'll see you out. Dennis will take you to a tube station."

On the way down Geoff was already thinking about how he could get another controller, but for the moment he was satisfied. He could go ahead with the next step of his plan, a visit to the Australian embassy to get a visa.

CHAPTER FOURTEEN

Geoff knew that he could not risk taking a new controller off the factory floor, it would certainly be missed. Instead he went to his old office where there was a working unit on the experimental bench. It was an old model, but it would do. He modified it, tested it with the remote and took it away. He would bring it back on Thursday evening, confident that it would not have been missed in the meantime.

On the Thursday the meeting went well. Naylor was impressed by Geoff's demonstration of the remote, insisting on trying it himself and chuckling like a child when he caused the indicator light to switch off.

"Right," he said to Norman. "We'll do the first one tomorrow. Get the lads organized."

He turned to Geoff. "Be here at nine tomorrow night. We'll have a little run-through before you leave. It'll be a long night, for you."

The following night the team was on the road in an unmarked blue Transit van, heading for the venue. They had been driving for only ten minutes, when Geoff realised that they were heading west. It was not what he had been expecting.

"Where are we going?" he asked. "Sadlington Manor is in Kent."

Mac grinned. "There's been a change of plan." Mac was sitting at the end by the passenger door, with Geoff beside him in the middle. Geoff turned to look at Dennis, who was driving. Dennis stared at the road ahead, a hint of a smile on his lips.

They don't trust me! Geoff thought. At the meeting they had run through plans for all five venues but dealt with Sadlington Manor in greater detail. Norman had told Geoff that they would be going there first.

"OK, I get it," he said. "I'm guessing you've sent someone to Kent to see if there's a bunch of coppers waiting." He snorted. "Huh!"

Mac shrugged. "Could be."

They were silent for a few moments. "Then he's wasted his time," Geoff said, flatly.

Geoff checked his watch. "Nearly half past midnight."

Mac looked down the deserted high street. They were in Longford, an old town on the upper Thames. As expected, all was quiet. He turned to look at Dennis, who was driving.

"Go round again," he said. "Slow, but not too slow."

"Right," Dennis replied.

The van cruised silently past the jewellery shop for the second time. All three occupants in the front swivelled their heads for another look at the shop and down the narrow alleyway adjacent. A pair of stray cats engaged in a yowling standoff skittered into the darkness when the van approached.

"Looks like it's still clear," said Dennis.

Mac nodded. "OK, we'll go in."

Geoff took the remote out of his jacket pocket. The shop occupied the front part of the ground floor of a two-storey building at the end of a terrace. Above the door was a sign saying, "Babcombe and Horsfield, Quality Jewellers since 1928."

Mac swivelled in his seat and addressed the two men who were sitting on cushions in the back. "Kit on and check your tools."

"Done it before we left," said Ted, the taller of the two.

"Well, do it again," Mac growled. He turned to Geoff.

"You ready with your gizmo?"

Geoff held it up. "Ready when you are." The confined space inside the van seemed to heighten the tension and his mouth had gone dry.

The van went around the block again, to enter the alley from the opposite end. Dennis drove slowly, stopping twenty yards short of the high street, where he parked against the perimeter wall of the building. The rear store room, they knew, was on the other side of that wall.

Dennis switched off the lights but left the engine running. Mac opened his door, slipped out quietly and walked to the corner, where he stood still and looked up and down the street. The van was in shadow with only an oblique shaft of light slanting into the alley from the street lamps.

Geoff watched as Mac came back to the van, opened the passenger door and said quietly, "All clear."

He then went around to the back and opened the rear doors. Inside, the two men were dressed identically in black long-sleeved pullovers, black jeans and black trainers. They pulled on black balaclavas and latex gloves.

"The ladder first," Mac hissed.

The men carefully and silently passed out to Mac a lightweight ladder, followed by a bag containing the tools they needed: a pair of heavy duty bolt cutters and two hessian sacks. They stepped out and Mac closed the doors gently and then went to the front passenger door again.

He pointed to the remote in Geoff's hand.

"You sure that thing works?"

"Positive."

"You'd better be right, mate, or you're a dead man." Mac's words were loaded with menace. He nodded. "Right, switch the alarm off."

Geoff keyed in the code and pressed the button. "Done."

Mac walked to the end of the alley, where he stood to check the road again. He took out a small torch and flashed it twice. Dennis switched the engine off.

Muffled footsteps of the men above could be heard clearly inside the van. Geoff glanced at Dennis and saw that he was frowning and beads of sweat had appeared on his brow. Moments later the sounds ceased. Geoff knew that the ladder would have been lifted onto the top of the van. They would have used the ladder to climb onto the adjacent flat roof and, as planned, would pull it up after them. They would be less than four metres from the window.

Geoff and Dennis waited inside the van in tense silence. The gang had estimated that working swiftly the men in the shop would need no more than ten minutes to complete their task. Geoff could see Mac at the roadside in the shadows, checking his watch repeatedly. Quite suddenly he flashed his torch briefly and sprinted for the van.

"Oh shit, trouble," Dennis exclaimed.

Mac grabbed the door handle, yanked the door open and scrambled in.

"Cops. Get down," he hissed. "Down, down, *now!*" He crouched half on and half off the seat beside Geoff, peering apprehensively over the dashboard through the bottom of the windscreen. Dennis cowered low against the driver's door, and Geoff doubled over but he could still see over the dashboard. A police patrol car had stopped across the entrance to the alleyway.

In the cab of the van Geoff could almost smell the raw fear. Mac stayed rigid, not moving a muscle, Dennis was breathing heavily and seemed to be shivering.

Geoff whispered, "I can see them. Two coppers, the car is stopped. Wait, they're calling someone over. A couple of lads with beer cans. Now the coppers are talking to them." He thought of the men on the roof, willing them to stay where they were and to stay silent. After what seemed like an age the young men walked slowly away from the police car.

"The lads are leaving," Geoff said quietly. "The car's still there."

Mac whispered, "Are they looking at us?"

"Can't tell," Geoff replied. After a few moments he said, "They're going. The car is leaving."

Mac straightened. "Shit. That was close." Dennis sat up. His face was white, his eyes wide.

"I'll check on the boys," said Mac. "I'll give it a couple of minutes first in case the bastards come back."

Ted and Foxy had just finished their task and were about to lower the ladder when the police car appeared. They immediately flattened themselves on the roof and froze. There they stayed until they heard Mac calling to them quietly. Then they put the ladder in position and clambered down with their tools and the two cloth bags, which were heavy. Within two or three minutes they were loaded and on their way again.

On the way back the men in the van were ecstatic, they had got away, clean away. They babbled with excitement, and Geoff found himself being carried along on their euphoria. It was a mood that lasted all the way back to BST.

Geoff did not get back to Gamages until nearly four in the morning. He let himself in quietly and went straight to bed. He was tired but sleep eluded him because his mind was still buzzing with the events of the day and the plans he had for the week ahead. Finally, he fell into a deep sleep and did not wake until after ten the next morning.

At Warwick Motors receptionist Elaine spoke into her telephone. "There's a gentleman here to see you, Mr Warwick." She lowered her voice. "He's from the police, Detective Sergeant Rollo."

Rollo stood at the counter, a bleak expression on his face, his shoulders hunched. He was not a happy man.

Elaine spoke again. "Yes, Mr Warwick." She put the receiver down and pointed towards the glass-walled offices.

"Mr Warwick will see you now. It's the last room on the left."

Rollo mumbled his thanks and made his way towards Warwick's office. He knew that he was probably about to experience the most unpleasant interview of his professional career. Nobody called uninvited on Jim Warwick. Not even police officers and certainly not me, he thought bleakly. But he had no choice.

He paused outside the door and looked through the glass panel. Warwick was standing behind his desk, leaning forward on his outstretched arms, hands flat on the surface. His round, shaven head was thrust forward belligerently; the cold blue eyes stared out from a face as hard as set concrete. For the briefest instant Rollo had a vision of a male gorilla leaning on his knuckles, spoiling for a fight. He swallowed nervously, ran his tongue across his lips, took a deep breath and pushed the door open.

Warwick's face contorted. "What the *fuck* are *you* doing here?" he snarled. "I told you never to come here."

Rollo felt his heart hammering. "I'm sorry, I had no choice," he whined. "I was ordered to."

Warwick sat down. "Ordered? By who? And why

258

didn't you phone first? I'm running a business here not a fucking social club."

There was a chair on the other side of the desk but Rollo was not invited to sit. He stood, awkwardly. Rivulets of cold sweat ran down the back of his neck.

"My boss Chief Superintendent Powell. I have to get a formal statement from you."

"Powell? *Powell?*" Jim snorted. After I've had a word with Charlie Haddow, he'll be out on the streets on dog shit patrol, or if he's lucky, directing traffic. A statement on what?"

"Bellini. What happened when he came to see you," Rollo mumbled. "And what happened after."

Warwick leaned back in his chair, a half smile of disdain on his face.

"I've had just about enough of that shit. You already have all the facts." He leaned forward again and picked up a biro from his pen tray. "Here," he said, throwing it across the desk. "Sit down. You write the fucking thing, I'll sign it."

Rollo was appalled. He was about to protest, but Warwick spoke again, slowly, in a tone loaded with menace. His mouth widened into a sardonic grin, an index finger pointing.

"Do you know how to spell Mercedes? Eh? We mustn't forget to put in about the cars your wife's had from here, must we? Or the luxury cruises. Two, was it? Or three?"

Frank Rollo felt physically sick. Slowly he picked up the pen and began to write, shakily. Jim Warwick reached for his address book.

"Time to call my pal Charlie Haddow." He found

the number and dialled it. After a few moments he exclaimed in annoyance, "Shit, an answer machine." He tried again, then spoke.

"Hello Charles, Jim Warwick here. I'd appreciate a call back, when you can spare a minute. Many thanks." He replaced the handset. "Sorted."

Warwick's call was not answered. Neither were the other half dozen attempts he made over the next few days to contact the assistant chief constable. He began to realise, slowly, that in fact nothing was "sorted".

On the Monday morning Geoff made his next move. He went in to Melfords, where he handed his letter of resignation to Ken Lever. On the way back to his office he paused outside Samantha's room and put his head around the door.

"Can't stop," he said. "Just thought you'd like to know, I've done the deed, four weeks' notice."

She smiled. "Good luck."

Geoff closed the door and headed for his office. He and Samantha had not seen much of each other lately, which was not what he really wanted but it suited him perfectly. It would not do he thought, to start tongues wagging at this stage.

Later that day Sandy Macgregor came to see Geoff, something the Finance Director rarely did. They talked and Sandy had been trying to get Geoff to think again.

"You know," he said, "you are one of the very few

people who have been here longer than me. Shame to throw away all the benefits of your long service. Are you really sure about this?"

"My life is different now," Geoff replied. "With Penny gone things will never be the same for me. I'm going to take a long break somewhere, then see what turns up. Besides, to be honest Sandy, there's no future for me at Melford anymore."

Macgregor looked at Geoff for a long moment. "I don't think I could disagree with that," he said. "A real pity. Anyway, Adam wants you to take payment in lieu of notice. I told him I wanted to ask you to reconsider and he agreed to let me try. That's why I'm here. But it seems your mind is made up. Can't say I blame you, though."

"Thanks, Sandy."

"I'll have all the paperwork sorted for you now. You can leave whenever you want to." He moved towards the door, stopped and turned. "By the way, there'll be a bit of a bonus added to your pay."

"Thank you. Are you sure Adam won't mind?"

"I'm still the Finance Director. It's my decision."

That afternoon Geoff said his goodbyes to his colleagues at Melford and went into the town. He pulled up at the premises of a courier company and went inside holding five brown envelopes, each with an addressed label on the front. At the reception desk a young woman came over to him.

"Yes, sir?"

Geoff smiled. "I wonder if you can help me?"

"What can I do for you?"

CHAPTER FOURTEEN

Geoff put the envelopes on the counter. "I want these delivered by hand, please."

The girl picked them up and scanned them quickly. "No problem sir, I'll just get the forms."

Geoff held up a hand. "Just one thing. They *must* all be delivered on the same day, Thursday the eighth November, at or after seven in the evening."

The girl's eyes widened. "I'm sure we can do that, but it's three weeks from now."

"I know, but I'm leaving the country this week and I need an absolute guarantee that this will be done, exactly as I want. Otherwise I could have used the Post Office."

The girl seemed hesitant. "Look," said Geoff, "I know this is probably unusual and I expect you may be worried about what's inside them." He smiled. "Just letters, this is a business matter and the timing is critical. I'll pay you now, using my bank debit card, not cash." He inclined his head. "Traceable."

She got the point. "I'm sure that will be fine sir, I'll just get the forms."

Geoff headed back to Gamages where he cleared out his car. He drove it to a second-hand car dealers on the outskirts of the town, and sold it for cash. Then he took a bus into the town and went to a different used car lot where as John Jeffries he bought another, paying in cash. It was smaller, older and less conspicuous than the one he had sold, but it would suit his purposes perfectly. And he could at last use the private car park at Gamages.

Geoff smiled when Robbie Naylor said, "Nice job, smooth. You done good."

"I'm glad you're satisfied."

Norman interjected. "We are extremely satisfied. You fulfilled your part admirably, just as we expected."

In response to a phone call from Norman the previous evening, Geoff was attending a meeting at BST. They were sitting at the table in Naylor's office and Geoff saw a distinct improvement in their attitude towards him. They seemed more relaxed. Was this a sign that they no longer regarded him with suspicion?

Norman had his elbows on the table, a notepad between. He locked the fingers of his hands together and rested his chin on them, looking directly at Geoff.

"Now that we know how – er, effective your system is, we have a proposition for you. Since it works so well, why stop at only five jobs?"

They were both looking at Geoff and Norman was using the faux smile again. They're watching for my reaction, thought Geoff. Absolutely no deal, fellers.

He shook his head. "I'm sorry, but that's just not possible. There were only five altogether. I told you that from the start."

"Come on Geoff," said Norman, adopting a reasonable tone. "There's always a way to achieve something, all you have to do is to know how." The smile widened. Was this Norman's version of a charm offensive?

Geoff shook his head again. "Gentlemen I'm really sorry, but it simply can't..."

Naylor interrupted sharply. "Don't give me that. You're a fucking boss there, you can easy find a way," he spat. "If you want a bigger cut, just say so."

"No, it's not that. I left Melfords yesterday. But even if ..."

"You *left? Already?* You was supposed to finish all the jobs first."

"That wasn't what I said. In fact, I made a point of saying that there were only five." He turned to Norman. "In the taxi, remember?"

Norman put his hands up. "All right, all right. We know you want to limit the number of jobs because you want to keep the overall time scale as short as possible. That makes perfect sense." He looked down at his notepad. "So, we've decided to do the next four as soon as possible. That should please you, and give us time to do a few more, before the balloon goes up." He sat back, a smug look on his face.

Naylor waved a hand. "We done the planning already for the next three. The fourth is being checked out now. We can easy fit in some more."

Geoff shook his head. "No, you don't understand. It's not enough for me to have the remote, the controllers need to have a small component altered to make them compatible with it. Since I've left Melford, it's just not possible for me to do that any more."

Naylor's eyes narrowed, and there was an edge to his tone. "You got mates, ain't ya? Don't tell me there ain't guys in there would be happy to do what we want, if there's bunce in it for them? All you gotta do is to tell 'em what to do."

Geoff stared ahead, saying nothing. If he stone-walled at this point it could all go wrong. He needed these people, at least for now. He knew he could not do what they wanted, so best to leave the door open and let them think he could. If he played his hand right, it could all be over by the end of the next week.

He sighed. "OK, I suppose it's possible. Let me think about it, I'll see what I can do." Geoff knew that Naylor had been watching him carefully. He wondered if he had said enough to buy some time.

Naylor smiled. "Good man." He turned to Norman. "Make sure he gets whatever he wants."

It was Geoff's turn to put on a smile. "Starting with fifteen grand, in cash, please."

Norman shot a glance at Naylor, who nodded his assent.

That afternoon Geoff was ushered into Roger Mantle's office. The solicitor rose to greet him.

"Ah, Mr Summers, do take a seat. How are you?"

"Fine, thank you. And you?"

"Can't complain," said Mantle. They sat down. "We are exchanging contracts on Friday, as planned."

"Good. I asked to see you because there's a slight change in my plans."

"In what respect?"

Geoff took out of his pocket a sheet of folded paper.

"Perhaps I should tell you first, that I have quit my job. I left on Monday."

"Uh-huh."

"To be honest I've had enough. No point in

265

staying on there, I need a complete break and I mean to take it as soon as possible."

"Sounds good. How can I help?"

"When you've done your final statement for the conveyancing, please give me a call. I want to put the proceeds into a more accessible bank because I'll be doing a bit of travelling." He handed the paper to Mantle. "Please transfer the funds to this account."

Roger Mantle scanned it. His eyes widened.

"Schneider Hoffman, Geneva? Who are they, may I ask?"

Geoff smiled. "Nothing sinister. They are agents in Switzerland who act for non-residents wanting to open a private Swiss bank account. There are conditions of course, the main one being that the minimum initial deposit needed to open the account must be in excess of twenty thousand Swiss francs. No problem there, we will have more than enough, with the exchange rate currently being about one and a half to the pound.

"Well, it's certainly a first for me," Mantle replied. "But, why not? The funds are yours to do with as you wish. I'm sure you will have checked these people out."

"As a matter of fact they are quite well known. They are one of the leading firms who offer this service, all regulated by the Swiss banking authorities. Their integrity I'm happy to say, is beyond question."

"Fine. I'll make sure it is done." Roger Mantle stood up and smiled. "Just one condition, Mr Summers."

"What's that?"

"Don't forget to send me a postcard or two from the exotic places you visit."

Ted was having a problem. He and Foxy were in a small blue van that was painted to look exactly like a British Gas service vehicle and they were dressed in British Gas overalls. They were parked outside the gate and the woman on the other end of the intercom was not cooperating. She was adamant; she would not let them in.

Ted spoke slowly, repeating what he had said before. "We're from British Gas, love. There's a pressure drop and we have to check your supply."

"I am telling you, Mr Granite is not at home. He is gone to America."

Patiently, Ted tried once more to explain. "We don't need to see him, we're here to check your gas supply. If we don't, there could be a serious problem."

"You know, I am thinking you should come back later. Tomorrow, Mr Jones will be here. You must go away now."

"We *can't* leave it till tomorrow. If there's a gas leak, there could be an explosion. That would be very serious. All we have to do is to check the supply; it will only take ten minutes."

"Mr Jones is, you know, the house guard. Come back tomorrow."

Ted sighed. "Bugger," he muttered under his breath. He tried a different tack. "What's your name, love? You don't sound English."

There was a pause before she answered. "My name

is Bernadette. I am coming from Sri Lanka. I am sorry, you know, I am not allowed to let anyone in."

Foxy was in the passenger seat of the van. He started to chuckle. Ted frowned and said, "Shush, you dork. This is important." He pressed the "speak" button again.

"Bernadette, my name is William. I know you have to do your job but it would be very bad for you and for us, if there is a gas leak. When you let us in, we will show you our identity cards. Then you can call the number on the card and speak to our office."

There was a longer pause, then she said, "All right, William. I am opening gate now, but you must be showing me identity before you can come in the house."

She was as good as her word. They drove up to the front door which Bernadette had opened, but only as far as the security chain allowed. They stood outside with their tool boxes while she carefully scrutinised their identity cards, frowning in concentration as she compared the photo images with their faces. Foxy was having a problem keeping a straight face. They had used the cards before and they knew that they were perfect fakes.

Finally the girl spoke. "I am just going to check." She went to a telephone in the hall and called the number on the card. In the office at BST, Steph let the phone ring for a full minute before picking up the handset.

"British Gas service," she drawled. "Sharon speaking, sorry to keep you waiting, how may I be of help?"

There followed a short conversation during which Steph, using a calm and practised off-hand manner, was able to convince Bernadette that the men were genuine gas engineers.

"But you were right to check," she said. "That's why we give them identity cards. These days, you can't be too careful."

Ted and Foxy did what they came to do and were off the premises within fifteen minutes. They learned that Bernadette had her own room at the back of the house and that Mr Jones lived in the nearby village and doubled as the butler when the pop star was in residence. Most weekdays when Granite was out of the country Bernadette was the only person on the premises.

Geoff called it his "Jeffries" mobile and he kept it separate from his original phone. He was in the solicitor's car park, about to get into his car, when it rang. He took it out and glanced at the display.

"Hello, Norman."

"Good morning, Geoff. How are you getting on?"

"Fine, thank you."

"Any progress with the, er, electrical panel matter?"

"I'm working on it," he lied. "Give me time."

"Excellent, excellent. Regarding our discussions yesterday, we have decided to move everything forward. Are you all right with that?"

"I should think that would be OK. What did you have in mind?"

"We want to do the Surrey job tomorrow night. Can you get here about the same time?"

CHAPTER FOURTEEN

"Nine o'clock? Yes, no problem."

"We'll take a break on Friday and then do Birmingham on Saturday. Can you manage that?"

So, Geoff thought, they really do want to get on with it. Good, it suited him.

"Sounds fine."

"Excellent. We'll run through the plans for those tomorrow. On second thoughts, it might be better if you could perhaps get here a little earlier."

"Shall I make it half past eight, then?"

"Yes, much better. There's a lot to get through."

They broke off, and Geoff thought about the new plan. There had been media coverage about the pop star's current tour in America, so he was out of the country. As for Stork Hill, if you want to break into an art gallery perhaps the best time to do so would be on a Saturday night.

Things were heating up. He felt a frisson of excitement and looked forward to getting full details the next day. In the meantime, there were a few things he needed to get on with, to move his own plans forward.

CHAPTER FIFTEEN

Part of the county of Surrey is known as the Stockbroker Belt, for good reasons. Houses are large, of individual design and positioned for privacy. They are also expensive.

It had taken singer-songwriter Matthew Pratt several years to make it to the top of his profession. As "Granite" he was now a superstar with houses in California, Switzerland and Surrey. But there was more to Matthew Pratt than that. A one-time art student, he had a real appreciation of modern art and over the years he had supported new British artists, thus acquiring a collection of contemporary paintings now valued at millions.

"No street lamps," Dennis observed when they turned into the rural lane.

Mac grunted. "Don't matter; better for us."

Norman's instructions had been clear. They could do nothing about the gate, so they would have to go in over the eight-foot perimeter wall. The road which snaked past the house was narrow and it petered out half a mile further on. The nearest neighbour was several hundred yards away, beyond open woodland.

The gang was well prepared. Geoff's layout drawing had identified the best point of entry, a door into the utility room at the side of the house. This time their equipment included two lightweight three-metre ladders and two large hessian sacks, plus a roll of gaffer tape.

They were to take only paintings that could be handled easily, nothing too large. The paintings were to be left in their frames and packed in pairs face to face, before being taped and placed in the bags.

Mac instructed Dennis to slow down and turn the van's headlights off, although they were still some distance from the house.

"Single track road," he said. "Bugger-all traffic, probably even in daytime. Drive on sidelights, we don't want to attract no attention."

"OK, but it'll be slow," Dennis replied.

He drove down the road leading to the property, with the van's headlights off. About twenty metres beyond the wrought iron gates Dennis stopped and did a three-point turn. The van was now facing back the way they had come, an expedient to save time if they were unfortunate enough to have to leave in a hurry. He switched off the engine and the side lights.

For a few minutes they waited, listening with the windows open. An owl hooted in the nearby wood and in the distance a dog barked, otherwise there was an eerie silence. Finally, Mac stepped out and walked back to the gates. After a good look around to make sure that all was clear he returned to the van.

He spoke quietly. "All clear. No lights on." He moved to the rear and opened the doors, again speaking softly.

"You ready?"

Ted was pulling on his latex gloves. "Yeah, OK."

"Come on." Using a shielded torch Mac then went with Ted into the undergrowth. "How far is it?" he whispered.

"Fifty or sixty yards. There's a break in the bushes, on the left."

They found the place that Ted had identified as being suitable when he and Foxy had checked out the house as gas men.

Mac moved the beam of the torch around the wall. "Yeah, this'll do."

They returned to the van where Ted and Foxy picked up the ladders and their tools, and disappeared into the undergrowth.

Mac nodded to Geoff. "Turn the alarms off," he whispered. "I'm going to give them a hand with the ladders, you keep watch at the gates." To Dennis he said, "Stay in the van. Engine off, but be ready if we have to scarper."

Geoff punched the code into the remote and pressed a switch. "Done," he whispered.

Dennis was sweating. He pointed at the remote. "You sure that thing always works?"

"One hundred percent certain. The only thing that could fail is the battery and that's not going to happen, so stop worrying." He opened the door. "Don't fall asleep," he said, as he closed the door softly.

Geoff went over to the gate. All was quiet, a half moon providing a pale, shadowless glow onto the building and its garden. Suddenly the garden at one side was flooded in light. Geoff blinked and saw two figures dressed in black and clearly visible, scurrying towards the house. The taller one was carrying the tool bag and the other the hessian sacks, all of which they set down hurriedly by the wall of the house, before immediately flattening themselves against it.

They had activated an infra-red sensor that turned a floodlight on automatically. But Geoff knew that as long as the light had not woken the maid, there was no cause for concern; lights like that were often triggered by small animals. He held his breath and looked around cautiously. Apart from a ladder leaning against the wall at the spot where they had come over, there was nothing to betray the presence of the two men.

After a minute the floodlight went out. Geoff could not see the side door but he assumed that the removal men would be working to let themselves in. Nothing more to do then, but wait.

Less than fifteen minutes later they emerged and again triggered the light. Geoff had a perfect floodlit view of the action and he saw Mac's head and shoulders above the top of the wall. Ted and Foxy were each carrying an unwieldy, bulging sack and Ted also had the tool bag. They shuffled across to the ladder, with Ted leading. In under a minute both men with Mac's help succeeded in getting themselves and their haul over the wall, taking the ladder with them.

There appeared to be no activity in the house and all was quiet. Geoff breathed a sigh of relief and returned to the van.

The next morning Geoff made his way in to BST. He was late, having overslept. The adrenalin and the stress had taken their toll and the Friday morning traffic jams he encountered on the way did not help.

Geoff sat at one end of the long table with Naylor at the other. Mac was not present. Naylor had a large, bulky envelope on the table in front of him. Across the room, Norman had placed three of the paintings upright against the back of the settee.

"Two John Pipers," he enthused. "Two!"

"What's the other one?" Geoff asked.

"Ken Kiff."

Naylor was scornful. "My six-year-old grandson can do better than that."

"An acquired taste," said Norman. "You either get it, or you don't."

Geoff said, "I take it you're happy, then."

"Happy? What do you think? And there are all these others." Norman gestured at eleven other paintings stacked against the wall. "What a result," he croaked. "*What* a result!"

Naylor appeared unmoved. "Take a good look, 'cos after tomorrow you won't see them no more."

Geoff wondered what would happen to them. "Where will they go?"

Naylor frowned. "Never you mind," he growled.

Norman came back to the table. "They're going to the States. A specialist wholesaler." He sat down, opened a note book and took a gold-topped pen from inside his jacket.

"Now let's get on with this," he said. "Tomorrow night, the gallery in Birmingham. Everything's in place. Then the Kent job, two nights later on Monday."

"The lawyer's gaff," said Naylor. "Should be a

good haul there. I got a thing about silver."

Norman nodded. "It's all going smoothly so we can crack on. Two nights after that, on Wednesday we'll do the Essex job, Warwick's." He looked at Geoff. "All right so far?"

"You're doing the schedule. You're calling the shots. All I have to do is turn up and press a button."

Norman put the pen down and sat back. "Not quite. You also have to give us the new list."

Naylor interjected suddenly, leaning forward and slamming the heel of his hand on the table. "And we want it *now*. We need time to suss the jobs. All gotta be done soon, before the balloon goes up."

Geoff looked steadily at him. He had been expecting something like this and had prepared for it.

Speaking quietly, he said, "You know I don't work at Melfords anymore and only two or three people there could do what needs to be done. That's why I need time. I'm talking to the one I think most likely to cooperate and he's thinking about it. But he'll want paying, otherwise he has no reason to take the risk."

"What's his name? Give us his name and we'll deal with him," Naylor barked.

Norman reacted. His face showed the visual equivalent of a sharp intake of breath.

Geoff shook his head gently. "No, I don't think so. I'm certain I can talk him round, but it'll take a couple more days while he's getting used to the idea. I'll find out how much he wants, then we'll take it from there."

"Very well," said Norman. "Give us an update tomorrow night when we load for the Birmingham job."

Naylor tapped the envelope. "Fifteen grand. Used notes like the last lot." He narrowed his eyes. "Tomorrow night. You get this tomorrow night, if you got good news for us."

There was a brief, awkward silence. Norman stood up. "I'll come downstairs with you, Geoff."

On the way out he said, "Mr Naylor is a hard man but that's because he's had a hard life. Talk to your contact. If the news is good, I'll see you get your money."

The following night the briefing meeting was held earlier than usual, because of the distance they had to cover to get to the target site in Birmingham. Geoff was the last member of the team to arrive at the office. When he walked in Norman was running through the plan, with the drawing of the Stork Hill Galleries premises in front of him on the table. Geoff listened as Norman ran over the details. There were no questions so Norman concluded, checking the time on his Rolex.

"You will need to be away in about twenty minutes. Get yourselves a cup of tea, lads." He turned to Geoff. "A word please, Geoff."

Geoff knew what was coming. When they were alone, Norman came straight to the point. "Have you got the new list?"

Geoff smiled. "Good news. Our man is on board and his price is ridiculously cheap, two grand. He can get three controllers done by the end of the week."

"That is good news. Have you got the names?"

"It's the weekend, I have to wait until Monday for

details but I'll be able to give you a list when I come in on Monday night. I'm hoping to have the drawings for them by Thursday."

"Thursday? Can't we get them sooner?"

"Actually, I think we are doing well to get them at all. It's not his department and I don't want to spook the guy by pushing him. One way or another it'll be fine, don't worry."

Norman did not seem too disappointed. "Very well. We'll look at the list together on Monday." There was a document case on the table. He opened it, took out the bulky envelope that Geoff had seen the previous day, and put it down.

"Yours," he said, pushing it across the table.

To Geoff's great relief they had bought his story and accepted that the drawings for the new jobs would not be available until Thursday. Only, there were no new jobs and no drawings, and never would be. He could promise them anything they wanted for Thursday. All was going to plan and if it stayed that way, he would be finished with Norman and company by Wednesday night. He picked up the envelope. It had a comforting, bulky feel.

Stork Hill Gallery was on a well-lit main road near the centre of the city. As they approached the site, Geoff pointed to a sign.

"There. Dennis, take that turning, on the left."

Dennis turned into the road. Fifty yards further on, Geoff said quietly, "Turn right now, into the service road."

PAYBACK

Dennis manoeuvred the van into the large parking bay that served four premises adjacent to one another on the main road.

"Which door is it?" Mac asked.

"The red one."

Dennis pulled up and with the engine running they unloaded Ted and Foxy with their tools.

"Right," said Mac as he climbed back into the cab. "Alarms off."

Geoff keyed a number into the remote and as Mac watched, he pressed a button.

"Alarms now off."

Mac turned to Dennis. "Come on, come on, don't hang around," he said, "We need to get out of here."

The van left to cruise the streets, awaiting a call from the men when they were ready to be picked up. Geoff was again impressed by the attention to detail which had gone into the team's preparation. This time apart from the two hessian sacks and gaffer tape, their toolboxes also contained a number of bags of differing sizes, all made from plastic bubble wrapping, convenient for quick packing of small objects.

Twenty minutes after they left, Mac's mobile rang. He had been holding it in his hand.

"You done?" he asked tersely. He paused to listen and then said, "Five minutes. Stay out of sight."

Five minutes later the van swung into the service road again and pulled up behind the building. Mac got out quickly and opened the back doors. The two men scrambled in with their sacks now laden with booty. They fell onto their cushions and ripped off their balaclavas.

Mac shut the rear doors and hurried around to climb into the passenger seat.

"Go, go," he urged Dennis. The van rocked as Dennis lifted the clutch and stamped on the accelerator pedal.

"Careful," Geoff warned, hanging on to the seat. "We don't want to get stopped for speeding."

Foxy leaned forward and tapped Geoff on the shoulder.

"Bloody fantastic!" he enthused. "Fab, no problems at all. In and out, great!"

"Sweet as a nut," said Ted. "You should see the stuff we got. Amazing. The boss should give us all a bonus."

Dennis glanced over his shoulder. "OK, *you* ask him, then," he said drily.

All the way back to their base the talk was of the extraordinary success they were enjoying. Once again Geoff got a buzz from sharing the excitement of their euphoria. He even wondered if it was such a bad thing after all, to feel part of the team.

They phoned Norman when they were about ten minutes away and he was waiting for them when they arrived. The sacks were taken out, with Foxy and Ted enthusing about the contents.

Geoff did not want to linger so he told Norman he was leaving.

"Fine," said Norman, who appeared delighted at the success of the venture. "An excellent job, again. I can't wait to see the merchandise. You get off then, and we shall see you again on Monday night for the next job. Around nine o'clock would be fine."

Geoff spent most of the next day relaxing in his room at Gamages, where he used his laptop to scan through the Sunday newspapers. Nowhere did he find any mention of the burglary at Granite's house; it would be tomorrow's news, Geoff surmised. But the jewellery shop job was mentioned in two of the newspapers. According to both reports the local police were convinced that the alarms had not been switched on. It was suggested that a member of the shop staff had been negligent.

Around mid-day he went downstairs looking for Gloria and found her in the dining room.

"Hello, Gloria," he said, "I'm sorry to disturb you."

"No problem Mr Jeffries. I'm just setting the tables for tonight's dinners. What can I do for you?

"I know it's a bit of a cheek, but could I please trouble you for a couple of sandwiches and a cup of tea?"

Gloria put down the handful of cutlery she was holding. "We don't do lunches," she said, "but as it's you, I'm sure I can manage that. What would you like? I've got some nice ham."

"That would be lovely, thank you. Shall I come down for it?"

"No need, I'll bring a tray it to your room."

Geoff thanked her and went back up to his room where he picked up his "Jeffries" mobile. He had two calls to make and he started by calling Samantha.

"How's it going?" she asked.

"It's going fine. It's a different world, Sam."

"Well, you're still here, that's a relief."

"Are you doing anything this evening?" Before she could answer he added, "I'd love another steak dinner at the King's Head. Even better if I'm having it with you."

After a moment's hesitation Samantha said, "In that case, I'm just going to have to cancel all my other engagements for the evening."

"Great. Sam, I'm sorry to have to ask this but would you mind if we met there, like last time? I'll explain over dinner."

"OK. And no need for an explanation, I think I know why. Just one thing you should know."

"What?"

"I've not decided, yet. I need more time."

"You know my feelings about that, but I promise to keep off the subject, if that's what you want."

They agreed to meet at the bar and Geoff said he would book a table for around seven o'clock. He then called Harry Mortimer. The phone rang for a little while before he answered.

"Hello," he said in a disinterested tone.

"Harry? It's Geoff."

"Hi, Geoff. Sorry, I thought it was the bloody office. Don't like it when they bugger me about on a Sunday."

"There's an easy answer. Why don't you invest in a new phone? Then you'd see on the display who it is. Or better still, you could always switch it off."

"No, couldn't possibly do that, unfortunately. I

might miss something. But I like the idea of a new phone, might do that. What have you got for me?"

"It's happening, exactly like I hoped it would."

"Good. Tell me more."

Geoff went on to give him details of the progress he was making and concluded by saying that it would all be done and dusted on Wednesday night when, with luck, Harry would have his big story, the scoop of the year.

As expected for a Sunday night the restaurant was busy. When asked, Geoff confirmed that they had reserved a table for two, booked by Mr Jeffries.

The waiter checked his clipboard and then looked up. "Yes, Mr Jeffries, table for two."

"Somewhere quiet, please."

The man checked his clipboard again. "I'm terribly sorry, Mr Jeffries, we're very busy tonight." He shook his head. "Sunday, you know."

Geoff reached into his pocket, leaned forward and proffered his hand, in which he was holding a twenty pound note. "It's really important. It's my fiancée's birthday today."

Samantha's eyes widened. She turned her head and covered her mouth with her hand.

The man beamed. "Ah, that's different, sir. A special occasion." He palmed the note and said to Samantha, "May I wish you a very happy birthday, Miss. This way, please." He led them to a quiet table in a corner of the room, then held the chair back for Samantha who sat down.

After the waiter was out of earshot, she smiled.

CHAPTER FIFTEEN

"Liar!" she said, softly.

Geoff's eyebrows arched. "Who, me? OK, I lied a bit, because it's not your birthday. So it was only a half-lie."

"It was a one hundred per cent fib." She pushed a lock of hair behind her ear. "It's not my birthday, and I'm not your fiancée. I told you, I have not made up my mind. And I meant it, Geoffrey Summers."

"Er, Jeffries, please."

"All right. I meant it, mister Summer Jeffries, or whatever."

They laughed. Geoff had not felt so relaxed in weeks. They chatted easily over the meal, and when the coffees arrived Samantha struck a serious note.

"What will you do? I mean, when it's all over."

He did not answer immediately, but stirred his coffee for a few moments.

"When I was fourteen my best friend Barry invited me to join him and his parents on a holiday to South Africa. He was an only child; his mum thought it would be good for him to have company his own age. My parents paid my fare, of course."

"Did you enjoy it?"

"It was fantastic. They rented a house on the coast south of Durban, in a town called Southbroom. The whole town is like a tropical garden, a beautiful place. There was a pathway from the back garden, down between bushes, to a sand dune. Behind that," he made a sweeping gesture, "was a huge, empty beach. And the Indian Ocean. You can get used to the sound of the ocean, just yards away."

"It sounds wonderful."

"It was, probably still is. I might go back there, if..."

"If what?"

"If I could afford it and if I had the right company." He was looking directly at her and once again his heart missed a beat. "And I don't mean Barry," he said softly.

Samantha dabbed her mouth with her table napkin, but she said nothing. Later, Geoff would come to look back on this as being a seminal moment. He now knew that he loved this woman and that he wanted to share the rest of his life with her.

He reached into his pocket, took out a mobile phone and placed on the table.

"I want you to do something for me," he said. "Take this; it's new and unused. Keep it just for calls to me and if I need to call you, I'll call you only on this phone. I have a new one too, or rather Jeffries has, and I've already put its number in for you. They are 'pay-as-you-go' and I've loaded them to last a while. Both have the same unlock and voicemail passwords. The unlock code is S-A-M-B and the voicemail one is J-E-F-F."

She raised her eyebrows. "Is all this secrecy really necessary?"

"I'm hoping not, but I'm swimming in shark-infested waters at the moment." He looked at her steadily. "Both new phones are secure but I don't want to take any chances. I can't bear the thought that they might try to harm you because of me. I don't really think it's likely, but I want to make it impossible."

When they left Geoff walked Samantha to her car. She unlocked it with the remote, and Geoff took hold of the door handle.

"Drive carefully, you're important to me." He held the door open for her.

Samantha stooped to get in, then paused and straightened. She placed her hand on his arm and kissed him on the lips.

"You take care, too."

Dave Merchant lived in the hamlet of Les Saules, about twenty kilometres south of the city of Lille. The house he shared with his wife Glenda had been built in the nineteenth century as a farmhouse but now it was a domestic dwelling, at the end of a rural track. Before they moved in, the house had been modernised and extended to include a new double garage and a wide, gravelled turning area to the front.

On this sunny late autumn Monday with just a hint of chill heralding the winter to come, Dave hummed to himself, easing his Transit van out of the garage. Glenda appeared at the front door, carrying two empty shopping bags and her handbag. Dave poked his head out of the window.

"Shut the garage door, will you, love?"

She frowned. "Lazy sod," she muttered. She shut the door, came over to the van and climbed into the cab, settling herself on the passenger seat.

"That's the only thing I can't get used to, living here."

"Eh? What?"

"Everything shuts on Mondays," she complained.

The gravel on the drive crunched as they moved off.

"Oh that. Hardly a problem, though. The hypermarkets are open or you wouldn't be coming with me today."

"But all the way to Lille, just to get some groceries. Lucky for me you were going to pick up the heater anyway. When are the boys coming?"

"Wednesday. I could have picked it up tomorrow but its best to get everything ready in good time. That way, if there's a problem I've got an extra day to sort it." He turned the wheel to negotiate a narrow bend. "Can't afford to risk letting Jim down."

"No," she agreed. "Not after all he's done, helping us with the move and everything." She was looking out of her window. "You know, I did wonder at first why he wanted us to have such a big parking area at the front." Her mouth moved into a twisted smile. "But removal vans need a lot of space for turning around, don't they?"

Dave glanced at her. "You love it here, don't you?"

"Beats Dagenham." She lifted her chin. "And just look around. It's so beautiful, and peaceful."

The track snaked between tall oaks and woodland, heading towards the centre of the village. She's right, thought Dave. As always, he was struck with the beauty all around. He felt that they were fortunate to live in such idyllic surroundings.

"Yeah, you're right."

Dave was enjoying the drive as he drank in the

beauty of the countryside, but he might have felt differently had he known about the policeman who, from the cover of the same beautiful woods, had watched them leaving the house.

Chief Superintendent Andy Powell looked at the man standing in front of him on the other side of his desk. Frank Rollo was seriously worried, and it showed. The statement he had taken from Jim Warwick was on the desk between them.

Powell put his hand on the document. "Before we talk about this, Sergeant, is there anything you want to tell me?"

Rollo averted his eyes. "Sir?"

"Jim Warwick. This statement reads like a fairy tale. Snow White springs to mind."

"It's what he said sir, word for word."

Powell paused and stared into Rollo's eyes. "Are you quite sure that you have nothing to say to me about Warwick?"

Rollo shifted awkwardly. "I know he gives to police charities."

Powell stood up, turned and walked slowly to the window behind his desk. He looked out onto the car park for a few moments. Without turning around, he said, "I take it you've seen the CCTV disc?"

"Yes, sir," said Rollo, addressing his Chief's back.

Powell swung around sharply. "So, did you tell him what was on it? Did you ask him why his employee Conroy was seen destroying the tracking device? Did you ask him where that tracker had come from?"

By now sweat was plainly visible on the brow of

Rollo's miserable face.

He whined. "Conroy works for him, sir, he admitted that. But he said he has no knowledge of the tracker. He said he paid Bellini off and he knows nothing about what happened to him after that."

Powell stared at his sergeant, saying nothing. After several long moments, Rollo looked downwards, breaking eye contact.

"And he showed me the cheque stub. The one he mentions in the statement. It was twenty grand, like he says."

Powell sat down. "Have you checked with the bank to see if it has been cashed?"

"No, sir. I mean, yes, sir, I checked. It has not been presented."

"Doesn't that surprise you? It's been nearly four weeks. Has it not occurred to you, Sergeant, how odd it is that a man who is supposed to be a gold-digger has not, in four weeks, *taken the money?*"

Rollo's face was ashen, his brow beaded with sweat. He passed his tongue over his lips, saying nothing.

Powell leaned back in his chair. He picked up a pencil and slowly began to tap the edge of the desk.

"You know, Sergeant, for the past couple of years there have been rumours about your relationship with the suspect." He tapped the desk with the pencil again and again, faster and faster. Rollo stood still, and mute. He appeared to have shrunk in stature and to be on the verge of collapse. Powell wanted more time to investigate. Without solid proof, there was a limit to what he could do at this stage. He pointed the pencil at Rollo.

"Sergeant," he said, speaking slowly and deliberately, "I am suspending you from active duty as of today. Go home, now. Do not come back until we tell you to. If Mr Warwick communicates with you in any way, you are to tell me immediately. And, under no circumstances are you to contact him at all. Is that clear?"

"Yes, sir," Rollo mumbled in a voice scarcely louder than a whisper. He turned to leave.

"Oh, and Sergeant," Powell said, "*Don't* clear out your desk, and do not touch your computer. I advise you also to think very carefully about what you may wish to say when you are questioned officially about this matter. Do you understand?"

Rollo merely nodded bleakly. Shoulders hunched, he trudged slowly out of the room. His eyes were glazed and as the door closed behind him he was already reaching for his cigarettes.

CHAPTER SIXTEEN

The following evening Geoff was seated at the long table at BST with the others, with the plan drawings of Sadlington Manor and Warwick Hall on the table in front of him. The team had completed their check list and loaded the van, ready to go. Geoff looked at his watch.

Mac was sitting with his arms crossed on the table. He scowled at Geoff.

"You got a problem?"

"No, why do you ask?" Geoff replied evenly.

"We got plenty of time. Norman's gonna be here in a minute."

Norman was with his chairman. Apart from Mac the men were cheerful, but Dennis complained.

"I'm telling you," he said, shaking his head, "sooner or later something's gonna go wrong." He rotated his teacup and looked into it. "Stands to reason, don't it? I mean, it can't go on being easy forever."

Mac shook his head. "No worries. Long as *you* ain't in charge, it'll be just fine."

In the next room, Robbie Naylor was sitting in his favourite recliner chair. Norman sat opposite in an armchair.

Norman said, "I really don't think it will work. It's too big a risk."

Naylor waved a hand dismissively. "What risk? The guy is a cheap loser. He'll fucking wet himself. He'll do exactly what we want."

"I have a problem with it. This is a man who has

said openly that nothing and nobody can hurt him. He doesn't care if he lives or dies."

"Don't be too sure about that. Believe me, when push comes to shove nobody wants to die. Nobody sane, anyway. The guy's got brains. He's only, what – forty-four, forty-five? And he's got a new woman. Course he'll do what we want. What's the worst that can happen?"

He went on to answer his own question. "You think he'll grass?" He snorted. "Not a fucking chance. I'm *telling* you, he'll fold." He smirked. "But first, he'll wet himself."

Norman sighed. "Very well, I'll do it."

Geoff looked up as Norman came in through the connecting door carrying his document case, which he placed upon the table.

"Right," he said, looking around. "Does anybody have any questions about tonight's job?"

There were headshakes and mumbled negatives around the table.

With a twisted grin Mac said, "Tell Dennis the meat ain't for him."

The others laughed out loud. Except Dennis, who scowled and muttered, "Very funny."

Norman smiled, then picked up the drawing of Sadlington Manor, folded it and put it aside. He pointed at the layout drawing of Warwick Hall. "That's Wednesday's job. Geoff will give us a few pointers about it now, but we shall be going over it in detail again on the night." He nodded to Geoff, who stood up.

PAYBACK

Geoff explained the general layout and the fact that the building was effectively in two parts. "We know, thanks to the firm's research, that the main house is going to be unoccupied that night, but we aren't sure about the extension." He indicated the outline on the drawing.

Ted interrupted. "If we're not sure about that bit, how do we know if it's OK to go into the house?"

Geoff looked at Norman, but it was Mac who answered. "The main man got an assistant guy called Clive." He grinned, eyes wide. "He told me, and for sure he wasn't lying. His boss mostly hangs out in the office at the other end and Wednesday his missus and daughter are going up west. All night, so Clive said. But he didn't know if the boss was going as well."

Geoff was slightly taken aback by Mac's remark but tried not to show it.

"Thank you," he said. "The two best places to get in are here," he pointed, "and here. The back door of the utility room and the double patio doors at the side of the lounge. The gold coin collection I told you about is here," he indicated, "in the living room. The coins are in two cabinets, in trays. You'll need to drill out the locks to slide out the trays but the coins are all in plastic envelopes."

Mac interrupted. "They're gold." He looked at Ted and Foxy. "No point getting sticky fingers, you can't use them to buy pints in your local." The others laughed.

Geoff traced the outline of the perimeter with his index finger. "The wall is about eight feet high, and the gates are electric, opened only from inside. Ted

293

will give Foxy a leg-up over the wall and Foxy will open the gate by pressing the button on the post inside."

Geoff looked around. They were all paying attention although they had heard all this before.

He went on. "The gate is programmed to close automatically after a minute or so, but as soon as it is open, I'll go in and disable the mechanism so that it stays open. Ted will come around and he and Mac will join Foxy inside. Any questions?"

There were headshakes all round, nobody had any questions.

Norman said, "Thank you, Geoff." He folded the drawing and put it aside, before picking up the second one. "Tonight, Sadlington Manor. You all know what to do." He looked at Mac, "Is everything loaded?"

"Yeah, loaded and ready to go," Mac replied.

Norman looked at his watch. "Off you go, then, and good luck."

On the way to the job Geoff thought about what Mac had said. He knew that these people were professionals, but learning that they had the means to find Clive and lean on him was a nasty shock. Clearly, they were every bit as ruthless as Harry Mortimer had said.

Traffic had been light on the M25. On the Dartford crossing bridge Dennis slowed the van as they approached the toll barriers.

Geoff checked his watch. "We're making good time."

Sitting beside him, Mac rubbed his chin. "This manor, you been inside it?"

"Yes, I did the survey."

"Norman says he's a big shot lawyer."

"Sir Stanley Blake-Wellings, QC. Sadlington's been in his family for generations."

"How come they got a lot of silver?"

"Old money. One of the ancestors was an ambassador. Diplomatic corps, apparently he started the collection. It's been added to over the years."

Dennis turned to glance at them. "Could be some tom as well then, in the bedrooms."

Geoff knew that Dennis was using cockney slang to describe jewellery.

"We're keeping out of the bedrooms," Mac shot back. He swivelled in his seat to address the two men in the back. "You hear that? No scouting. I mean it," he growled.

"OK," Ted responded. "We wouldn't anyway."

Mac turned back. "Better not," he snarled. "Not if you know what's good for you."

Sadlington Manor was a minor stately home set in six acres of landscaped gardens. BST's reconnaissance had revealed that when Sir Stanley and his wife were away, the only occupant of the manor was an elderly maid.

At the briefing Norman had said, "She's in her seventies, but that doesn't mean that there is anything wrong with her hearing." He had looked around at the team, adding, "And the two Rottweilers will be noisy. That's what they are for, so make sure it's all clear before you go in."

Geoff looked down the road when Dennis stopped the van a hundred metres from the gates to the premises. There was nothing in sight.

Mac picked up the parcel that had been at his feet and opened the door. He turned and said, "Engine off, Dennis, but be ready to start it up sharpish. Everybody stay here, and keep quiet. The dogs'll make a racket because I'm going to make sure they come to the gate. I'll be back when I've given them their dinner."

Mac closed the door softly and moved off. Dennis asked, "What about Sir Blake and his missus?"

"Norman said they're in Scotland," Geoff replied, "so they must be."

A minute later all hell broke loose. Geoff was surprised that two dogs could make so much noise, snarling, yelping and barking like they were spoiling for a fight. Surely, he thought, in the still night such a cacophony would not go unnoticed in the house.

Sitting beside Geoff, Dennis nearly leapt out of his skin.

"*Christ.*" he exclaimed. Eyes wide, he turned to Geoff. "I'm starting up, that racket's enough to wake the dead." Dennis' fingers were on the key about to start the engine, when Geoff put a restraining hand on his arm.

"Calm down. Dogs like that are easily spooked. If the maid hears them she won't do anything, unless she also hears your diesel engine."

Dennis paused and said, "Maybe you're right."

Moments later the din ceased abruptly. Geoff

surmised that the dogs were busy with their treat.

Mac scuttled back to the van, opened the passenger door and climbed onto the seat. He held up a hand. "Everybody, *quiet!*" Then he lowered his window and listened. "Give it five minutes," he said, "then we'll know if it's OK."

Geoff had learned from Norman that the tranquillizer in the beef steaks that Mac threw to the dogs was powerful enough to knock the animals out within three minutes. Mac was just making sure, Geoff thought.

In the eerie silence of the night five minutes seemed more like an hour. Finally Mac left the van again and went over to the gate. He flashed the torch beam once, signalling that all was well.

Geoff disabled the security alarm and the men climbed over the gate and went into the house. Mac stood at the gate keeping watch, with Geoff beside him.

The men were out again in less than fifteen minutes, returning with bulging sacks. Foxy moved cautiously around the recumbent guard dogs.

Through the gate Mac hissed. "Come on, get a move on. The dogs'll be out for hours."

"All right for you, you're outside," Foxy muttered as he and Ted passed the sacks over the gate and then climbed over.

Two minutes later they were all back inside the van, with their booty.

When they got back to BST, Geoff was surprised that

Norman had come downstairs to meet them. As before, the sacks were taken upstairs immediately by Mac and the others. Geoff did not go with them, because Norman took him aside. He had another fat envelope in his hand.

"Your remuneration," he said, holding it out.

"Thank you," said Geoff, taking hold of the envelope.

Norman did not release his grip, holding on firmly to one end of the packet. "You have earned it, but make no mistake. It is *essential* that we have the new list on Wednesday. You promised three more jobs, we want the names and locations of the venues, and your drawings. I cannot stress too highly the importance of this. Time is running out, for us and for you. Wednesday, without fail." He released his grip on the envelope.

"You'll have it," Geoff said, wearily. He was tired, and all he wanted was to get back to his room and his bed. He walked over to his car, opened the door and threw the envelope unopened onto the passenger seat.

Driving back to Leigh he reflected that he had not done badly even though this would be the last payment, whatever Naylor and Norman might believe. He would be giving them a list of three new target venues on Wednesday to keep them at bay. But the difference this time, he thought smugly, was that the controllers would not have been modified. He had done nothing at all about arranging anything like that.

Geoff turned off the road and drove through to the

parking area behind Gamages. The old Victorian guest house was in darkness, save for a dim glow from the low wattage night light in the hallway. Geoff let himself in and quietly shut the door. Clutching his document case and the bulky envelope, he started up the staircase. In the background the familiar "bongs" of the mantle clock echoed in the dining room, chiming three times.

In his room Geoff put his case and the unopened envelope on top of the chest of drawers. He did his toilet and went to bed, exhausted. He was too tired to bother to open the envelope; he decided to leave it until the morning.

Chief Superintendent Andy Powell was sitting in the passenger seat of an unmarked police car, with Detective Constable Eddie Smith driving. It was raining, the windscreen wipers swishing rhythmically as they swept back and forth across the screen. Smith turned the wheel to guide the car into a side road and Powell peered out through his rain-spattered window.

"This is the road," he said, pointing. "There's number four, there's six, so sixty-four will be on this side a bit further on."

Smith slowed the car as they approached the semi-detached house and drew up at the kerb outside number sixty-four. A concrete drive led from double gates which were open, to a single garage attached to the house. The area to the front of the house was concreted, its purpose revealed by black oil stains on the surface.

"Have you got an umbrella?" Powell asked.

"On the back seat."

Powell swivelled in his seat and reached for the umbrella. "Just the one?"

"I'm afraid so, sir."

"Then you're going to get wet, lad." Powell climbed out, shut the door and raised the umbrella.

"Thank you very much, sir," Smith muttered quietly as he stepped out. He turned his collar up and slammed the door shut. Powell was already standing in the shelter of the half porch. He pressed the doorbell as Smith joined him. After a few moments the door was opened to a gap of about six or eight inches. From behind it, a freckle-faced small boy with tousled hair frowned up at them. He looked to be about eight or nine years old.

"Hello," said Smith. "Is your dad in?"

The boy stared, unblinking. He shook his head. "No."

"Your mum, then?"

"No."

Powell leaned forward. "What's your name, son?"

"Ben Conroy. What's yours?"

"I'm Andy. Shouldn't you be in school?"

"I'm off sick." He frowned and added, "Prob'ly infectious."

With a straight face Powell asked, "With what?"

The boy inclined his head and rolled his eyes. "Doh! *Sickness*, of course."

Powell smiled. "OK, but we really need to speak to your dad, Ben. When will he be home?"

"He's gone to France, on business. Prob'ly won't be back till tomorrow. Late."

PAYBACK

Smith cut in. "Does he go to France a lot?"

The boy shrugged. "Some. Every couple of months, maybe."

"Does he go in his car? A Range Rover, isn't it?" Smith asked.

"No, he goes by boat." He nodded. "Yes, he's got a Range Rover. It's crap. My mum's got a Merc," he said proudly, "a blue one, only a year old."

"Really?" said Powell. "Cool. Anyway, Ben, we have to go, we'll call back another day."

They turned to leave, and Ben called after them. "Who do I say came?"

Smith was hurrying around to the driver's side. Powell put the umbrella up. "We're old friends. Sorry, have to go, we're getting wet." He collapsed the umbrella and got into the car.

Smith started the engine. "France? Why France?"

Powell lobbed the folded umbrella onto the back seat. "Who knows? But it's interesting."

A minute later Smith said, "Sir?"

"What?"

"Do you say 'Cool' a lot?"

"No, but my eight-year-old does." He grinned. "Drive on, Constable."

Despite having had only six hours' sleep, Geoff was alert. Amazing how quickly a hot shower and a decent shave could revive one, he thought. He strapped on his wristwatch, noting that he still had ten minutes to get downstairs for breakfast. He was hungry but if he hurried he could get to the dining room before nine-thirty, the time at which Gloria

301

stopped serving breakfasts.

Fifteen minutes later Geoff was finishing his meal.

"Everything all right Mr Jeffries?"

Geoff would have preferred to have his breakfast in silence but Gloria had come in and he thought it would be churlish not to respond politely.

"Fine, thank you," he said. "The scrambled eggs are delicious."

Gloria beamed. "I do them in butter, with just a smidge of garlic and black pepper." She pointed at his cup. "Would you like some more coffee?"

"Yes, please."

"I'll just get it for you."

When he had finished, Geoff left the table and slipped away when Gloria was out of the room. He did not want to be buttonholed by her as she seemed always to be looking for opportunities to engage him in conversation. He had things to do in the town, but wanted to speak to Samantha first. He went to his room, took out his "Jeffries" mobile, sat on the bed and called her.

After a short delay, she answered.

"Hi, Geoff, how did it go?"

"Fine, no problems. How are you?"

"OK, but I can't wait to get out of this place."

"Hang in there, it'll all be over by this time Thursday."

"When will I see you?"

"I'll call you tonight."

"What are you going to be doing today?"

"Got to do the rounds again. Banks, travel agents, building societies, buying travellers cheques. Not in my name of course, they'll be signed by John Jeffries."

Samantha chuckled. "You really are a devious devil, aren't you?"

"I have my moments. Anyway, I've got to go; I'll call you again later."

"Bye. And take care."

Geoff put the mobile in his pocket, stood up, went over to the chest of drawers and picked up the envelope with the cash in it. He sat on the bed, tore open the envelope, and tipped the contents out onto the bed. As before the cash was in bundles of twenty and fifty-pound notes, each with a rubber band around it.

This time however, there was also something else. Another, smaller envelope. Geoff opened it and found that it contained six photographs. They appeared to have been taken in quick succession, showing a woman entering a car that was parked in front of a block of low-rise flats. They were excellent pictures of Samantha Bowen.

In France Dave left home in the Transit and at the crossroads in the hamlet he turned right. The road ran alongside a wide stream, on both banks of which were the lines of willow trees which gave the place its name, Les Saules, the Willows. The stream went on to join the great River Deule, which flows through the ancient city of Lille. Dave checked his watch. He was making good time, and would soon be on the

A25 which would take him to the port of Dunkirk.

He was on the motorway when his mobile trilled. He fished it out of his pocket and pressed a button to take the call.

"Yes, mate," he said. "I'm driving but without looking, I'm guessing it's you."

"Just checking, everything all right?" Dave had guessed right, it was Jim Warwick.

"Yup, no probs, I'm on the motorway, next stop Dunkirk. The heater's in the back. Any news about my passengers?"

"I called Shaun just now. The boat left on time, should be OK."

"You worry too much. You don't need to call every five minutes. What's the point of being filthy rich if you're going to kill yourself with stress?"

"I didn't know you cared. Now bugger off and get on with it. I'll call you again when I've checked with the Dutch guy."

"OK, bye."

On the Channel ferry Kevin Flynn was seated in a corner of the passenger lounge. He sighed audibly.

"We should get season tickets," he muttered.

Across the aisle two tables away, Shaun Conroy heard the remark and ignored it. He appeared to be concentrating on the sports page of his tabloid paper. From where he was sitting he could see the holdall, it was tucked into a corner at Flynn's feet. They were on a winter sailing schedule, not too many passengers about, and none within earshot of Flynn's comment. The vessel shuddered as it slowed, and the ship's public address announced their imminent arrival at Dunkirk. The vessel would be docking in ten minutes.

Flynn waited a few minutes and then picked up his briefcase and the holdall. He looked across at Conroy before making his way towards the queue of passengers waiting to disembark. Again Conroy ignored Flynn, but he was right behind him in the queue.

Fifteen minutes later they were on the road in Dave's Transit. It was an uneventful journey, with little to break the monotony of the motorway driving. Dave's attempts at making conversation went unrewarded, and he reflected that it would be difficult to find three such disparate characters anywhere. This was not something, he thought, that he would do from choice. But the reward of a good bonus in cash made it worthwhile.

They had been on the road for close to two hours, when the mobile in his pocket rang. He fished out the instrument.

"The boss, I expect," he surmised. "Yup," he said, glancing at the display. He pressed the button to take the call.

"Friendly French courier speaking."

"Cut the crap. Where are you?"

"Heading for the Antwerp bypass. We should be at Henk's in a couple of hours, give or take."

"Good. I'll let them know you're on schedule."

"On schedule, on budget, on target. But definitely not on speed, if you get my meaning."

"Silly bugger. Take care and do it right."

"Yes sir, boss. Wilco, over and out."

Nearer their destination, Dave was getting fed up with Flynn who was complaining again.

"Give it a rest for God's sake," he said.

"We should have stopped. It only takes ten minutes," Flynn whined.

"Stop moaning. I told you, there was a burger van near the factory, it's sure to be there again. You can stuff your face as soon as we finish loading. Or you can wait until we drop you off at the Eurostar. You can get a meal on the train."

On previous trips they had stopped to pick up sandwiches and drinks from a motorway service area. This time Dave had kept going; partly, he admitted to himself, to annoy Flynn. Also he himself was not particularly hungry, and Shaun had said nothing.

Fifteen minutes later they turned into the cul-de-sac and pulled up in front of the roller door. Dave climbed out, went across to the side door and pressed the bell. As he waited to be let in, he turned casually to look around the cul-de-sac. He was reassured to see that there was no sign of anything untoward. No sign even, of the burger van. On the last visit he had dismissed the possibility that it had been parked in the cul-de-sac for any covert purpose. Unlikely, it had been selling food, at lunchtime.

Henk came to door. "Hello my friend," he said. "Good to see you."

"Yeah, you too."

Dave climbed back into the van as Henk raised the

shutter. He drove in under the partly raised door and Henk brought it down immediately.

They carried out the transaction, packed and loaded the heater back into the Transit, and were on their way again within thirty minutes.

The observer sitting behind a screened window in a factory unit across the road put down his camera and switched off the video unit that was set up on a tripod. Sitting beside him, his colleague logged the time of the Transit's departure. Then he called a Rotterdam number on his mobile.

In the hotel Geoff sat on his bed, holding his head in his hands. "God, what have I done?" he whispered. "What *have* I done?" It took him only seconds to grasp the enormity of the threat. He was angry and frightened. His immediate reaction had been to pick up his phone to call Norman. Then he thought better of it, he needed time to work out how best to deal with this. He paced the room, trying to think clearly, rationally. His feelings now for Naylor and his gang were only of pure hatred. And he hated himself for seriously underestimating them. How could he have been so stupid?

It took him some time to calm down and to work out a plan. He checked his watch. Ten twenty, he had enough time, just. Using the Jeffries phone, he called Samantha.

Her phone rang for a few moments before she answered.

"Hello again, did you forget something?" She

307

sounded anxious.

"Sam there's a problem, I must see you. Now."

"What, right now? I'm in the office. Oh, by the way, I gave Adam my notice yesterday, couldn't wait. You should have seen his face."

He tried to stay calm but could not keep the edge out of his tone. "It's a big problem. We have to meet as soon as possible."

"What sort of problem?"

"It's complicated, I'll explain when we meet. You take your lunch at twelve-thirty, don't you?"

"Such as it is. Sandwiches, here. But if it's that important, I can leave now. What are they going to do, fire me?"

"Lunchtime would be better for me, Sam, I've got a couple of things to do before we meet up. Can we make it around one? Mario's in the high street?"

"OK. I'll be there."

"Good. And about giving in your notice, well done. It's going to help."

"See you there, then."

He left the guest house and drove to the town, where he found a space in the town centre car park. After a visit to the bank, he walked down the high street towards Mario's. He was apprehensive as he approached the restaurant. It had been bad enough when he had to tell Samantha that he was about to get involved with criminals, but this time it was much worse. He was deeply worried about how she might react when she learned that he may have put her life in jeopardy. With a sick feeling he acknowledged that he was likely to lose her forever. He pushed the door open and entered.

The restaurant was busy, and filling up. He saw Samantha sitting alone at a table set for two. She looked up and waved him over, and Geoff eased his way between the tables towards her. Samantha was smiling, but her smile faded to a look of concern as he approached.

"Hi," he said, "been waiting long?"

"About five minutes. What's up? You don't look happy."

"I'm not." He slipped his jacket off and placed it over the back of the chair. "It's a balls-up, Sam, and it's all my fault."

"Sit down and have a drink, and tell me about it."

Geoff slumped onto the chair. He put his elbows on the table and wiped his face with his hands.

"It's not good news," he said. "There's a problem with the people I've been working with."

"Are you in trouble?"

At that moment, a waiter came over, looked from one to the other and asked, "Would you like to order?"

Geoff said to Samantha, "I'd rather not have a drink just now." To the waiter he said, "We'll have a bottle of your house red with the meal, please. Can you give us a couple of minutes before we order?" The waiter nodded and left.

Geoff's mouth turned down. "The short answer is yes, I am in trouble, but I'm going to get out of it." He picked up the menu, although he had no appetite at all.

"Lunchtime specials. What are you having?"

"The minestrone and ravioli sound good," she answered.

"I'll have the same." He put the menu aside. "You know we decided that the less you know about what I am doing, the better?"

"Yes."

"What I did tell you was that there were only ever going to be five jobs. I've left Melford, so I can't set up any more even if I wanted to, which of course I don't. We'll be doing the last job tomorrow night. I've planned it so that I can get away and call the police while the others are still on the premises."

"Then what's the problem?" she asked quietly.

He shook his head despairingly. "They refuse to believe that I can't organize any more jobs. No matter what I say, they are insisting that somehow I must conjure up more. These people are greedy, Sam, and ruthless. They will stop at nothing to get what they want."

"Have they threatened you?"

He nodded. "In the worst possible way," he said bleakly.

The waiter returned bringing a bottle of wine and two glasses. He placed the glasses on the table and poured wine into each. Geoff thanked him and gave him their order and the waiter left.

Geoff said, "I have to get away until the dust settles. And so must you, my darling."

It was the first time he had addressed her as "darling".

"Me?" she exclaimed, not responding to his

endearment. "Why me?"

"To keep them quiet, I had to get them to believe that I would be carrying on. I can't of course, so I gave them a few names, just to buy time.

"I still don't understand why I should be..."

Geoff interrupted, holding up a hand. Speaking slowly, he said, "Their way of guaranteeing my cooperation, Sam, was to put photographs of you in my pay envelope. Nothing was said, but the threat..."

"*What?*" Samantha sat up, clearly horrified. "Are you saying that they – that *I'm* in danger?"

"Sam," he pleaded, "you've got to believe me, I had no idea they would do anything like this. I'm sorry, really, dreadfully, sorry."

Geoff had never seen Samantha angry. "So you *should* be," she fumed. She had raised her voice enough to draw the attention of people at the nearest tables and one or two turned to look at her. Samantha reached down to pick her handbag up off the floor. "I'm leaving," she said.

Her other hand was on the table and Geoff immediately leant forward, put his hand over hers and pleaded with her.

"Sam, stay," he pleaded. "We will get out of this. Please, just give me a minute to explain."

She withdrew her hand, put her bag in her lap and sat still, glaring at him.

"Thank you," he said. "Firstly, nothing will happen before the day after tomorrow. At the moment they think they've forced me to cooperate, and that suits us. By the time they realise that I'm no longer around, the gang will be busted."

CHAPTER SIXTEEN

Samantha did not seem satisfied. "I'm upset, Geoff. I don't like being a target. This was nothing to do with me. What are you going to do about it? Getting involved with criminals was a stupid idea from the start. It hasn't helped you and it was never going to bring Penny back."

He put his head in his hands. "Yes I know, I know. My only excuse is that at the time, I was too screwed up to think straight. You're right; I never should have started this." In a tone of despair he pleaded, "Forgive me, Sam."

For a few moments neither spoke and Samantha seemed a little calmer.

"I don't know if I can ever forgive you for this, but one thing I do know is that I can't go through the rest of my life looking over my shoulder."

"I wish to God I could turn the clock back, but I can't. Not being with you would be the heaviest price I could pay for my stupidity."

The waiter arrived with their soup. They leaned back and he placed the bowls before them, leaving with a cheerful "*Buon appetito.*"

Sam quietly put her handbag down on the floor again. Meanwhile Geoff reached into his jacket pocket and withdrew a small piece of paper.

"I can't turn the clock back, but if we can get away for a few days, I'm sure it will all blow over." He passed the paper to her.

"This is the address and phone number of Mallins Wood Hall," he said. "It's a four star country hotel, not far from here. It's quiet and safe. I have booked two rooms there for us, one in your name and the other in mine, as Jeffries. The rooms are ours from today but I won't be checking out of Gamages just yet. I'm keeping it on for a few days, better if they think I'm still there."

Samantha said nothing for several long moments. Then she picked up her spoon and slowly started on her soup.

"Will you be staying at the hotel or at the guest house?" she asked.

"I can use either but it'll be the hotel tonight and definitely tomorrow night, after the job's done and I've slipped away."

"And after that?"

He inclined his head. "I've still got a couple of things to sort out but I'll be able to answer your question properly tonight. If my plan works, it will all be over tomorrow night anyway. But I'd like you to go to the hotel this afternoon, after you've picked up what you need from your flat. I'll join you there this evening."

Samantha looked distinctly unhappy. "I really don't like the sound of this at all. Is it going to be safe? You said they'd been watching me."

"It'll be fine. They believe they've blackmailed me into cooperating, so they have no need to watch you. Besides in the very unlikely event that they might, they will expect you to be at work this afternoon."

"I really don't have any choice, do I? There doesn't seem to be any other way out. But I can't just — disappear."

"You don't have to. Just stay away from any place where you would normally go. It'll only be for a few days, a week at most and maybe only for the next two days." He looked at her tenderly. "Right now, your safety is all I care about. Nothing else matters."

They finished their soup in silence. Geoff was beginning to hope that all was not lost with Samantha, who appeared to be deep in thought. She dabbed her lips with her napkin and put it down.

"When it's over, where will you be going?"

"I want to settle in South Africa. On the coast, the place I told you about. But if the plan goes pear-shaped," he said quietly, "it won't matter where I am."

"When will you know for certain?"

"Tomorrow night. Or rather, the early hours of Thursday morning."

There was another short silence. Finally, Samantha nodded.

"All right. Like I said, you haven't left me any choice." Geoff was about to interrupt, but she went on. "I'll go home, pack a few things, and check in to the hotel. You can tell me tonight what you'll be doing after Thursday," she paused, "and for the rest of your life."

Before they parted, Samantha telephoned Melfords and asked Sheila to tell Adam Ford that she was going home because she was not feeling well, but that she hoped to be back at work the following morning.

Geoff went back to Gamages and packed an overnight bag. Then he used his laptop to book a flight on Qantas to Sydney, travelling overnight from Heathrow two days later, on the Thursday. He arranged to collect his ticket at the check-in desk before the flight. If his plan worked he would be on it and if not, it would not matter anyway, he thought grimly. He then booked a room for his first night in Australia, at the Sydney Hilton. He made both bookings in the name of Geoffrey Summers.

CHAPTER SEVENTEEN

Samantha was in an armchair in her hotel room reading a magazine and trying to relax, when the bedside phone rang. She went over to it and picked up the handset.

"Yes?"

"This is Reception, Miss Bowen. Mr Jeffries has just arrived, you asked us to let you know."

"Thank you. Please tell him that I'll be down in a minute."

Samantha put the magazine aside and checked herself in the full-length mirror. Then she picked up her room key and went downstairs. Geoff was seated in the reception hall and at his feet were a small bag and his laptop in its case. He stood up and smiled. Samantha thought that he looked a bit weary. She went over to him and kissed him on the cheek.

"What news?"

"So far, so good." He nodded towards a door at the end of the hall. "I'm told there's a bar in the lounge. Let's find a quiet corner and unwind." He picked up his bag and the laptop and they made their way through to the guest lounge.

Samantha looked around. It was a large room, with comfortable chairs and sofas set around low coffee tables, only a few of which were occupied. She led the way to a corner table.

Geoff put his bag and laptop down. "G and T?" he asked.

"I'd prefer a fruit juice. Orange or something, please."

He nodded and went to the bar, returning a few minutes later with the drinks. He placed them on the table and sank into a chair.

Samantha picked up her glass and raised it. "Here's to your new start."

Geoff raised his beer glass. "I wish it could be our new start, not just mine."

"I told you, I need time."

"Sorry. I don't want you to feel under any pressure. But when this is all over I'll be there, if you want me."

"You are opening a new door for yourself. But you've had months to close all the old ones. It's different for me. I have friends and family, I can't just up sticks and leave."

"I hadn't thought of that." His mouth turned down at the edges.

Samantha took a sip from her glass. "How did you get on with your final plans?"

"All done. At least, the first part. I'm leaving for Australia on Thursday night."

"Australia?" She was surprised. "You said you would be going to South Africa."

"There's a reason, it's part of the plan. I'm going to Sydney first, then a week or so later John Jeffries will fly from Sydney to Durban, via Dubai. Emirates has direct flights from Dubai to Durban."

"So it will look like Geoff Summers stays in Australia." Samantha was impressed. "You've got it all worked out, haven't you?"

"Not quite all." He leaned forward and Samantha wondered what was coming next.

"Why don't you just – pack up and come with me,

all the way?" he said, softly. "I really wish you would."

She looked into his eyes. "No, I don't think so. I told you, I'm not sure I can spend the rest of my life in a sort of limbo, always looking over my shoulder."

After a brief silence he capitulated. "As you wish. But I won't give up trying."

Samantha felt that she was perhaps being too hard on him. "Just give me some time. If it all blows over I could change my mind." She picked up her glass and finished her drink. "Now, tell me, are you hungry?"

Geoff's expression showed that the question had caught him unawares. "A bit. You?"

"We had a good lunch today. Do they do light meals here?"

"I expect so, but I'd like to shower and freshen up first."

"OK, call me on the intercom when you are ready to come down again. Room 104."

He picked up his bag and laptop, and smiled. "I know, mine's 103."

They went down to the restaurant together and Samantha had linked her arm through Geoff's as they made their way there. Their conversation during the meal was relaxed and easy, although Geoff could not dispel his feeling of deep despair at the thought that he might soon lose her forever. They had taken their time over the meal. When the waiter came to take their dessert plates away, he asked if they would like coffees.

Samantha answered. "No, thank you. I think we'll be going into the lounge for a drink."

The waiter left and Geoff asked, "A drink?"

"Coffee," she said. "But not in the lounge. The coffee in the room is quite good, and I'm good at boiling water. Come to my room." As they got up to leave, she added, "Give me about five minutes, I've a kettle to fill."

Samantha smiled when she saw the bemused look on Geoff's face. She leaned in to him and whispered, "Bring your toothbrush."

At the Rotterdam office, Marta had taken the call from the observer at the factory.

"They've just left," she said to her boss, Annika van Houten. "Shall I call Joss?"

Annika nodded. "I want them tailed, all the way. They'll probably be heading for Lille. I'll call the French office, see if they want to join in; they can liaise with Joss, if they want to. My guess if that the stuff is going to be loaded onto another vehicle, on its way to a port."

She made another call first, to her Belgian counterpart. The drugs would be travelling through Belgium so it was a minimum courtesy, as the vehicle was not expected to stop anywhere in that country. The Belgian office simply asked to be informed if it did. After making the phone calls, Annika sat down to compose an email to Commander Blake in London.

In France on the morning after they had collected the

drugs, Dave and his wife Glenda were sitting with Shaun in their kitchen after breakfast. Shaun's overnight bag was at his feet. Outside, the wind was howling and rain hammered down in torrents.

"Looks like you're in for a choppy crossing," Dave observed. "The forecast is not good."

Shaun almost responded with a four-letter word. But he never swore in front of ladies.

"Hate boats, specially ferries," he said.

"How do you get on with the Mounts?"

Shaun shrugged. "They're OK."

"Do they give you any problems?"

"No."

Dave thought that as always, trying to make conversation with Shaun was a bit like trying to open a can of beans with a screwdriver, you had to work at it. He was about to try again, when they heard the distinctive throb of the pantechnicon's big diesel engine.

"They're here," he said, getting up.

Glenda said, "I'll make the coffees." She knew that the brothers liked strong French coffee.

The two gendarmes parked in a Renault Clio in the woods saw that their quarry had arrived at last. They had been forced to endure four hours of incarceration in the car, with the windows barely open and steamed up with condensation. The driver switched on the windscreen wipers.

"Take as many shots as you can," he said to his colleague, who was wiping the inside of the glass with a cloth in one hand, while holding his camera in the other.

The driver then picked up his phone and, against the background of rapid-fire clicking of his colleague's camera shutter the man spoke to his headquarters. He gave them a detailed description of the moving van, starting with the registration number, as Peter Mount made a three-point turn on the gravel. The shutter kept on clicking, recording the opening of the rear doors and the loading of the water heater and later, Shaun climbing into the cab to join the brothers.

Within twenty minutes of the van's departure, Annika van Houten had all the details. Ten minutes later, so did Superintendent Ron Standish of Scotland Yard's Drugs Unit. It had all come in by email from Holland. Standish took the information to Commander Blake.

Martin Blake, a six-foot-tall barrel-chested veteran of the force, was galvanized into action.

"Good," he said. "Been expecting something like this. Get on to the ferry companies with the van's details. I want to know exactly where they're arriving and when."

As usual the four mobile phones on Jim Warwick's desk were laid out neatly, like soldiers on parade. One of them trilled. He picked it up and glanced at the display, which confirmed that it was Shaun calling. Jim jabbed at the button.

"Yes, Shaun."

"Boss, we got a problem."

For an instant Jim's stomach tightened. "Is the

shipment all right?" he snapped.

"It's OK. No, the problem is the ferries. Lots of them is cancelled, 'cos of the weather. We're in a queue, but it's miles long."

"Do you know how long you'll be delayed?"

"They reckon about five hours, could be more."

Jim was thinking fast. Five or six hours meant that, allowing for the time spent in Canterbury, they would not get to him until midnight at the earliest.

"All right," he said. "No problem. Call me again when you're actually on board. I'll call Stubby now."

"OK, boss."

Just after eight o'clock UK time, they finally boarded the ferry to Dover. The bad weather had abated and although it was still raining, conditions were calmer.

Shaun and the Mount brothers were on their way up from the vehicle deck to get some food in the passenger lounge, when he remembered that he had to call Jim Warwick.

"What time will we get to your depot?" he asked Pete.

"Depends on traffic. If we aren't held up at Customs, I reckon we should be there around half past ten or eleven."

They joined the queue at a burger bar in a lounge full of people milling around. Shaun took out his mobile and called Jim Warwick.

His call was answered immediately.

"Yes, Shaun. You on the ferry?"

"We boarded about fifteen minutes ago. Just queuing for some nosh."

"Is the consignment OK?"

"Locked in the van. Nobody's allowed on the vehicle deck, so it's safe."

"When will you get to Canterbury?"

"Pete reckons some time between ten-thirty and eleven. Depends on traffic."

"I'll tell Stubby. When you leave don't hang around, you should get here about midnight."

"OK, Boss, see you then."

"Fine. Give me a call if there's a problem."

They docked in Dover, and vehicles were streaming through the checkpoints more quickly than usual, Pete thought.

"Looks like they're waving them all through as fast as possible," he said.

"Good job, too," said Charlie. "My bum is sore from sitting around so long."

Pete, who was driving, slowed the van for the border checkpoint. "Let's have the passports then," he said.

Charlie nudged Shaun. "Hey, it's the same bloke. The copper who clocked you last time."

Pete grimaced. "Shit. Just keep schtum, maybe he's forgotten."

He passed the documents into the officer's outstretched hand. "There you go."

The officer scanned the passports, then looked into the cab.

"Well, well," he said. "You boys again." He raised his voice to speak to Shaun. "You working for this lot now, Shaun?"

Pete grinned. "Nah, he's just hitching a free ride again."

Shaun leaned forward. "It ain't free," he shouted. "I got a mate lives near Lille. The boys give me a lift 'cos I help with loading stuff."

The policeman picked up a pen and scrawled something on a pad, then handed the passports back. "Off you go, then," he said.

Pete drove forward. "Not good. We'll have to put you in the back with the furniture next time Shaun."

The queue of vehicles that had built up behind them was held up a little longer because the officer had picked up his phone to make a call. He stayed on the phone for several minutes, whilst the waiting drivers grew ever more impatient. They were not pleased.

Detective Sergeant Tom O'Brian and his partner Constable Gary Scott, both of Scotland Yard's Special Drugs Unit, had been waiting in an unmarked estate car for the Mounts' van to appear. They were parked in a lay-by just outside Dover. Scott was in the driving seat and he had pushed it back so that he could sit more comfortably. They had taken up station early and had been there some time.

The policemen knew it was going to be a long night and had come prepared. O'Brian picked up his vacuum flask and unscrewed the top. He was about to pour himself a cup of coffee when Scott straightened and pulled his seat forward.

"Ay up," he said, "that's them, Mount Continental something." He glanced at his colleague. "I wouldn't do that just now, if I were you."

"Bugger." O'Brian re-capped the flask.

They watched the pantechnicon grinding its way up the long rise towards the main A2. Scott started the car and merged into the line of slow lorries.

"Keep him in sight," said O'Brian. "These trucks all look the same from the back at night."

"OK."

O'Brian called the office. "They've just gone past. We're following."

"Right," said Vanessa. "A2, as we expected."

They rang off. O'Brian said, "It's the Canterbury address, odds on."

Scott pulled out to overtake a slow lorry. "Do you want to get there before them?"

"Yeah, but don't pass them yet. Once we're sure they're heading for their depot we'll nip ahead and find the best place to park up."

Commander Martin Blake was a hard-working officer, dedicated to his job. Nevertheless, he disliked being away from home at night, something that was necessary occasionally. His unit had two major cases ongoing and this was one of them. He was at his desk reading a copy of an emailed report from Kent Constabulary on the recent activities of Mount Continental Removals when Vanessa came into his room. He looked up.

"Sergeant O'Brian's just been on, sir. The moving van's on the A2 and they're following."

"Excellent. Thank you, Vanessa."

"Something else, sir."

He swivelled his chair. "What is it?"

"The third man in the van. We've had a call from Kent, his name is Shaun Conroy."

"Anything known?"

"No recent form. Only a conviction for affray, some years ago."

"Do we have an address?"

"The officer at the border got the passport number. They checked. His last known address is in Becontree Heath, Essex."

"Hmm. Not Kent, then. Interesting."

"Do you want me to check with Essex?"

"Yes, do that. He's been with the shipment all the way from Holland. We need to find out if there is any connection with trafficking. Or anything else they want to tell us about him."

Chief Inspector Andy Powell was relaxing at home watching a football match, when the phone in his hallway rang. Powell was a keen fan, and the match featured his favourite team who were playing away in eastern Europe.

He did not get up, he knew that his wife Nora would pick up the phone. A few moments later she came into the room.

"It's for you," she said. "Pat Nolan."

Powell groaned. "Oh hell, not tonight." He muted the TV. "It better be important."

He went into the hallway and picked up the handset. "Yes, Pat."

Detective Sergeant Nolan apologised. "Sorry to disturb you, sir."

"What is it?"

"A call from the Yard. Commander Blake's office. They're doing a pursuit and want to know if we have anything on Shaun Conroy. I thought it best to call you."

Powell was instantly alert. "What? The drugs squad? What's the story?"

"Apparently Conroy's in a removal van on its way from Dover to Canterbury."

"Canterbury? What the hell is *that* all about? Did they leave a number?"

"Yes, sir."

Nolan gave him the number to call, and Powell wrote it down. Nolan asked, "Do you want me to do anything?"

"Let me talk to them first. I'll call you if I do. Is Eddie Smith about?"

"Just left. Shall I get him to call you?"

"No, not yet. I want to see what this is about first."

When Powell called Scotland Yard he was put on to Superintendent Ron Standish. Powell explained why he was interested in Conroy. He said that he was investigating a missing person case and that he had no knowledge of Conroy's possible involvement in drugs trading.

"We tried to get hold of him yesterday, but he'd left for France. What's he doing going to Canterbury?"

"He's on a lorry we believe is carrying a load of happy pills."

Powell was trying to process this information in his brain, whilst still maintaining the conversation. "Why Canterbury? And in a moving van? The guy lives and works in Essex."

"The moving people have a depot there. Anyway, we'll soon know, we're in pursuit."

Powell needed time to think. He also wanted to get back to the match on TV.

"Anything we can do?"

"Thanks for the offer. It's OK for the moment. We'll call you if we need to take you up on that."

Powell went back to his chair in the sitting room. He was thinking about the implications of the information he had just received and his brain was in overdrive. He was looking at the television, but his mind was not on the football. He sensed a result coming up. A real result, concerning Jim Warwick. He looked at his watch. Still time to get a warrant, if he phoned first. Better to have it and not need it, than not to have it at all.

When Geoff arrived at BST that evening Norman came out to meet him, which was unusual. Something else struck Geoff, the usually unflappable Norman looked anxious. This encouraged Geoff who was feeling a little apprehensive. He knew it was imperative that they believed he was going to cooperate fully; he could not afford to give them the slightest cause for concern. Geoff was holding a plastic grocery bag.

"Hello, Norman," he said calmly. "I've brought along a few bits I'll need to sort the gate tonight."

Norman stopped. The anxious look disappeared, to be replaced instantly by the faux smile.

"Good evening, Geoff. I trust that all is well, and

that you have the list?"

"Yes, I have." He handed Norman a piece of folded paper. "Here it is."

Norman took the list and scanned it quickly. "Excellent," he said, "this looks good. What about the drawings?"

"My man on the inside is in the production department, nothing to do with designs. He can alter the controllers, but he wasn't able to get access to the site drawings."

"Oh."

Geoff waved a hand. "Don't worry, I can do them. But drawings are not just knocked out in minutes you know, they take time. And I've not had too much spare time lately."

"Of course, of course." Norman was almost conciliatory. Unusual, and unexpected.

They clunked up the echoing metal staircase and Geoff asked, "Are we loaded yet?"

"All done. We are not using the van tonight. The car will be better for this one."

On the A2 about four miles south of the city of Canterbury Scott closed the distance between their car and the Mounts' van.

O'Brian was looking at the satnav. "I reckon we're about ten minutes from their depot. Time to push on," he said, pointing forward to indicate that Scott should overtake the lorry. Scott eased the car out and accelerated. As they passed the lorry, O'Brian glanced at the side of the vehicle, but there was not enough light to show details of the lettering.

CHAPTER SEVENTEEN

Shortly after, they turned off the main road and headed for the industrial estate, turning again to enter the road where the Mounts had their depot. It was one of a dozen or so units in a communal courtyard just off a wide curve in the road. Scott pulled into the car park of one of the factory units on the opposite side to Mounts' depot.

"Will this do?" he asked.

"Yeah, fine."

They had a good view of the Mounts' premises. Although it was dark there was enough light from the street lamps for their purpose. They saw two vehicles in the parking area in front of the Mounts' unit: a Volvo car and a small van. O'Brian picked up his radio transmitter.

"On site Canterbury address," he said. "All quiet. There's a Volvo saloon parked up at the unit, and an Escort van."

"OK. Details?" Vanessa asked.

"We'll get back to you."

The men settled themselves and O'Brian unscrewed the cap of his Thermos again.

Scott turned and reached behind to pick up a pair of night vision binoculars that were on the rear seat. He removed them from their case and peered forward.

"There's a bloke in the van. Having a fag, looks like."

"Oh yes? Do you think he's clocked us?"

"No. He doesn't seem worried."

Moments later headlights approaching around the bend heralded the arrival of the pantechnicon. It slowed and turned into the courtyard. O'Brian hurriedly finished his coffee and put the Thermos down. He picked up his radio transmitter. As he spoke into it the man in the Escort van stepped out, dropped his cigarette and ground it under his heel.

"The moving van's just arrived," O'Brian said. "And there's a man in the Escort. He's stepped out of the vehicle."

Scott was peering through the binoculars. "White male, stocky, mid-forties, glasses, moustache."

O'Brian said, "Scotty's observing. The Escort driver's male, mid-forties, stocky build, wearing glasses and a moustache."

Scott read out the number plates of the small van and the Volvo, and O'Brian repeated them into his transmitter.

"Hey," Scott exclaimed. "The moving van's got French plates. But the lettering on the side is English. Mount Brothers Continental Removals, Canterbury address."

O'Brian spoke into his handset. "The moving lorry is French registered. English lettering, Mount Brothers."

"Yes, we know," Vanessa replied.

Scott read out the number plate and O'Brian repeated it.

"Good. Thanks for the confirmation."

"Maintaining station," O'Brian said. "I'll take some photos and call in again." He leaned forward to open the glove locker and removed a camera.

They watched as two men climbed down out of the lorry. One walked over to open the side door of the unit and enter the premises. A light was turned on inside, outlining the roller door through the gaps around it. The other man went to speak to the driver of the Escort van. Shortly after, the roller door ascended, squealing in protest as it rose. The pantechnicon moved forward into the unit and the Escort van reversed up to the entrance. The policemen watched as the water heater was transferred from the back of the big van into the smaller one.

"Gotcha!" said O'Brian as he took yet another clear shot of the men.

Commander Martin Blake was recovering from a bad cold and he was not well. He felt tired as he drew his hands over his face. His deputy Superintendent Ron Standish had just finished a phone conversation. He came over, looking concerned.

"Why don't you take a break, sir? You need a rest. If you want to go home, I can deal with this."

"I might take you up on that Ron, but it's just getting interesting. I'll give it another couple of hours. Any info on the Escort van?"

"Just heard back, it's registered to Warwick Motors in Essex."

Blake raised his eyebrows. "Well, now. Isn't that the same outfit that our man Conroy works for?"

"You don't believe in coincidences, do you, sir?"

Blake rubbed his chin. "Where do you suppose the Escort is heading for now?"

"Could it be coincidentally, somewhere in Essex?"

"Sharp as the proverbial blunt instrument, Ron."

"Just making a joke."

"So am I." Blake smiled. "There are three possibilities," he said, counting them off on his fingers. "The driver's home, or Conroy's home, or somewhere else. Their destination is unlikely to be either of the first two. Why not the driver's home? Because Conroy is a passenger, transferred from the moving van. Unlikely that he has a reason to go home with the driver. Why not Conroy's place? Because Conroy will have left his car at the place they're headed for, which would be the third option."

He paused to honk into a handkerchief. "See if you can turn up the names and addresses of the top people at Warwick Motors. Owners, directors, you know what to look for. Chances are the van is headed for a private residence."

"We'll get on it now," said Standish.

"I want to find out where they are going, and I want you to get there before they do. It'll be somewhere in Essex, so we probably have a couple of hours. See what you can turn up. And tell our men to stay with the small van."

"They're following it now, sir. When they left, the moving van was locked inside the factory unit. The Volvo is registered to Charles Mount at a Canterbury address."

Blake nodded. "Can you bring Kent up to speed on the operation and ask them to pick up the Mounts. But not yet, tell them to wait until we give them the nod."

"OK."

Ten minutes later Blake looked up as Standish came back into his office.

Standish was holding a notebook. "It's a private limited company. The directors are James Warwick and David Merchant. The company secretary is Sandra Warwick. The shares are owned by Warwick and her only."

"Narrows it down a bit doesn't it?" said Blake, with a wry grin.

"Yes, sir. I reckon they're heading for Warwick's house. It's a posh address near Braintree."

Blake looked at Standish. "Well, what are you waiting for? You've got a head start. Ask Vanessa to give O'Brian the good news."

"Wouldn't you prefer to go home, sir? I can hold the fort, we can button it up now."

"What? And miss all the fun? You must be joking again, Ron." Blake nodded towards the door. "Off you go, now. Keep us posted."

CHAPTER EIGHTEEN

Andy Powell was driving his Audi. He had picked up Eddie Smith, and they were now getting close to Warwick Hall.

"In answer to your question, Smith," he said, "the reason I picked you to come along tonight is that when we find out what happened to Tony Bellini, whatever it turns out to be, you can be the one to give the news to the family. A first-hand account." He looked towards the right as they entered a roundabout.

"You know, lad, it's not usually a good idea for a police officer to get involved with victims on a personal level." He glanced across at his junior. "But for you this is personal, isn't it?"

Smith was looking straight ahead. "It just seemed so unfair. Nothing's being done and they're blaming us. I really want to help them."

"Well, let's see if we can settle a score for them tonight." Powell swung the wheel to turn into Heather Lane. Two hundred metres further on there was a right turn into a close with four large properties, one of which Powell knew, was Warwick Hall. The lane was a cul-de-sac and he also knew that although there was a bridle path at the bottom end, for cars there was only one way into or out of the close.

They entered Heather Lane and saw two dark BMWs parked one behind the other, close to the turning into the cul-de-sac. The cars were perfectly positioned to intercept traffic from Heather Lane into and out of the close.

"The heavy mob from the Yard," Powell explained. "I'll just have a word."

He pulled up behind the rear car and got out, telling Smith to stay where he was. Powell spent the next few minutes with his hand on the roof of the lead BMW, leaning forward and talking to the two men inside. Then he straightened, walked back to the Audi and climbed in.

"They say there's a Range Rover parked at the end of the drive. I told them it was probably Conroy's. I wanted to take a look myself but they weren't happy about that."

Powell started the engine and looked over his shoulder as he reversed the car. "We'll park a bit further down, we don't want to spook their quarry. Might spoil their fun and that wouldn't do at all, would it?"

They moved forward towards the junction. Smith asked, "Are we going in first, sir, or are they?"

"Neither, just yet. They're expecting the carrier's van, so they'll wait until it's gone in and they're sure it's unloaded. The electric gate could be a problem but they'll get in, one way or another. We'll wait until they swoop. Once they're in we'll follow, with the help of a bit of back-up." He smiled. "I didn't tell them about that bit, though."

"That won't please them."

"No, it won't. The guy I spoke to is Ron Standish, one of the senior officers in the squad. Actually I out-rank him, so we *could* go in ahead. Ours is a separate case and we have our warrant. But in the spirit of cooperation I took the hint when he asked me to bugger off."

Seeing the surprise on Smith's face, Powell grinned. "Well, he did say please."

Sitting quietly at the back of the seven-seater car, Geoff was on edge. The gut fear that had at first paralysed all other emotions had eased, because it looked like his plan was working. Nevertheless, he found himself unable to join in banter with the others. No longer did he feel the slightest connection with these people, any feeling of camaraderie he may have had before was now dead.

They were still treating Geoff like one of the team and all seemed normal and friendly. All except Mac, who maintained a sullen demeanour when speaking to him. Geoff knew that he would need to watch him carefully.

Dennis turned the car into Heather Lane and drove forward at low speed. "Nearly there," he said. "Another couple of minutes."

Heather Lane with its respectable middle-class detached houses on both sides was quiet, which was only to be expected at one o'clock in the morning. Two BMW cars were parked near the entrance to the cul-de-sac and an Audi further down. None looked out of place in such a neighbourhood, and the men in the BST seven-seater took no notice of them.

In his BMW, Standish reacted immediately when the headlights of the BST car came around the corner into view.

"They're here," he said tersely. He and his driver

slid low in their seats. Standish saw that in the Audi parked thirty metres further on and facing them, Powell and Smith had crouched low, below the line of the dashboard. The beam from the headlights swept over their heads as the vehicle, moving slowly, turned into the cul-de-sac. Standish and his driver sat up.

"Now, who the hell are *they*?" Standish had been expecting the Escort van.

"Visitors?"

"What, in the middle of the night? Not likely."

"You want me to follow?"

"No. Whatever's going on, we stay here until the stuff arrives. Once it's inside the house we can block the road off if we need to."

Standish got out of the car and looked down the cul-de-sac. The BST car was moving slowly towards the end. He put his head down and sprinted across the road towards Powell, who was coming forward.

Standish hissed angrily, "What the hell is going on?"

Powell answered in a loud whisper. "You tell me."

The two policemen stayed out of sight behind the perimeter wall and put their heads around the corner to follow the progress of the BST car. When it reached the end of the road, it slowed and did a three-point turn. It was now facing them and its lights were turned off.

"They can't be visitors," Standish observed. "It's stopped outside."

Inside the seven-seater Geoff watched as Mac got out

of the car and moved cautiously to the gates, where
he looked around, checking through the gates the area
around the house and also glancing down the road.
Apparently satisfied, he returned to the car and
slipped back onto the front seat.

"Looks clear," he said. "There's a light on in the
extension but the house is dark." He turned around
in his seat. "OK, we're ready," he said quietly.

Geoff had the remote in his hand. Mac looked
directly at him and said, "You. Turn off the alarm. I
want to see you do it." Geoff punched in the code,
then held the device up.

"Done," he said, calmly. He opened his door and
stepped out of the car, carrying his plastic bag with
the tools.

Mac stepped out and motioned to Ted and Foxy,
who climbed out silently, wearing their balaclavas and
latex gloves. Ted picked up their tool bag and two
empty sacks and went with Geoff to the gates. As
planned, Foxy and Mac went around to the side of
the perimeter wall where Mac was to give Foxy a leg-
up onto the wall.

Through the gate Geoff and Ted watched
anxiously as Foxy appeared at the top of the wall and
briefly lay prone, before dropping down soundlessly
into a flower bed. He stood up, looked around
quickly, then scrambled across the gravel towards
them. He pushed the button on the concrete post
and slowly the gates squealed open. Mac came
around to the gate and he and Ted moved off to join
Foxy, who was already at the side door of the
building.

CHAPTER EIGHTEEN

Geoff stood rigidly still, his heart pounding, dreading a response from inside the building. In the still, dark night, the noises of the gravel and of the gate opening seemed magnified to an alarming degree. And he knew there were cameras. Geoff hoped fervently that at that hour, Warwick would not be watching any monitors. The game would really be up if Warwick had a view good enough to recognize him.

Geoff knelt by the electrical junction box which was set low down on the wall and took the tools out of his bag. Using a torch and screwdriver, he removed the cover of the box and set it down. A quick glance in the beam of torchlight showed him where the power cable was and he cut it cleanly. The gates were open and would now stay that way.

Geoff turned around to see Mac standing by the patio door, while Ted prised it open and stepped inside. Foxy followed him.

At the top of the cul-de-sac Powell and Standish waited and watched. They were looking at the BST car.

"Beats me," Powell whispered. He's turned the lights off."

Standish asked earnestly, "You *sure* they're not from your lot?"

Powell snorted. "Huh, how would I know? I'm only the Chief Super of CID."

"OK, sorry."

Geoff moved around the open gate and looked

towards the BST car. Dennis gave him a "thumbs up", and all seemed quiet down the road. Geoff turned his back, took his mobile phone out of his pocket and pressed a button.

Holding the phone to his ear, Geoff waited for the response, and then whispered, "Harry? You there?"

"Of course, dear boy. Did you doubt it?"

Geoff exhaled in relief. "Good, I'll be with you in five or ten minutes."

That was the moment, with Ted and Foxy inside drilling out the lock of the coin cabinet, Mac outside keeping watch over the garden, Dennis watching the road, Geoff at the open gate, and two separate lots of policemen at the top of the cul-de-sac; that was the precise moment when Stubby's Escort van turned into Heather Lane.

Standish reacted first. Grabbing Powell's sleeve he said, "It's here. Quick, behind your car."

The two policemen crouched behind the Audi, inside which Smith ducked below the dash. They watched the van with its headlights on full beam, as it turned into and then drove down the cul-de-sac.

In the BST car Dennis, dazzled by the approaching headlights, could see nothing beyond. He reacted instantly, flinging himself sideways to flatten his body across the front seats. In his panic he dropped the phone that he had been holding in readiness to alert Mac to any threat. He scrabbled around desperately searching the floor with one hand while lying semi-prone across the seat. Even if he had found it and been able to hit the call button, he was too late. The Escort van was already approaching the open gate.

"That's nice," said Stubby. "Looks like he's opened the gate for us."

Shaun peered at the seven-seater. "Who's that?"

Stubby was dismissive. "Snoggers, probably. The boss is always complaining about them." He grinned wickedly. "Is it rocking?"

Meanwhile, the instant he saw the headlights, Geoff had dropped to the ground and lay flat against the inside of the wall. As the van turned in through the gates, Geoff saw Mac crouching in the shadows, against the side wall of the house. The occupants of the van cannot have noticed anything amiss, it headed down the curved drive towards Warwick's office suite.

At the top of the road, Standish hustled to his car and climbed in and Powell got back into the Audi. Moments later O'Brian and Scott's car came down the road towards them at speed. Standish got out again and the estate car screeched to a halt beside him. Scott leaned out of the driver's window.

"Got him sir, we tracked them all the way." He glanced around quickly. "Where is he?"

"Gone into the premises." Standish pointed. "This house on the left."

Powell and Smith had hurried across to join them. "Are you going in?" Powell asked.

Standish looked at his wristwatch. "Give it a few minutes. If he's just unloading, he'll be out again shortly and we'll grab him. If he's staying we'll get them all together, inside."

"Fine, we'll wait," said Powell.

Standish had the last word. "You do that. Don't be getting any ideas. This is *our* collar. You can have him when we're done."

Powell and Smith walked back to the Audi and climbed in. Smith seemed disappointed.

"What do we do, sir?"

"I told him we'll wait, so we're waiting." He looked at his watch. "But I didn't say how long."

Five minutes later, Stubby's Escort van reappeared at the bottom of the cul-de-sac, coming through the gate. Immediately, Standish's BMW pulled out and blocked the road. The second BMW pulled up behind.

In the Audi, Powell reached for the radio microphone. He pressed the "send" button. "All units move in now. No sirens, repeat, no sirens."

Moments earlier, when Stubbs' van was coming back up the drive heading for the gate, Geoff had slipped outside and flattened himself on the ground. After it passed, he scrambled to his feet and looked down the road. The van had stopped, its path blocked by the two BMWs. Behind it, police cars with flashing blue lights were pulling up all around. Dennis stepped out of the seven-seater, clearly in a state of panic. Geoff glanced at the house and saw Mac leaning through the patio door.

Dennis rushed over to Geoff. "What's happening?

CHAPTER EIGHTEEN

What's happening?" he squeaked.

Geoff saw that at the top of the road, the driver had been hauled out of his van. Stubbs was shouting, protesting and declaring his innocence loudly in technicolour language. Two detectives had wrestled him onto the bonnet of the van.

"God knows," Geoff answered tersely. "I'm getting out of here."

He sprinted for the bridle path, casting a last look over his shoulder. He saw Dennis doing an involuntary impersonation of Buster Keaton, undecided as to which way to turn. Geoff ran down the path; he knew exactly where he was headed, as he wondered briefly who had summoned the police, saving him the trouble.

In the surreal flashing blue light from several police cars, Standish strode over to Powell, who was talking to a uniformed officer from the first police patrol car.

"What the hell is all this?" he fumed.

"This is the back-up you didn't know you were getting. Go in now, and we'll be behind you."

Standish paused briefly and then nodded. "OK." He climbed into his car quickly and motioned his driver forward. "Through the gate, right now."

His driver executed a smart three-point turn and slammed the accelerator down. The car rocketed forward, its tyres screeching. It scorched through the gate, trapping in the beams from its headlights three men scurrying at the double towards them. The driver immediately rammed on the brakes. The car slewed to a stop, showering gravel everywhere.

Standish and his driver jumped out and ran forward. They saw two men drop what they were carrying, turn and flee towards the back of the house. The third stood still, seemingly immobilised in the beams of the headlights.

"Police, *stop!*" Standish shouted.

The large black man standing frozen in the lights did not move. "Oh shit!" he exclaimed, "This is baaad."

Close behind Standish's BMW was Powell's Audi, followed by two patrol cars, both with blue roof lights flashing. They all pulled up and Powell and Smith leapt out, leaving the doors open and sprinting through the gate. Standish, who had seen two men standing at the other end of the drive outside the glass door, pointed at them and shouted to Powell.

"I want those two." He nodded towards Mac. "This one's all yours."

Outside his office, Jim Warwick could not believe his eyes. Beside him, Shaun Conroy was speechless, Warwick not so. Eyes wide, he growled. "What the fuck...?"

CHAPTER NINETEEN

After only a few minutes of rapid jogging Geoff came to realise, painfully, how unfit he had become. He was out of breath, his chest was heaving and he felt dizzy. Head spinning, he slowed, stopped and doubled over. No sounds on the pathway and no sign of a pursuer.

Thank God, no one following, he thought. Got to get on. Breathing deeply he continued at a slower pace, until he emerged from the wood onto a pavement at the end of a road on a housing estate. The road was a dead end, the pavement encircling a turning area. There, at the end of the road was his car, exactly where he had left it that morning. And parked immediately in front of his car was the tiny Fiat saloon much loved by its owner, Harry Mortimer. Geoff breathed a huge sigh of relief.

The little Fiat rocked as Harry eased his bulk out. When he stood up, beside him the car looked like something from a fairground ride.

Geoff stumbled over to him. "Harry," he said, panting, "You are not going to believe this. Coppers everywhere."

"Yeah, I guessed. Down the road I stopped at traffic lights and somebody in a big hurry pulled up alongside. I looked across just before he took off like a bullet. Ron Standish of the Yard. Looks like you guessed right about Warwick."

"But squad cars turned up, quite a few, with lights flashing. Did you call them? I didn't."

Harry shook his head. "No. Somebody else must

have tipped them off. Or maybe Standish asked the locals for back-up."

"Saved me the trouble then. I'm in deep shit with the removals firm, but I would have been anyway."

Harry leaned against his car. "Not necessarily. Hop in and tell me all, dear boy."

Geoff opened the passenger door to climb into the Fiat.

"I got away, Harry. They're bound to think it was a set-up and they'll be after me now." He climbed into the car, which rocked again as Harry heaved himself into the driver's seat and grinned broadly.

"Not if this is a drugs bust. When I file my copy, we'll be on the front pages of the morning dailies, for sure. So the Yard's heavy mob chose the same night to move in, nothing to do with you at all."

"I hope that Naylor and his mob think so too."

"Oh, don't worry. I'll have a word with them. I owe you that for finding Warwick. And I'm guessing there's more to come out, when I've looked into how Warwick moved his money around using Mr Flynn to pay for the merchandise."

"Thanks, Harry."

"Tut, no thanks necessary. Just doing my job, old son. Now, tell me what happened tonight but make it quick, I have work to do."

Geoff quickly ran over the events of the night. When he finished, he strolled over to his own car and climbed in. He looked up and saw that Harry was already on his way out of the housing estate, headed for Warwick Hall.

CHAPTER NINETEEN

Geoff took out his mobile and pressed a speed dial button. She answered immediately.

"You do know how to keep a girl guessing, don't you? Where are you and how are you?"

"I'm fine, I got away. I didn't call the police but they turned up anyway. I'll explain later. For the moment you can relax and go to bed. You'll be quite safe. Me, too. It's over, Sam, it's really all over."

"Well done, you." She sounded hugely relieved. "Go to bed? I can't do that. Not on my own, on your last night."

Andy Powell was watching Jim Warwick closely. So far, the man had stonewalled stubbornly. His resistance showed no sign of slipping, but Powell was not worried. During questioning Powell discovered that Warwick had been staggered by the appearance of the drugs squad, and with Standish questioning Shaun Conroy in the next room, Powell knew that it would be only a matter of time before he got what he wanted.

Jim Warwick was sitting stiffly in one of the armchairs. On the other side of the low coffee table, Powell was perched on top of an arm of the settee, one leg on the floor and the other casually swinging free. He was relaxed and enjoying the encounter.

"What really puzzles me, Jim," Powell said, "is why your cheque to Bellini was never presented. Help me out here. Can you think of any reason for that? Seems odd, doesn't it?"

Jim on the other hand, was far from relaxed and it showed. He sat stone-faced and rigid, with his arms across his chest.

"I told you, I'm saying nothing until my lawyer gets here."

Powell's eyes stayed fixed on Warwick, but he spoke to Smith. "You might as well put your book away, then, Constable. Have a poke around to see what you can find."

Warwick's head swung around sharply, his glare transferred to Smith who was sitting in the other armchair. Smith tossed his pad onto the table and stood up.

"What am I looking for, sir?"

"Anything to connect – no, I'll re-phrase that – anything to add to the evidence we already have, connecting Mr Warwick with Anthony Bellini's disappearance."

Instantly, Warwick's expression changed. He was on the point of saying something, but stopped.

Powell smiled. He had nearly got the response he was seeking. "All right, Jim," he said. "You're going to be talking to Scotland Yard about your other activities, so why bother with a little thing like murder, eh?"

That hit the spot. Warwick snarled, "It wasn't – I didn't –" But then he clammed up again.

Powell leaned forward, eyebrows raised. "Wasn't what, Jim? Murder?"

Warwick's face reddened. The effort to keep silent seemed almost more than he could contain.

Powell inclined his head. "Manslaughter then," he said in an even, reasonable tone. "Just as we suspected. You're a nasty bastard, but we don't have you down as a murderer."

Eddie Smith was busy at the big desk. He flicked through the pile of papers on top, then tried the drawers, pulling open the three in the right-hand pedestal. Suddenly Warwick reacted.

"Leave that alone," he snarled. "You don't have the right to stick your filthy noses into people's private papers."

Smith ignored him as he tugged at the handle of the top drawer of the other pedestal.

"This one's locked," he said. "Can we have the key, please, Mr Warwick?"

Jim Warwick stood up, then slowly sank back into the chair as his knees buckled. Until that moment he had forgotten what was in that drawer. Pieces of the torn and crumpled cheque. His body slumped as his face at last betrayed his defeat.

Geoff Summers opened his eyes to glorious sunshine streaming through open curtains. He looked around. Did all that really happen last night? Wow!

Samantha was not in the bed. Probably showering, he thought. He swung his legs off the bed, sat up and looked around. He checked the bedside clock. Five to nine, plenty of time to shower, have a leisurely breakfast with Sam and enjoy her company for the rest of the day. He reminded himself that he had to be at Heathrow that evening.

Samantha emerged from the bathroom wearing the white robe provided by the hotel. Her head was wrapped in a towel.

"Oh, you're awake. How are you feeling this

morning?"

"How am I feeling? Lucky, and relieved."

She loosened the towel, shook out her hair and began to rub it dry.

"Last night," Geoff said, "The police turning up out of the blue was a real stroke of luck. But we could still be in trouble with the firm. Especially as I got away."

Samantha went over to the dressing table. "But somebody must have called them. A neighbour?"

"No, I don't think so. The drugs squad came to the same house, on a raid."

She picked up a hair dryer that was on the dressing table. "What? At the same place?"

He nodded. "And Harry was there. Harry Mortimer, the reporter I told you about. He said that when the story hits the papers this morning, the firm would know it wasn't me who called the police."

"It'll be fine then, surely?" She sounded anxious, as she plugged the lead into a socket.

"I won't be relaxing until I know that for certain."

Samantha stood up, holding the dryer. "Wait a minute. Maybe there's something on the radio. It's set on the local BBC station, just time to catch the nine o'clock news." She pointed. "You can put it on. Turn the sound up."

Geoff turned the radio on. Moments later they heard the Westminster chimes, followed by the newsreader's announcement that the headline for the morning was a successful raid by Scotland Yard's anti-drugs squad on a private house in north Essex, in the early hours of the morning. A haul of Ecstasy tablets believed to have a street value of over a million pounds was recovered and there had been several arrests.

Geoff stood up. "We're in the clear," he exclaimed in delight. "We're in the clear, Sam." He rushed over, took her in his arms and hugged her.

Geoff's flight arrived in Sydney early on the Saturday morning. He was tired and bleary, standing at the luggage carousel waiting for his suitcase. He checked his watch, then called Samantha as he had promised to do. She answered immediately.

"Hi, Geoff, how are you?"

"Tired, jet-lagged, and missing you. I know it's probably quite late in England, so I'll keep it brief."

"It is," she said. "Any immediate plans?"

"The way I feel right now, I think the only plan is bed and a long sleep."

"OK, give me a call when you've surfaced."

"I will. Probably tomorrow, when it's late evening here, so it'll be about nine or ten in the morning, your time."

"OK, take care."

Geoff left the terminal and took a taxi to the Hilton, where he spent the rest of the day recovering and relaxing in the hotel's leisure facilities.

On the Sunday morning he woke refreshed, alert and eager for news coverage of the drugs raid. He switched his laptop on and found the website of the *Daily Mail*, where he was relieved to discover that the Essex drugs bust was a major story. He scanned the report quickly, then decided that he would read the details later. He checked the websites of some of the other hotels in the city, finally deciding on one with rooms available. Then he went downstairs for a leisurely breakfast.

After breakfast Geoff went back to his room and packed his case. He took the lift down to the ground floor and went over to the concierge's desk where he ordered a taxi. At the main reception desk he had to wait his turn for a few minutes. A pretty, blonde young woman looked up and smiled as he put his plastic door entry card on the counter.

"Room 307," he said. "Can I have my bill, please?"

"307, certainly sir." She tapped the number into her keyboard, and a minute later his bill was deposited into the tray of her printer.

She picked it up, glanced at it and handed it to him. "Your account, Mr Summers."

He checked through the items, then handed it back to her with his credit card. She processed the transaction and gave the card back to him.

"Thank you, Mr Summers. Have a nice day."

"You, too."

Geoff had left a few hundred pounds in his UK bank account. He reflected wryly that this was likely to be the last card transaction that Geoffrey Summers would ever make.

The Rocks Plaza Hotel was a more modest establishment than the Hilton but it was clean and comfortable. Geoff had arrived by taxi from the Hilton and checked in as John Jeffries, saying that he

353

would be staying about a week.

That evening he went out to have dinner at a Greek restaurant that he had found when wandering around as a tourist earlier in the day. He had resolved not to telephone Samantha until eight o'clock that evening, when it would be nine in the morning in England. He had finished his meal and was enjoying a coffee when he made the call.

"Good morning," she said. "How are you feeling?"

"Hi, Sam, good evening, which it is here. I'm fine, just finished a tasty dinner in a Greek restaurant. I've seen the press coverage of the raid on the internet."

"It's been in all the papers and on the TV news."

"Any problems? With the bad guys, I mean."

"No, nothing. I've been thinking about going back to my flat."

"I'd rather you didn't, not just yet. It's too soon. Can you leave it a few more days?"

"You're still worried, aren't you?"

"Logically they have no reason to harm you, but we can't be sure. Better safe than sorry."

"What are your plans now?"

"Geoff Summers left the Hilton this morning. John Jeffries checked into another hotel and will be leaving for South Africa at the end of the week."

She laughed. "OK, John, so you'll be doing some sightseeing, then. Are you going to see Penny's sister?"

"No. I'd like to, but if she is ever asked about me it would be better for her to say that she has not seen me. Besides, they live in Adelaide, a long way from here."

"OK, that makes sense." She paused. "If we keep making these calls, the phone credits will soon run out."

"That's going to happen, sooner or later," he replied glumly.

"Call me again when you've firmed up your travel plans."

"I'll do that. This will all blow over soon, Sam. In the meantime, be careful."

"You too."

With a heavy heart he rang off, then dialled the number to check how much credit was left on the phone. She was right, it was running out.

The following day was Monday, so the shops were open. Geoff went to a travel agents to book his flight to Durban. As Jeffries he could not risk making any bookings on the internet using his laptop. He booked a flight to Durban on Emirates via Dubai, and paid in "Jeffries" travellers cheques. That evening he called Samantha again.

"Sam?"

"Hi, Geoff, everything OK?"

"Fine. Any problems at your end?"

"No, all OK. I've decided to stay in the hotel, but only to stop you worrying!"

"Great. That's a huge relief."

"Have you been sightseeing?"

"A bit, and I'll be doing some more the rest of this week. I booked my flight today. I'm leaving Australia on Saturday night, arriving in Durban about five the next afternoon."

"Sounds like a long haul."

"It is, but there's a stopover in Dubai for five hours. I'll call you again from there, it'll be about eight in the morning your time." He desperately wanted to tell her that he loved her and missed her. Instead he said, "I don't think there's too much time left on the phones and I want to say goodbye properly. Without having to rush it, I mean."

After a moment she replied. "We'll stay in touch, anyway, so it'll be au revoir, not really a final goodbye."

"Thanks, Sam. Let's save the phones, we'll speak again on Saturday." He rang off, feeling drained of emotion, missing her.

Despite the relative comfort of business class, during the fourteen-hour flight on the Saturday night Geoff slept only fitfully. After landing at Dubai, he made his way to the transit lounge to await the departure of his onward flight to Durban.

The five days he had spent on his own without any contact with Samantha, had dragged on interminably. He was desperate to speak to her again if only to hear her voice, but he left making the call until his flight was about to board, when it would be just before eight o'clock in the morning in England.

He pressed the pre-dial button, and her phone rang several times before she answered.

"Morning, Geoff, how are you?"

"I'm fine now, but I was starting to worry when you didn't pick up."

"Oh, sorry, I was just coming out of the bathroom.

Where are you?"

"I'm in the transit lounge in Dubai, the flight to Durban has just been called."

"You sound tired."

"I am. It was a fourteen-hour flight to get here, and that was five hours ago."

"You can get your head down on the next bit. How long is it going to be?"

He groaned. "Another eight hours."

They were silent for a few moments, then she said, "The phones are running out. Just time to say another au revoir rather than goodbye, because I'm sure we'll talk again when you are sorted."

"Save the phone time. I'll call you again as soon as I get a South African mobile."

"OK."

"Bye for now. And Sam..."

"Yes?"

His voice cracked. "I love you and I'm going to miss you."

He was desperately disappointed when she rang off without another word.

Samantha, on the other hand, smiled. In the background the hotel radio was playing a rumba: "The Girl from Ipanema." She put the phone down, and swaying her hips gently whilst humming along to the melody, walked out into the sunshine on her hotel balcony, to savour the sea air and the magnificent view over the Indian Ocean.

At King Shaka international airport Geoff joined the queue of weary passengers clutching their hand

CHAPTER NINETEEN

luggage, leaving the aircraft. He put on the polarized sunglasses that he had bought in Australia and paused at the top of the boarding steps. He was struck by a wall of searing heat that was like suddenly being shoved in front of a furnace. But he was glad to get off the aircraft, it seemed as if he had been on aeroplanes for a month.

In the queue waiting to pass through South African immigration, Geoff reflected on how different it would have been, if only Samantha could have been with him to share his new life. He was starting again with nobody to share his experience, in a country where he did not know a soul. Am I completely mad he thought? During the past week he could think only of Samantha and bitterly regretted his stupidity in losing her. Just when he needed her, a loving companion, to share his new beginning. He felt thoroughly miserable and depressed.

Geoff passed through the last set of doors into the arrivals lounge, his eyes scanning the semi-circle of expectant faces, some holding up cardboard signs with names scrawled upon them. People were embracing, their chatter augmenting the volume of background noise. He moved forward slowly. He could not blame her for refusing to join him. He was after all, a criminal on the run.

Looking up, Geoff picked out the sign showing the way to the taxi rank. He stepped out of the air-conditioned building through automatic glass doors and was again assailed by the wall of heat. There was a queue of people, businessmen, couples and families,

358

waiting. He dragged his wheeled case behind him and joined them to take his turn.

The heat was getting to him. Sweat trickled down the back of his neck and down his forehead. What had he done, he asked himself bitterly. What on earth was he going to do in this place, without the one person who would have made it all worthwhile?

A minute later he felt a gentle tap on his shoulder. "Taxi, sir?"

He turned around, and Samantha fell into his arms.

On a balmy evening two days later, with arms entwined they were strolling in the tropical garden of Shaka's Beach Hotel, only a low wall between them and the Indian Ocean. A gentle breeze off the sea cooled the air and the rhythmic, hypnotic slap and hiss of waves breaking on the beach provided the perfect backdrop.

"Isn't it gorgeous?" Samantha asked. "Just look at the plants, reds, yellows, orange and green. Lush, verdant green. So *much* colour!"

"Stunning. You'll soon have a garden like this of your own, you know. Just be nice to me, you'll see."

She looked at him sideways. "I've not heard you complaining lately."

They were approaching a rustic bench at the side of the pathway. Geoff slipped his arm out of hers. "Let's just sit here for a bit and enjoy the view." He held her hand and they sat down.

"It's Penny's birthday," he said, "she would have been thirty-nine today."

Samantha squeezed his hand. "I know."

CHAPTER NINETEEN

Geoff looked at his watch. "Half past seven in the evening in England. I've left her birthday present to be delivered. Actually not one, but five."

Samantha turned to look at him and frowned. "Whatever do you mean?"

Geoff told her.

Sandy Macgregor's wife Moira was in the kitchen when the doorbell chimed. Moira was wearing her oven gloves and she had just opened the door of the oven.

"Can you get that, Jenny?" she asked her daughter.

Fifteen-year old Jenny did not respond. She was at the kitchen table, her eyes locked into an electronic games device.

Moira removed a pyrex dish from the oven and put it down carefully on the worktop. *"Jenny.* Can you get the door, please?" She pointed with a gloved hand. "Dad won't, he's working in the study."

Jenny dragged herself off her chair with a show of reluctance. "All right, I'm going." The doorbell chimed again.

"I'm *coming,"* she exclaimed, shaking her head. "Some people!"

The man on the doorstep was wearing the uniform of a well-known courier company. In the crook of his arm was a clipboard, with an envelope in the clip.

"Hello," he said, "is Mr Alexander Macgregor in?"

Jenny looked him up and down as if he was from another planet. Finally she said, "Yes. Wait, I'll get him." She moved into the hall and called, *"Da-ad.* There's a man at the door asking for you."

PAYBACK

Two minutes later Sandy Macgregor closed the door gently and turned. He had signed for the letter and was examining the envelope in his hand. His name and address were printed on an adhesive label that was also marked "Confidential."

"Strange," he muttered.

From the kitchen Moira called. "Who was it?"

Sandy tore open the envelope as he entered the kitchen. "Courier with a letter." He removed the contents and turned the papers over in his hand. "Two pages, plus an enclosure." He sat down at the table beside Jenny.

"What is it?" Moira asked.

Sandy's elbows were on the table. His head was tilted back slightly and he was scanning the letter through his bifocal glasses. He then read the second page and the enclosure.

"Well," he exclaimed. "How about *that?*"

Moira was standing by the cooker. "What is it?" she asked again.

Sandy handed both documents to her without a word. She took them from him and started reading. The letter was dated for that day, the eighth of November. It was addressed to Adam Ford and it read:

Dear Mr Ford,

I'd like to say that it was a pleasure working for you, but I cannot. Throughout the twenty-two years of service I gave to Melford Electronics, I was always treated by my superiors and colleagues fairly and with respect. That was the currency that bought my commitment and unswerving loyalty over all those years.

When you joined the company, you had a different agenda, one which it soon became clear, required that I should not be around. Not the end of the world; I have skills which are in demand in our market. And of course, as the new managing director you have a perfect right to choose your own staff.

My wife Penny was diagnosed with a tumour on her brain. It was a serious condition, but not immediately life-threatening. Nevertheless, she wanted to see her sister in Australia before her surgery, just in case the operation did not succeed and we needed to borrow money to pay for the trip. These facts I imparted to you reluctantly when you told me you had received an enquiry from my bank requesting information about my ability to repay a loan. You promised me a good reference in exchange for my immediate voluntary resignation from the company. You will recall that I declined but conceded that I realised that my career with Melford was over. I told you I would leave within a few weeks and that is what I did.

All would have been well had you not then, for your own ends, sent a gratuitously poisonous reply to the bank's enquiry. What is much worse is the fact that before you wrote that letter, *you knew* about her pending surgery and the reason why I needed the loan. That I can neither understand nor forgive. Penny died without seeing her sister.

I understand that there have been some problems with equipment failure recently and I cannot help wondering whether poor reliability has been the cause.

If so, doubtless the principals and directors of the company will decide whom to blame, particularly when they learn that you have a substantial shareholding in Stalmann Electronics. That fact, together with sight of the content of your letter to the bank, may give them cause to question your integrity.

Today is Penny's birthday. Had she lived she would have been thirty-nine today and this letter to you, copied to your colleagues, is my birthday present to her.

Yours sincerely,

Geoffrey Summers
Enclosure: Copy of your letter to the bank, also copied to your colleagues.
Copies: The members of the board of Directors of Melford Electronics Ltd.

Sandy watched as Moira then read the second document. She handed them back to him with a half-smile on her face.

"I'm not surprised," she said, "not a bit surprised. What do you make of it?"

"Well, I wouldn't want to be in Adam's shoes right now."

Moira turned her attention to the cooker again. "I hope they kick the swine out, it's what he deserves. They should have given you the job in the first place."

AUTHOR'S NOTES

Thank you for buying this book. *Payback* was my first novel.

It is based loosely on some unusual and arguably bizarre incidents that really happened.

If you enjoyed it, I would be grateful if you could please leave a review on www.amazon.co.uk, www.amazon.com or on my publisher's website: www.3ppublishing.co.uk/bookshop.

Since the publication of *Payback* I have completed three more novels, *My Brother's Keeper, Celeste Three is Missing and Kismet*. I am now working on two more.

I try never to lose sight of the fact that readers of fiction expect to be diverted and entertained. Please feel free to contact me to let me know if I have succeeded in this endeavour with *Payback,* or if I have not. Either way it would be a pleasure to hear from you.

I am always grateful for feedback from my readers and I read and respond to all to emailed messages. You can contact me by visiting www.chriscalder.com.

Chris Calder - December 2018

ACKNOWLEDGEMENTS

'Payback' was my first novel. I am hugely indebted to a few kind people without whose help, encouragement and severely tested patience I could not have completed the work.

For that I shall be forever grateful to Laura Lawrie, Karen Davies, the late and much missed Lance Callaghan and my long-suffering spouse, Joan.

Special thanks also to my mentor, editor Doug Watts.

Chris Calder

Have you enjoyed *Payback*? If so here is a taster from Chris' second book: *Celeste Three Is Missing* – coming soon from 3P Publishing.

OCTOBER 2002

"All done?" Test pilot Mathew Wallace glanced over his shoulder at his colleague, first officer Richard Palfrey, on a test flight of the prototype space plane *Celeste Two*. Palfrey had been carrying out the pre-descent checks.

"Uh-huh. Just gimme a sec," he replied, scanning his instrument display panel again. "Yep, all good. I'm telling you, this is one sweet aircraft."

"So far, but this is only the third flight of *Two*. Better than *Celeste One*. I like the extra power but you can't make a judgement yet. How far to engine burn?"

"Re-entry burn in about three minutes. Time to cross-check with FCC," he said, referring to the Flight Control Centre at their base in Benson Flats, Arizona.

In the captain's seat Wallace sat up suddenly. The instrument panel displays had just switched off. "What the hell…?"

Palfrey reacted immediately, flicking the switch to open the communication channel to the control centre. "FCC, *Celeste*. There's a problem, all displays are out," he said crisply.

In the flight control centre director Gus Mead had been relaxed, watching over the routine test flight when the call startled him. Did he hear right?

366

His stomach knotted as he jabbed at the send button, his words sharp and clear.

"*Celeste*, FCC. Say again, please, we do not copy. Repeat, we do not copy."

The reply came from the usually laconic captain Matt Wallace.

"Matt here, Gus. I say again, we have no telemetry readings. The screen is blank." In the background the voice of Rich Palfrey could be heard swearing as he tried desperately to resuscitate the dead display.

Mead immediately turned to Robin Stevens, another of the test pilots who was on monitoring duty in the control room.

"Any suggestions, Robbie?"

Stevens looked horrified. "Blank display? Shit, I thought they'd fixed that. Right now *Celeste's* on the primary glide path, too close to re-entry burn."

"Oh, God," Mead muttered. He took a deep breath and pressed the send button.

"We're on it, *Celeste*, we got you on GPS, we can count you down to the burn. What have you tried?"

"Everything. Gus, we gotta have attitude info. The screen is blank."

Mead was staring at one of the three monitors at his console. To Stevens he said, "Get on to Pickard, *right now*. I want options, fast."

Stevens grabbed his intercom phone to call the systems and electronics expert as Mead pressed the send button again.

"Copy that, *Celeste*. We're checking with Pickard."

"Too late for that. Count us down, I'll give it my best shot. We don't want to go exploring outer space just now."

Mead's heart was pounding. He knew that the only alternative was an attempt at re-entry, with Wallace relying on his experience and skill to get the entry attitude exactly right. Chances were not good. His mouth went dry as he made the effort to stay calm.

"You are precisely one hundred fifteen seconds to engine burn, Matt; keep trying, here we go."

With the room now silent and all present watching, Mead started the countdown. He kept his eyes fixed on the monitors as the seconds drained away.

"…..fifteen, fourteen, thirteen…"

From *Celeste*, Wallace cut in. "See you guys later."

"…five, four, three, two, one, ignition."

The tense silence of the control centre was shattered by the familiar roar of the engine's blast. It confirmed that the burn was working and for a few heart-stopping moments all seemed well. Four seconds later it ceased abruptly. Instantly Mead reached out and stabbed at the intercom button.

"*Celeste?* Come in, *Celeste*. FCC to *Celeste*, come in." The director's voice cracked as his anxiety increased. "Come in, *Celeste*. Matt, come in, dammit."

There was no response. With his staff watching in complete silence, Gus Mead's face reflected the horror they felt. He sank into his chair and put his head in his hands.